HIGH TIDE
BIKINI

Lyla Dune

HIGH TIDE BIKINI
A Pleasure Island Romance

http://www.lyladune.com

ComposeSum@gmail.com

Cover art from Shutterstock
Photography by Mast3r

This book is dedicated to my father, the man who has shown me what unconditional love really means.

Table of Contents

CHAPTER ONE
Drawbridge

Kendal Duvall awoke to the ringtone "I Fight Authority, Authority Always Wins" and immediately covered her face with a pillow to muffle her groan of dread. Dealing with her mother before sunrise required more patience than Kendal possessed this morning. Rita Duvall thought running out of milk for her Cheerios was a family emergency.

Kendal answered. "Mom, are you okay?"

"Yes, I'm fine. Hello to you too."

"Mom, it's barely light outside. Can this wait? I'm not up to talking."

"What kind of greeting is that? You will talk to me, young lady. I am your mother! You never used to disrespect me this way. Get an apartment, and now you're too good for your own mother."

"Sorry. Running on two hours of sleep here. We gig at the Blues Shack in Myrtle Beach on Thursday nights and don't get home 'til the wee hours of the morning. I'm just tired. I love you, Mama, but--"

"It's okay. I know you're just a little grouchy when you're sleepy. But this *is* an emergency. I have a doctor's appointment in Wilmington this morning, and I don't have enough gas to get there and back."

"For crying out loud, Mama. That's *not* an emergency.

Drive over to Filly's and ask someone to help you work the gas pump. You know everyone on the island."

"Please, Kendal. I don't want to have to beg favors from people. You know how uncomfortable that makes me."

"You seem pretty comfortable asking me to do stuff."

"That's different. You're family. I'm sorry to disrupt your beauty sleep, Sugar. Tell you what…fill my tank up this morning and then go with me one day next week and teach me how to do it myself. Okay?"

That was a first, an apology from her mother followed by a willingness to learn to do something for herself. Progress.

Ever since Kendal's folks split, all the things her dad used to take care of suddenly became Kendal's duties. Sometimes she felt more like a servant than a daughter. But she didn't have the guts to tell her mom that for fear of coming off as disrespectful and never being forgiven.

She pushed herself up from the bed. "Fine. I'll be there in a few minutes." She loved her mother. Most days. Well, every day, but some days the loving came easier than this morning. The woman could be incredibly sweet at times, but Kendal desperately wanted to loosen the apron strings from around her neck enough to catch some air.

Fifteen minutes later, she opened the back door to her mom's house without going inside. She grabbed the car keys off the hook by the light switch and left, saving the face to face greeting with her mother for when she returned the vehicle.

It only took her two minutes to get to Filly's.

With the gas nozzle set to continue pumping, she groggily shuffled toward the entrance of the store and came to a halt when Ted Davis drove into the parking lot in his blue work truck. A magnetic sign on the side of the truck read: *Ted's Handy - Give him a Call - 791-FixU.*

Crap. There she was wearing a plaid housedress her mom

had given her. It was loose, comfortable, and ugly as sin—but it was laundry day, and it happened to be one of the few things clean. However, she had no excuse for her fuzzy blue bedroom slippers or the fact that her hair was a tangled mop of dark tresses piled on top of her head and held in place with a pair of green chopsticks from Sushi Mama's. Lack of sleep left her eyes so puffy she squinted worse than an old lady who had misplaced her bifocals.

Ted climbed out of the truck and all her sleepy little nerve endings sprang to life, eager to play with Ted—as always. He'd probably ignore her, as always.

Since she looked like she was dressed for a comedy skit, being invisible would be a blessing today.

She took a brief moment to admire the full-body view of Ted Davis while he had his back turned to her. Mmm. He could be a male model—sun-streaked hair, golden tan, broad shoulders, athletic build, not an ounce of fat anywhere and muscles galore. *Ding, ding.* Bonus! His equally gorgeous, hard-bodied brother Dirk was with him, soaking wet in nothing but a pair of board shorts. He'd most likely just come in from his morning surf. Dirk was seriously ripped, even more so than Ted. Whew. Yep, not one, but two of the island's most eligible bachelors were going to see her in all her granny glory— if she didn't find a place to hide, and fast.

As Ted waited for his brother to put on a shirt and some flip-flops, Kendal darted inside.

Ashley, a twenty-year-old blonde who caused heads to turn anytime she walked by in a bikini, laughed from behind the register as Kendal made a mad dash for the restroom. "Dang, girl. You wearing Louise's hand-me-downs these days?"

Kendal put a finger to her lips and gave Ashley the shush signal.

Ashley shrugged with a "what's going on" expression.

To Kendal's horror, the ladies room door was propped open with a mop bucket, and Mr. Benson stood in front of the lavatory with a plunger in hand. So much for that hidey-hole.

Panicked, she crouched behind some shelves.

Ashley whispered, "What are you doing?"

Kendal mouthed, "I'll tell you later."

With an eye roll, Ashley shook her head.

Okay…so Kendal was acting as crazy as the hermit lady, Miss Judy, who lived in a shack on the south end of the island. She even looked like Miss Judy this morning.

Kendal rose just enough to peer over the shelving. Ted and Dirk entered. Dang it! Why couldn't they just get some gas, pay at the pump, and go? She duck-walked to the end of the aisle, as far from the front door as she could get.

Ted spoke to Ashley upon strolling by the register, "Hey. What's up, Ash?"

"Good morning, Ted. Hey, Dirk." Kendal couldn't see Ashley, but she could hear the syrup in her voice. Which one of the Davis brothers was she flirting with?

Dirk said, "Hey, hey, hot stuff. Aren't you a sight for sore eyes?"

Ashley giggled. "Thanks, Dirk. Are you two going to the party tomorrow?"

Dirk stepped into the aisle where Kendal was hiding. She stiffened and wished she were invisible.

His attention was directed toward Ashley, and he didn't even glance at Kendal squatting near the coolers. He flashed his winning playboy smile at the cute blonde and said, "Do I ever miss a party?"

Ashley giggled again. "Nope, but that's a good thing. You make things fun." Gag. That was cheesy. No mistake about it; that girl had a thing for Dirk. Not surprising, almost every girl on the island did, and rumor had it he'd slept with most all of them too. Apparently, he was talented in between the sheets. Judging from some of his prize-winning dance moves, he had the whole hip action thing down pat. A dance called the shag was popular in their neck of the woods, but Dirk, a.k.a. Mr. Shag-a-thon, had turned it into an art form.

Ted coughed. "Thanks." Kendal detected sarcasm in his voice.

Ashley laughed. "Oh you're fun too, Ted, but you don't shag. You need to let Dirk teach you how to do it."

Ted grumbled. "I've got plenty of shagging moves. I just prefer to keep mine private."

Dirk chuckled at his brother's grumpy comment then lumbered in Kendal's direction.

She stayed in a crouched position and waddled, trying to round the corner of the aisle before he saw her, but her big butt bumped the end of the shelf. Several boxes of tampons rained down on her.

Dirk busted out laughing. "Little House on the Prairie, is that you? You okay?" He came to her aid and picked up a box, then looked at the label and dropped the box like it was too hot to handle.

She fought back the urge to laugh. Little House on the Prairie? He hadn't called her that in years. "Yes, Dirk the Jerk. It's me. I'm fine." She bit her lower lip to keep from grinning.

Paint splattered work boots came into her line of vision. She slowly let her gaze crawl up the drool-worthy body of Ted Davis.

Ted held out his hand to help her up.

She accepted his offer. Eyeing his throat because eye contact would've made her even more nervous, she said, "Thank you."

"You're welcome." His Adam's apple bounced up and down while he had a good laugh. What he found so funny, she could only imagine. Probably her Brady Bunch dress.

Dirk busied himself by putting the fallen boxes back on the shelf. When she turned to thank him, he stood with his hands in his pockets, looking around the store as if he hoped no one saw him touch those feminine products or do a kind deed.

Picking on her one second and being sweet the next, that pretty much summed up their whole relationship. He was annoying and charming all in one. Annoying enough she never developed a crush on him and charming enough she could never get mad at him. "Thank you, Dirk."

He gave her an upward nod and smiled. "Nice shoes."

Of course he couldn't just say you're welcome and move on. No. He had to make some sort of jab.

Ted pressed his hand against the small of Kendal's back. The warmth of his touch sent a tremor of excitement through her entire body. Ted was more her type—never made wise-cracks at her expense and always treated her like a lady even though she knew he wasn't attracted to her. He went for bossy extroverts, not quiet bookworms like her. Those were the facts, and she'd accepted them. She kept her crush in check. Nothing would ever come of it, but he sure was fun to fantasize about. She spun toward him and found herself practically in his one-armed embrace. His breath was soft and sexy by her ear.

He whispered, "You're standing on my foot."

"Sorry." How did she not feel that? She was so flabbergasted she hadn't even noticed? She readjusted herself so he could free his foot. He stepped away and gave her an awkward smile, then looked over her head. Laughing again, he covered his face quickly, turned, and strode to the drink cooler. His shoulders shook as if he were laughing even harder than before.

She twisted to see Dirk scrub his hand down his forehead

and nose, hold that hand over his mouth, and study her from the top of her head to her fuzzy feet, his gaze lingering an uncomfortable second too long on her slippers. She was sure he was coming up with all sorts of jokes about her appearance and was struggling to hold them in. Grateful for his silence, she'd be even more grateful for his disappearance. Why didn't he just walk away like Ted had?

Dirk finally lowered his hand and said, "Sesame Street called. Someone's abducted Cookie Monster. Pieces of him have been showing up all along the east coast. They haven't found his feet yet. Is there something you'd like to tell me, Kendal?"

"Yes. I'd like to inform you I have a pair of scissors in my pocket, and I've got an urge to start snipping a wagging tongue." If she could have said that without a smile on her face it would have been a lot more effective.

He laughed. "Gruesome. I'm scared!" He jiggled his knees and pretended to bite his nails.

She scowled like she meant it. There. Now, maybe he'd take her seriously, even though she was cracking up inside about the image of Cookie Monster feet.

"Oh come on, I was just joking, Little House. Don't get your panties in a bunch."

She picked up a lightweight tampon box and tossed it at his head.

He ducked, and the box hit the ball point pens hung in clear packs from a peg on the opposite side of the aisle. The peg dislodged, and the packs of pens slid to the floor.

He lunged to pick them up.

She held up her hand to stop him. "I'll get this. Just leave me alone, would ya? I've reached my limit of humiliation before coffee."

He had a sad expression, as if he actually felt sorry for teasing her, which was weird, because teasing her had been one of his favorite things to do their whole life. She was convinced of it.

Ted called out, "Come on, Dirk. I got our stuff. We're gonna be late. See ya, Kendal. Take care, Ashley." The bell that hung from the door jingled, and out he went.

Dirk gave her a nod and a wink, then jogged out of the store, waving to Ashley as he passed by. "Save a dance for me at the party, hot stuff."

Ashley giggled. "I will. Bye, Dirk."

Thank the Lord. They were gone. Finally.

Kendal knelt to pick up the pens. Her face throbbed with prickling heat, and her hands shook. Embarrassed didn't even come close to how she felt. She should've stuck to her guns and made her mother get her own gas this morning. Once again, caving in proved to be the wrong thing to do. When would she finally learn this lesson? Obviously, not today.

Cookie Monster feet? She pursed her lips to keep from laughing. Leave it to Dirk. She'd never be able to wear these shoes again, which might be for the best.

Dirk crawled into the passenger seat of Ted's truck. "Whoa, Kendal was looking unusually rough this morning."

Casting a bemused look Dirk's way, Ted pulled onto Lunar Avenue. "Why she wears those big ugly ass dresses baffles me. She isn't ugly, but her clothes are."

"You think she's pretty?"

"Yeah. I mean…she has a cute face. Who can tell what she looks like from the neck down?"

"You could find out what's under those tents she wears."

"Give me a break. I never even know what to say to her." Ted retrieved a Yoohoo and a honey bun from the bag that sat between them and passed the items to Dirk.

Their mother's voice invaded Dirk's thoughts. "You

don't need all that sugar. You need some protein."

The good son, Ted, opened his protein bar, the show off.

Ted wasn't into Kendal. She was too quiet and "goody two shoes". He needed someone edgier who enjoyed a walk on the dark side.

And like the good little brother Dirk was, he saw the opportunity to push Ted's buttons and went for it. "You should ask her out." That thought was hysterical. He could imagine it now. Their whole date-night conversation probably wouldn't even fill a single tweet #awkwardsilence.

Ted growled then barked, "Not happening." He tore the lid off his coffee.

"What's with the werewolf routine?"

Ted glared at him. As he slurped the dark elixir, he slowly transformed back into a human. A smile twitched in the corners of his mouth. "How much you want to bet she wears granny panties?"

Dirk got a clear mental image of Kendal in some old-fashioned bloomers with ruffles on the butt paired with those electric blue slippers that looked like she'd scalped a tribe of troll dolls to make them, and her face twisted into a "I'll get you, my pretty, and your little dog too" grimace.

Dirk tried to shake the image out of his head. "Whatever kind of panties she wears, they stay wadded."

"Ha!" Ted's first laugh of the day. One syllable, but it still counted. Score for Dirk. Coffee dribbled down Ted's chin onto his white T-shirt. Bonus points! And…the good son dropped the f-bomb. Game over. Dirk won.

Once parked in the front of the house scheduled for the day's renovations, Ted reached behind the passenger seat and pulled out a clean shirt.

No way. "Anal much, Ted?"

"Never hurts to be prepared."

"True. I get it. Mom still needs to send you off to school

with an extra set of clothes, in case you have an accident."

"Hey, as I recall you were the one who stood in the middle of your first grade classroom when you were picked to be Simon for Simon Says and got so excited you peed yourself and told everyone, 'Simon says, don't laugh at me.' Name one time I had an accident in school."

"I was brilliant even then. Who else can get the entire class out in one?"

Ted rolled his eyes.

"Okay then, I've got an example of a Ted accident for you. How about the time you spilled your spoiled milk science project all over Kendal on the bus?"

"The bus hit a bump. That's not the same thing as pissing yourself, and you know it."

"Right…cause Kendal was the one who needed the extra set of clothes."

"Give it up. I won this one. Anyway, Kendal was a real sport about it. Bottom line—she's a nice girl. I like her, but anyone who goes out with her better be prepared to enter into 'relationship zone.' She's the serious sort."

Serious sort was code for proud member of the "if you like it then you shoulda put a ring on it" club. "You think she's ever__"

Ted arched an eyebrow and cut him off. "I'd be surprised if she's even kissed. And that's sad, man. Really."

"True." Between her shyness and the way her mom controlled the poor girl's life, Dirk had never seen Kendal actually cut loose and have fun. "Think she'll go to the party?"

"Didn't she sit off to the side by herself last time and read a book on her iPhone?"

"Oh yeah. I forgot about that." He'd asked her to dance that night, but she turned him down, claiming she couldn't dance. Any girl who could play the piano like Kendal could knew a thing or two about rhythm. With that much music coursing through her veins, she could dance. She just needed to loosen up.

"Parties aren't her thing. Even if she does go, I doubt she'll enjoy herself. Anyway, let's get to work." Ted scanned his to-do-list. "What time do you need to fill in for the bridge tender today?"

"Between four and eight. Tomorrow, I'm covering his whole shift though. The chemo takes it out of him, and no one else is available."

"That's nice. Amazes me how you can do any and everything on the island."

"Except hold down a steady job?"

"Hey, I didn't say that. You stay busy. You make money. That's a steady job in my book."

A twinge of jealousy ran through Dirk. Ted had gone to college and gotten a degree in engineering and was offered a high paying job in Raleigh, but he passed it up and came home to help Dirk and their mother take care of their father, who was diagnosed with early onset dementia.

Dirk never went to college, wasn't even sure what he'd major in if given the opportunity. Plus, after Ted graduated high school, their dad started showing signs of memory loss, and Dirk stayed close to home to keep an eye on him. Luckily, people on the island kept tossing odd jobs Dirk's way. However, he didn't have anything close to what you'd call a career. Now that so many of his friends had graduated college and were embarking on full time jobs, he felt like a loser who still lived with his Mama.

Ted had his handyman business. It was a legitimate business—tax number, ad in the yellow pages, an official website. What did Dirk have? The ability to do just about anything that needed to be done on the island, but no actual career.

He'd help Ted this morning and fill in for the bridge tender later in the afternoon and tomorrow. Next week, he'd work the Sea Tow boat a few days and bartend at the local resort a few evenings.

If his buddy who ran the marina didn't get out of jury duty, he'd be handling the marina the following week. And this was normal for Dirk. Jack of all trades, master of none.

Dirk settled into the bridge tender booth and adjusted the radio to his favorite station. The late afternoon sunlight bounced off the calm water below. A couple dozen boats motored up and down the channel, but none were so large they'd require him to raise the bridge, which was a good thing. People always got irritated when traffic backed up. Unfortunately for him, it meant not having a damn thing to do but look out the window, listen to some music, and drink Red Bull to keep from dozing off on the job.

He liked to keep moving. This job was as sedentary as they came, which was perfect for Harvey, the guy he was working for. But for Dirk, it was torture.

Whenever a message came in over the control panel, the radio went silent—a safety feature built into the system to make sure no contacts were missed. A lot of the larger boats called in their requests. However, he had to be alert, because some of the sailboats were small, but had tall masts and didn't always have the ability to contact the control booth— or simply didn't realize the height of their mast was an issue.

About an hour into his shift, a shrimper requested clear passage.

Dirk had it down to science. When the boat got to the flag in front of the marina, he raised the bridge. When he saw the back of the boat, he lowered the bridge. The timing worked out perfectly.

He eyed the approaching shrimp boat. It was a good five

minutes before it reached the flag.

Jet skis and speedboats zipped up and down the waterway. A few small fishing boats trolled near the grassy areas along the shore. A paddle boarder glided toward him.

As the paddle board got closer, he gawked at the curvaceous woman paddling. He picked up the binoculars to get a closer look.

Yum. The young lady in a red bikini had full breasts that appeared soft and natural, luscious round hips, tiny waist, thighs he'd like to squeeze and nibble, and dark wavy hair that shined in the sunlight. He zoomed in on her face. And she had a face like Kendal Duvall!

Holy shit! *That* was Kendal? Oh my God. It couldn't be. She'd been hiding that body under those sack dresses? Jesus.

His mouth went dry. She stared straight ahead. He got another good look at her face. It was definitely Kendal…and she had a body like Jessica Rabbit. Who knew? Not him, that's for sure. Kendal was a hottie!

The shrimp boat blew his horn. Oh shit. He raised the bridge just in time.

He zoomed back in on Kendal. She was gorgeous with curves in all the right places. He loved a woman with some meat on her bones. Kendal was Grade A. Damn!

The shrimper blew his horn again and snapped Dirk to reality.

He had a clear view of the back of the shrimp boat. Time to lower the bridge.

The metal jaws of the drawbridge began to descend and car horns started blaring. *Geez, people. Be patient.* Next thing he heard was a loud crunch and the bridge got stuck midway.

What the hell? A tall mast was lodged in the mouth of the drawbridge. No! Had he closed the bridge on a sailboat? Where'd it come from?

He raced out of the booth and up the walkway, peering

over the edge of the rail into the angry face of the guy manning a sailboat with its mast broken like a twig. The guy yelled something up at him, but Dirk couldn't make out what he was saying. Nonetheless, he was pretty sure there were plenty of f-bombs being flung his direction. Oh, man. This was bad. What was he supposed to do?

He ran back to the controls and raised the bridge just as Sheriff Meyers tapped on the window of the booth.

Dirk squeezed his eyes shut, his heart racing, hands trembling, and a rock the size of a bowling ball in his stomach. What kind of idiot lowers the drawbridge on a sailboat? How could he do something so stupid?

She wore an itsy, bitsy, teeny, weeny, really smokin' hot bikini.

Now, *he* was afraid to come out of the tower.

CHAPTER TWO
Sheriff

Thanks to all the nightmares about the demonic drawbridge that ate sailboats, Dirk barely slept the night before. Now he faced Sheriff Meyers for "the final verdict talk" that would most likely end with Dirk being fined more money than he earned in a year.

From behind a mahogany desk, the young, dark-haired sheriff with a friendly manner and brawny physique gestured for Dirk to take a seat. "Dirk, breathe, man. Everything's fine. Turns out Brock Knight owned that sailboat you tore the mast off of, and he didn't want to file a report."

Brock Knight, an ex pro rugby player from Wales, was a super nice guy with plenty of dough from doing sporting good endorsements. Regardless, Dirk didn't feel right about Brock having to pay for everything. "I still need to reimburse him."

"Nah. Addison down at the marina salvaged an awesome replacement from an old junker. The sailboat was useless, but apparently, it had a fairly new, high dollar mast on it that fit Brock's boat perfectly. They already made the switch and gave it a test run this morning. Don't fret about a thing."

No way. He barely slept a wink all night from worrying about how he was going to pay for his mistake. Now the sheriff was telling him he was off the hook, completely?

How'd he manage to get so lucky? Was this too good to be true? There had to be a catch.

Meyers leaned forward. "Why don't you seem happy? You're sitting there all stiff-jawed. I figured you'd be dancing around the room."

"Sorry. Hard to believe this is real. This is my stunned face."

Meyers leaned back in his big leather executive chair with duct tape across the headrest. "I won't lie...I wasn't expecting things to fall into place so easily either. But if I were you, I'd be doing cartwheels."

He *was* doing cartwheels on the inside, but he was also trying to sniff out traces of b.s. "You sure I don't owe anything?" Didn't seem to be adding up to him. He had to have a fine or something. "Was there any damage to the bridge?"

"Damage to tons of steel? No, Dirk, the bridge came out of this without a scratch on it. I think your pride is about the only thing that got damaged, but you'll bounce back from that. Give it time. Something else will happen around here, and everybody will stop talking about the day you turned the bridge into a wood chipper." He pointed to the walls in his office that were adorned with memorabilia from odd things that had happened on the island. By the window hung a bent up hubcap from Trent McAllister's SUV that burnt to the ground last summer after chasing Mazy Washington through the ostrich farm. Over the fax machine was the melted hula hoop Myrtle Pinkerton had used last year at the hula contest. The poor old woman had wiggled too close to the bonfire. With her fuzzy blue hair, and the way she'd sprung out from that flaming hoop she'd looked like a poodle in the circus jumping through a ring of fire.

The sheriff pushed to his feet and walked over to the door. "The real reason I called you down here is to get your autograph."

His autograph? Was this a joke?

Sheriff Meyers closed the door that had been hiding part of the infamous broken mast, wedged in the corner of the room. With the splintered pole in his grip, he walked over to his desk and pointed to a black area on the teak wood. "I painted this section here for ya. Even went out and bought a metallic gold sharpie that should show up nicely on that dark background." He pulled the pen from a cup by his laptop. "If you don't mind, put a little description about what happened, the date, and your name. Take your time and write neat."

Dirk stared at the pen and couldn't quite wrap his brain around what was happening. This was surreal. The most disastrous event of his life was being immortalized by the sheriff himself? A brief description? *I got distracted by hooters and lowered the bridge on a sailboat.* No way was he going to tell the truth. Instead, he scrawled something about how the sailboat was tail-gating a shrimper, and due to the afternoon glare, Dirk didn't see the second boat when he lowered the bridge on top of it. He was tempted to sign it Dirk "the Jerk" Davis, but left off the alias Kendal had given him years ago.

"Thanks, man. Now, if you'll help me hang this 'half-mast', I'd be much obliged." Sheriff Meyers laughed at his own joke, opened up a step ladder, then pointed to the area over his office door.

Dirk climbed the ladder, and the sheriff passed him the unexpected souvenir. Hooks were already in the wall, waiting to receive the relic.

Just as Dirk lifted the heavy pole, he heard Kendal's voice in the lobby. "Spencer, stop it. I'm not telling him his zipper's down. You do it."

He was too close to the ceiling to see under the doorjamb

and into the lobby. He glanced down at his fly. Shit. She was talking about him, and he was going commando because he forgot to bring underwear to change into after his morning surf and hadn't had time to go home and get any before his meeting with the sheriff. He craned his neck to see if he was revealing his goods. Nope, just a few curlies and a patch of lower abs. He was in luck. Thank goodness his zipper was only down a couple of inches.

Clunk. One end of the mast hit something hard.

"Would you watch what the hell you're doing?" The sheriff fumed while rubbing the top of his head.

Oops. That had to hurt.

"Sorry, Sheriff. You okay?"

"I'll live. Hurry up and get down from there before you drop that thing."

Dirk finished his task as fast as he could, zipped his pants, and descended. When he had both feet back on the floor, he made eye contact with Kendal. Her brown eyes were sparkling with bemusement, and she looked like she was about to bite a hole in her bottom lip. Her best friend Spencer, the local florist, sat in an electric wheelchair with her back to him.

The sheriff pushed the intercom button on his phone. "Denise, would you mind bringing me a ziplock baggie of ice. I just thunked my head pretty hard."

Dang. He hoped he didn't hurt the guy too badly. That was a hard knock. "Sheriff, I really am—"

Meyers held up a hand, and Dirk went silent.

A grumpy female voice answered back. "Again? I swear you need a helmet."

Dirk couldn't help but grin at the idea of the sheriff walking around town wearing a helmet.

"Just bring me the ice would ya? And some Advil if we got any left."

Myrtle Pinkerton burst through the front door wearing a white top, tennis skirt, and highlighter-yellow running shoes. A tuft of frizzy pale blue hair looked like it had exploded through the top of her white ball cap, but he knew she was actually wearing a visor. Her Jiffy Pop head bobbled and her aged, wrinkled flesh quivered as she jogged past Kendal and Spencer giving them a little wave. The spunky old woman made a bee line straight for Dirk.

She curled her orange, lipstick-stained mouth into a smile. "So glad I didn't miss you. I was afraid you'd already be gone."

Was she talking to him? He pointed to himself and gave her a questioning look.

"Yes, you, honey. Who else? You're the talk of the town. Now, I'm gonna need a few pictures of you on the bridge. One for the Island Gazette and one with your shirt off for my craft club, if you don't mind. Louise wants to use your image for some new seat covers. Oh, and she said something about pillowcases with your smiling face on them too. I'd also like to interview you for my blog."

Myrtle's blog was the gossip column/news central for the island. It was one of those things everyone loved to read, but no one wanted to be featured in, unless you'd won a prize of some sort. Most of the time, however, it was the equivalent of a dunce cap. Whoever screwed up the biggest got top billing and an interview. Guess he was the big screw up of the week.

Myrtle poked her head into Meyers' office. "Sheriff, mind if I borrow Dirk for a bit?"

The sheriff leaned back in his chair, still rubbing his head. "You can have him."

Myrtle hooked her little bird-wing arm in Dirk's. "Come with me then." She speed-waddled toward the front door in that short white skirt and bright yellow shoes like a duck jacked up on espresso. Dirk had to damn near jog to keep up, until she came to an abrupt halt by Kendal and Spencer.

Myrtle chirped, "Y'all delivering flowers to Deputy Litton?"

Kendal shyly looked away when Dirk smiled at her. She was so freaking adorable, and she didn't even know it. He could look past that loose black dress she was wearing that covered her from collar bone to ankle. Now that he knew what she was hiding, he could recall the luscious vision beneath anytime he wanted. Like now.

Spencer pointed to a vase full of roses on the counter. "Yep, there they are right there. How'd you guess?"

Myrtle reached over and plucked the card from the bouquet and had it opened before Spencer could snatch it away from the nosy woman. "That's private. You can't do that."

"It ain't that private. You know what's on the card."

"That's different. He dictated what he wanted put on there." Spencer covered her mouth like she wished she hadn't said that.

While Myrtle and Spencer had it out, he inched closer to Kendal and caught a whiff of her jasmine scent. She flashed him a quizzical look. He let his gaze fall to her glistening ruby lips, and her face went bright pink. Absolutely adorable.

"So, he's not a local guy. I kind of suspected that." Myrtle tapped a finger on her chin. "It's one of two fellas. Does he have a French accent?"

"Myrtle, I am not telling you anything. If Deputy Litton or her suitor want you to know, they can tell you. You're overstepping here."

Myrtle grinned. "That's the only way you get anywhere in life, honey. You step over everything in your way. Mark my words. That's a lesson worth learning while you're young."

Myrtle tugged his arm. Guess that was his cue it was time

to go.

Before he left, he needed to know one thing. "You girls going to the party tonight?"

Spencer answered first. "You bet."

Kendal just smiled and said, "Plan on it."

"Good. Save me a dance, both of ya."

Spencer pointed down at her wheelchair and gave him the you're-crazy face. Kendal wrinkled her nose and tucked a strand of hair behind her ear. He'd take that as a yes from both.

Good. Kendal *was* going, and if he had anything to do with it, she wouldn't have time to read. She was going to be far too busy shaking her groove thang.

Ted jokingly shoved Dirk, causing him to bump into the kitchen table and nearly knock over their mom's favorite glass pitcher. Quick-reflex Ted, righted the pitcher without missing a beat. "Punk. You always make out. Here I was all worried, and you got the sheriff asking for your autograph like you're some kind of celebrity. You screw up and get a medal. What the—"

"Damn it! Y'all better listen to me!" Their father bellowed from the living room.

They rushed to see what had upset the man and found him standing in front of the T.V., holding up a handwritten sign that read: *Somebody talk to me.*

Ted pulled the sign from his father's grasp. "What's this all about, Dad?"

"These crazy people keep yammering away, and I can't get their attention. All I want is another peanut butter and jelly sandwich. None of them will lift a sorry finger. We should fire them. They ain't done a damn thing all day besides talk, talk, talk."

Dirk stifled his laughter. Laughing at their father would be inappropriate. It was sad his sense of reality was so fractured. When Dirk locked eyes with Ted, there was no holding it in. They both burst out laughing.

The look in Ted's eyes, in spite of his laughter, mirrored Dirk's own conflicted emotions. They had to either laugh or cry sometimes, and laughter helped them keep going. Crying just broke them a little more, and they needed to stay strong for their mother's sake, if not their own.

"What's wrong with you people? You think I don't know when two grown men are giggling like teenage girls that drugs are involved?"

Ted straightened up. "Sorry, Pop."

"I don't want no damn pop. I want a peanut butter and jelly sandwich and a glass of milk."

Dirk said, "I'll make you a sandwich, Dad. Come on into the kitchen."

"I'm not your dad. My boys are still in grade school. See there." He pointed to an old family photo. "I don't know what you people are trying to pull around here. I might be sick, but I haven't lost my mind."

In black leggings and a lime sports bra, their mom came through the patio door, her blonde hair pulled away from her slim, angular face. She removed her pink earbuds that matched her pink and lime running shoes. She had to color coordinate just to go for a jog. Dirk was convinced it was a sickness. "How nice, both sons in the house at the same time. Seems like that rarely happens these days."

Their dad, George Davis, squinted at them then eyed his wife. "These are your boys?" He pointed to Dirk and Ted.

"Yes, George. They're yours too."

They're dad stared at the old family photo then swiveled his gaze back to the brothers with his mouth twisted into a pretzel. "Kizzie, I don't want to take any more of those purple pills you've been feeding me."

She frowned at him. "The Prilosec? It's for your acid reflux."

"They aren't sitting with me too well. No more of those. You hear me?"

"Of course, George." She dabbed her face with the towel draped around her neck. "No more Prilosec. Bring on the indigestion. Let me go get supper started. I'll make it as bland as possible."

Dirk and Ted looked at their dad, the silence between the three men was uncomfortable, to say the least.

Picking up his remote control, and flopping back down into his recliner, their father aimed the clicker at the T.V. "Y'all still like Bugs Bunny? I get the cartoon channel."

Ted grinned. "Bugs is my favorite."

"Good Lord, Louise. What have you done?" Their mom cried out.

Dirk rushed to the kitchen. There stood Louise Moore, Myrtle's best friend. Louise was nearly six feet tall in her wedge heels, shoulders as broad as a line-backer's, bouffant puke green hair. And apparently she'd been crying cause she had black mascara tracks down her reddened, wrinkled cheeks. She touched her head. "I made a mess of it this time, Kizzie. You think you can help me out?"

Ted came up behind Dirk. "At least she doesn't have a bald spot on her crown in the shape of a penis this time." He whispered so low his voice was barely audible.

Dirk choked down a laugh, remembering how many variations of pecker-head the islanders had come up with the last time Louise dyed her own hair.

Their mom gave them a stern look then took a deep breath. She ran her fingers through Louise's green locks. "I'll have to strip the color out, but I can fix you up."

"I know it's after hours, but do you think you can fix it this evening? I'm desperate, Kizzie. Tonight's the big party, and I can't go like this. Myrtle will make me queen of the day on her blog."

"Oh dear, okay. Go on down to Curl Up and Dye, and I'll meet you there in a few minutes."

When Louise disappeared out the side door, Dirk sang, "Ho, ho, ho…Green Giant."

Ted elbowed him in the ribs and smirked.

Their mom stared at both of them, straight-faced, then broke out in a smile that set her blue eyes sparkling. "I've told y'all not to make fun of others, but sometimes…" She shook her head and never finished her sentence. "Lord, help me. Never a dull moment around here. That's for sure. Can one of you stick around 'til I get back, keep an eye on your dad and make sure he gets fed? There's a chicken and rice casserole in the freezer."

Ted lifted his hand. "My shift for dad-duty."

"Thanks, Sugar. I don't know what I'd do without you two. Best sons on the planet. I do know that." She gave them each a peck on the cheek then hurried out the door.

Once alone in the kitchen again, Ted turned to Dirk. "You're still going to the party tonight, right?"

Heck yeah, he was going to the party. Kendal said she was going be there, and he was eager to have a chance to get close to her, do a little slow dancing. Sure, he had to keep things casual with her so as not to lead her on, but nothing wrong with a little harmless flirting. "Yeah, probably. You going?"

"I might swing by later on. Did you hear that Mazy and Trent are now officially engaged?"

"Good for them." Dirk studied his brother's face. He knew Ted had carried a torch for Mazy for a while. Even though he claimed he was over it, still, hearing she was getting married might hit him hard.

"I didn't like Trent much at first, but damn if he hasn't grown on me. We hung out at the pier the other day. He's a decent fisherman. Good all around guy, and he loves Mazy to pieces. That's the main thing."

Ted didn't appear upset a bit. Good. "He's a decent surfer too, but what the hell man, he's an ex-Navy SEAL. He knows his way around water."

"Plenty of that around here. This place seems to suit him. Oh, I also heard Heidi was back in town." Ted licked his lips. Ashley's cousin, Heidi, had spent her summers on the island for the past four years, and each summer she and Ted had gotten together at some point.

"Every summer you hook up with that girl only to get your heart broken when she goes back to Michigan. You sure you want to go down that road again?"

Ted shrugged. "She's a blast to be around. What can I say?"

He had no business giving Ted a hard time. Dirk was the poster child for just having a little fun with the ladies. And if he was lucky, maybe he could convince Kendal into having a little fun with him tonight.

CHAPTER THREE
Party

Kendal stopped by Big Kabloom flower shop to pick up Spencer, who took one look at her and said, "Unless you're hiding a band of clowns on tricycles under that tent you're wearing, you're going to have zero fun at the party tonight."

Some greeting that was. Spencer was usually nice. When had she morphed into Kendal's mom? "I don't know what you're talking about. This dress is pretty and brand new."

"Pretty? It makes you look pregnant."

Ouch. That hurt. Kendal had recently lost some weight, nearly twenty pounds. She'd even found the courage to wear a bikini the day before and thought she'd looked okay in it. Now, was her best friend calling her fat? Spencer had never teased Kendal about her weight before.

Her pain must have been visible, because Spencer's expressions softened and she said, "Kendal, seriously, you have a great body. You're not fat. I know you think you are, and you're hyper sensitive about it, but you're *not* fat. I promise. That dress simply isn't doing you any favors. It's a muumuu. I thought we agreed you were done with muumuus."

"Whatever. I just want to be comfortable. We're going to a party on the beach, not some fancy nightclub." Muumuu? Really? Her dress was on trend. She bought it at Forever

Young in the mall last week. "Since I didn't bring anything else to wear, it'll have to do. I don't pick on your wardrobe."

She eyed the little black dress Spencer wore. There was nothing to pick on. Spencer was about as cute as they come — skinny as a rail, thick dark hair that she'd flat-ironed, flawless porcelain complexion, and makeup applied beautifully, including false eyelashes and red lipstick.

Spencer motioned her to follow as she drove her electric wheelchair out the back door of the shop and toward the house she shared with her folks. "Come with me. I'm sure I have something in my closet that'll fit ya."

"Are you nuts? You wear a size zero. I wear an eight."

"Never underestimate the power of spandex." Spencer grinned as she rolled through her living room and down the hall to her bedroom. She wheeled into her walk-in closet and pulled out a sherbert-orange tube dress. "Try this one. It's too big on me. It'll probably fit you just right."

"How am I supposed to wear a bra with this?"

"You aren't. It has a built in bra."

Kendal turned the bodice of the dress inside out and tugged at the flap of fabric trimmed with elastic that was suppose to be a bra. "This won't be enough support for me. Get real." Without underwire her girls would be a pair of jiggling water balloons.

Spencer shoved the dress toward her. "Try it on before you rule it out."

"Fine." She yanked the dress from her friend's hand and stepped into the bathroom to put it on, just to prove her point. Once she squeezed into the dress, she looked in the mirror. The dress showed every curve and dimple. She looked like one of those orange marshmallow candies shaped like a peanut. Well, maybe not quite that many dimples. She turned sideways and touched her lower belly. If only that little pooch was completely flat. "It shows my tummy too much." She opened the bathroom door and Spencer snapped her picture. "What are you doing?"

Spencer held out her camera so Kendal could see the snapshot. "Before you tell me this dress makes you look fat, I want you to take a good look at yourself."

Actually, in the picture the dress flattered her curves nicely. She'd always heard the camera put on ten pounds, but apparently, in her case, the mirror did that, not the camera. Yeah, mirrors had a long history of deception where she was concerned.

Spencer pulled the camera back and flipped something on the device then held it out again. "This dress *does* make you look fat."

Kendal gazed at a picture of herself standing on the sidewalk outside of Spencer's front door. The white billowy maxi dress did make her appear as wide as she was tall. That *was* a tent, for sure. She really did need to hang a *Ringling Bros. and Barnum & Bailey* sign around her neck.

"See what I mean? You aren't fat. That dress is just too big. Be brave. Show off your curves, girl. I wish I had them."

Kendal scanned Spencer's bony frame. She thought about the car accident that had left her friend paralyzed from the waist down at the age of sixteen. The drunk driver who had hit her barely had a scratch on him. Talk about unfair. Spencer had endured a lot of health complications due to that accident, one being digestive troubles. A wave of guilt washed over Kendal. She had no business whining about her body to Spencer of all people.

She had to admit, the orange dress was a lot sexier than the long white one. But after a lifetime of her mother telling her to keep her body covered so she didn't give guys the wrong impression, it was hard to convince herself it was okay to dress a tad racy. Combine that conservative mentality with years of being referred to as chubby, and you have the ingredients needed to create body dysmorphia, as the pros called it.

Add an encounter with a group of teenage boys who played grab-boob and didn't take no for answer, a cousin who claimed having your boobs grabbed by high school football players when you were in the sixth grade was some kind of accomplishment, and a mother who would've blamed you for the incident because you wore a tight shirt—now, you have the recipe for creating a twenty-five year old virgin who hides in baggy clothes and panics when placed in intimate situations with the opposite sex, just like Kendal.

But tonight, Kendal was on a mission to slay her demons. Granting herself permission to dress however *she* wanted was a step in the right direction. Those teen boys had been wrong to touch her years ago. Her cousin had been wrong to imply their inappropriate behavior was a compliment. And her mother had been wrong to make her believe her attire excused or invited sleazy male actions.

Furthermore, a size eight was not fat. That orange, body-hugging dress was flattering without being so skimpy she felt uncomfortable. It wasn't low cut or extremely short. It made her feel sexy, and maybe it was high time she felt that way.

She blew out a breath. "Thank you, Spencer. Mind if I wear your dress tonight?"

Spencer beamed. "I insist. Heck, you can have it. Maybe it will be your lucky charm and help you land someone to have a summer fling with."

Laughing the comment off, Kendal said, "Very funny. You knew I wasn't serious about that."

At the time she'd confessed to Spencer that she had decided to have a summer fling to help her get over her anxiety of intimacy, specifically sexual intimacy, she had just downed half a bottle of wine and was on her second Corona. She couldn't be held to the craziness she'd blabbed while intoxicated. But the truth was, she'd put a lot of thought into that fling idea while sober, and secretly, she wished she had the guts to pursue it.

"Girl, I can read you like a book, and you weren't joking. Besides, I'm all for it. I think it's a great idea. And if you can't go all the way, at least make out with someone before the summer's over."

Spencer was the only person who knew for a fact Kendal had never even French kissed a guy. Being that inexperienced would be cool, if she were say…fifteen instead of twenty-five. At twenty-five that "never been properly kissed" fact was an embarrassment. It made her feel like a freak. Whether it should or not, it did.

Now it was time to kick her fears to the curb. She wasn't going to let her mother's over-protective ways or one bad experience with a group of idiot teen boys with raging hormones prevent her from having a healthy life—a life in which she wore what made her feel attractive, a life that included a boyfriend and sex, if she chose.

However, taking those first steps into that lifestyle was scary. But she had to power through, because the truth was —sitting at home alone wasn't doing it for her anymore.

Spencer grabbed her hand and gave it a squeeze. "You're gorgeous. And I'm not just saying that because you're my friend. You've been hiding your flame under a haystack for far too long, just like Myrtle said."

"You mean light under a bushel. I'm pretty sure it's impossible to hide a flame under a haystack. Well, maybe not impossible, but the fire you'd cause would give you away."

Spencer laughed. "Whatever. You have a smoking bod."

Kendal took a deep breath and smiled. "Thanks. You're the best." She looked around for Spencer's service dog. "Where's Benny?"

"Playing in the yard. Bring him in for me?"

"Sure." Kendal opened the door and Spencer's golden lab bounded toward her, his tail wagging. "Hey there, Benny. How you doing, boy?" Scratching the friendly dog behind the ears, it sat at her feet attentively.

Spencer drove her wheelchair over and placed the service harness on the dog. "Does Benny wanna see Myrtle?"

Benny's ears went back and his tail wagged at turbo speed upon the mention of the island's favorite pint-sized senior citizen.

"Myrtle will be at the party." Spencer had the dog's undivided attention. He tugged on his leash until her chair started rolling.

Kendal opened the door. "Myrtle needs a fan club. I swear."

"What makes you think she doesn't have one? What do you call all her blog followers? She's already a world-wide celebrity. Make no mistake about it."

Kendal leaned close to Spencer. "I really like your new beach wheelchair. It's a lot easier to push in the sand than the old one."

Spencer patted the armrests, "This one's more comfy too."

When they crested the highest dune along the sandy path, the beach opened up before them. Tiki torches formed a barrier around the group of more than fifty people already present—mingling, dancing, laughing. The aroma of burgers on the grill was carried on the breeze and made Kendal's stomach growl. Music and laughter filtered through the air.

Spencer sat up straight. "This party is going to be a whopper. Come on. Push faster!"

Kendal's palms pooled with sweat and her heart raced. She hoped her apprehension wasn't noticeable to others.

Parties weren't her thing. She sucked at making small talk, dancing, telling jokes, and most of all flirting. If they'd offered a "How to Party 101" class in college, she would've gladly taken it.

Spencer, on the other hand, never met a stranger and could knock mugs with the best of them. She had a way of making everything fun. Kendal figured she'd be okay as long as she played sidekick to Spencer tonight.

Halfway down the beach path, redheaded fraternal twins Mazy and Earl from Kendal's graduating class at Island High strode toward them. Mazy waved, her long hair whipping about her pale, smiling face. Earl kept his hands shoved in his pockets, a slight grin curling the edges of his mouth.

Spencer glanced back at Kendal and said, "Does Earl look like he's in a bad mood to you?"

Kendal studied his expression. When they were kids, she was able to read him at a glance. But after spending a little time in jail, he'd developed mad skills at putting up a tough-guy front.

She caught his gaze with hers. He winked. "Nah, he's just trying to act cool. He's fine."

Earl held a special place in her heart. After his mom died during his senior year of high school, he and Mazy struggled to make ends meet, while their dad rode off into the sunset on his Harley, instead of taking care of them. Earl got mixed up with the wrong crowd, robbed a couple of vacation homes while the owners were away and sold off the goods to pay the electric bill and buy groceries.

Even though Earl had made some bad decisions, Kendal truly believed that he would have avoided jail time if he had been able to afford a decent lawyer. That jail time had done more damage to him than good. Once he'd served his sentence and was released, she thought he'd come back home and pick up the pieces, and he'd tried, but he ended up wandering off. She was so glad he'd found his way back home again and was finally getting his life moving in a positive direction. She'd really missed him. She realized he was Mazy's twin brother, but in some ways, it seemed like he was hers too, even though they weren't related.

When the gap closed between them, Mazy said, "Holy Cow, Kendal. You look amazing tonight."

Earl nodded. "Smokin'."

Kendal's face warmed. As much as she appreciated the compliments, they did little to calm her jitters, if anything, they made her more anxious. "Thank you." Not wanting the attention to be focused on her, she said, "Show us your ring, Mazy!"

Mazy held out her hand and showed off her engagement ring, a teardrop-shaped one-karat diamond set in yellow gold. "Trent surprised me last night. I had a feeling he was up to something. We'd never taken that dinner cruise from Crystal Cove to Wilmington before. When he got on one knee and held out that little ring box, I almost keeled over into my chocolate mousse."

Kendal and Spencer made a fuss over the ring and Mazy ate every bit of it up then pushed her red hair from her face. "Y'all are just in time. Myrtle and Louise are about to battle it out for the hula hoop championship."

Spencer laughed and cracked an invisible whip. "Giddy-up. I don't want to miss this."

Earl motioned Kendal to step aside. He grabbed the handles of Spencer's chair, tilted her back, and tore off running. Spencer squealed with glee. Mazy and Kendal ran after them.

Kendal's boobs nearly bounced right out of her dress. She clutched the fabric to her bosom and stopped, pretending to need to catch her breath while she readjusted herself. When Mazy looked back, Kendal waved her on.

A deep voice sounded behind Kendal. "You okay?"

She spun around. Dirk Davis stared down at her with a tense expression, like the sight of her hurt him.

She straightened her spine. "Yeah. I'm fine. Just out of shape, I guess."

His gaze slowly traveled the length of her body. "You're far from out of shape."

Was he suggesting being in shape was so far out of her reach it wasn't even funny? She sucked in her stomach and tightened her jaw. "Don't you start picking on me, Dirk. Not every girl is meant to be a toothpick."

"Thank God for that. You don't hear me complaining. What makes you think I'd pick on you about your figure?"

"Well, you pick on me about everything else." She studied his face.

His mouth twitched like he was fighting back a grin. "Girl, you have no idea."

"No idea about what?" Was he patronizing her? Was that a smug expression on his face or was he amused? Either way, his weird smirk annoyed her. "Since you don't think I have any idea, how about you clue me in."

A slow smile replaced his smirk, but he didn't respond.

She reached out to shove his arm and demand he tell her what he meant by "no idea", but when her fingertips touched his firm bicep, she froze. An unexpected surge coursed through her veins. Instead of shoving him, her hand lingered as if held in place by a magnet.

His eyes met hers. "You have no idea...how sexy you are."

What? She jerked her hand away from his arm, as if he'd just burned her. In an instant, he'd somehow managed to turn her bones to jelly. Her heart beat double time. Did he really just call *her* sexy?

She took a deep breath. Why did hearing him say that

suddenly make *him* the sexiest man alive? Maybe it was true that flattery gets you everywhere.

Whew. She was kind of dizzy. Well, not exactly dizzy, just woozy. Was woozy even the right word? Whatever this sensation was called, it felt strange. But a good kind of strange.

Did he *really* think she was sexy?

Wait. This was playboy Dirk. She'd finally caught a glimpse of why so many girls were wild about him. He had some sort of magical charm. This was just the first time he'd used it on her. He wasn't being serious. He was yanking her chain, and she wasn't going to fall for it.

She tossed her hair and put her hand on her hip. "That's where you're wrong. You're the one who doesn't know *exactly* how sexy I am." Of course he'd know she was joking, but he'd been joking, so she had to volley back. Otherwise, he'd think she bought that b.s.

"I'm starting to get an idea." He grinned.

"It's about time. I'd hate for you to go through life having no idea." She wasn't completely sure that made a dang bit of sense, but it was all she could do to keep from laughing.

"I'm with you on that one. I'd hate to have gone through life having *no* idea either." There went that head-to-toe gaze sliding down her body again, accompanied by that slow, easy smile of his.

Good grief. She was downright panting. How'd he do that?

Who cares how. This was fun.

She turned and sashayed toward the party, making sure her hips were swinging hard. Every time she glanced over her shoulder at Dirk, who followed close behind her, he had a big cheesy grin on his face, but he didn't say a word. And he wasn't laughing at her antics. In fact, he seemed to be quite enthralled with her hip action.

So this was what it felt like to flirt.

Good grief. She was actually biting her bottom lip like some sex-kitten taking a selfie. At least he didn't see that. But as far as the flirting thing goes, maybe she *could* do this after all.

Twist those hips, girl. Ouch. Rib pain. Yeah, maybe don't twist quite so hard.

CHAPTER FOUR
Hula

When they reached the crowd, everyone had formed a circle around Myrtle Pinkerton and Louise Moore. Myrtle's fuzzy pale blue hair was backlit by the moon, and she resembled a Q-tip. Louise stood nearly a foot taller than Myrtle and had a figure like Julia Child, hair the color of tomato juice, slightly more crayon-red than normal. They wore matching neon pink bikinis and held glow-in-the-dark hula hoops.

Kendal knelt in the sand beside Spencer's wheelchair. "I'm glad they had the sense not to do this by the bonfire this year."

Spencer started laughing. "Did you notice Sheriff Meyers had Myrtle's melted hula hoop from last year hanging up in his office?"

"No way."

"Yep. I saw it when we delivered flowers to deputy Litton. I'm surprised you didn't see it."

Kendal had been checking Dirk out too hard to notice much of anything. She'd been seriously distracted seeing him standing on a step stool, his arms raised just enough to cause his shirt to rise and reveal his rock hard abs, and his zipper down a little. Whew. That was enough to throw anyone off their game. She'd stood there in the lobby, concentrating, trying to invoke telekinetic powers to inch that zipper down farther. Alas, she possessed no such powers. But it'd been worth a try.

"Shake Your Booty" by KC and the Sunshine Band blared from a nearby boombox, and Myrtle and Louise began to dance with their hula hoops.

Spencer whistled and cheered. "Come on, ladies. Shake those thangs."

On the opposite side of the circle. Dirk sipped a beer. He caught Kendal's attention and lifted his long-neck bottle as if to say, "cheers." She gave him a nod in return, and tried to ignore the trembling sensation that swirled in her tummy.

Yep. The other girls on the island were right. Dirk really could do things to a woman without even touching her.

The two old ladies entertained the crowd, shimmying with all their might. Normally, Kendal wouldn't have been able to take her eyes off the women, but tonight she kept watching Dirk. He had a great smile. Why hadn't she ever paid attention to his smile before now? He stood beside Ted, and they were both laughing at the way Myrtle nearly did a split to keep her hula hoop from reaching the ground, but Dirk's laughter was more raw and real than his brother's. Ted looked like he was holding back, afraid if he laughed too hard he wouldn't look cool or tough. Dirk didn't seem to care what he looked like. He threw his head back and let the laughter rip from his gut, enjoying the moment to the fullest. She bet he didn't hold back in bed either, just threw his head back and enjoyed. She'd like to know what that was like.

Spencer leaned toward Kendal. "I see who you're eyeing tonight. Excellent choice. He'd be the perfect summer fling."

"I wasn't serious about the fling. I told you that."

"Dirk never kisses and tells." Spencer waggled her brows. "I hear he's awesome in bed."

"Spencer! What's gotten into you?"

Spencer looked over Kendal's shoulder and folded her

lips inward, indicating they best hush about this for now.

Earl sauntered toward them, carrying three beers. "Hey, figured y'all could use a drink. Looks like the hula girls are going to be at it for a while."

"You're such a nice guy." Spencer cooed as she reached for a beer.

Earl frowned. "Those are not words a man wants to hear a woman say. 'How did you know exactly what I need?' That would be much better."

Spencer spewed her beverage all over the front of his shorts. Earl froze, didn't move a muscle, didn't crack a smile, didn't say a word.

Spencer's eyes grew wide, and she covered her mouth with her hand. A muffled, "I'm sorry," leaked between her fingers.

Kendal couldn't hold it in. She threw her head back and laughed full force like Dirk.

Earl narrowed his gaze at her and held up an index finger. His lips pinched into a disapproving pucker, but the flicker of amusement in his eyes gave him away. He handed Spencer his Corona and proceeded to march straight to the ocean and into the breakers.

Spencer appeared nervous. "I didn't mean to do that. I hope he isn't mad. What's he doing?"

"My guess would be he's just rinsing off. Better to have his shorts completely wet than just his crotch." Another chuckle bubbled out of Kendal.

"Oh." Spencer took a swig of ale with her brow furrowed. Kendal could almost hear her tender-hearted friend's gears whirring, no doubt trying to figure how to best handle the situation.

"Relax, Spencer. He's not upset. I wish I'd thought to snap a picture of him before he got in the water, though. Man, you had good aim."

Spencer beamed. "I did nail him right in the fly, didn't I?

"Yes, you did." Kendal looked up just in time to witness Myrtle's hula hoop hitting the sand. Louise let out a woohoo and jumped around clapping her hands. Myrtle had won the past three years. It was nice to see Louise win for a change.

When the crowd began to scatter, Bikini Quartet's leggy, blonde bass player Sam and her gorgeous British husband Brock walked over. Mazy Washington, the band's drummer, and her hot new fiancé Trent McAllister were close behind.

Mazy said, "Why are your pants wet, Earl?"

He shrugged. "Went wading in the ocean. That all right with you?"

"You did see the port-a-potties on the hill, right?"

"Ha. Very funny." Earl cocked his head as if irritated by Mazy's sisterly digs.

Dirk joined their tight circle of friends and stood between Brock and Kendal as the gang continued to chatter away.

Her pulse kicked into high gear. When Dirk's arm brushed against hers, she scooted away to give him more elbow room. He looked at her with that laid-back smile of his and motioned her to move back over. She inched back to her spot, and he motioned her closer still. As she fought back a snicker, Spencer gave her a little shove, and she stumbled toward him. Kendal glared at Spencer.

Dirk caught Kendal with one arm and snugged her up close. "Hey, Little House. I'm happy to see you too."

She couldn't contain her giggle-snort. Embarrassing! She lowered her head and accidentally bumped it against Dirk's shoulder. He wrapped his arm around her tighter and clinked his beer with hers. "Great party, huh?"

She smiled up at him. "Yeah." Dirk's relaxed manner, how he enveloped her without a care that they were in a group and everyone could see what he was doing, helped her calm down. Because he was being so nonchalant, she was able to keep her trembling to a minimum, which shocked her. Normally, when in the flirt-zone, she shook like every bone in her body was a vibrator set on high.

Dirk acted like cuddling her up was the most natural thing to do—relaxed old friends, ultra-casual. Yet, he'd never done it before. No guy had ever done that before, not even Earl.

Brock nudged Dirk. Dirk dropped his arm from around Kendal, and she immediately moved away from him a few inches.

Spencer waggled her brows again. Kendal tried to pretend she didn't notice, but dang, Spencer needed to cool it.

Brock spoke to Dirk, "If you wouldn't mind helping me repair the pier, I'd appreciate it. But I insist on paying you. Stop feeling guilty about the sailboat. Really. It's been the highlight of my summer. Nothing brings me more happiness than seeing terror in my brother's eyes. Scratch that. Nothing brings me greater joy than recording my brother screaming like a toddler and having something to blackmail him with for the rest of his life. I'm indebted to you."

Sam draped herself across her handsome husband and touched Dirk's arm. "You've nothing to be ashamed of, Oh Mighty Bridge Muncher. You've served us well."

Kendal piped up. "Yeah, Dirk, be proud. You're Pleasure Island's very own weapon of mast destruction." That statement made everyone bust out laughing. Dirk laughed harder than anyone else. Yay.

When Dirk caught his breath, he said, "Little House, you cracked a joke, and it was a good one. I'm proud of you."

Sam grinned at her. "Weapon of mast destruction…oh, I'm so telling Myrtle that one. She'll roll with it. My dear, don't be surprised if you hear your punchline repeated on Letterman. Remember how she got that picture of Mazy on

Leno?"

Mazy's eyes flew open wide and Trent wrapped her up in his arms and said, "I'm not afraid."

Mazy looked back at him and smiled.

Dirk's face went pale. "No. No. Don't tell Myrtle. Come on, Sam. I thought we were friends. Don't do that to me. I'm already the butt of the joke these days on the island. I don't want any more attention drawn to me."

Kendal could practically feel the tension in his muscles as his voice escalated to a higher pitch. She could certainly relate to his panic about being Myrtle's target.

Sam and Brock shared a knowing look and grinned. Sam said, "Guess you don't want to know how many views that video Brock filmed of the bridge fiasco has received on Youtube today."

Dirk covered his face. "Y'all didn't post it. Please say you're bluffing."

Aww, he was really embarrassed. She'd never seen him this way. She wanted to put her arm back around him and console him, but people might read too much into that. She wasn't the touchy feely kind like Dirk was.

Brock cleared his throat. "No bluff, mate. I posted it a couple hours before the party. Right before we left the house, it had over a hundred thousand views."

"Nooooo." Dirk's mouth fell open. He squeezed his eyes shut. "I'm never going to live this down, am I?"

Earl stepped forward, his expression dialed to gloat. "Nope. And I'm loving it."

That was mean.

Kendal glared at Earl. He gave her a "what?" look.

Dirk opened his eyes and met Earl's gaze. "Come on, Earl. I never expected you to get stuck with the nickname Squirrel. We were just kids. You were caught stealing nuts, for Christ Sakes. I couldn't resist."

Spencer spewed her beer again. "That's how you got that name?"

Earl's face turned bright red, and he raised one eyebrow. "Y'all don't want to know what squirrel means to some of the guys in prison. I'll give ya a little hint. Think: tail and mouthful of nuts."

Spencer gasped. Kendal made eye contact with her, and they shared their "uh-oh" face.

Yikes. Poor, Earl.

Dirk got serious. "Oh shit."

Earl nodded. "Yeah. My thoughts exactly when I found out on my first night behind bars. Luckily, I had sense enough to act insane so no one wanted to come near me. I'm pretty sure you'll survive this."

Mazy stood with her arm linked in Trent's. She playfully kicked Earl. "Jesus, Earl. You really know how to be a buzz kill."

Trent said, "You aren't in jail anymore, Squirrel. Feel free to stop acting insane anytime you'd like."

That made everyone laugh again.

Dirk caught Kendal's eye once more, as they both enjoyed the humorous moment with their friends. He gave her a little wink and her heart became a skipping stone across the water.

When the gang meandered over to the grilling area. Kendal found herself alone with Spencer once again.

"You should give some serious thought to hooking up with Dirk. He's been flirting up a storm with you." Spencer's gaze was intense, as if she'd been reading Kendal's mind. "He'd be discreet, wouldn't push you into anything you weren't ready for, and wouldn't try to get too serious."

Kendal couldn't deny the notion held appeal. He certainly had her hormones doing their own version of the hula. Maybe Spencer was right. If she didn't want to end up an old maid, she needed to learn how to assert herself.

"What do I do? Just walk up to him and suggest we have a fling?"

Spencer shook her head. "Maybe something more subtle. How about you ask him to come fix your leaky faucet?"

"I don't have a leaky faucet."

Spencer rolled her eyes. "I know that, but he doesn't. Unscrew something. Make it leak. Whatever. Just find some excuse to get him alone. Once you're alone with him, you can ease into the conversation, and see how he feels about it."

"You mean lure him into a trap."

"It's not a trap. It's just a chance to talk in private. It's not like you can discuss it with him here in front of everyone."

Earl walked toward them with a couple plates of food. Kendal whispered, "Here comes Earl. We'll talk about this later."

Spencer jerked her head toward the freckle-faced redhead and bit her lower lip.

Earl smiled down at Spencer. "Chill out. I'm not mad about you for spraying me like a human fountain. I brought you girls a couple cheeseburgers."

Spencer's eyes twinkled.

Kendal said, "Thanks, Earl, but I'm not really hungry. You and Spencer go ahead."

Earl shrugged. "More for us."

Spencer grinned. "How did you know exactly what I need?"

Earl chuckled. "I always know what you need, darling. Never doubt it."

Wow. Earl was getting bold these days. It was like watching a frog sun himself on a rock, puckering up for a smooch. Cute, goofy, and totally cartoonish, but she couldn't deny there was a touch of Prince Charming in him tonight. Was he seriously hitting on Spencer?

Warm breath tickled the back of Kendal's neck.

"Care to dance, Little House?"

Dirk. Goosebumps popped out all over her. She faced him. "I'd like to, but I'm a really bad dancer, and you're… you're a freaking dance champion."

"Shh. It's a slow song. Just wrap your arms around my neck and sway."

She loved how his smooth, easy-going way set her at ease. Normally, she would have been a wreck. She trembled a little, but her muscles weren't jumping like jack rabbits. This was okay. She could handle it.

He sat her drink down, took her hands in his, and led her toward the area where other couples were dancing. His eyes never left hers. Placing her hands behind his neck, he said. "Don't be nervous. It's just me." His tone was gentle and coaxing.

When he slipped his hands around her waist and drew her close, she rested her head on his chest and exhaled a breath she didn't even realize she'd been holding.

Here was a guy who'd picked on her for years, who'd made her laugh in spite of it all. He'd done sweet unexpected things for her all her life, like hold her hand and guide her around the skating rink the first time her mom let her go skating. This flirting stuff was new for them, but trusting each other wasn't.

When he almost failed algebra in high school, and needed help, but didn't want anyone else to know how close he was to failing, he'd come to her. She kept his secret, spent hours tutoring him in private for his final, which he passed.

They had never been super close, not nearly as close as she was with Earl, Mazy, and Spencer, but they had always been friends.

She closed her eyes and let him lead her. The faint scent of his cologne was exotic, and his heartbeat thumped steady and strong. She reveled in the comforting pressure of his hand at her lower back, tender and reassuring.

Spencer was right. He was the perfect choice for a fling.

"What are you thinking?" He whispered as they rocked side to side to the music.

She looked up into his eyes, his pupils appeared to float in tiny golden suns surrounded by blue skies. "How we've never been close friends, but we've always been friends. I feel safe with you."

His gaze deepened, those suns lit from within. "Yep. We've always been friends, and we always will be friends. You feel safe with me, because you are."

"But there's something different tonight." She had the urge to wax philosophical as she tended to do when she pondered something heavily. But she didn't dare flash her nerd card right now. She'd scare him off.

He pressed his forehead to hers and said. "Yes. There's definitely something different tonight."

He caressed her back. Her breath hitched, as she rose to her tip-toes to get her face a little closer to his. A few strands of her hair got stuck in his stubble, and his lips brushed against her brow.

In her mind, she'd bravely lifted her head and kissed him on the mouth. Oh, to be so brave. Mmm. One day, maybe.

The music changed and a fast song came on. She was thrown off by the loud bass shaking the ground beneath her. She dropped her hands from around his neck, and he let go of her. Glancing around at the other people nearby, she tried to regain her composure after being pressed against Dirk in a sweet embrace that had left her dizzy.

Ashley from Filly's tapped her on the shoulder. "Mind if I cut in?"

Yes, she minded, but she didn't dare say that. Kendal stepped away from Dirk. "Of course not. Y'all enjoy yourselves."

Dirk quirked an eyebrow as if to ask, "are you sure?"

Kendal nodded and rejoined Spencer. When she glanced over her shoulder at Dirk, he was a staring back at her, even though Ashley was twerking right in front of him.

Spencer asked Earl to get her another beer.

Earl got up. "How about you, Kendal. Care for another cold one?"

She glanced down at her half-full beer in the cup holder of Spencer's chair. "I'm good. Thanks."

When he was out of earshot, Spencer said, "Did you invite Dirk over to fix your faucet?"

"No. We just danced. That's all."

"Girl, what are you waiting for?"

Kendal didn't respond, she just watched Ashley grind Dirk in front of everyone. It got so raunchy, Dirk backed away from the girl. Good for him.

The song ended and Dirk broke away from Ashley. He stood alone by the fire.

"Now's your chance before another girl comes up." Spencer jerked her head toward him. "Go talk to him."

Kendal stood and Earl came up behind her. "Where you running off to?"

She checked to make sure Dirk was still standing near the fire, alone. He was, but that was likely to change in a split second. She didn't have much time. "I'll be right back."

Earl gave her a look like he thought she was acting strange.

He was right. She was acting odd, but wasn't going to tell him why. She needed to get this over with before she lost her nerve.

She approached Dirk, rehearsing what she'd say in her

head. "Hey, I was wondering if you could swing by my apartment tomorrow and take a look at my kitchen faucet. It's been leaking." Hmmm. Sounded good in theory, but once she started stumbling over her own tongue, like she did when she lied, he'd see right through her charade.

A girl Kendal didn't know, but recognized from some shagging contests, approached Dirk, shaking her hips as she neared.

Dirk looked at Kendal. A bewildered expression flashed across his face when Kendal walked right by him and kept on trucking down the beach.

He had plenty of girls throwing themselves at his feet. Did she really want to be one of them? This wasn't how it was supposed to go. She didn't really want to *ask* a guy to kiss or make love to her, did she? Was she that desperate? That pathetic?

She was only twenty-five. She wasn't desperate for a boyfriend. There was nothing wrong with being single, nor did she believe she was pathetic for still being a virgin, but she had every right to feel it was time to take matters in her own hands. She was determined to get the ball rolling in her romance sector. It was empowering.

Who was she kidding? She was *so* empowered. *Right.* That's why she'd just chickened out and lost the nerve to ask Dirk to fix her imaginary leak.

Rah. Go, me.

She plopped down amidst the seagrass crowning a soft dune and admired the way the moonlight glittered on the surface of the dark water.

Something large moved to her left. She turned to see what it was.

Dirk marched straight toward her. *Eep.*

She dug her fingers in the sand as if searching for buried treasure, but jewels and money weren't the kind of treasures she longed for. No. Right now, a stream of perfect words to express what she wanted with dignity, strung together in eloquent sentences, these were the things her heart desired most—and the things farthest from her grasp.

She chewed on the inside of her cheek. *It's just Dirk. Don't get so rattled. Breathe.*

CHAPTER FIVE
Proposition

Dirk thought Kendal was coming over to talk to him, but then she gave him a long look and headed down the beach. On the off chance she wanted him to follow her, he tossed a couple of cold waters and a beer in a pail and trailed after her. He hoped he made the right call; he'd had enough of looking like a damn fool tonight.

The bright full moon illuminated the beach as he made his way toward Kendal. With her head on her knees, staring at the water, she looked troubled.

"Little House, why are you sitting out here all alone, girl?" Taking long strides, he trudged up the dune and sat beside her. When he offered her a drink, she chose water. Since she was driving Spencer's van tonight, he figured she'd forego another beer.

Two was his limit when he was driving, and he'd already consumed those. Having a friend like Spencer in his life made him realize the importance of drinking responsibly.

Kendal took a sip. "Thank you. I like the quiet, I wasn't planning on staying out here too much longer."

She had a weird tone in her voice—the tone most girls used when something was bugging them, but they tried to pretend nothing was wrong.

He scooted over and draped his arm around her. She

didn't move away, instead, she leaned into him. She was a perfect fit with her soft curves nestled against his side. As her long dark hair tickled over his arm, he got a whiff of her apple shampoo, all-American sweetness. Kendal was the epitome of the wholesome, girl-next-door, and he wanted to eat her up.

She trembled. What in the world? He rubbed a hand down her arm. "Are you cold?"

She shook her head and stared at her bottle. "Dirk, can I ask you something personal?"

Uh-oh, she'd never wanted to ask him anything before. There was definitely something up with her. "Of course." He couldn't resist stroking her silky hair.

She pulled away from him.

Whoa. He didn't like the vibe she was throwing his way. Had he done something to offend her?

She twisted so her shoulders were squared with his. Those big brown eyes of hers leveled him. "Would you ever consider having a summer fling with a friend?" Breaking eye contact, she blew out a breath.

Do what? He scratched his head, wondering what brought that question on. "You mean friends with benefits for the summer?"

"Yeah." She faced him again and blinked up at him, serious as can be.

"I don't see anything wrong with it, why?" Was sweet, innocent Kendal considering a summer fling? Impossible.

Dang, her hand was shaking so badly she nearly dropped her water bottle.

With her eyes downcast, she stammered, "I…I was thinking it…umm…it was time I did something like that, and…and I wondered if you and I—"

He drove his fingers through his hair, making sure his head hadn't just exploded. "Are you suggesting *we* have a fling?" This was crazy. Had to be a dream. Had to be.

She hugged her knees to her chest. "Yes."

He couldn't believe his ears. She said she wanted to have a fling, but she'd pulled herself into the fetal position. Something wasn't right here. Was this a practical joke? Had Ted put her up to this?

He wasn't going to fall for it. "You expect me to believe that? Very funny."

She hid her face in her arms. "I knew this was a dumb idea." He could barely hear her.

"Kendal, look at me, Sweetie."

She slowly lifted her head. The look of embarrassment was all over her face, from her pinched brows to that plump, bottom lip she was gnawing.

He caressed her arm. "Are you serious?"

She nodded. Goosebumps erupted all over her arms, and she shuddered.

The poor girl looked scared to death. He wasn't sure what to make of all this.

Was he in an alternate universe? Wasn't this precisely what he'd secretly dreamed of ever since he saw her in that bikini? But Kendal wasn't the fling sort of girl, was she? Little House on the Prairie gone wild? Or more precisely, wanted to go wild with him. No way.

"*You* want a no strings attached, fooling around, friends with benefits…fling?" He wanted to make sure he wasn't misinterpreting anything here.

"Of course. I know you never get too involved with any one person. That's the way you've always been. Everyone knows that." Her tone was so….so…Siri for android flat.

"Is that right?" She sure had his number. He couldn't deny the facts. He liked to keep things light, no commitment. Until he figured out what he wanted to do with his life, he didn't think he was in the position to offer more to the sort of woman he'd want to be with long term. But still the word "fling" and Kendal Duvall didn't fit well together.

Sure, he'd intended on rubbing up against her and dancing a little bit tonight, getting his flirt on, but fling implied...sex. That was a whole different ball game. Sex had a way of changing things between friends. A girl like Kendal would definitely change after they'd slept together. She'd either hate him or want him to stop seeing other people. He wasn't interested in either one of those options.

As much as he'd love to do the horizontal mambo with her, he didn't want to be responsible for breaking her heart.

Maybe he just needed to get to the bottom of this proposal. Help her work through whatever was really at the root of this unexpected notion of hers.

He eyed the beer in the pail; it was calling his name. Nah. Better not. He took a big gulp of water. "What's brought all this on, Kendal?"

"Promise not to tell anyone?"

No one would believe him if he did tell, but betraying a friend's trust wasn't his thing. "I'm a man of my word, you know that."

"You are. That's one of the many things I like about you."

There were things she liked about him? Do tell.

She closed her eyes and held her breath. "I'm twenty-five and still a virgin." The words tumbled out of her so fast she could have been an auctioneer.

He was surprised she had the guts to tell him that personal tidbit, but he wasn't surprised she was a virgin. In fact, he would've been shocked to discover she wasn't.

She waited silently, like she thought he'd say something to her newsflash, but what was there to say? It didn't make her seem undesirable, quite the opposite. He just couldn't figure out why she'd want to lose her V-card so casually. Wouldn't she rather wait for Mr. Right?

He wasn't anybody's Mr. Right, not in his current state, at least.

Mr. Right was a guy ready for a wife and 2.5 kids, the three bedroom house with the picket fence, the minivan, a guy who could keep his family fed and safe, home for dinner every night. Dirk was the guy who drove an old used car, called it a classic to not draw attention to the fact it was…an old used car. He was the guy who not only didn't want a wife, but had never even had a serious girlfriend. As far as a three bedroom house…he still lived with his folks. Yes, he paid them rent for the garage apartment, but they gave him offspring rates, and if he fell behind on rent, there was zero chance of eviction.

When she exhaled a shaky breath, she eyed him curiously. Probably wondering why her confession didn't get much of a reaction. He waited for her to continue, giving her his full attention.

She tapped a seashell onto another one, creating a funky little rhythm like she used to do with her pencil during tests —which had annoyed him to no end when they were in school and he'd been seated right behind her. Now, he just read it as a clue she was really nervous.

Eventually, she began to speak again. "I know there isn't anything particularly wrong with virginity. It's something to proud of, actually."

Yes, it was. Most of the girls he knew had lost their virginity in high school, granted, not necessarily to him. Come to think of it, he'd only been with one virgin, and she didn't bother to inform of that until afterwards, which had pissed him off, because had he known upfront, he would've handled things differently.

Kendal paused, the shell fell from her trembling grasp.

Geez, this must be really hard for her to talk about.

Without looking at him, she said, "But the fact that I haven't even so much as French kissed a guy seems weird, doesn't it?"

Yes. Truth hurts. How could he respond to this tactfully? She grew up on the island just like he had. So far as he knew, she wasn't overly religious, no more so than half the other girls he'd been with. To have never had a proper kiss at twenty-five? Yep, it was definitely unusual, but he wasn't about to say that.

He cleared his throat. "I wouldn't call it weird. If you told me the only guy you'd ever kissed was some salesman who showed up at your house offering a free Hoover vacuum cleaner demonstration, I might think that was weird."

Her chin shot up, and she crinkled her nose, as her gaze met his. "Yeah. That would suck."

"Ha. Yeah." She really had a cute sense of humor. Why hadn't he ever noticed that before? That weapon of mast destruction joke she'd made earlier had been awesome. What cracked him up most was that it'd come from her, the person he'd least expected to nail a one-liner.

She went back to her nervous shell tapping. "I'm starting to think there's something wrong with me."

Damn. He felt bad for picking on her all these years. So what if she was a little odd sometimes. That's what made her so adorable. "There's nothing wrong with you, Kendal. To my knowledge, you haven't dated much. The two go hand in hand. Dates lead to kisses." The way her lips glistened in the moonlight made him want to take care of that "never French kissed" dilemma right then.

"No. I haven't dated much, and that right there is reason enough to feel like a freak. I know I'm not the most beautiful girl in the world, but am I that unattractive to guys?"

Unbelievable. She *couldn't* really think she was ugly. Come on. "Unattractive? Dang, girl. Slow down. Didn't you notice how all the guys at the party were checking you out tonight?" He certainly noticed, that's why he put his arm around her and slow danced with her the first chance he had. He wanted to call dibs, nonverbally.

"No. None of them approached me."

That was his plan.

"Well, besides you." She blushed and gave him a sweet smile.

God, she was killing him.

"That doesn't mean they weren't checking you out. Believe me. They were. Why? Because you're beautiful."

The corners of her mouth quirked. All right, she was on the verge of a smile. He was on the right track.

"But truth is, Kendal, you don't normally show it off. This is the first time you've ever worn anything remotely revealing to a party. You look great, by the way. I have to tell ya, you're far from unattractive. Why do you think I followed you out here?"

"You followed me?"

He started laughing. She was so clueless. "Of course. How did I know exactly where you were? Why did I bring drinks? I followed you, hoping to get some one on one time with you."

"So you really do find me sexy? You weren't joking earlier?

"Very sexy. No joke."

She beamed. "Then we can have a fling?"

He coughed. She was so matter of fact about it all. "Well, it's not an algebraic equation, babe."

"I know that. I'm sorry. This is just awkward."

Awkward for him too. He didn't know whether to take notes or take her clothes off, but he figured taking notes was the safer option. "Okay, tell me what you're hoping to get out of this. What are your expectations?" Note to self, the next time his mother was watching Oprah, he needed to leave the room, cause he just sounded like a talk-show host.

"I want to learn to be more comfortable in my own skin and more confident. I want to learn what I like and don't like in bed so when the time comes, I'll be able to communicate that with my partner."

Hearing her say "what I like in bed" made his manhood spring to life. He was glad they were sitting in the darkened dunes so she couldn't see how much he liked this notion of finding out what she liked in bed.

"I think I need to get comfortable with intimacy in general, but I also need to assert my independence. I'm not looking for a serious relationship, but I don't want a one night stand or to hook up with a stranger or someone who might leave me feeling slutty or bad about myself afterwards."

Her bookish tendencies were showing themselves. It was like she was reading a list off of the back of some self-help book. But, he got what she was saying, and any man who'd leave her feeling slutty deserved a swift kick in the groin. Sad truth was, a lot of guys out there wouldn't think twice about bragging after bedding her, or leaving her cold and alone in the morning. He didn't like the thought of that one bit.

"I want someone I can trust, someone who will treat me with respect and dignity, someone who will be discreet and patient, someone who knows what they're doing in bed, and someone I can talk to comfortably."

There goes that "in bed" phrase again. He adjusted his pants to ease the pressure as nonchalantly as he could. That phrase was gonna be the death of him. But damn. She'd definitely given this a lot of thought. She probably made a spreadsheet and a graph while she pondered the whole thing.

He took her hand in his. "And you view me as this someone?" Knight in shining armor, he was not, more like gigilo in board shorts.

She gave his hand a squeeze then released it. "Yeah. You've always been easy-going around me, which makes me feel relaxed, well, more relaxed than usual. The girls on the island brag about your skills in the bedroom."

"They do?"

"Yes. You know that. Stop acting all surprised."

Actually, he didn't know that. It was nice to hear.

"Anyway, I know you aren't the kiss and tell type. The girls sometimes blab, but you never do. I also know you've managed to remain friends with everyone you've slept with, or at least the ones I know about."

She was right about that. Mutual respect was part of the deal. He couldn't imagine sleeping with someone he didn't genuinely like, and that like didn't just disappear in the morning light.

"Okay…I'm flattered you view me as a decent guy, but what makes you think you can't explore these things with a boyfriend?"

"I probably could, but I'm so uptight when put in romantic situations I can't seem to get to the boyfriend stage, you know? "

She just hadn't been with the right guy. Maybe he needed to take the high road, avoid the temptation of playing with her, and instead, help her find someone who'd treat her right.

She leaned back on her hands, the curve of her bosom made him do a double take.

With her head tilted back and the moonlight on her angelic face, she said, "I want to take the prospect of a serious relationship out of the equation so I don't make everything such a big deal. I've made it out to be such an enormous thing in my head, I can't seem to get past it. The longer a person puts something off that they dread facing, the harder it becomes, the bigger it seems. I think once I've had a little experience, I'll be able to be more open to romance." Her hair blew across her face, and she pulled the dark strands from her eyes. "You think my idea is crazy?"

He was so glad there wasn't going to be a test, because he was too busy looking at her to even remember half of what she'd just said. "No. I think it's surprisingly mature and level-headed, which is just the opposite of what fling means." And he needed to do the mature thing too and stop ogling her tits and concentrate on her heart. "The thing is, flings aren't therapy sessions. They need to flow naturally."

"So, I've ruined it by talking about it?" She looked hurt.

"No. I wouldn't say that." Crap. Now that she'd made the offer, he was too curious about what it'd be like to actually make love to her, he had to push on. Forget helping her find a boyfriend. High road, low road, who cares, he just wanted to be on the road that led to that bed she kept talking about. He didn't want to miss his chance to be with her, even if it was just for a couple of months. Not a proud moment, but damn. He was only human. "Alright let's lay some ground rules here. We'll talk all the business stuff out tonight and then we won't say anymore about rules. Deal?"

"Deal."

"Okay. Summer fling. Does that mean there is an expiration date?"

"Sure. Let's say we end on Labor Day, the Wing Fling race."

Dang, she was being so cut and dried. "And you want this to be our little secret?"

"Yes. I'd die if Myrtle broadcasted it. And I don't think I could handle my mother finding out, or people gossiping about us. No one else needs to know.'

"You realize keeping a summer long fling hidden isn't going to be easy."

"I know, but if we're careful, don't you think we can manage?"

"It's doable. I have skills when it comes to being discreet."

"I know. That's what I'm counting on."

"Fair enough." She was already counting on him. God, he hoped he didn't let her down. "And we're free to see other people while we're being 'intimate'?"

"Of course. I wouldn't ask you to commit to me."

"What if I don't want to share you with other guys?"

She rolled her eyes. "No need to flatter me. Besides, if that were a possibility, I wouldn't even be thinking of doing this in the first place."

Ouch. "So, I'm your last resort?"

"No. That's not what I mean. It's starting to sound like I'm asking you to 'do me' as a charity." She stared up at the moon. "God. Maybe I am. Let's just forget it." She buried her face in her hands.

He pried her hands away and ran his finger down her nose. "I'll call you in the morning."

Those big puppy dog eyes of hers drew him in. Next thing he knew, his lips were on hers. He planted a brief, soft kiss on her delicate mouth.

She sighed and licked her lips. A shy smile crept across her face.

He gently bumped his forehead against hers. "Spending time with you in any capacity could never be called a charity." Planting another tender kiss on her brow, he pulled back and gazed into her eyes. "You're being with *me* might be considered a charity."

She released a sigh and seemed more at ease.

After a few quiet moments, she smiled at him again. She

had an awesome smile.

He stroked her face. "From where I'm sitting, being near you is an honor and a pleasure. I'm not convinced you know exactly what you're offering, or how it might make you feel about yourself and me later on down the road, though. I don't think we need to go too far too fast. Trust me?"

"Yes."

Damn those big brown eyes were slaying him. This was torture. "Let's take things really slow. Baby steps." He didn't know if he'd be able to hold back long, but overwhelming her wasn't something he was willing to do. She needed to be treated with tenderness, whether she thought so or not. He knew better. She was a special lady, emphasis on lady.

But heaven help him, he was so damn stunned by her offer his brain was on the fritz. Nothing could've shocked him more than her proposal tonight. Nothing. And if she said she wanted to find out "what she liked in bed" one more time, he was going to have to jump in the ocean to get himself back under control, or he'd climb on top of her right there in the dunes and give her a sampling of it all so she could make an informed decision about what she liked.

CHAPTER SIX
Milk

How stupid could he be? He promised Kendal he'd call, but didn't have her phone number. Getting it wasn't a problem, but he'd have to ask someone. That someone would wonder why he was calling her. He'd have to make something up. Rumors would start flying around the island.

Damn it. He had the number of every girl in their graduating class except Kendal Duvall's. Why didn't he think of that last night? The only time he'd ever called her was when he'd needed a math tutor in high school. That was what, six, seven years ago? She didn't even have a cell phone in high school. Her mom wouldn't agree to it. The only reason he knew she had one now was because she was always reading on it at the restaurant when her jazz band took breaks. The girl loved to read. And sad truth was, he had no idea what kind of books she liked best. Probably nonfiction, literary, historicals—the kind of stuff that made text books look interesting.

He did know she moved into the apartment above the Laffy Taffy candy shop a couple of months ago. It had a private entrance on the ocean side. If he parked near the boardwalk and walked over, he might be able to slip under the radar without anyone figuring out where he was going. Lots of reasons to hang out at the boardwalk. No one would think too much about seeing him down there.

Seven o'clock on Sunday morning might make people a bit suspicious though. He should probably wait a few hours.

His phone vibrated. His mom's number flashed on the screen.

"Morning, honey. I'm making blueberry pancakes for your father and thought you might like some. Come on down and join us since you're up. You pace the porch anymore, and you're gonna wear a hole in the floor."

He peered over the rail of the deck connecting to his garage apartment and waved to his mother who stood at the kitchen window with her phone to her ear. "Thanks, Mom. Blueberry pancakes sound good. I'm starving."

It was nice to be so close to his folks, but he had zero privacy. That's one of the reasons why he never brought any girls to his place. His mom would probably bring them some cookies right in the middle of a rocking good time.

Great. He suddenly had a vision of his mother knocking on his door at the worst possible moment, holding a basket of condoms, each with a tiny bow. She'd say, "I just thought you might need a few of these. Help yourself. I have plenty more."

No. He'd never bring a girl to his apartment. Nope. Never gonna happen.

Thank God Kendal no longer lived at home. Otherwise this fling wouldn't even get off the ground.

He entered the kitchen of his parents' house. His dad sat at the head of the table naked as a jaybird. This was new. His dad wasn't a fan of nudity. He'd protested against the senior citizen nudist colony, Bare Point, for years.

His mom whispered, "He claims the chemicals in the laundry detergent I use are making him sick. I've been using the same detergent for twenty years. He refuses to get dressed. Last night, he said his toothpaste was poisonous so he refused to brush his teeth. Otherwise, he's doing pretty well. No point making a fuss and getting him all riled up."

"Morning, Pop."

"No pop with food. The carbonation messes with your digestion. You'll drink milk like the rest of us."

"Yes, Sir. Milk it is. Have any big plans for the day?"

"Going to the mall. I need some new clothes. Sears is having a sale."

An old Sears catalog, thick as a phone book, sat on the table. His dad gravitated to things from the past, things that triggered memories he could catch glimpses of amidst the contorted visions bumping around inside his head.

Dirk flipped through the catalog. "Sears has some nice things. Good prices."

"Yeah. It's my favorite store. Last time I went shopping, your mother tried to get me to buy my underwear in the grocery store."

"George Davis, that's not true. We were in the Walmart superstore. That is not a grocery store."

"They sell eggs there don't they?"

"Yes."

"They even had a meat counter. And live lobsters in a fish tank. Who buys their underwear in a place that sells seafood? What kind of looney bin do you think I am?"

"No one called you a looney bin. Here's your pancakes. Butter and syrup's on the table."

"You going to Sears naked, Dad?"

"Hell no. I ain't gonna get out of the car 'til you mom brings me a set of clothes. If I feel like it after I get dressed, then I might go in. I need a new drill."

"Who buys clothes in a place that sells hardware?"

His dad cracked up. "You know. You got a point. Never thought about it like that. You wanna come with us?"

"I'll take a pass. Promised to help someone out."

"Female?"

"Why you ask?"

"It's Sunday. Only time you take a job on Sunday is if a pretty girl is involved."

"Mighty observant for an old geezer, aren't ya?"

"Whatever gave you the notion I didn't keep my eye on you?"

Dirk looked deep into his father's bloodshot eyes. All the lights were on, and his dad was definitely home. It was good to connect. "I'm glad you do, Dad."

"Yep. And I'm glad you keep your eye on me."

Heat rose to Dirk's face, and his eyes began to sting. He was *not* going to get emotional right here at the breakfast table.

His dad reached over and grabbed his hand, tears were in his dad's eyes.

Shit. Yes he was. Dirk was definitely going to get emotional. Right now. Moments like this were too few. He squeezed his father's hand. "I think I change my mind about going to the mall."

His dad pulled away. "What's in the mall?"

"Sears."

"Sears? I can't stand that place. They wouldn't honor the warranty on our washing machine." He twisted in his chair. "Kizzie, are them clothes dry yet? Or do you expect me to sit around naked all day?"

His mom gave Dirk a weak smile and told his father, "I almost forgot about those clothes in the dryer. I'll go get them for you right now."

"Thank you. I'd appreciate it. By the way, good flapjacks." His dad dug his fork into the pancakes. "You like your breakfast, son?"

"Yep, Dad. I love it."

"Your mama's a good cook."

"Yes, sir. She sure is."

His father looked around the kitchen with a bewildered expression. "Where'd she go anyway? Family's supposed to eat together. That's what's wrong with America these days. Family's don't have their meals at the table, where they can talk eye to eye. People don't seem to understand, without your family, you got nothing."

Kendal checked her phone again, making sure it was fully charged, volume set to high. Checked her call log. Nope. No missed calls. It was ten o'clock. Was Dirk a late sleeper?

She knelt by the tub, flipped her head upside down and rinsed her hair with apple cider vinegar. It was her weekly ritual to keep her locks shiny and healthy. Her mom swore by it, and she had the prettiest head of hair of any woman her age, when she didn't plaster it down with hairspray.

There was a knock on the back door. She grabbed a towel, wrapped her tresses in it, and darted to the kitchen. Dirk Davis. No. He said he'd call. He never said he'd just stop by. She ducked behind counter.

"Kendal, I saw you in there. Don't freak out. Just come to the door. I won't bite." He sounded amused.

She peeped over the counter. He was looking right at her through the window in the back door. He gestured her over, crooking his index finger in a c'mere motion.

She slowly pulled herself upright. Her nipples pebbled. She glanced down. Oh crap. No bra. And her T-shirt was damp.

And there Dirk stood, mouth hung open, gaze fixed on her chest, and all she could picture was a big thought bubble over his head. "Got milk?"

She spun around and grabbed the cow print apron with

Udderly Delicious embroidered across the bib in bright pink thread. She put it on and adjusted the top so it covered her breasts, then faced Dirk and went to the door, opening it about three inches. "What are you doing here?"

His face twisted into a puzzled expression. "I came to see you. You gonna let me in?"

"Now's not a good time. Come back in thirty minutes."

His brows rose so high on his forehead, he reminded her of Mr. Potato Head after an encounter with a three year old. "Are you serious?" His voice was squeaky, not his usual baritone with a delicious drawl.

"Yes." She owed him no explanation.

Nostrils flared, he sniffed and made a sour face. "What's that smell?"

"My hair treatment."

"Smells like a Greek salad. Got any feta? Everything's betta with feta." He waggled his Potato Head brows.

She was too flustered to put up with his wise-cracks. "Don't start on me, Dirk Davis. Come back in thirty minutes."

"Alright. Alright. I'll come back. Want me to bring you a milkshake?"

"Before lunch?"

"Why not?"

He had a point. There was no milkshake law like no alcohol before noon on Sundays. Heck, people drank breakfast smoothies all the time. What was the difference? "That'd be nice. Strawberry, please."

Her towel-turban unraveled, and she reached up to catch it. Her wet T-shirt clad boobs poked out from behind the bib of her apron. Dirk made a strange, whimpering noise and stared straight at her chest. Again.

He nodded like he was in a trance. "I'll be back in thirty minutes." That was not the voice of Dirk either; that was the voice of Robby the Robot.

She turned her back to him once more. "Strawberry."

"Right. Right. Strawberry."

Pushing the door closed with her backside, she released a giant sigh of relief at the sound of his footfalls descending the stairs.

She bounded toward the bathroom, stripped, and jumped in the shower. Oh. My. God. What am I gonna wear? Besides a fricking bra?

Hair thoroughly washed with her favorite apple shampoo, skin scrubbed clean with orange blossom body wash, she rinsed. The scent of vinegar was gone. She now smelled like a fruit salad. Everything's betta with feta. Ha.

Two minutes later, she stared into her closet full of "nothing to wear," and had to sit on edge of her bed to catch her breath before she hyperventilated.

Overreacting much? Yes. Still breathing like a fat English bulldog going for a run in the park? Yes.

Most girls wouldn't struggle with something as simple as deciding on an outfit, *but* most girls didn't have her knack for always wearing the wrong thing.

If the hosts from *What Not to Wear*, Clinton Kelley and Stacy London, had a love-child, it'd be Leah, the saxophonist from Bikini Quartet. In desperation, Kendal dialed her up. "Hey, Leah. Sorry to bug you, but I'm in a bit of a crisis. I have a casual date, and I have no idea what outfit to choose."

"Congrats on the date. Where's he taking you?"

"We're just hanging out at my place."

"Is this a first date?"

"Yeah."

"What kind of guy are you seeing? Does he have a girlfriend or wife?"

"He's a great guy, and no, he doesn't have a girlfriend or

wife.

"You're positive?"

"One hundred percent."

"Good. But still, don't let him think it's okay to just hang out at your apartment on a first date. Make him take you somewhere. I don't care if it's just a walk on the beach. Listen to me carefully, do not entertain that man in your apartment this early in the relationship. It makes it seem like he's ashamed to be seen with you. If he balks at the idea of actually going somewhere, he's only interested in a booty call. Is that what you want?"

Hell yeah! No? Crap. She didn't know. Jesus. She'd called Leah for fashion advice not dating advice. What the heck? The fat little bull dog in Kendal's chest began to wheeze again. She took a deep, cleansing breath. "So, if we go do something, then what should I wear?"

"Depends on what you're going to do."

"Fine. Say…we go for that walk on the beach like you said, maybe get a milkshake, hang out around the boardwalk. Something like that."

"Well, in that case, wear a pair of shorts, a cute top, and some flat sandals. You don't want to appear like you're trying too hard."

"Shorts?" She only owned two pair of shorts. One pair was missing a button, and the other pair were baggy since she'd lost weight. "Why shorts? Why not a sundress?"

"Sundresses are nice, but if you decide to go on any rides they can be tricky. Plus, they're easy access for roaming hands, if you catch my drift."

"Right." Roaming hands…sundress it was.

"Who's the lucky guy?"

"I'd like to keep that to myself for now. See how it goes first."

"So it's someone I know. Well, well. I'll let you keep your

secret. I can understand wanting privacy around here, but I insist you give me an update later. No names needed."

"Will do."

Okay… deep breaths…her heartbeat was returning to normal. She tried on six dresses before finally deciding on the first one she'd pulled from the hanger. It was 50's vintage, pink with black piping and little buttons down the front, fit and flare, to the knee, sleeveless, and it matched her new bra and panty set. She slid on a pair of black sandals and pulled her damp hair in a high ponytail.

She left the top four buttons undone. A little cleavage was okay.

As soon as Dirk climbed the back stairs, she rushed out to greet him. "Hey. Sorry about earlier. Let's go for a walk."

"Uhh…all right." In jeans, a white T-shirt, and flip-flops, he reminded her of a young Brad Pitt. With a nod, he said, "You look pretty." He handed her the strawberry milkshake.

"Thank you." Dang it. Her face burned. She was totally blushing.

"So you wanna go for a walk, huh?"

"Yeah. It's a beautiful day."

"You're not worried about people seeing us together? You know how people love to talk."

"Oh, right. I didn't think about that." She did think about, but she also thought about what Leah had said, and the big sisterly advice had won the battle. So did his response mean he was embarrassed to be seen with her like Leah suggested, or was he trying to protect them from gossiping neighbors, or just sticking to their fling rules?

Overreacting—check.   Hyperventilating—check. Overthinking—check. Hands shaking like a tambourine player's—check. Being a paranoid wreck—check. Yep, she was officially in date-mode. And *this* was a prime example of why she'd never had a boyfriend.

She had to get a handle on herself. They had agreed to stay out of the public eye. He was just following their rules. "I thought it might be nice to be outside, fresh air, sunshine. But you're right about me not wanting people to know our business."

"Fair enough. We can work around that. Why don't you meet me at the point where you tutored me in high school? Remember?"

"Oh yeah. The old treehouse on the south end."

"Yeah."

He had a smile on his face, but it looked fake, and the way his gaze was narrowed made her think he found her behavior very odd. And it was. It was beyond odd, and she didn't seem to be able to help herself. Maybe she should have filled the prescription for anxiety meds that doctor wrote out for her.

Something she'd read on Facebook flashed through her mind. "There's a fine line between crazy and free spirited and it's usually a prescription."

She didn't want to have to rely on pills to handle her issues. She wanted to be able to do it herself, without meds as a crutch. She'd been fine last night, why was she freaking out today? Maybe because she'd been obsessing about being with Dirk ever since their talk? Yeah, that and the fact that she'd downed about ten cups of coffee that morning, checking her phone every twenty seconds.

She took a deep breath. "Meet there in thirty minutes?"

He nodded slowly then immediately shook his head. "Kendal, you do realize you're acting a bit nuts, right? I mean…you say you want a fling and don't want anyone else on the island to know about it. Then you want to go traipsing around town. Not to mention, I stop by and you send me away like you're scared to even let me in your apartment."

"I know. You're right. I'm just nervous. I'm sorry. This *is* crazy. Wanna just come in?"

"Yes!" Finally a sincere smile from him.

She sipped her shake and opened the door. "Mmm. This shake is delicious."

He sighed and drove his fingers through his hair as he stepped across the threshold. She could sense his exasperation. Who could blame him?

Why'd she have to always get so nervous whenever in any sort of "date" situation? This sucked. Just once, she wished she could handle herself with grace and confidence around a guy. She'd done so well last night, for her anyway. What was different then? Beer? No. She hadn't even drank a full one. Maybe it was the fact she hadn't expected him to flirt, didn't have time to overthink things, got caught up in his casual, laid-back manner. Who knows. She sure didn't have the answer, but she knew she had to get a handle on herself now or he'd bail on her.

CHAPTER SEVEN
Piano

This girl is insane. As soon as I'm done with this shake, I'm outta here.

All that…come back later, let's go here, there, then finally wanna come in? Hair treatment that smelled like pickles? Yeah. No doubt about it; she was nuts. Pretty, but quick to play the crazy card.

He checked out her apartment. It was cheerful and old-fashioned with distressed furniture painted bright colors. Peach chairs encircled a turquoise table in the kitchen. A set of pink bookcases in the living room were loaded to the hilt. A mint green desk hugged the back of the couch. Positioned in front of a large bay window, a yellow baby grand piano was bathed by the mid-morning sunlight. "Cool place. Did it come furnished?" Furniture contributed from the Cartoon network to be precise.

"Thanks. I like it. All this stuff is mine. I hit the yard sales, picked up some 'mistake' paints from the hardware store, got the piano from the nursing home where I volunteer. They got a new one. This one still plays well, but the veneer was peeling pretty badly. I sanded it down and painted it. Now, I can't imagine it being any other way. I love it. Getting my own apartment brought out the crafty side of me. I even learned to do a bit of sewing." She covered her mouth, like she wished she could stuff some of those words back in, which was funny, because in all the years he'd known her, he'd never heard her say all that much, 'til lately.

He picked up a patchwork owl pillow off the couch. "You make this?"

"Yeah. Made the white slipcover for the couch too. That was a challenge, but I was determined."

"I didn't know you were so…domesticated." She was a regular Martha Stewart. She probably had her future wedding all planned out, some of the stuff already made. If he could slap a label on the yawn-worthy vibe her place was giving him it'd be—insta-family, just add husband and stir. He was *not* interested. He knew last night the word fling and Kendal didn't go together. He should have said no then and been done with it.

Her eyes widened. "You say domesticated like it's a bad thing."

"No. It's cool. Especially if you're a beer." She didn't laugh. Maybe his tone was harsher than he intended. But something about this basket of Easter eggs she called home was messing with his head. "Where's your T.V.?"

"I'm not a T.V. watcher. I prefer to read or play the piano."

Good luck finding a guy willing to give up T.V., especially during playoffs.

"Have a seat." She motioned to the couch.

"I'm good." He sauntered over to the bookcase and sucked on his milkshake hard as he could. Ouch. Brain freeze.

The books were alphabetized by author. Jesus. This girl really needed a life. Odd that she didn't have any pictures sitting around. In fact, she didn't have a single thing sitting out besides books and a lamp or two. Everything was neat and tidy. Not a speck of dust to be seen. She'd flip if she ever stepped foot in his place.

"Dirk, please, sit down. You're making me nervous."

She made him nervous too, and he wasn't used to it. He didn't quite understand why he was suddenly so jittery. His gut must be trying to tell him something. A man should listen to his gut.

He sat on one end of the sofa, she sat on the other, the owl pillow between them. Only a third of his shake was left. He'd give her five or ten minutes then make up an excuse to leave. He didn't want to be rude, but between her crazy antics earlier, the Donna Reed get-up she was wearing, and this happy homemaker apartment—the writing was on the wall. This was a crazy girl's boyfriend trap, and he wasn't gonna take the bait no matter how tempting the bait might be. And Kendal's body was definitely tempting.

"You want to go, don't you?" Her voice was quiet and airy.

He met her gaze. She didn't appear upset. "What makes you say that?" Oops. Guess his body language gave him away.

"I can just tell. I have that effect on guys."

"What do you mean?" She'd probably scared away quite a few guys, if he had to guess.

She shrugged and gave him a weak smile. "I get flustered and can't think straight when I'm around a guy one on one in a date kinda situation. Never fails. I end up making a fool of myself somehow. Next thing you know, the guy trumps up some lame excuse and makes a run for it."

So much for that plan. He'd be a real jerk if he cut out now. "But you know me. I'm not some guy you're crushing on. Why would you get flustered around me?"

She blew out a breath. "I wasn't going to tell you this, but I think I need to, because it's at the root of all my anxiety."

Root of her anxiety?   It was official. She'd definitely overdosed on Dr. Phil. No doubt about it.

She swallowed loudly. "I'll make this as brief as possible."

Oh Lord, that was girl-code for prepare for an hour-long explanation.

"The summer before seventh grade my family went to visit relatives in Kentucky. My cousin, Emily, was fourteen. I was twelve."

You're kidding me? We're going back to age twelve? He closed his eyes and sipped his shake, hoping patience was somewhere in the cup and would find its way up his straw.

"One day she convinced me to go to the creek with her to meet some boys. Once we got a block away from the house, she pulled out a set of clothes for me to put on—a tight T-shirt and short-shorts."

Short-shorts. Okay, now she had his attention. Maybe this story would be better than he thought.

"My mom always told me to not wear things like that because it would give boys the wrong idea, and they might try things with me that weren't 'right.' I was hesitant, but I put the outfit on anyway. We went down to the creek."

Wait, this was a story about her at twelve, short-shorts, and boys at the creek. His body tensed just imagining what awful thing could have happened at the creek, but he didn't interrupt her. He was listening intently now.

"We met up with four teenage boys. They were all in high school, football players. One of them was nice to me and said he'd show me how to catch a fish. I pretended I didn't know anything about fishing and followed him down the creek, alone. Next thing I knew, he had me pinned to the ground and was squeezing my boobs and butt. I screamed and his buddies and my cousin came running up. I thought Emily would make him stop, but she just stood there and watched, while the other boys came over and copped a feel.

I was so stunned, I stopped screaming. I don't know. I think I was in shock."

Dirk couldn't contain himself. "I hope you blew the whistle on those assholes. They had no right doing that to you. No right at all." He was scared they'd done more than touch her, but was hesitant to ask her.

"I knew what they did was wrong, but my cousin told me to keep my mouth shut about it or we'd both get in trouble. She said for high school boys to want me, a girl not even in the seventh grade, wow, I must be hot."

"Hot? You were twelve. What the hell was wrong with your cousin?" What kind of backwoods bullshit was this?

"She ended up getting pregnant later that year and Mom never let me hang out with her again."

"Good. Well, not good that she got pregnant, but good you didn't have anything more to do with her. What'd your mom say about all of this?"

"I never told her. I had disobeyed her, and I didn't want to get in trouble. Plus, I knew she'd say it was my own fault for wearing those skimpy clothes."

"Like hell it was your fault. Look, I grew up at the beach. Girls paraded in front of me in very, very skimpy outfits, and I knew better than to touch without permission. For one guy to be an ass is on him, but for his friends to join in shows it was a group mentality. It's like gang banging. It's disgusting, and there's no excuse for it. None."

"But all they did was touch me over my clothes."

"I don't care. You were twelve. They shouldn't get by with that." He'd known Kendal at that age, and she did *not* give off the vibe she was interested in being fondled by a group of boys.

"Too much time has passed now to do anything about it, and since it was just groping, I doubt anything would've been done to them anyway."

"Good thing they aren't locals. I'd beat the shit out of them for that. I don't care how much time has passed. That was wrong. Way wrong."

"I know it was. I've come to terms with it, somewhat. But it's partly why I've always dressed so conservatively, and why I haven't really dated."

So this is why she'd dressed like a granny most of her life. "Aww, Kendal. I'm sorry it scarred you so badly. You can't let the past keep you from your future, you know?"

"I do know. That's kind of why I wanted to…be with you."

"And that's why you got so nervous when I showed up like a 'date'?"

"Yes. My doctor offered to write me a prescription for my anxiety, but I didn't want pills. I figured it was better to face my fears head on and learn to get a hold of my nerves on my own terms, like I did with stage fright."

"You're a brave girl. I probably would've taken the drugs." He winked at her.

"A lot of women have been through much, much worse, and they've managed to get over it."

"You can't compare your experience, or how it impacted your life to what anyone else went through. It's like you're feeling guilty for being upset about what happened. You have a right to be upset. It's understandable. It happened to you and has left its mark. Everyone deals with shit their own way."

She smiled.

He hit the bottom of his shake with a slurp and slammed the empty cup on the end table a little harder than he'd intended.

"It's okay if you want to leave. You don't need to explain. You don't have to hang out. I shouldn't have pushed the whole—"

"You haven't pushed anything Kendal. I'm here because I want to be." And he'd leave when he wanted to leave. The fact that he suddenly wanted to stay surprised him. But now that she was baring her soul so openly to him, he wanted to stick around, help her through all of this.

Most girls didn't come right out and tell him what was going on with them. Heck, most girls played head games. Kendal didn't seem to even know what those games were. It was refreshing.

Maybe she wasn't trying to hook a boyfriend. Maybe she wasn't actually crazy, much. *Maybe* she just needed a friend. He could be her friend, a better friend than he'd been in the past. There was a loneliness about her he couldn't ignore. It tugged at his heart, made him want to pull her close, emotionally. He couldn't put his finger on it. She had friends and family, but she was somehow detached, alone.

She placed her shake on the end table and pulled the owl pillow into her lap, as if she needed it to comfort her. "I wish I were different, you know?"

He didn't say anything, just listened.

"I mean…I see how couples interact. I've read romance novels. I've watched movies. I know it isn't supposed to be this hard. But I can't help it. I just get so worried that I'm going to…to…I don't know." She tapped her fingernail against the button eye of the owl, creating a crazy little rhythm again.

"When do you feel most relaxed, most comfortable being you?" He sincerely wanted to know.

"Playing the piano." Her eyes reddened, and she blinked several times, batting back the welling wetness forming in the corners of her eyes.

Man, he didn't want her to cry. He hated when girls cried around him. He stayed quiet, and she managed to get her emotions under control within a minute or so. No waterworks. Whew. That was a close one.

Chin up, she drew in a slow breath. "Ever since I can remember, the only times in my life I've felt strong and free, proud of who I am, were when I was playing the piano. When I'm performing, I don't have to talk to people. The music talks for me. I don't have to worry about what to say, or what to do with my hands, or what I look like. I can just let go of all of that, and my fear and awkwardness disappears."

He pointed to the piano by the window. "Play something for me."

Her brows pleated. "Now?"

"Yes." He wanted to help her get to her happy place where she was calm and free.

"Geez. What do you want to hear?"

"I'll leave that up to you."

Playing piano was like breathing for Kendal. She wasn't the least bit nervous about performing for Dirk. He'd heard her tickle the ivories many times, but he wasn't asking her to play because he wanted to be entertained. He was offering her a chance to find her center again, after being thrown for a loop by his unexpected visit. She'd shared a lot about her past with him, things that stirred up a multitude of emotions within her. She'd been hit by an emotional hurricane and debris was still flying around in her heart. Some things whizzing about in her mixed up world were funny, like the sight of an udderly delicious mooing cow floating by with strawberry-shaped spots. But she couldn't ignore the twelve year old girl she once was, curled into a ball with her breasts strapped down by ace bandages, bound so tightly her tender flesh bruised. Nor could she pretend to not see the sixteen year old that child grew into. The teen who watched her father turn his back on her and her mother, leaving behind man-sized shoes Kendal couldn't fill, even though she'd tried.

An old standard song like the ones requested of Bikini Quartet wasn't strong enough to stop the storm inside her. She needed to play something that tapped into her veins, something that had her DNA all over it.

Dirk's strong fingers curled into her palm, as he pulled her to her feet and guided her to the piano. His eyes never left hers. She imagined they were in another time, a distant reality, dancing at a grand ball, that out of all the ladies present, he only wished to dance with her, only her.

He pulled the piano bench out. She took a seat and lifted the lid to reveal the keys. Her fingertips caressed the slick, cool, ivory and ebony. The tension in her shoulders eased. She had a sense of wholeness, as if she were rejoined with a missing part of herself.

The forlorn clarinet solo from the symphony she'd composed in college and won national honors trickled through her thoughts and manipulated her fingers. In a flurry of motion, her right hand flitted across the keys, causing that solo to ring in the belly of the piano. She adjusted her posture and placed her foot on the small brass damper pedal. With little effort, she depressed it and reveled in the way the notes lingered in the air.

This was who she was, this intangible mixture of high and low, major and minor, loud and soft. Her spirit was a wordless, faceless mass of energy and sound. This symphony she'd created with a million moving parts was her home, the place where she could be her true self. And with the sounding of each note, the churning within grew quieter and slower, until it was so faint she paid it no mind at all.

Lost in the music, she'd almost forgotten Dirk was there, until he placed his body against the feminine waist of the piano, where he could witness the hammers striking the strings and still see her face.

He gazed her direction with a piercing, almost hungry flicker in his eyes as she played. She wanted to share this part of herself with him, to open the doors she'd barricaded since childhood and invite him in, leaving all her troubled memories behind.

He stared at her face, seeming to study it.

She lifted her chin, unafraid and attacked the chords and runs as if they were dragons she skillfully slayed. And when the song grew calm again, she allowed her eyelids to close as if velvet stage curtains. She blocked everything else out. Movement after movement of her symphony poured out of her and into the piano like a waterfall, a constant stream, bubbling, sparkling, alive beneath the surface.

Every intricate passage on the violin and thunderous blast from the tuba sang in her head. Thousands of notes and chords clicked through her brain effortlessly, vivid as childhood memories. She wanted him to feel her, hear her heartsong in the melody.

The music moved through the room like invisible smoke, embedding itself into every fiber. The vibrations of sound kissed and penetrated each surface, causing inanimate objects to transform into conduits for harmony.

She released the final chord and opened her eyes. His face glowed in the morning light. His gaze held hers tenderly.

A ragged sigh escaped her lips, a release, both victory and surrender. She'd wanted to touch him in the only way she *knew* how.

His expression told her that in her own special way, she *had* touched him, deeply. The exquisite tension between them was unmistakable. In that moment, she felt closer to Dirk than anyone else in her entire life, and for the first time she knew she'd been seen, really seen. And she wasn't nervous. She was calm, at peace in the presence of a man, not just any man—Dirk.

He moved to her side and crouched by the bench. She turned to face him, eye to eye. He cupped her hands in his. "God, I felt you in that song. Was it Beethoven or Mozart?"

"It was a Kendal Duvall original."

"Wow. It was brilliant. You have a magical gift, Kendal. Never wish you were different. Who you are is breathtakingly beautiful, inside and out." He leaned in, his eyes searching hers, as if asking permission to kiss.

She didn't withdraw or look away. She lifted her face to the sunshine in his blue eyes. And as his mouth found hers, she savored the sensation of their lips enfolding, caressing, expressing their hearts without words or music. His kiss told her everything she'd longed to hear, and more. It told her she was desired, safe, respected, and cherished, as is.

When his tongue petted her lips, she opened her mouth and invited him deeper. He didn't plunder like she'd imagined. Instead, he caressed and created in her a desire to give and explore. Without thinking, she found herself mimicking his actions, her tongue dancing with his so sweetly she didn't know where her mouth ended and his began.

He pulled her to him, and she slid off the bench. In an instant, he had her on her back on the plush area rug, their kiss unbroken. A moan escaped her, and he lifted his head to gaze into her eyes.

She murmured, "Don't stop."

He claimed her mouth again and something in her changed. It was as if she'd melted on the inside, and it was the most gorgeous sensation she'd ever experienced. And like a great nurturer, he kept feeding this need growing within her, and she hoped he never stopped.

He whispered, "I could kiss you forever."

CHAPTER EIGHT
Lasso

Dirk dove in for another greedy taste of Kendal's sweet mouth. For someone who didn't have much experience, she was doing everything right.

After hearing about how she'd been groped, he wanted to tread carefully, but, as their passion rose, keeping his hands under control was a struggle. Her lips and soft moans were driving him slap out of his mind with desire.

His cellphone vibrated. Grrr. Not now.

Reluctantly, he pushed away from Kendal and rested on his side. If he had his way, he'd trail his fingertips over her breasts and tease her nipples into tight beads through the fabric of her dress. Her plump mouth, reddened from making out for so long, made him want to ignore the incoming text and keep doing what they were doing, but he needed to make sure the message wasn't important. What if something was up with his dad? He fished his phone out of his pocket.

The text was from Carl, Myrtle Pinkerton's boyfriend and local ostrich farmer.

Carl: Spike's out. Bare Point. Need help.

'Not again! One of Carl's ostriches is running around Bare Point. I gotta go." He held up the phone in front of Kendal's face so she could see he wasn't making up some excuse to leave.

It took her a few seconds to take it all in. "You better get going before Sheriff Meyers shows up with his tranquilizer gun. Carl hates when his birds get tranqued." She was a sport about it. Some things were too strange to be made up stories. This was one of them.

He jumped up and smiled at the fleeting thought: *Only a local girl would understand my life.*

People claimed music could alter a person's mood, even ignite passion. Being a dancer, Dirk understood the concept of how songs could seize control of emotions, if only briefly. But never had he experienced such an otherworldly connection with another person like he'd just shared with Kendal.

What's more, he hadn't "just" kissed a girl since… since…okay, so this was a first for him too. He hadn't expected a first of his own, nor had he expected to enjoy kissing Kendal Duvall so much. There was such depth to her that he'd never realized lurked below her timid surface. He could drown in that depth and die happy.

Enchanted by her talent and ability to reveal so much of herself through her art without needing to rely on lyrics, he was in awe.

He couldn't wait to see her again, but first, he had a giant bird to catch.

Atop his favorite ostrich, Robirrrda, Dirk rode up to Bare Point with the taste of Kendal's strawberry mouth still on his tongue, her song in his head, and his body still thrumming with arousal. Fortunately, that arousal was no longer obvious.

Brock Knight and Trent McAllister were running after

the rogue ostrich named Spike and having no luck at all. No wonder Carl called him. Those guys didn't know how to handle these birds. But they sure turned all the old ladies into screaming fans.

He ought to be used to seeing these old people naked, but he still found himself gawking. It was like Madame Tussaud's wax museum rejects got over-heated and melted. It creeped him out, but he couldn't help but stare.

Spike trotted around the tents on the beach. Louise jiggle-jogged toward the bird, reaching out as if she was going to catch it with her bare hands. Crazy lady. Brock must not have seen her, because he ran right into her and knocked the woman flat on her back. His muscular Mr. Universe body landed right on top of her, nose to nose. She wrapped her tanned, leathery arms and beefy legs around Brock and gave him a big smooch. Gross. Ha. Dirk wouldn't be surprised if Brock swam back across the pond to Wales in horror after that one.

Trent stopped and put his hands on his knees. His shoulders heaving. Was he okay? He straightened and held his stomach, laughing so hard he seemed to be having trouble breathing. Yeah. He was fine.

Dirk adjusted himself in his saddle, readied his lasso, and whispered to Robirrrda. "Ready, girl?"

Robirrrda made a clucking noise and scratched the ground.

He gave her hind end a light heel kick and off they went, full speed ahead. Everyone turned and cheered when he came charging up the dune on his two-legged, avian steed, lasso circling above his head like Roy Rogers.

Weaving around lounge chairs, and coolers, knocking over three umbrellas, and demolishing a sandcastle—the chase was on.

When Henry, a chubby old man with bigger boobs than

his wife's, tripped while trying to get out of Dirk's way, Robirrrda flapped her wings and was airborne, briefly. She changed directions with her long neck outstretched horizontally, parallel with the ground. Dirk was jostled side to side, as her claws scratched up clumps of sand and sent the globs flying behind them.

Spike slowed down to a trot when he reached the fence, searching for a way around it.

Dirk tossed his lasso and hooked Spike on the first try. "I got you, you rascal."

Cheers and whistles sounded behind him. He got off Robirrrda's back and walked over to Spike and petted his neck. "Why you got to always cause trouble, huh?"

The bird looked at him, then rubbed his head on Dirk's shoulder. "Crazy bird. I'm not mad at you. I reckon if I was trapped behind a wire fence all the time, I'd try to make a break for it every chance I got too. Freedom's important to a guy."

Ted rolled up in his truck and parked beside the barn, while Dirk closed the latch on Spike's pen.

Robirrrda galloped over to Ted. He opened his arms and gave her a big hug as she rubbed her fuzzy face against his.

Dirk said, "Should I give you two some privacy?"

"Very funny." Ted sauntered over to the pen area. Robirrrda high-stepped all happy-like at his side.

Dirk got a kick out of watching Ted interact with Robirrrda. "That bird is in love with you. You know that, right?" They both laughed when the pretty ostrich nodded her head maniacally. "See? She agrees."

Ted reached up and gave her a scratch on the back. "She's a looker, and sweet as can be. Yes, she is." He petted her head, and she batted her long lashes. "Glad you were able to catch Spike for Carl. I was in the attic of Reel to Real Good when I got his text."

"In the attic?"

"Yeah. They had a leak. All squared away now." Ted snapped his fingers and pointed to the field. Robirrrda bounded for the wide open, for one last run before she'd be corralled into her pen for the evening. "Guess who was at the restaurant?"

"Who?"

"Ashley and her cousin Heidi, and we're all going out for a few drinks this evening."

Dirk wanted to clarify who "we" referred to. "You, Ashley, and Heidi?"

"And you."

"Me?" Dirk didn't like how his brother included him without asking first. Normally, it wouldn't have bothered him a bit. Ashley was a wild one and easy on the eyes, but tonight he wasn't interested. "I'm gonna pass, man."

Ted couldn't have looked more surprised if Dirk had said Heidi was a dude. "You can't do this to me. Heidi just got here. She's not going anywhere without Ashley, and Ashley's not going to play third wheel. Come on, man. They were so excited about it when I offered. I can't back out now."

Crap. Ted rarely begged. This must be pretty important to him. What was a few drinks with his brother and a couple of pretty girls? It wasn't some huge sacrifice. He didn't have to *do* anything with Ashley if he wasn't into it. The girl wasn't gonna jump his bones or anything. Okay, so this was the first time he didn't secretly want that to happen.

Damn. He really needed to snap out of the spell Kendal's strawberry kisses put on him. Their rules stated that they were going to keep things casual and see other people.

Why did he suddenly want nothing more than to see

Kendal again, and no one else? Her kisses? Her piano playing? The way she blushed around him? The way she'd bared her soul to him? All of the above!

And he hadn't even mentioned how stunning she was. There were so many things he was discovering he loved about her as a person, her outward beauty was just a bonus. That's what really floored him. He was no longer focused on her appearance. He was too mesmerized by all the intrinsic qualities she possessed that made her Kendal Duvall.

Kendal was still in a daze from her encounter with Dirk. She stared at the shelves in the back room of Spencer's flower shop, but everything in front of her was a blur. Her mind was too busy conjuring up images of Dirk.

At last, she could say she'd been kissed, really kissed. A lot. And it'd surpassed all her fantasies.

When he'd left, she'd danced alone and barefoot in her living room, and she'd *never* done that before. But today, she'd cranked up the jams and performed her own clumsy version of the shag.

Ever since she'd played the piano for him, she'd been in a dreamy bubble. He'd allowed her to use music to get her nerves under control. Miraculously, it'd worked.

Then, he'd proceeded to kiss her into an intoxicated state, where she still remained, floating and smiling.

Spencer had asked her to come over to help move some things around at the shop, and Kendal had gladly rushed over. She had every intentions of doing whatever Spencer wanted, but she'd soon discovered she couldn't focus to save her life.

All her mental energy was locked on Dirk, his lips, how all her fears had dissolved in his arms. For years, she'd imagined the physical aspects of what it would be like to be kissed, but nothing had prepared her for the euphoria she'd experienced.

Unburdening her heart, sharing a piece of her past—a piece she'd kept hidden—had left her emotionally naked. And to her astonishment, for the first time in her life, she felt free.

He'd seen who she was when she was a nervous wreck and when she was her most vulnerable, and he'd embraced her, completely. Her awkwardness, insecurities, fears, naivety and loneliness had all made an appearance. And after he'd taken *all* of that in, he *chose* to kiss her, instead of abandoning her like every guy she'd gone out with.

She absently rearranged some vases on a shelf while Spencer made bows at the work table.

Stepping away from the shelf to admire her handiwork, she asked, "How's this, Spencer? Can you reach these vases better now?"

Spencer rolled over and extended her arm until she touched a vase. "Yep, that's perfect." She went back to unwrapping the cellophane from a new spool of ribbon and gave Kendal a mischievous grin. "You've had a goofy look on your face for the past thirty minutes. You gonna tell me what's up or what?"

Busted. Kendal didn't want to be one of those girls who *only* talked about guys with her friend, but she couldn't hold it in any longer. "Dirk stopped by today."

"Were you expecting him?"

"Nope. He surprised me."

"I bet you flipped. Especially since he didn't have an 'appointment' with you."

Yep, Kendal was a planner, but in all fairness, there was no way she'd be able to keep everything straight if she didn't stick to a carefully planned schedule.

Spencer worked 9 to 5. She didn't need to post every hour of her day on a chart. Kendal had private lessons, gigs, volunteer work, not to mention the things she did for her mother.

However, Kendal was still too giddy from being with Dirk to get defensive about her need to plan. "He definitely caught me off guard. I'd just finished doing my weekly vinegar hair rinse, too. I was a mess." She shuddered at the memory.

Spencer laughed. "I bet he *loved* that. Vinegar is such a turn on, you know?"

Everything's betta with feta. He'd joked it off, in his fun-loving way, but her hair had reeked—a definite turn-off. "It was pretty bad. I made him leave to give me a chance to clean up."

"Leave?" Spencer's slapped the ribbon onto the table. "Please tell me you're joking."

"No joke. I made him leave while I showered, had a meltdown, called Leah, then had another meltdown. When he returned, I tried to get him to go for a walk with me. Within thirty seconds of that suggestion, I invited him in. *Finally.* And he looked like he wanted to call the whole thing off so bad he couldn't stand it. I shook, felt nauseous, broke out in a sweat, and did everything in my power to make sure he'd never want to see me again." She was tensing up just thinking about it.

"Man. That sounds painful."

"Oh, the painful part came later, when I told him about the boys in Kentucky." She still couldn't believe she'd blurted all that out to Dirk.

Spencer had a look of concern on her face and locked eyes with Kendal. "That must've been hard on you. What'd he say?"

"He was ready to hunt those boys down and punch them out."

"Good. That's what those boys deserve." Spencer smiled

at her.

Kendal smiled back, thinking about how he'd reacted to her story.

He'd demonstrated that he believed those boys had done Kendal an injustice. Dirk was on her side. It felt good. She already knew the boys had been wrong, as well as her cousin and her mom, but it was wonderful to have those sentiments echoed by a guy, Dirk specifically. She loved how he'd mentioned that he'd grown up around girls who dressed skimpy, and yet, he'd known better than to touch without permission. It showed his character, and that he respected women.

She'd never told anyone else the story about the Kentucky boys besides Spencer, and the counselor she'd gone to right after her dad left.

Her parents' break-up had been a hard time for her. The one man she thought she could count on, her dad, up and decided he no longer wanted be a part of their small family. Instead, he filed for divorce and moved to Miami. Her poor mom couldn't function for a while after that. Kendal stepped in and picked up the pieces, took care of the bill payments, the taxes, the yard work, the car maintenance, all of the things her dad did prior to his withdrawal from their lives. The last time she heard from him was on her eighteenth birthday, and that was just a card with nothing personal written in it.

She tried to put all of that hurt behind her. Her father knew where she was. He chose to walk away. It was up to him to reach out to her, and he'd made his choice.

The counselor tried to convince her she'd been taking on responsibilities way beyond her years and her mother needed to step up to the plate. She also told her trust issues when it came to males would most likely plague Kendal for years because of her past experience in Kentucky and the way her father had practically abandoned her. At the time, being only sixteen, Kendal wasn't able to fully grasp what the counselor was trying to tell her, but the woman had been right. Kendal did have issues when it came to males, in general. The whole idea of getting close to any man, emotionally or physically, triggered unpleasant responses throughout her system, like those God-awful nervous tremors.

When Dirk had shown up, she felt like she was on the Disney tea cup ride internally, until she'd sat behind the piano and was able to find her center again. She was so grateful he'd suggested that she play, because it'd really helped her calm down.

Spencer arched a brow. "Did you do your 'thing'? You know. That thing you do where you put your brains in a blender and your insides on a tilt-a-whirl whenever you have a date?"

"Oh yeah. I did my 'thing' all right."

"Aww, I'm sorry, Kendal. Maybe I shouldn't have pushed you to pursue him at the party."

Kendal walked over to Spencer and put her hands on the armrests of her friend's wheelchair. She leaned in, her face a foot away from Spencer's and grinned. "I'm so glad you pushed. Dirk is amazing. We ended up making out on the living room floor for a long time."

Spencer let out a squeal.

Kendal jumped up onto the work table, swinging her dangling legs.

"No wonder you're red from nose to chin. Was this make out session just kissing?" Spencer's entire face seemed to be glowing.

Kendal suspected her own face was glowing even more than her friend's. "I wouldn't call it *just* kissing. It was amazing kissing, but if you're asking if we went all the way... nope. He was a perfect gentleman." She wanted him to be less of gentleman, but had been too shy to say so. The kissing was mind-blowing though. She was definitely *not* complaining.

Spencer didn't ask, but Kendal knew her friend was curious about what it'd felt like. Spencer had never French kissed either. Kendal figured it wouldn't hurt to describe it a little bit, but she didn't want to make a habit of giving explicit details about everything she and Dirk might end up doing. Lord help her, she hoped they ended up doing a *lot* more. "It was really nice. Not what I expected. I thought it'd be a little gross, slobbery, kind of invasive feeling, but it wasn't like that at all. It was sweet, and exciting, kind of like communicating in a physical way. Makes you feel really close to the other person. I don't mean physically, even though you're super close to one another that way too. I mean—"

"While your lips are touching, it feels like your hearts are holding hands…" Spencer had a faraway look in her eyes. "That's how I've always imagined it."

"Yes. That's precisely what it feels like." Kendal hoped Spencer would experience it for herself one day.

The roar of an engine got Kendal's attention.

Earl pulled into the parking lot of Spencer's flower shop on his Harley. Spencer whirled around, her eyes twinkling like sparklers on the fourth of July.

Kendal asked, "What's Earl doing here?" Earl wasn't the kind of guy to buy flowers.

"I called him. The refrigerating system for the lilies in the back is acting up. Since he's going to tech school for his heating and refrigeration diploma, I figured he might be able to fix it. He's bound to charge me less than that crook who supposedly fixed it last time."

Spencer's dark eyes shifted back and forth from Kendal to the window like a couple of black ping pong balls. When Spencer untied her stained white apron and removed it,

Kendal noticed she was wearing a new dress in Earl's favorite color, emerald green.

"Spencer…did you pull a leaky faucet on Earl?"

Her friend whirled her wheelchair back around, her eyes as big as a lemur's. "How'd you know?"

"Lucky guess." Busted. "What'd you do to your cooler?"

"I just pulled a couple wires loose in the back. I didn't break anything."

Kendal held back her laughter. "You little vixen. Earl doesn't know what he's walking into."

Spencer appeared worried. "You're not going to tell him, are you?"

"Heck no. I think it's awesome. I'm just going to skedaddle out the back so you two can be alone."

"But he's bound to have seen your car. He'll want to know where you are."

"You can tell him I went out back to play with Benny before heading over to my mom's house for Sunday supper, and you won't even be lying." Without giving Spencer a chance to respond, Kendal rushed out the back door into the small, fenced-in yard between the flower shop and the cottage Spencer shared with her folks. Benny bounded around the corner at the sound of the slamming screen door.

She squatted by the blue hydrangea near the side gate and welcomed the golden lab into her arms. "Hey there, Benny." He licked her cheek. "You being a good boy?" The dog wagged his tail. Ted's truck and what looked like Dirk's car turned into Provisions night club across the street. Seven p.m. was a bit early for partying. The only other cars in the bar parking lot belonged to the bartender and the D.J.

"Gotta get on down the road, Benny. You watch out for Spencer." With one last pat on the dog's back, Kendal went through the gate and secured it behind her. She eased alongside the shop and crouched beside her car, peering through the side windows like a cop on a stake-out.

Ted and a brunette got out of his truck. Ashley and Dirk got out of Dirk's car. A double date! That double-timing… wait, she told him he could see other girls. But that didn't mean *she* wanted to see him with other girls.

"Boo!" Someone jabbed her in the ribs and she nearly jumped out of her skin. She popped up.

"Ouch!" Earl cupped his chin, blood trickling from his lip. "You made me bite my lip. Damn, girl."

"I'm sorry. You scared the pee out of me."

He laughed and looked at her legs.

"Not really." She smacked his arms.

"I got you good, didn't I?" She hated seeing him hurt.

He sucked his bottom lip into his mouth, brows arched. "Yes. Mission accomplished." He touched his bloody lip and looked at his finger.

"Sorry, about that, Earl. Do you want me to go get you some ice?

"Nah. It's no biggie. What were you doing hunkered down by your car?"

And the interrogation began.

She had to think fast. "I…I…I dropped my keys."

He pointed to her purse. "They're hooked to her purse strap like always. Come on now. Fess up. You weren't even looking at the ground. You were looking through your window like some peeping Tom. What's going on?"

Dang it.

Her gaze traveled back across the street. Dirk was staring right at her and Earl. She waved. Earl waved too.

Dirk waved back.

So much for being discreet.

She sighed. "Okay. I was being nosy. Who's that girl with Ted?"

Earl squinted at the couples across the street. "I think

that's Ashley's cousin, Heidi."

"Oh yeah. I forgot about her. I think you're right."

Earl leaned in and whispered, "You still got the hots for Ted? I thought you were over that."

"I am over it. I was just curious."

He narrowed his gaze like he didn't believe her. The couples disappeared into the bar. "Kendal, I know you've had a thing for him for a long time, but he's just not that into you. I know that hurts to hear, but somebody's got to say it. This has gone on long enough."

If he only knew the truth, he'd really flip out, but she wasn't about to tell him. "I know that. I got it. Really. Now, if you'll excuse me, I better get on over to Mama's for supper before she sends Sheriff Meyers out looking for me. I'm all of seven minutes late."

Earl entered Big Kabloom with his toolbox in hand. He was really starting to worry about Kendal. She'd developed a slight crush on Ted in high school. Ted had been a senior, a football star, and most of the girls at Island High had swooned over him. It wasn't surprising that he'd caught Kendal's eye too. But, damn, that'd been eight years ago. High school was over. She'd even graduated magna cum laude from college. Besides, Ted had openly chased after Mazy for two years, and Kendal had egged him on, even tried to talk Mazy into going out with the guy. Earl really thought Kendal's crush was ancient history. But seeing her spy on Ted like that? That was obsessive, borderline stalker. She needed help.

Spencer rolled into the showroom at the sound of the

bell on the door. She wore an emerald green dress and a beautiful smile, her wavy dark hair fell softly around her angelic face. "Hey, Earl. Thank you for coming right over."

"No problem. Glad to be of help." Truth was, he didn't come right over. After he got her call, he showered, shaved, put on cologne and his best shirt. Sunday go-to-meeting duds to come work on her refrigerator. Yep. He'd keep that information to himself.

She sat there looking up at him like she expected him to say something else. So he said the first thing that popped into his head. "Did you see Kendal out there spying on Ted?"

"Ted?"

"Yeah. He was on a double date with Dirk and Ashley. Ashley's cousin Heidi was with him."

"Double date? Are you sure?"

Why did Spencer look so damn shocked? Horrified to be exact. "What's going on around here? Something happening between Ted and Kendal?"

She fiddled with the locket around her neck. "No... nope...nothing I'm aware of."

Spencer didn't sound too convincing. If Ted had fooled around with Kendal and then flaunted another girl right in front of her, he was going to go have a talk with him. That wasn't right. He had to know she had it bad for him for years. Her heart wasn't a toy. "I'm not gonna stand by and watch Kendal's heart get stomped on. You hear me? If something's going on, you best tell me now." What the hell was he doing? Threatening Spencer? Might as well slap a name tag on his chest that read: "Hello, my name is Ass Hat."

Spencer smiled wider than when she first greeted him. "I love how protective you are. If I find out anything is going on between Kendal and Ted, I promise, you'll be the first and only person I tell."

Did he just score brownie points for acting like a dickwad? Women…he'd never figure them out. But hey, as long as it was points in his favor, he'd take it. "So you got a cooler on the fritz?"

"Yeah. Right over here." She rolled toward three big refrigerators in the back with glass doors. The one in the middle was dark. The other two were lit from within. Must be an electrical problem. Flat out not getting power at all.

He needed to get behind there to have a look. With one hand on top of the refrigerator and the other on the side, he tugged the machine forward. It didn't budge. Determined to not look wimpy in front of her, he threw his back into it… and right out. Holy shit that hurt.

"Earl, what are you doing? I have an access door so you can get behind the coolers. Come here. I'll show ya."

He gritted his teeth, and sucked in a breath. Slowly, very slowly, he straightened his spine. There was no way he could take a single step. Not right this second.

"What's wrong, Earl?"

"I pulled a muscle in my back. Give me a minute. I'll be okay."

"You need to lie down? I got a cot in the back room. Come on back here and stretch out for a minute."

Stretching out was a great idea, but that cot might as well have been in China. He attempted to take a step and his back spasmed on him. "Damn it." He'd injured himself years ago, pushing a tow truck uphill. Oh, the irony. Ever since then, one wrong twist or pull and that old injury flared up.

That's what he got for trying to show off in front of Spencer. He ended up showing his ass. Again. *Shoot me now.*

She patted her thighs. "Sit on my lap. I'll roll you back there."

He looked at her lap, her tiny shins protruding from the

hem of her dress. The weight of him would probably snap her legs in half, even though he only weighed just over a hundred and fifty pounds. "I'm too heavy."

She rolled her eyes. "Earl, you're a lot of things, some of them quite wonderful, but you are *not* heavy. Be real. You aren't going to break me. I'm not that freaking fragile. Damn. And think about it…I'm not going to even feel you on my lap. There's no way you can hurt me. Come on. I insist." She tugged his hand.

If he could relax his back for a few minutes that would really help. He wrestled with the thought. She jerked his hand harder and threw him off balance. He ended up falling into her. Their foreheads almost bumped.

She grinned up at him. "There. Now just turn a little."

He did as instructed, and she wheeled herself right under him, causing him to flop down into her lap. Dang. He hoped he didn't bruise her or anything.

As much as his back was hurting, that didn't stop him from focusing on the way her breasts felt pressed against his shoulder blades, or the way her breath tickled the back of his neck.

CHAPTER NINE
Bicycle

Spencer breathed in Earl's cologne, her heart about to beat right out of her chest and into his back. "You smell good. I love that cologne."

Earl's muscles tightened. "Thanks."

Did she embarrass him? Turn him on? Make him mad? Without being able to see his face, she had no idea, but the mention of his cologne definitely had some sort of effect on him. "Mind driving my chair? I can't see where I'm going."

"Sure." He had to tinker with the controls on the armrests a little, but he got the hang of it. He rolled them into the back room.

She pointed to the far corner. "See the cot? It's got a bunch of floral foam on it."

He drove them across the room and slid the green styrofoam pieces toward the foot of the bed. He eased off her lap, giving her a close up view of his cute little butt, lovingly cupped in a pair of Levi's. She wanted to pinch that tush so bad, she dug her fingernails into her palms to fight the urge.

He didn't groan, or wince, but as he sat down on the cot, she saw his pain etched into the lines across his forehead and the taught muscles drawing his lips into a straight white line. Where was that Tylenol? There it was, right beside the stack of bills on the counter. She rolled over and grabbed the pill bottle then went to the water cooler. As she drained water into a paper cup, Earl gave her a weak smile. Poor guy. He looked miserable.

She went back to him and handed him the medicine and water.

He said, "You're an angel."

An angel? Is that how he saw her? Darn. She was Florence Nightingale instead of Marilyn Monroe in his eyes, not that anyone could ever mistake her for Marilyn, but a girl could dream. Still, angels weren't sexy. She felt kind of deflated, and without meaning to, she released a little huff.

"Did that upset you?" He picked up on that mighty fast. She was going to have to be more careful about disguising her emotions.

"No. No. I just get called things like 'angel' a lot and sometimes I just…" Holy crap. What was she doing? She didn't need to tell him she'd rather be called something a bit more naughty.

"Just what?"

She bit her lower lip, not sure what to say.

"Sometimes you get tired of being labeled the good girl, little miss perfect?"

"Yes."

"Well, if it's any consolation, I'd like to see your devilish side." He tossed a couple of tablets in his mouth and gulped down the water. "I can't believe I just said that." He covered his face and laid flat of his back on the cot.

Stunned, she soaked up the silence that grew between them. He wanted to see her "devilish" side? Did he mean what she thought he meant? "I'd like to see your devilish side too." There, let's see what he has to say to that.

His big blue eyes peered out at her through his spread fingers, his ears and forehead blending in with his red hair, the backs of his pale, freckled hands a stark contrast to the deep pink hue of his cheeks.

She pried his hands away and leaned her face close to his. "May I see your devilish side, Earl?"

He ran his fingers into her hair and held her head gently. Before she could even process what was happening, he had his mouth on hers and their tongues were…were…wow.

This kiss was so much better than she'd imagined it would be. Hearts holding hands? More like inner animal unleashed. Whew.

Kendal scolded herself for being jealous of Dirk's date with Ashley. The entire six mile drive from Spencer's flower shop in Crystal Cover to her mom's driveway, Kendal's focus was on Dirk. She wished it was a longer drive, because she needed more time to stew before facing an evening of her mother's nonstop criticism. In Kendal's current discombobulated state, it wouldn't take much to make her snap. Snapping at her mother always ended with a big blow out and Kendal apologizing amidst tears. More times than not, *she* was the only one crying. Her mom tended to glare, in arm-crossed, deafening silence while Kendal groveled for forgiveness.

A wreath made from nautical rope hung on her mother's front door. The longer Kendal stared at that wreath, the more it resembled a noose. She put her car in reverse. No way was she ready to go in. She needed to watch the sunset on the water, smell the ocean, clear her head. Just ten minutes was all it would take.

As she eased back out of the driveway, her mother ran out of the house in a royal blue tent dress, waving her pale, plump arms hysterically. Her shiny, light-brown hair was sprayed into a solid mass, her bangs waving in one piece like the flap on a cardboard box.

"Kendal. Where are you going?"

Kendal stomped the brakes. Crap. She rolled down her window. "I forgot the dessert. I meant to bring you some fudge. Pam made a great batch today for Laffy Taffy and gave me a box of it." Part of that statement was true. Pam had made a batch of fudge and Kendal intended on sharing it with her mother, but had chosen to leave it at home so it wouldn't melt while she visited with Spencer.

I just saw the guy I kissed today on a date with someone else, and I can't deal with you right now. That wasn't a very pleasant thing to say. Telling her mom she wanted to bring her candy was much nicer.

"That's thoughtful of you, but I don't need any fudge." She motioned her back into the driveway.

Reluctantly, Kendal rolled up to the bumper of her mother's car.

As soon as she opened her door, Rita Duvall was on her. "Look at your hair. It's a pure mess. You left a headband here. It's dark blue. A black one would match your outfit better, but it'll do for now."

Kendal closed her eyes and stood, bracing herself for the comments her mother was bound to make about her dress.

"Kendal Duvall, since when do you let your boobies hang out for all the world to see?"

"They aren't hanging out."

"Button up farther."

Kendal glared at her.

"Kendal, That dress is so tight I can see your heart beating. My lands, child, can you even breathe?"

Don't say a word.

"I do like those sandals though, darling. Are those the ones I bought you in Myrtle Beach last year?"

She nodded, but kept her mouth shut.

"I thought so. We had such a good time that day, didn't

we?"

If you call hauling all the shopping bags around while her mother browsed every store in the outlet mall empty-handed fun, then yeah, they had a freaking blast.

Her mom grabbed her hand. "I'm doing it again, aren't I? I don't even give you a chance to answer before I'm asking you another question."

Once more, Kendal nodded, but kept her mouth shut.

"I'm sorry, honey. I don't know why I'm like that. My mother used to do the same thing to me. I do understand how frustrating it is, but I just can't seem to stop myself."

"Try."

"No need to be sassy."

Nod.

They stepped into the living room and her mother whispered, "I still can't get over how your boobies are just hanging out for all the world to see. Go put on one of my dresses. That purple one fits you good. I just washed it today."

Kendal spun on the heel of those flat sandals her mom liked so dang much, gripped the neckline of her own dress with both hands. "I'm not wearing one of your dresses. My boobs are not hanging out." She ripped her dress wide open, sending buttons in all directions, and revealing her brand new polka dot push up bra. "Now, my boobs are hanging out. See the difference?"

"Maybe I should come back another time." An unfamiliar male voice came from the kitchen. Kendal turned toward it. Standing in front of the table set with flowers and the fancy dishes was a tall, thin young man with jet black hair and a look on his handsome face that was a unique mixture of oh shit, hell yeah, and every expletive in between.

All the air in Kendal's lungs leaked out of in one long, "uhhhh."

Her mom grabbed the front page of the Raleigh News and Observer she'd clipped the coupons out of earlier, opened it, and slapped it against Kendal's bared bosom to hide her breasts. "Go change. Now."

Kendal didn't argue, didn't even take the extra second to nod. She clutched the paper and rushed to her old bedroom, slammed the door behind her, then slid down the door. The sound of her dress ripping even farther was barely audible over the rapid pulse thumping in her ears.

She lowered the paper from her chest and read the headline: *Girl Stands Up to Bully Twice Her Size.*

Kendal repeated the headline like a mantra as she bumped the back of her head against the door until her backbone turned to steel.

With determination coursing through her veins, she pushed to her feet, sat the paper on the desk, and marched herself straight into the kitchen—ripped dress and an attitude to match. The young man's back was to her, but her mom faced her. When Kendal stepped into the kitchen, her mother's mouth fell open so wide the woman could have swallowed an ostrich egg whole.

Kendal took a big breath and said, "I'm sure you're a very nice guy." The young man turned toward her and attempted to advert his gaze, but…yeah…his attempt was futile. He stared at her tits. So what if he could see her new bra. Why wear beautiful lingerie if you never get a chance to show it off. Let him look away. That bra covered more than most bikini tops anyway. "Please don't take this personally, but I'd like you to leave. I need to have a talk with my mother."

"Kendal!"

A smile played at the corner of the guy's mouth. "Good luck."

"Jeremy, don't you dare go anywhere. I'll handle this." Her mother chased after him.

He darted out the door, didn't even look back. In one fluid movement, he zipped down the front steps, hopped on a blue bicycle beside the corner azalea and he was gone. She hadn't even noticed that bicycle earlier. Dang.

Kendal blocked her mom from reaching the front door, and squared her shoulders with her. "A bicycle? You tried to set me up with a guy on a bicycle?"

"Jeremy's a nice boy. He's repented for his DUI, and he'll get his license back soon."

"Mama, I don't need a nice boy on a bicycle! I need a man with enough sense not to drink and drive in the first place, and I don't need your help to find him."

Kendal stormed to the kitchen table and pulled out a chair. "Mother, sit." She pointed at the seat. Surprisingly, her mom didn't protest. She crept over and plopped her behind down right where she was instructed then proceeded to fold her arms across her chest, stubborn nose in the air and lips pinched.

Kendal took a seat beside her and pulled one of her mother's pudgy hands into hers. "Some things have got to change, Mama."

"Let's start with your dress." Her mother didn't look at her, but she didn't tug her hand away either.

"Yes. Let's. This is my favorite dress. I feel prettier in this dress than anything I've ever worn. It flatters my figure without being raunchy."

"That's a matter of opinion."

"Agreed. And since I'm the one wearing the dress, my opinion is the only one that matters."

Her mother tried to tug her hand away after that comment, but Kendal held on. "I've always respected you, Mama, and I always will. I love you. But I love me too, and it's time I start doing what makes *me* happy, instead of bending to your every wish."

"Does flashing your bosom to a visitor in my home make you happy? Does embarrassing me in front of company bring you great joy? Do you think you're the only one who bends? Do you? Let me tell—"

"Stop it." Kendal released her mother's hand. "You will not turn this around on me. You didn't tell me that guy was coming to dinner. You took it upon yourself to arrange a blind date you could supervise like you always do. How many times does this make? Seven? Eight?"

Her mother's jaw twitched but she didn't deny that Kendal spoke the truth.

"My life doesn't need supervising. You've taught me right from wrong. I'm a smart and kind woman, Mama. I volunteer at the nursing home, help kids with autism, share my music with others. I graduated with honors. You did a great job raising me. But you need to accept the fact that I'm grown. If you can't ease up on me, let me be my own person, you're going to drive me away, just like Grandma drove you away. Is that what you want?"

Her mother gasped. "No. No. Don't you dare run off. I'd...I'd fall apart, baby. You're my everything. Please. Your father left. You're all I have in this world." Tears filled her mother's eyes. "I'm sorry. I'll really try to mind my own business. I will."

This was bizarre. Her mother was the one apologizing amidst tears. Why didn't this make Kendal feel any better? She kissed her mother's cheek. "I'm here, Mama. I haven't gone anywhere."

Her mother hugged her tight. "I love you...and...I'm so proud of you. So very, very proud. I don't care about the dress."

"I love you too, Mama." She meant it. And Kendal was proud of herself too. Very proud.

Today, she'd made out with Dirk Davis and stood up to

her mother. Even though she wasn't thrilled about Dirk being out with Ashley, she still felt pretty darn good.

Her mom pulled away and said, "I'd like to mend this dress. I won't raise the neckline or lower the hem. I promise."

Kendal smiled. "Thank you." She leaned in and clapped a hand on her mother's shoulder. "Did you see the look on that guy's face?"

Her mother giggled, actually giggled. "I haven't seen a look like that since the time your father caught me skinny dipping in Miller's pond when we were in high school."

"Wait a minute. When we went to Miller's pond back when I was in the third grade, Daddy said it was his first time there."

Her mother's eyes grew wide. "I meant my first boyfriend, not your father."

It was fun to watch her mother squirm for a change. "Mama, I can't believe you let your boobies hang out for all the world to see!"

CHAPTER TEN
Ashley

Ashley's laughter plucked Dirk's last nerve. She giggled at everything he said. He could've said his dad had a stroke and she probably would've giggled like that was a punchline.

He massaged his temples. "I hate to be a party pooper, but I'm gonna have to call it a night. I feel a migraine coming on."

Ted glared at him. "I think there's some Goody powders behind the counter. Sophie, you got some of those headache powders back there?"

Sophie, the bartender, moved some junk beside the register and held up a couple of packets. "Got'em right here. You need'em?"

"Nah. Dirk does, though."

Ashley gently raked her fake fingernails through Dirk's hair, causing a shiver to run down his spine. She said, "Poor baby. I know the perfect stress reliever to get rid of that headache. Let's go back to my place. My roommate's gone for the night, and I'm sure Ted and Heidi can find something to do on their own."

Was she serious?

The last time he went home with Ashley, she moaned so loud during sex, her roommate had to knock on the bedroom door and ask her to keep it down. Dirk was glad

Ashley enjoyed herself, but he was too embarrassed to speak to her roommate the next morning when he slipped out before Ashley woke up. Her roommate offered him a cup of coffee, and he didn't even bother to say no thank you before he bolted out the door, shirt and shoes in hand, jeans half-zipped.

Dirk waved Sophie away when she held out the powders to him. "Sorry folks. I'm out. Ted, can you drive Ashley home for me?"

Ted said, "Yeah," through clinched teeth.

Dirk locked eyes with his brother. "I'll see you in the morning. Still got that job on the Henderson place, right?"

Ted scowled. "Right. I'll pick you up at eight."

Ashley popped off the barstool. "I'll walk you out."

The girl couldn't take a hint. "I'm fine. You stay put."

She shimmied up beside him and linked her arm in his. Against his better judgment, he didn't pull away from her. Instead, he let her walk him out. But so help him, he wasn't going to make plans to see her again. He knew how her little mind worked.

When he climbed into the vehicle, she said, "Come by my place tomorrow night around nine. I'll be home alone."

"I'll be working."

"Tending bar at the resort?"

"Yep. And you know Mr. Treadway doesn't like locals hanging out down there."

"As long as I'm a paying customer, he won't mind."

"I'll be working, Ashley. I won't be in the position to jabber-jaw."

"Why are you being such a grouch?"

"Sorry. Like I said. I got a migraine coming on, and I need to get home. See ya later." He closed the door and started the engine, ignoring the fact that Ashley was motioning him to roll down his window. He pulled away without giving her a second glance. Instead, he eyed the parking lot across the street. Kendal's car was long gone, but Earl's motorcycle was still out front.

He thought about texting Kendal—now that he actually had her phone number—but he reconsidered. Probably better to let her cool off and call her tomorrow, talk to her instead of texting.

Even though there was nothing wrong with him going out with other girls, and vice versa, he could tell Kendal was upset when she saw him with Ashley. Kendal had waved to him, but her frown conveyed unhappiness.

No strings attached had sounded like a good idea originally, but maybe they needed to rethink things. He didn't want a commitment, but there was nothing wrong with them giving each other a warning before dates with other people. A little heads up just to be considerate so the other person wasn't caught off guard might not be such a bad idea.

Dirk waited 'til nine the next morning to give Kendal a call. "Hey, there."

"Hi." Her voice was clipped.

He pushed on. "What are your plans for the day?"

"Nursing home, piano lessons, and a gig tonight." Short and to the point. Ouch.

"Sounds like you're going to be busy."

"I am."

She sure as hell wasn't making this easy on him with her

tight-lipped responses. "Listen, I just wanted to clear the air about last night when you saw me with Ashley."

"Don't worry about it." The coldness in her words was driving him nuts. He knew she was mad, and she was trying to act otherwise.

"Come on, Kendal. I could tell it bugged you. I'm not stupid. I just wanted you to know that going out wasn't my idea. Ted roped me into it."

"Dirk, you don't need to explain yourself. You're free to go out with whoever you want, whenever you want. Just because you kissed me, doesn't mean I expect you to pledge your undying devotion. I'm a big girl. I get it, and I'd rather not talk about it."

Damn. "Now hang on a minute. I know you're a big girl, but that doesn't mean I don't owe you some consideration. I'd like to make an amendment to our rules."

"I thought we were never going to discuss our rules again after the night of the party."

"Things change, Kendal. Cut me some slack here. I have your best interest at heart."

"Say what you gotta say."

He wanted to shake some sense into her. She was as stubborn as he was. "Okay, thank you. Now, I was thinking maybe we should tell each other anytime we're going out with someone else."

"Oh great. So, each and every time you go out with another girl, you want to be sure to rub my nose in it?"

"No. I didn't mean it like that." He pushed up from his chair in his living room and tunneled his fingers through his hair.

She said, "Well, you're the one hound-doggin' around town. How did you mean it?"

Hound-doggin'? He hadn't done a damn thing wrong. "I just thought if we knew what was up, we'd be prepared, in case we crossed paths like we did last night."

"Get over yourself, Dirk. I said I was a big girl and could handle it. Be a big boy and accept the fact that I don't expect you to change on my account, nor do I want to know each and every time you go carousing around town."

"You're being a little—"

"Say it."

He would not say it, because he'd regret it. She was being sensible. Bitchy, but sensible. He was the one creating the drama.

Maybe what he needed to say was what was on his heart. "Kissing you yesterday got under my skin. The whole time I was sitting across from Ashley, all I could think about was your sweet strawberry mouth and big brown eyes. Take it for what it's worth. I left at 7:30 p.m., and Ted took Ashley home. I know I don't owe you an explanation, but damn it, there it is. Make of it what you will."

She was quiet. "Kendal?"

"Kissing you got under my skin too. I didn't like seeing you with Ashley."

He smiled. Finally, they were getting somewhere. "Fair enough. I care what you think, Kendal, and I don't want to play games with your heart."

"You aren't. I know we just kissed and it shouldn't be a huge deal, but it was for me. It was good that I saw you with Ashley, because it reminded me to keep myself in check. I needed that reminder. Everything's fine, Dirk. Really."

"So, we're good?"

"Yes. We're good."

"And you want to keep seeing me?"

"Yes, but I'm super busy for the next few days."

"All right then, we'll make a date."

"Oh, God. Let's hope I don't turn into a nervous wreck again. Something about the word date messes with my head."

"Ha. Yeah, don't get all wiggy on me. Relax. We're friends. We've kissed. It'll be fine. When are you free?"

"Next Wednesday my schedule is pretty clear."

"Good. I don't have any plans for Wednesday either. Let's have a picnic at our old stomping ground on the south end around two in the afternoon. We'll have sunshine and fresh air. What do you say?"

"It's a…da….day I will circle on my calendar."

He chuckled. She really had a thing about that date word. It was cute. "Kendal, I just want you to know, I really do care about your feelings. Just because we're keeping this casual and our little secret, doesn't mean I don't care. Okay?"

"I know you do, and I care about you too. That's why this is going to be a good thing this summer."

"It's already a good thing."

"You say the sweetest things sometimes. I swear."

He grinned, loving the smile in her voice. "I'm not sweet to everybody, babe. See you Wednesday."

CHAPTER ELEVEN
Spicy

Wearing a white bikini and a new pair of shorts, Kendal packed her beach bag. She zoomed to the south end in her silver Toyota Camry, windows rolled down, radio blasting. Dirk's classic, green El Camino was parallel parked on the side of the road, his surfboard in the back. She drove on by and chose to park near the gazebo a little farther down so it wouldn't look like they were there together. With beach bag in one hand and flip-flops in the other, she padded across the warm sand and down the beach access that led to the old fort. Not another living soul was in sight. Perfect.

She ran through her list of what-not-to-do. Don't talk about virginity or being groped as a teen. Don't talk bout anything depressing or heavy. Don't get emotional or swept up in romance.

Now for what-to-do. Remember this is casual, purely physical. Keep the conversation light. Try to have fun.

As she neared the cluster of trees on the tiny spit of land that jutted out into the Atlantic farther than the rest of the beach, reggae music filled the air—steel drums and Bob Marley, a winning combination.

Marley's voice rang out. "Don't worry…about a thing…'cause every little thing…gonna be alright." Yes indeed, Mr. Marley. She couldn't help but sing along.

Dirk rushed up behind her and wrapped her in his arms, his mouth close to her ear. He sang, "This is my message to you-ooo-ooo." He twirled her around and kissed her full on, playfully at first, but he quickly intensified the passion. She dropped her bag, her shoes, and threw her arms around his neck. Bring it on.

She wasn't bashful about kissing him this time. She welcomed the chance to show him she could match his passion with her own. When they finally tore their mouths from one another, he pressed his forehead against hers and said, "You're one hell of a kisser."

She beamed. "You're not half bad yourself."

He gave her another quick peck on the lips and led her over to a blanket spread on the sand with a cooler and a duffle bag smack-dab in the middle of it. "I wasn't sure what you'd like, so I brought a little of this and a little of that. There's fresh fruit, cucumbers and tomatoes soaked in Italian dressing, chicken salad, crackers, chips, soda, beer, chocolate chip cookies, and cajun pork rinds."

Ewww. Nasty. "Cajun pork rinds?"

He grinned. "I love'em. You ever had'em?"

"No." They looked disgusting.

"You're in for a treat."

"I don't eat pork rinds, but the other stuff you mentioned sounds great. A bit too much food, but delicious all the same."

She knelt on the blanket and helped him unpack the paper products from the duffle bag. After loading their plates, they dug right in. She was glad he wasted no time, because she'd overslept and missed the chance to eat breakfast before going to the nursing home. Afterward, she was in too big a rush to meet Dirk to even think about grabbing a bite.

As she shoveled a fork full of chicken salad in her mouth,

she looked up and found him staring at her. Was she being a pig? How embarrassing. She was normally self-conscious about eating in front of guys, but she hadn't flinched at the thought of chowing in front of Dirk.

He said, "How do you like the chicken salad?"

She chewed quickly then swallowed. "It's scrumptious."

"Made it myself. Boiled the eggs. Cut up the onions, the works. My first time. I was worried you wouldn't like it. I can't tell you how happy I am to see you gobble it right up."

He'd really gone all out for her. How sweet. "Your chicken salad is better than mine. I don't know what you put in it to give it that sweet, tangy flavor, but it's fantastic."

"Sweet'n'hot banana peppers. I forgot to pick up salad pickles, figured the banana peppers would give it a little kick."

"You were right." She took a few more bites then confessed. "I've never had a guy cook for me, or anything like that. I really appreciate this."

He smiled. "I've never done anything like this before either. My mom jokes that I'm allergic to cooking. Ted's good at it, but I avoid it like the plague."

"Yet you did this for me today. You could've just bought some stuff ready made."

"I know, but I wanted to put forth a little more effort than that. You're worth it."

She'd always heard that actions spoke louder than words. The fact Dirk had taken the time to do this for her said so much about his character and what he thought of her. Who knew chicken salad could be so romantic?

She was going to buy a diary and document every aspect of their time together, because these were the most beautiful moments of her life, and she didn't want to forget a single thing. She treasured every second with him.

"Thank you, Dirk." She wanted to thank him for

respecting her, not rushing the physical stuff, and for making their fling something sweet instead of dirty, but she opted to keep the conversation light. "Next time, I'll do the cooking."

He opened up the bag of pork rinds, popped one in his mouth with a loud crunch, and raised his brows. "Mmm."

She wasn't sure if that "Mmm" was because he liked the idea of her cooking, or because he was enjoying that nasty looking stuff he was munching, but it didn't matter. He seemed perfectly comfortable with the notion of "next time," and that's all she needed to know.

They had a relaxing lunch, and she was actually able to participate in "small talk" without turning into a rambling idiot like she usually did. She ate her fill and rubbed her tummy. They had enough food left to feed a family of ten, maybe he could take the rest home to his mom and dad and share some with Ted. They packed the cold items back in the cooler.

Even though she had a beer with her meal, when he offered her another, she declined. She wasn't really in the mood for it. "No thanks. I brought some fresh squeezed lemonade. Want some?"

He nodded. "Sure. I don't believe I've ever had the real deal. Mom always uses the powder."

"You're kidding me. You've *never* had real lemonade?" At least she wasn't the only one experiencing things for the first time. Trying new things seemed to be a theme for them.

She poured him a cup full and handed it to him.

He took a sip and made a face. "Man, that's tart. I need something to sweeten it up." He leaned close and kissed her.

She savored the zing of lemon on his soft lips still cool from the iced liquid. His head shadowed her face as he followed her down until she rested on her back. She giggled when she realized her toes were wiggling like a happy child's.

"What's so funny," he murmured, his mouth hovering

above hers.

"Nothing's funny. I'm just so happy right now."

He caressed her cheek and smiled. "Me too. Last time your kisses tasted like strawberries. This time lemons. For the rest of my life those two flavors will remind me of you."

Oh, God. She just sighed, loudly. And now he traced her lips with his finger, and she wanted to suckle it.

Don't get swept up in the romance. This is just physical.

But…he was so…so…he was so affectionate and kind. And he said the sweetest things and touched her tenderly. And he was thoughtful. He'd cooked for her. And…he was looking at her like she was the most precious thing on earth. Dirk Davis was making it *impossible* for her not to swoon and be caught up.

Dirk paid close attention to Kendal's breathing and all those subtle signals that told him she was becoming more and more aroused as they kissed. She'd asked him to help her learn what she liked. It was obvious she enjoyed kissing, but it was time to find out what else turned her on.

The way her nipples hardened beneath her bikini top and the arch of her back was an unspoken invitation to let his hands roam.

Propped on one elbow, he ever so lightly fondled her soft breasts. She kissed him more feverishly.

Yep. She liked that.

As he squeezed her delicate flesh and pinched her nipples through the fabric of her bikini top, one, then the other, she moaned and gently placed her hand on the back of his, caressing his knuckles affectionately. She was practically urging him to continue. He had no problems doing that. No problems at all.

Working his mouth back to her ear, he whispered, "You're so beautiful." She sighed and turned her head, exposing her neck to him. He trailed wet kisses and nibbles from her earlobe to her collar bone, his hand continuing to massage her bosom.

She bent her outer knee and began to grind her hips slightly. Untying the bow at the nape of her neck, he bared her gorgeous breasts. Her areolas were pale pink and taught, perfect. He held her gaze in his and lowered his head until he could hear the rapid pounding of her heart. One lick across her hardened nipple followed by a gentle suckle and she rewarded him with a sultry "ahhh."

Blowing hot breath across her creamy skin, he slid his hand between her thighs, pressing his palm firmly against the crotch of her shorts. He held his hand still and returned his focus to her upper body, feasting, devouring, teasing, until he kissed his way back up to her face.

She smiled. He enveloped her mouth with his own and began to move the hand cradling her womanhood, dragging his fingertips over the seam of her shorts. Up and down he stroked her. She grabbed his bicep and shuddered. Her breathing was a series of held breaths peppered with whimpers. Those whimpers were causing him to become even more excited.

As he slid his fingers beneath the waistband of her shorts, her abdomen trembled. He softened his kiss, showing her more tenderness, less passion, reassuring her through his hesitation that she could stop this any time she wanted.

She closed her eyes, "Please, please touch me."

That sweet little beg. Damn. He loved that.

At her request, he drove his fingers inside her bikini bottoms and caressed her moistened lips, gently parting them, finding her swollen center, circling.

She sucked in a sharp breath, her brows furrowed. "It's so hot."

"Yes, baby. You're so hot." And wet. Holy shit was she

wet.

She cried out and bucked. Jesus, he wasn't expecting her to be so close to orgasm this fast. Just witnessing her responsiveness had him rock hard.

"Dirk…"

"Yes, baby, I know." He rubbed faster. "I got you. Does that feel good?"

"Dirk, I'm on fire."

Shit. So was he. But right now he just wanted to make her come, hard, show her how good it could be, make her first experience incredible.

She pushed up, her entire back springing off the blanket. "Thatta girl. Let it go, baby." She was so slick. He couldn't wait to taste her.

She pressed her hand against his chest and shoved him back. Whoa. She wanted to be in the driver's seat. All right. Kendal was a little wildcat. Hell yeah.

Next thing he knew, she was on her feet and running for the water, holding herself between the legs. "It burns. Why does it burn so bad?"

He looked down at his hands. Residue from the pork rinds coated his fingertips. Aww shit! The cayenne pepper!

Kendal sat in the breakers, the cool ocean gradually easing the burn of her most private area.

It wasn't supposed to feel like this. Was she injured? She peeked inside her bathing suit. Everything looked fine down there. But it'd never burned like this when she'd touched herself. Something was definitely wrong. Very wrong.

A shadow fell over her, and the splashing against her back signaled Dirk was coming up behind her. She couldn't bear to look at him.

"I'm so sorry, Kendal." His voice was tender and quiet. "I should have washed my hands after eating those cajun pork rinds. Cayenne pepper is some pretty potent stuff."

The spices? That's what lit her up like a bonfire? She whirled around. He was rubbing his hands together in the foaming water.

Concern filled his eyes. "Are you okay?"

"Okay? How about I take a blow torch to your dick and ask you if you're okay?"

His eyes nearly bugged right out of his head.

Breathe in. Breathe out. Everything's gonna be alright just like Bob Marley said. At least there wasn't some strange medical reason for her pain. She could tell her inner hypochondriac to chill out. "It's getting better."

"I'm so stupid." He sat beside her. "I ruined it." He wrapped an arm around her.

She wiggled away. Maybe she was being a big baby, but she really didn't want him touching her at the moment.

He dropped his hands to his lap and shook his head, eyes cast downward. "I don't know what to say. I'm just...so... so...sorry."

"It's okay." She'd probably laugh about this later, but right now, she wanted to stop the ride, get off the crazy train, and go home. "But if you don't mind, I'd like to call it a day."

"Sure. I totally understand." He stood and helped her up then followed her back to the blanket.

She gathered her stuff in silence.

"I'll walk you to your car." He reached for her beach bag.

"We can't run the risk of anybody seeing us together. Our little secret, remember?" She kept her tone flat, very matter of fact.

He didn't say anything, but the tension in his face, the sad look in his eyes, and the way he swallowed loudly told her those words had stung him almost as badly as the pepper had stung her.

She considered apologizing, but for what? The truth?

CHAPTER TWELVE
Necklace

Dirk cursed under his breath and hauled his stuff down the beach. Could he have ruined the moment with Kendal any more? She'd probably never want him to touch her again.

He tossed the remainder of the pork rinds in the garbage can along the edge of the dunes. No sense keeping those cursed things. He sure as hell would never eat any more of them.

A few yards away, Miss Judy's run down hermit shack leaned into the wind. Her front door had come off again. Miss Judy never liked it when he came by or did minor repairs to her place, but somebody had to take care of her. He didn't mind doing it.

He trudged toward her shack, and she staggered out into the open, shielding her eyes from the sun. She wore a ripped white pillowcase as a dress, her waist-length gray dreadlocks barely moving in the breeze. She waved a bony arm like she was swatting a fly then she proceeded to flip him off. Well, that beat mooning him like she'd done the last time he paid her a visit.

She turned, limped back into her shack, and draped a cast net across the doorway. He chuckled. She knew darn well he wasn't going to pay her grumpy ways any mind.

Dirk peered into the shack through the weave of the net.

She was huddled in the corner peeking around a pink, translucent raft she held upright as a shield, but had probably been using for a bed.

He reached in and unhooked the net from a nail in the doorjamb. "How you doing, Miss Judy?"

"You git outta here. Git."

"I thought you might like some yummy vittles. I made chicken salad and a few other things, turned out good. Now there's eggs and mayonaise in the chicken salad, so eat your fill quick. Once the ice melts in the cooler, you'll need to toss out any left over food, but the sodas will keep. I'm gonna take out the beers though. I know you don't drink alcohol. I got some paper plates and stuff I'll put right here on this little table."

She inched over to the cooler and opened the lid. "Why you got so much?"

"I had a picnic date with a pretty girl, got a bit carried away."

"Where's the girl?"

"She wasn't feeling well, had to cut out early."

Miss Judy straightened her spine and looked him up and down slowly. "Something's different about you."

"What do you mean?"

"I'm not sure. Can't make up my mind if you look like you been tasered or lovestruck."

He laughed. "Aren't they the same thing?"

"Nope. You ever been tasered?"

"No, Ma'am."

"I have, it don't hurt near as bad as being lovestruck."

The sadness in her eyes when she mentioned love was a hit to his chest. She'd never told him her story, but rumor had it, her rich father ran off the sailor she'd fallen in love with. Soon after, her lover's ship went down, his body never recovered. She got depressed, suicidal, was locked away for a spell, but was eventually released. She'd moved to the beach and kept her eye on the horizon.

He worried about her being out here all alone, but it was her choice. She had money in the bank and had inherited a nice house she refused to live in. Strange as it seemed, this was how she wanted to live, and people let her be.

He saw her life alert necklace and said. "Glad to see you're still wearing that necklace I gave you."

She touched the plastic pendant. "You told me to never take it off."

"That's right. I did. If you're ever in a jam, hurt, or what have you, you push that button and help will come."

She nodded and studied the pendant, then looked at him with a lopsided smile.

He smiled back. "Listen, I'll be back in a day or two and level your roof back up, put your door back on. Want me to bring you anything?"

"No. I don't need you to come back either." She shoved his arm playfully.

"Oh, I know you don't need me to. I want to."

She picked up a rusty coffee can from a shelf and fished around in it. She stuck out her fist, something small was in her grasp, but he couldn't see what it was. "Take this."

He held out his palm, and she dropped a necklace in it, a heart-shaped diamond pendant on a gold chain. "What's this for?"

"When you figure out whether or not you're lovestruck, you give it to your girl."

He smiled. "You don't need to do this, Miss Judy."

"I know that. I want to. It's real so keep it safe."

He knew better than to argue with her. She was being unusually friendly today. He pocketed the necklace. "Thank you. I'm sure she'll love it."

"You give it to the right girl on the full moon, and she'll

cherish your heart forever. You give it to her at the wrong time, or to the wrong girl, she'll toss it aside and fall in love with another."

What sort of nonsense was that? Miss Judy wasn't a witch or anything of that nature. He'd never known her to speak such hippy-dippy crap. "Okay, Miss Judy. Thank you."

"Go away." She pointed to the door with a grimace that contradicted her smiling eyes.

"Yes, Ma'am." He exited her shack and put the net back in place.

He felt much lighter as he trudged up the beach access, and it wasn't because his duffle bag was nearly empty, or the fact he was no longing carrying the cooler. His lightness came from within. And he was whistling a melody from that song Kendal had played for him on her yellow piano.

Spencer was making patriotic bows for Reel to Real Good's fourth of July bash. She dropped the blue and white polka dot ribbon when Earl burst through the front door of Big Kabloom with some funky, black, strappy thing in his hand.

He grinned and rushed over for a quick smooch. "I got a surprise for you."

She tried to figure out what he was holding, but for the life of her, she had no idea. "What's in your hand?"

"You'll see, but first, I need to ask you something."

"Go ahead."

"I just saw Kendal driving with her face all scrunched up, mad-like, and she was coming from south end. She didn't even turn her head when I beeped at her. Two seconds later, Ted comes barreling down the road from the same direction, and he ran a stop sign. I cornered him at the gas station a few minutes ago, and he swore up and down nothing was going on between him and Kendal. And I'm sorry, but, I just don't believe him. Neither one of them hang out on that end of the beach normally. It just looks fishy to me. So I want to know once and for all...Is Ted messing with Kendal?"

"What do you mean by messing?"

"Putting the moves on her without doing right by her."

"Earl, I honestly don't follow you, but if you're suggesting hanky panky or something like that, I can assure you Kendal is *not* interested in Ted and he is *not* messing with her like that."

Earl twisted his mouth in contemplation. "You wouldn't break Kendal's confidence no matter what."

"Earl Washington! Give me some credit. If I thought my best friend really needed help, I would tell you. We've been over this before. She is not into Ted anymore. You need to chill out."

Earl's face turned red. "My life wouldn't be complete if I didn't make an ass of myself at least once a week."

"Aww. You just care about her. So do I. But Everything's fine. I promise. I know the scoop with her, and it has not one thing to do with Ted Davis. Not one cotton-picking thing. And what it does involve is nothing she needs any assistance handling. Give her some privacy. Trust me. Now, give me a real kiss."

He leaned over and kissed her gently. That wasn't what she wanted. Sweet? Heck no. Bring on the fire.

She pulled him closer and showed him how it's done, using her lips and tongue and breath to do the talking for her. When they parted, his eyes remained closed, his mouth opened, and a dopey expression on his face like he was in another world.

"Earl?"

He moaned and cracked his eyes open.

"You okay?"

"I am now. Do it again." He leaned close, a sly grin playing in the corners of his mouth.

She swatted his arm, then tugged him down for another electrifying kiss.

He wrapped something around her and pulled her up out her seat. Before she knew what hit her, he had some sort of black nylon contraption between her legs and was pulling a flap up to match one on the side like some sort of diaper. "What the hell are you doing?"

She wrestled to see what he had her in, but his head was in the way.

He chuckled. "You'll see." When he stood, he had her in some sort of harness that was hooked around his shoulders and held her upright, face to face with him.

He put his arms around her waist, maintained eye contact, and walked her over to the mirror.

She studied this funky seat she was in, strapped to his chest. Her feet were dangling a few inches from the ground, but she was eye to eye with Earl and seemed to be secure as could be. It was pretty darn cool. "Where'd you get this thing?"

"Made it." He turned on the radio and found a channel he liked, country two-stepping music. Placing one of her hands on his shoulder, he held the other in his and commenced to dancing her around the work room.

She was dancing, actually dancing, upright, in his arms. She couldn't stop smiling. Her cheeks hurt.

He mirrored her joy. "Having fun?"

"Yes! What possessed you to make this thing?"

"I saw something like this on the internet. A mother had made it for her disabled child. I took the idea and ran with it. Like it?"

"Yes!"

"Good. Cause we're going to be doing a lot of things

you've missed out on. Make a list."

As he whirled her around the flower shop—heart to heart, eye to eye—tears filled her eyes, happy tears.

He paused. "Am I hurting you? Are you in pain. What's wrong, baby?"

"You're magic. This is the most wonderful thing anyone has ever done for me."

He swallowed hard and said, "You're the one who's magic."

When they danced their way outside into the backyard, Benny bolted around the corner of the house, wagging his tail, running circles round them like he wanted to dance too.

Spencer started singing a version of "Benny and the Jets" to her dog. "She wore electric boots, a mohair suit, you know I read it in a magazine…uh-oh, Benny is my pet."

Her parents stepped out of their house onto the front porch, huddled close together, faces alight with smiles. Her mother pressed a hand to her heart, love in her eyes. Her father kissed her mother's brow.

Spencer reached up and plucked a peach from the tree and held it to her nose, enjoying the fresh fragrance, and the pleasure of picking right off the branch.

She rested her head on Earl's chest and dreamed of all the things she wanted to do again, and for the first time since the accident, they felt obtainable. No, she might not be able to do them in the exact way she'd hoped, but she'd do them in a way more beautiful than she'd ever imagined, because Earl would be there to share those experiences with her.

CHAPTER THIRTEEN
Duet

Hunter had unusually small hands for an eight year old boy. Kendal gripped his right hand and placed it on the piano keys. He slapped at the keyboard and shook his head of blond curls. She'd learned that when he did that, he was frustrated not angry. Each of her autistic students had their own unique ticks, and this was one of his. He sometimes struggled to work his fingers independently like he wanted. That's why he slapped with his palms, his way of letting her know he needed more help.

She placed his thumb on middle c then lined his other fingers up on d, e, f, and g. Hunter cooed and bounced on the bench. He was adorable with big dimples in his cheeks when he smiled. His big doe eyes, bright blue, reminded her of Dirk's, honest and happy.

"Is that what you wanted, Hunter?"

A jubilant squeal escaped his smiling mouth.

His mother, Mindy Lancaster, laughed and rose from the couch. "You're so good with him. You read him better than I do."

Kendal pushed Hunter's fingers one by one to help him play "Row, Row, Row Your Boat," his favorite song. Once the first few notes of the melody were sounded, he began to move his fingers on his own, continuing the song. "He's a smart boy. He shows me what he needs." She removed her hand from Hunter's and waited for him to finish playing.

His mother said, "I never dreamed he'd take to piano lessons so well. Hope you don't mind, but I've distributed your number to Hunter's class. Several of the other mothers are interested in your services."

"Mind? I'm grateful. Thank you so much."

"You're welcome. I know you said your schedule is getting pretty full, but I hope you can squeeze in a few more autistic students."

"I can always squeeze in a few more. I love doing this." If Kendal had her way, she'd specialize in working with special needs students. There were lots of piano teachers in Crystal Cove and in Wilmington to handle the basic piano teaching needs of the area, but to her knowledge, none of those teachers took on students like Hunter.

Her dream was to set up a studio in Crystal Cove, midway between Pleasure Island and Wilmington, where she could teach lessons in one location instead of traveling from house to house. That would give her more time to teach. Now, her hours were very limited. Everyone wanted lessons after school and before supper. She understood that, but when she was using an hour of that three hour daily block driving, it created a challenge to work all her students in. Piano lessons on the weekends were out, because invariably there were too many cancellations to keep things consistent. Plus, that's when she played for weddings and stuff like that, in addition to gigging with Bikini Quartet.

Luckily, she could fit in the nursing home volunteer work she did during school hours. She tended to swing by Silver Dreams, the local nursing home, after lunch three times a week to play the piano for the residents. She always passed out tambourines, maracas, and other small rhythm instruments for them to play too. The residents had a ball.

Even though some of them rarely held conversation, most of them sang the old songs from their youth, including the patients whose memories were shattered.

Music had healing properties. She was convinced.

Mindy stood by the back door of her cottage and said, "Is that Dirk and Ted's father?" She pointed toward the beach.

Kendal peered at the man walking near the waves. It *was* Mr. Davis, and he was alone. What was he doing this far from home? "Yes, it is. Please excuse me. Let me go check on him."

"Absolutely. Need me to call anyone?"

As Kendal rushed down the back steps she said, "I don't know yet. Let me see what's going on first."

Dirk's father ambled toward the boardwalk. He kept glancing around with a bewildered look in his eyes, as if he had no idea where he was.

Kendal approached him slowly, being careful not to startle him. "Hey there. I don't know if you remember me ─"

He looked at her and smiled. "There you are, Sissy. I thought you'd run off. Where's that boyfriend of yours? Brian, right?"

Dirk had an uncle named Brian, married to his father's sister Diane. Kendal had worked with enough patients who suffered from dementia to know, when they are mixed up like Mr. Davis seemed to be, it's best to go along with their version of reality and not argue. Correcting them only confused them more and sometimes caused them to get violent. "I'm surprised you remembered his name."

Mr. Davis grinned. "Just cause I remember him, don't mean I like him." He laughed.

Kendal was a bit unsure what to say, so she did what had worked for her in the past in similar circumstances. She started singing "Fly Me to the Moon."

Mr. Davis joined in. He knew all the words too. He twirled her around and did a little shuffle in the sand.

She held his hand and said, "Let's go back up to the house."

"Good idea. I'm thirsty." He followed her back to Mindy's house.

Mindy whispered, "Want me to call his wife, Kizzie, at Curl up and Dye?"

"No. I'll call Dirk. I think he's on break right now." She was glad Mindy didn't bat an eye at the fact Kendal knew Dirk's schedule. Kendal dug her phone out of her purse and said, "Mindy, could you keep an eye on Mr. Davis for a second?"

"Of course." Mindy walked toward him, and he took a seat next to Hunter on the piano bench.

Kendal dialed Dirk.

Dirk answered, "Hey, sexy, about time you returned my calls. When are we going to meet again?"

"Umm…Er…I'm not sure. Anyway, that's not why I called." Yes, she'd been avoiding him. After how things went the last time, she was nervous about being touched again. She'd set out to do this so she could feel more confident, but now she was even more skittish. So, she wrestled with the notion of ending the fling, but she wasn't a hundred percent sure that's what she wanted. She hated when people were wishy-washy, and she didn't want to be that way. So she'd decided not to say much about it to Dirk until she felt more secure about her decision. Truth was, if she wasn't having such strong feelings for him, she wouldn't have a bit of trouble ending things.

"You aren't still mad about the pork rinds are ya? I've apologized a gazillion times. It was an accident."

"I know that. You're forgiven." She couldn't have this

conversation right now. "Listen, your dad was wondering around the beach alone. I brought him into Mindy Lancaster's house, because I happened to be in the middle of Hunter's piano lesson."

"Is Dad okay?" His voice sounded alarmed.

"Yes. He's just a little disoriented. I believe he thinks I'm your Aunt Diane."

"Aunt Di? Oh boy. Thanks for looking out for him. I should've known something like this was going to happen. Ted stayed out all night with Heidi. He probably fell asleep on his watch today. Anyway, I'll be there in a flash. Mindy Lancaster's, right?"

"Yep. The pink cottage next to the resort."

"Got it."

Kendal watched Mr. Davis closely. He didn't seem agitated. Actually, he seemed rather content as he plunked out the bottom part to "Heart and Soul" using both hands on the piano. Hunter added in a few bass notes of his own.

Mindy walked over and squeezed Kendal's arm gently. "I've got to record this. Let me get my camera." She disappeared down the hall.

Kendal eased over to Mr. Davis and began playing the upper melody to "Heart and Soul."

He grinned and said, "That's it, Sissy. What do you think, little buddy?" He nudged Hunter.

Hunter nodded repeatedly, his face aglow, and said, "Little buddy, little buddy, little buddy."

A flash went off. Kendal glanced back and Dirk was standing with Mindy in the archway leading to the living room. Dirk held up his phone like he was taking a picture of his dad. His mouth was slightly opened, the corners upturned in a look of amazement and joy. He punched a few buttons on his phone, still holding it up, and motioned for Kendal to keep playing.

Mr. Davis didn't even seem to notice Mindy or Dirk in the room. He was completely engrossed in the song. However, Kendal was completely distracted by Dirk's presence.

Dirk couldn't get over the fact his dad was playing the piano. His father hadn't done that in over a decade. Not only was he playing, he was playing from memory. Dirk couldn't wait to share the video of this event with his mom and brother.

Trying not to disturb the performance, he tiptoed into the living room.

His dad spun around and said. "Do you want to play too?"

"No, you keep going. I'm enjoying this."

"Suit yourself." His dad segued into Chopsticks and Kendal joined in. Hunter created his own accompaniment.

When the song ended, Dirk applauded and said, "That was great!" He established eye contact with his dad. "Ready to go home, Dad?"

His father scowled. "I'm not your father. Who are you? Is this some kind of joke?"

"No, sir, no joke. You *are* my father, and I need to get you home." Dirk's stomach tightened, sensing his father was on the verge of a meltdown, judging from the man's hostile tone. Dirk needed to get him out of there quickly before things turned ugly. "Say goodbye to these kind folks."

His dad grabbed Kendal's hand. "You know this young man? Is he a friend of yours?"

She gave Dirk a weak smile, almost apologetic. "Yes. He was in my chemistry class."

Dirk didn't know what she was up to. Besides, he and Kendal were in more classes together than chemistry years ago.

She patted his father on the shoulder and walked toward Dirk. In a hushed voice, she said, "I might have better luck getting him home. Why don't you let me give it a try? I'm afraid if you push too hard, he'll pitch a fit, and that might set Hunter off."

Keeping things calm was probably the best thing. Dirk chewed on the inside of his cheek in contemplation. "Okay. See if you can talk him into coming downstairs so I can load him in the car."

"All right." She nodded then went over to his father and whispered something in his ear.

His dad stood and playfully rustled Hunter's blond curls. "Time for me to get going, little buddy. My mom just made a lemon pound cake. My favorite."

Hunter waved bye. "Little buddy, little buddy, little buddy."

Dirk wondered how his dad was going to react when he got home and there was no cake. Lying to him was not a great plan.

His father followed Kendal out of the house and down the stairs. When they got in the driveway, Kendal opened the back door of her car, reached in and retrieved something covered in a towel.

She whispered, "Here's a lemon pound cake I just bought from Louise. I was going to give it to my mother, but I'll get her another one later. Take this one and go on home. I'll meet you there with your dad."

Dirk wasn't too keen on Kendal handling his father alone. His dad could snap any second. Dirk had experienced too many episodes to not be aware of how quickly his father's demeanor could change, and when he was not in his own house, he tended to get disoriented and emotional.

His dad put his arm around Kendal. "Diane, think Mom would like us to pick up some vanilla ice cream to go with that cake?"

Kendal didn't bat an eye. "What a great idea, George. We'll get some on the way home."

She jerked her head and widened her eyes at Dirk as if to say "get going." His dad appeared calm and happy.

Kendal had everything under control. It shocked the heck out of Dirk, but he was grateful.

He called his mom and gave a report on his dad then drove back to his parents' house. When he stepped into the kitchen, Ted was on his phone, panic in his eyes.

Ted slammed his phone down. "Bad news. I fell asleep and Dad got out. I can't find him, but I've already called Mom and was just on the phone with Sheriff Meyers."

Dirk tried to appear pissed. "Why didn't you call or text me?"

"I was going to do that next, but you're here now."

"You should've texted me before anyone else, and you know it." He also knew Ted didn't want to admit he'd fallen asleep on his watch. They didn't have many fights, but when they did, most of the time it was about their dad.

Ted shoved a kitchen chair out of his way and stormed toward the side door then came to a halt and faced Dirk. "I'm going to go look for Dad again. You stay here in case he comes home."

Kendal entered the side door, his father right behind her with a gallon of ice cream in his hand.

Dirk sat the pound cake on the counter. "Want some cake, Ted?"

The relief on Ted's face was priceless. He wrapped his arms around their father.

His father pulled away from him. "Cool it with the

touchy feely, buddy boy. You're not my type."

Dirk locked eyes with Kendal, and they both cracked up.

Dirk said, "Ted, you remember Diane don't you?" He motioned toward Kendal.

Ted looked puzzled. "Diane?"

"Yes. Diane Davis."

Ted's eyes widened. "Oh…yeah…Diane Davis." He nodded toward their dad. "And this must be George."

His father nodded back. "Nice to meet ya."

Their mother, Kizzie, came home, and the second she walked through the door, their dad said. "Where you been, honey? You nearly missed out on cake and ice cream. Dirk, cut your mother a piece of that pound cake."

His dad was back. Thank the Lord.

His mother looked around the kitchen and smiled at Kendal. "Hi, Kendal. It's nice to see you again."

Dirk fixed the plates and passed them around then sat at the round table in the only available seat, between Kendal and his father. "We owe a big thank you to Kendal, Mom. She gave us this cake." He made eyes to indicate Kendal had a hand in getting his father back home.

His mother got the message. "Oh, how nice. We certainly appreciate it *very* much."

Kendal smiled. "My pleasure."

His dad nudged him and said, "I forgot, tell me again, when are you and Kendal getting married?"

Dirk nearly choked on his cake.

Kendal dropped her fork against her plate with a clatter.

Ted howled with laughter.

Dirk wanted to disappear. This was a prime example of why he *never* brought a girl to his house. Invariably, his family would embarrass him, not to mention, not many girls would know what to make of some the crazy things his dad did.

His mom said, "George, where did you get that idea?"

Kendal patted her mouth with a napkin and straightened her spine. She looked at his father sweetly. "We haven't discussed it lately. We'll be sure to let you know when we finalize plans, though."

What the...? *Cough*. That cake wasn't going down. He coughed again. His mom stood and got him a glass of water and winked at him when she handed it to him. He gulped the water down.

His dad gave a satisfied nod to Kendal. "You do that, and make sure y'all send Diane an invitation. Lord knows, I haven't seen my sister in a month of Sundays. Kizzie, we should invite her and Brian down for the fourth of July."

With a knowing smile on her face, his mother kept looking from Kendal to Dirk and back again. "That's a good idea, George. I'll call her tonight."

As soon as Kendal finished her dessert, she stood and said, "Thanks so much for the hospitality. I hate to eat and run, but I have somewhere I need to be." Her voice was formal and distant, like she'd put up some sort of wall. What had flipped her switch and made her want to run off?

His family said their goodbyes to Kendal, but Dirk wasn't about to let her just walk out. He stood to escort her to her car, and she gestured him to stay.

As she backed toward the side door, she said, "No need to get up, Dirk. I can see myself out."

Determined to speak with Kendal in private, he ignored the looks his mom and Ted gave him, and he followed Kendal to her car. "Why are you in such a hurry to get out of here?"

With her hand on her driver's door, she spun around. "I'm not."

"Where do you need to be then? You don't gig at the restaurant for another two hours."

She glanced up at his apartment. "We said we were

keeping things casual. Me hanging out with y'all and your dad asking when we're getting married doesn't seem so very casual. I felt like I'd overstepped some boundary."

"You helped my dad today. You were amazing with him, Kendal. I appreciate what you did, and my mom and Ted appreciate it too. This wasn't a planned meeting. They don't even know you and I are seeing each other."

"Seeing each other? Is that how you describe it?"

"What's with you?"

"I don't know. What we're doing is immoral in a lot of people's eyes. It certainly would be immoral to my mom. I can't imagine you just hanging out with me and my mother, eating cake and ice cream. She'd be reading all sorts of things into us being together."

"So, what, you're scared my mother or Ted might think we're dating?"

"But we aren't dating, are we?" She crossed her arms over her chest.

"Technically, no." They weren't dating per se, but he didn't feel they'd done anything immoral.

"I'd be embarrassed to explain our arrangement to your mother or Ted. The way your mom looked at you and then me, I could almost hear her thoughts. She suspects something. I don't want to be faced with that awkward moment when you or I have to say…we're just fooling around. I know this was all my idea. I'm okay with that, as long as it stays between the two of us. Seated at the dinner table with your family didn't feel like just the two of us."

She had a point. But he wasn't buying it. She'd been avoiding him since the incident with the pepper.

He stepped into her space and put his hand on her driver's door. He wasn't going to let her leave without agreeing to meet with him again. "Okay, so when do you want to get together again, just the two of us?"

Silence. He knew it. She was scared to be with him now. He'd ruined it.

"Come on, Kendal. I feel bad about how things went down last time. Let me make it up to you."

Nose to nose, he gazed into her eyes. "Give me a chance to thank you properly." He put a hand on her hip.

Her eyes lowered to his lips.

That's better.

He slid his hand up to her waist and beneath the hem of her shirt to caress her bare flesh just above the waistband of her skirt.

She sighed and dropped her head to his chest.

"Do you want to see me again, Kendal?"

She looked up at him through lowered lashes, her lips parted slightly.

When he bowed his head to kiss her, she squirmed away and mumbled, "I'm running late. Sorry."

CHAPTER FOURTEEN
Better

Kendal brought in a bouquet of yellow roses that sat by her back door. She placed the vase on the kitchen counter and read the card that came with the flowers.

Dear Kendal,

I can't thank you enough for being George's guardian angel. He's been singing "Fly Me to the Moon" nonstop since he spent some time with you the other day. He's even started playing the piano again. It's such a joy to have the house filled with music and to see my husband happy. You are a special young lady, Kendal. You have a rare and wonderful way of bringing out the best in troubled souls through your gentle nature and your musical talent. I hope you'll visit us again soon. You're welcome any time.

Sincerely,

Kizzie Davis

Kendal couldn't stop smiling. She hummed "Fly Me to the Moon," and sniffed the roses. Mrs. Davis was such a thoughtful lady. Kendal had always liked her and admired her compassion for others, and the way she avoided gossip, even though she ran a popular beauty shop on the island. In addition to being a strong woman with integrity, Kizzie was known for her classy way of dressing trendy yet age appropriate. She changed her hairstyle often and tended to go for edgy styles that flattered her high cheekbones.

Dirk had inherited Kizzie's compassion, integrity, and those amazing cheekbones, but his jawline was firmer than his mother's, more squared and strong like his dad's. The whole Davis clan had svelte and toned bodies, including George Davis, who was in her early fifties, but seemed older because of his mental condition.

She took one more big whiff of the roses. Was yellow the color of friendship? She'd ask Spencer later. The only time Kendal had ever received roses was at a piano recital. Her dad had given her two dozen pink, long stemmed roses with baby's breath sprinkled in the mix. She still had a few of the buds pressed in a book as keepsakes.

A quiet knock snagged her attention. Dirk peered through the window of the back door, his light brown hair dripping wet, no shirt on. She could only see his upper half, but that alone was enough to make her weak in the knees. She'd always found him attractive, but the more she got to know him, the more handsome he became.

There was no way she could keep seeing him and not fall head over heels. No way. Heck, she was already a goner.

She opened the door, and he stepped right in, wearing nothing but a pair of black swim trunks. "Hi, Dirk. I wasn't expecting you."

"Hey, sexy. I thought I might catch you at home. You have about an hour before you need to go to the restaurant, right?"

"Yeah. The band plays at seven, but I like to get there early to warm up."

He glanced at the clock. "I think we have enough time."

"Time for what?"

He closed the door behind him. "You've avoided me long enough, darling." He stepped into her space, his gaze intense and filled with desire.

"I wasn't avoiding you, Dirk. I've been busy." Liar. She was sure he could see right through that.

"We've both been busy, but now we have a little time one on one. Isn't that what you wanted, Kendal? A little private time?" He placed his hands on her hips and guided her back to the counter.

"I…I…wanted a little fun, but I didn't want to have to rush." Dang. Her body was practically buzzing with desire just from the nearness of him. She breathed in his the scent of his fragrant soap and shampoo, clean and masculine.

"I want to show you a little fun." Hoisting her up without warning, he plopped her bottom on the counter and ran his hands beneath the hem of her sundress. With his palms, he pressed her knees open and stepped between her legs, his face close to hers. "Kiss me."

She gripped the edge of the counter and tried to keep her abdomen from trembling.

"Kiss me, Kendal." He stared at her mouth.

She felt compelled to obey. Scratch that. His sexy "take charge" attitude made her want to do whatever he asked. She lifted her lips to his. He stayed still and let her lead the kiss. Once her tongue began to timidly explore his minty fresh mouth, he pulled her to the very edge of the counter and deepened the kiss, his lips demanding, yet soft. She wrapped her legs around him without even realizing what she was doing.

Coming up for air after a dizzying kiss that lasted several minutes, he whispered, "You blew my mind the other day with the way you helped my dad. You're amazing."

"It was my pleasure."

He grinned. "I've dreamed about your pleasure, and that wasn't it."

A warm brush of his lips against her neck drew a moan from her. With an approving "Mmm" of his own, he trailed wet kisses to her earlobe and nibbled gently.

Woozy from his touch, she held onto him.

He stopped abruptly and stepped back. His brows pleated. "Someone sent you flowers?" He gestured toward the arrangement beside her.

"Yes. Your mother gave those to me. She's so sweet."

His eyes seemed to glow from within. "Yes, she is." He flashed a wicked grin. "But you're sweeter." He nestled his body between her legs once more and slid his hands up to her hips. Hooking his fingers into the waistband of her panties, he gave a little tug.

She gasped. "Dirk, what are you doing?"

"I'm going to find out how sweet you really are."

"Wait. We need protection."

"Not for what I have in mind." He lowered to his knees. "Last time, I caused you some severe discomfort. I feel really bad about that. Let me kiss it and make it better." He inched her panties down as far as he could. "Lift up for me."

Excitement swirled in her belly. How had he turned her on so fast? She lifted her hips.

He slid her panties off and tossed them aside. Her dress covered her lap, but she wondered if he could see up her skirt from his vantage point. The thought of him being able to see what no other man had laid eyes on aroused her.

He draped her legs over his shoulders and lifted her dress. "Mmm, baby. You look and smell delicious. May I?" He moved his face closer.

With his warm breath on her folds, she exhaled "Yes."

His mouth enveloped her, his wide flat tongue stroking from her opening then moving up and over her throbbing pink pearl. She couldn't stop watching his mouth, his tongue, what he was doing to her. He closed his eyes and kissed her folds like he'd kissed her mouth and seemed to be in love with what he was doing.

"You like that?" His voice was low, and vibrated against her moistened skin.

"Yes." She was mesmerized by the sensations he was creating in her, his cool wet hair against her inner thighs, his strong shoulders supporting her legs, his mouth melting every bone in her body. Her breathing increased to a quick pant. She couldn't think. All she could do was feel.

She relaxed and rested her back against the counter, eyes closed, her mind focused on the building orgasmic tension he was drawing out of her.

When she began to moan and writhe, he reached up and clasped one of her hands in his, entwining their fingers. As if he could read her mind, he concentrated on the precise speed and place that sent her mind spiraling into delirium. He spoiled her, giving her body just what it craved, in just the right spot. "Dirk, I'm going to…"

He locked his mouth on her and sucked her swollen clitoris then went right back to flicking it. She trembled and cried out as the muscles in her abdomen contracted. She climaxed, mind-boggling spasms rippling through her core. He kept his mouth on her, petting softly with his tongue as the orgasmic waves dissipated.

When her breath returned to normal, she said, "I never knew it could feel like that."

He murmured against her, "Come again, baby. I want more."

She raised up on her elbows to establish eye contact. Was he serious? She was sated. Every time she'd experienced an orgasm alone, once did her in. She *wanted* to give him more, but with the intensity in which he'd made her come, she wasn't sure she had any more to give, until…

Her body started to tingle again as he lapped her up.

"Oh, God, Dirk…I'm…"

He nodded. "Come on, Kendal, baby. Come again."

Hearing him practically beg made her quiver inside.

He spread her legs wider and fluttered his tongue barely touching her clitoris.

"Ahhh. Dirk…"

"More baby. I want more. Do you have more to give?"

"Yes." For the love of God, he was so good at that.

She reached down and opened herself with her fingertips for him.

"That'a girl. Feed me that pretty little clit." He applied more pressure with his tongue and she bucked, clenching his damp hair in her fist.

The emotion revealed in the depths of his gaze was more tender than she'd expected. She couldn't look away. She was shocked by the way her hips writhed greedily, wanton. She couldn't hold back, didn't want to hold back. She came harder the second time than the first. She didn't think that was possible, but she did.

Dirk didn't remove his mouth until she'd crested the peak of climax. Then he kissed her inner thighs, rocked back on his heels, and gently smoothed her dress back over her lap.

He stood and caressed her face.

"Dirk…that was…"

"Shhh." He kissed her deeply. "It was just a little taste. A taste I love." Placing his hands on each side of her jawline, he said, "No more avoiding me. Okay?"

"Yes."

"Any time you want more of what we just did, you call me or text me. Okay?"

"Yes." She held back a laugh, realizing she'd become the "yes" girl.

"I love when you say yes." He smiled. "Call me when you get home tonight?"

"Yes."

"Mmm." He teased her nipples over her dress with his thumbs. "You liked what we just did, didn't you?"

"Yes." God, she was practically whimpering again.

"Felt good, didn't it?"

"Yes." Her body temperature had risen to a fever.

"It's supposed to feel good, not hurt, not burn. Are you going to allow me to make you feel good again?"

"Yes." Yes, yes, yes that's all she could say. She wanted to toss her head back and forth like the Herbal Essence girl.

He brushed her hair from her face. "I feel like the luckiest guy alive. You're beautiful, talented, intelligent, and so damn sweet. You outshine all the other girls I've ever been with."

Upon hearing those words, her heartbeat fluttered. She hugged him tight, her face buried in the crook of his neck.

He stroked her hair. "I don't want to go, but I know you need to get ready for your gig, so I'm going to slip away. I'll talk to you later tonight."

"Okay. Thank—"

He put a finger to her lips. "Thank *you*, sweetness. What we shared has been one of the greatest gifts I've ever received."

When he walked out the door and down the steps, she fell back onto the counter. "That's what I've been missing? Wow…" She attempted to sit up, but barely raised her head before lowering it again. "I'm jello. Mello-Jello." She released a drowsy giggle and sang "Fly Me to the Moon," adding theatrical arm and leg movements while remaining flat on her back.

CHAPTER FIFTEEN
Paisley

Upon leaving Kendal's apartment, Dirk ran straight into the ocean for a swim. Luckily, no one was nearby to witness the tent in his shorts as he jogged toward the water. Diving under foaming waves and swimming close to the sandy bottom, he recalled Kendal's fingers in his hair and the sounds of her moans. He rose to the surface and looked up at her apartment, imagining what she was doing at that very moment.

Two orgasms in a row? Grrr. Sometimes he was jealous of girls. If he could have multiple orgasms, he'd be so addicted to sex, he'd need rehab.

But this was her first time being pleasured by a man, and he was determined to show her how it was supposed to feel. Judging from her I-can't-move-after-sex expression, he doubted she'd jump right up off the counter to get ready for her gig. He hoped she'd rested, soaked in the moment, and thought of him. Yeah, he wasn't too proud to admit it. He hoped she was still saying his name. God, he loved the way she'd said, "Dirk," in the heat of the moment. Damn. Could he have more of that, please?

With his thoughts still on Kendal and how erotic their experience had been, his erection refused to go down. She had him so turned on it had become painful.

He gazed out over the undulating horizon. Was that a shark fin? He shielded his eyes and squinted in the direction of the gray triangular shape protruding from the water. Holy shit. It was a shark.

He dove under and swam toward the beach at lightning speed. When he reached the shore, he collapsed onto the sand face-down. After he caught his breath a little, he rolled over and scanned the area for the shark. It was circling close to the breakers, and if he had to guess, that sucker was at least ten feet long.

He knew better than to swim during feeding time. His father had taught him as a child to avoid going in the water near dusk. What the heck had he been thinking? Ha. Oh yeah. How great Kendal tasted and how much he'd wanted to do more than just taste her. Well, he'd certainly found a cure for blue balls.

With his hand on his chest, he concentrated on bringing his heart-rate down.

For the most part, sharks left folks alone. Even though quite a few had been spotted near the shore of Pleasure Island through the years, there didn't appear to be any real danger of being attacked.

But knowing that didn't calm his nerves when that shark swam right toward him. His heart was still thumping like a jack-hammer.

He stood and brushed off as much sand as he could and headed to the boardwalk.

As he neared the marsh, a distant voice bellowed, "Dirk!" Ted stood atop a dune and waved him over. "Come join us!"

Heidi's head popped up from behind the sea grass. She fiddled with the straps on her bikini top.

You gotta be kidding. Ted was inviting him over in the middle of a make out session?

Ashley climbed up the dune and waved both her arms

like she was trying to flag down a rescue helicopter. "Over here!" She wore the smallest American flag bikini he'd ever seen. Even though it *wa*s the week of July fourth, he still thought the patriotic dental floss was tacky. Just something about it screamed "Look at me. I'm a hottie." Kendal wouldn't be caught dead in that thing. She was far too classy for a cheesy bathing suit like that.

As Dirk neared his brother and the girls, he spotted a couple of guys behind them on a blanket—a tall lanky fella with black hair and another dude with curly, light brown hair who looked like he could bench press a pickup truck. Who were those guys? He'd never met either one of them, and he knew everyone on the island.

Ashley struck some kind of crazy pose with one leg bent, one hand on her hip and one behind her head, chest thrust up and out. Did she think that stance looked remotely natural? Dirk wasn't in the mood to deal with Ashley. He'd turned down her invitations to dinners and to the movies three separate times since he bailed from the bar with a headache about a month ago.

Ted walked over to Dirk. "We got some drinks and food, enough to go around, if you'd like to join us." His voice was low. No way could the others hear their conversation in the wind.

"Nah. Looks like you've got quite a crew." Dirk inched closer to his brother. "Who are those two guys?"

"The big one is Carson. He's opening up a gym beside the Harley shop. He moved down here to be close to his fiancé' who works at the resort."

"The tall, skinny guy is some hot shot violinist from New York. I forget his name. It's something like Pansy." Ted laughed and shook his head. "He's getting his masters at Juilliard or something like that. Anyway, he and his family are staying at the resort for a couple of weeks on vacation."

"His family? So he's married?"

"Heck no. He's single. Something you might like to know though, he's been going on and on about Kendal for the past hour. He heard her play a few days ago at Reel to Real Good, and he's a fan of her piano playing and her tits." Ted's mouth twitched with amusement. Dirk's fist didn't think there was anything funny at all.

Ted quirked a brow. "You sure you don't want to stick around for a little while? Maybe you'd like to go with him to the restaurant tonight. He heard Bikini Quartet would be performing, and he's eager to see if he can strike up a conversation with Kendal between sets. I tried to tell him she wasn't much of a talker, but that didn't seem to sway him."

A hot shot musician from New York with an interest in Kendal? And the guy was going to hang around for a couple of weeks? Not good. But Dirk had agreed to the "free to date others" rule. As much as he hated it, Kendal could go out with anyone she wanted. Dirk stuffed his urge to get possessive down as deeply as he could. "Like I told you the other day, Kendal and I aren't dating." If she wanted to go out with some pretty boy from the city she could do so.

Ted laughed. "You're so full of it. The vein that pops out near your hairline when you're stewing about something looks like it's about to burst."

Dirk felt the elongated bump on his head. Dang. It was big, and he could practically feel his pulse when he touched it. He took a deep breath and released it slowly. "Maybe I got time to have a beer."

Ted patted his back. "That's more like it."

Dirk shook his head with a slight chuckle. "Tell me that violin guy is an asshole."

Ted grinned. "He's a smart, talented, rich, asshole."

"I only wanted to hear the asshole part. Thanks."

Ted clapped a hand on his back. "Did I mention he's rich?"

Why'd his brother have to rub it in that the guy was loaded? "Asshole."

"Yep, he's that too." Ted grinned.

Ha. "Nice deflect."

They headed up the dune. Ashley and Heidi sat side by side, the guys sat across from the girls on the blanket.

Ted gestured toward Dirk. "Carson and…ummm…." He snapped his fingers, while staring at the violin guy.

"Paisley." Heidi chimed in.

"Right, Paisley. Sorry about that, man. This is my brother, Dirk."

Dirk nodded toward Carson then Paisley. "Hey. Nice to meet y'all." He wasn't so sure it was nice to meet Paisley, but Dirk's parents had taught him to be polite. What kind of sissy name was Paisley anyway? Wasn't paisley some old-fashion fabric people made tablecloths out of? Who names their kid Paisley? Heck, plaid or tweed would've been better.

What's up, Tweed? Ha. Sounds like dweeb. The guy looked like a dweeb; how ironic.

Dirk snagged a beer from the cooler and sat between his brother and Mr. Tablecloth.

Ashley gave Dirk the evil eye, and he just winked at her, while keeping a safe distance.

To break the tension he'd apparently caused, he decided to tell everyone about the shark. He stood and acted the scene out as he recalled the details of how he'd panicked and scrambled out of the water with the shark a few feet away. He exaggerated to make it more fun and make them all laugh. It worked too.

Well, it worked on everyone but Ashley, who didn't crack a smile. She sat there with her mouth wide opened and terror in her eyes.

When everything got quiet again, Paisley announced he needed to take a leak. Just like that. Real dignified in front of the ladies. Yeah. Lots of money and no manners.

Dirk was looking for a way out of this uncomfortable gathering anyway, so he said. "There's a bath house by the boardwalk. I need to get going, and I'll be passing right by it. I can show you where it is."

"Thanks. That'd be great." Paisley stood and Dirk suddenly felt short. That was new. Dirk was 6'3". How tall was this guy?

Dirk said his farewells and led the New Yorker toward the boardwalk.

Paisley struggled to keep up, but Dirk didn't slow his pace.

Hassling for breath, Paisley said, "So, how well do you know Kendal?"

"Pretty well. We met in kindergarten. Had lots of classes together all through school. We were seated side by side during our graduation ceremony, Dirk Davis and Kendal Duvall."

"Wow. So you two are tight. Anything I should know about her?"

Dirk stopped on the edge of the marsh area where a lot of crabs tended to hide. He made eye contact with the dweeb. The thought of this stranger making moves on Kendal didn't sit well with him. His possessive side reared its ugly head and demanded to take the wheel. As far he was concerned, there wasn't a darn thing this guy needed to know about Kendal, except to stay away from her.

A blue crab scurried across the sand by Dirk's foot. "Watch out for crabs, man."

Paisley's eyes widened. "Crabs? Oh shit. I had a time getting rid of those things in high school. Learned real quick that you get what you pay for when it comes to prostitutes.

Thanks for the warning, dude. I owe you."

This Paisley fella was an idiot. He obviously hadn't even noticed the multitude of sand fiddler crabs inches from his feet.

Without missing a beat, Paisley said, "Okay, so Kendal's off limits. Tell me about Ashley."

Wait. Kendal's off limits now? Fine. Let him think she has crabs, if that'll keep him away from her.

"Ashley's a lot of *fun*." Dirk lifted his brows for emphasis.

"Now you're talking."

"But, she likes to be wined and dined and treated like a princess." Even though Dirk wasn't interested in Ashley, he didn't want some guy to sweep in and do her wrong.

"No problem there."

They continued walking. Their voices had scared the crabs away, for the most part. Paisley seemed oblivious to the few that did cross their path. Dirk pointed to the bath house. "There ya go."

"Thanks, man. Glad I ran into you. Whew. You saved me."

"Don't mention it." Seriously. Don't.

When Dirk got home, his mom was on the phone.

She held up a finger to him, as if she wanted him to sit tight for a second while she finished her conversation. "Don't you worry, Penny. It's no trouble at all. I raised two boys of my own. I got this. You just rest and leave everything to me. I'll pick your boys up in about thirty minutes. Everything's going to be just fine. I'll give you a call when I get them tucked in bed safe and sound. You're welcome, sweetie. Bye now."

Crap. That didn't sound good.

His mother sat the phone on the counter. "I'm so glad you're here. What would I do without you?" She gave him a hug. "I need you to stay the night and watch over your father. Penny had to have emergency surgery on her appendix. She's in the hospital, and I promised I'd babysit her boys tonight. Their father won't arrive until tomorrow. Anyway, her boys are sitting at daycare and need to be picked up. I told her I'd handle it and spend the night at her house with them so they sleep in their own beds. Bless their hearts, they don't need any more disruptions. I'm sure they're already worried sick about their mother."

So much for going back over to Kendal's after her gig. Damn. "You better get going then. Don't worry about me and Dad. We'll be fine." Dirk gave her a reassuring smile. He was disappointed about being stuck at the house all night, but Penny was in a jam. His mom needed to do this.

"Love Me Tender" was being played on the piano in the living room. "Is that Dad?"

"Yes. He's been picking out old tunes on the piano off and on all day long. Sometimes he's able to add in his left hand, but mostly he just plays the melodies with his right hand." She grabbed her purse off the back of a kitchen chair. "Supper's in the crockpot, beef stew. Lemon meringue pie is in the fridge. I love you." She squeezed his arm affectionately then dashed out the door.

And this is why he never left home. He needed to be close, for days like this. Yes, it put a damper on his social life. Yes, it sometimes felt like an anchor that held him back from really making something of his life, but he was doing the right thing. He knew it.

He also knew letting that guy think Kendal had crabs was *not* the right thing to do.

Maybe being forced to stay home tonight was karma.

"Take Me Out to the Ball Game." His father sang at the

top of his lungs while playing the song with both hands.

Dirk smiled and strode into the living room singing, "Take me out to the crowd." His father beamed and looked him in the eyes. His dad was all there tonight. Awesome. They continued singing the song in unison. When it was over, his father segued right into, "Look For the Silver Lining."

Dirk gazed at his father's silver hair, and the silver frames of his bifocals. *Found it.*

CHAPTER SIXTEEN
Phone

Kendal rushed home from the gig and called Dirk.

He answered. "Hey, sexy. I've been waiting for your call. How was the gig?"

She was dying to ask him to come over, but she didn't want to seem over eager. "It was the same ole, same ole. We played, people danced, Jack made the band a nice meal."

"What did he cook for y'all tonight?"

"Crab cakes, but I don't really like crab meat. Crabs give me the eebie jeebies."

"Crabs make a lot of people jumpy." He laughed.

"What's so funny about that?"

"Nothing, it just reminded me of some city boy I met today who got rattled at the mention of crabs."

"City boy? You mean the New York guy who plays violin?

"So, you've met him. Was he at the gig tonight?"

"No, but he was at the last gig, and he annoyed the crap out of me. He kept trying to show off how much he knew about classical music and wanted me to play a duet with him. Somehow I can't see Myrtle and the gang shag dancing to Mozart, and trust me, this guy wouldn't be able to play any songs with a groove."

God, she was babbling, but couldn't stop.

"He couldn't swing a quarter note if he tried. Have you ever heard an orchestra try to play jazz? Not good. Let me tell ya. Cellos don't know how to bebop, that's for sure." Kendal covered her mouth. *Shut up, Kendal.* Dirk probably didn't want to hear about bebop, jazz, or Mozart. "I'm sorry. I shouldn't be rambling on."

"Ramble away. All these years we've known each other, you've never talked much. I feel like I'm just now getting to know you, and I'm enjoying it."

"Aww. That's sweet. I'd like to get to know you better too." She understood exactly what he was talking about. They had been friends since grade school, but they'd never had a full length conversation until recently, and so far, sex had been their main topic of discussion. Casual, meaningless sex, which was so "unlike" her it wasn't even funny. However, it was exciting. "I know it's late, but you're welcome to come over, if you'd like. We could talk face-to-face."

"I'd definitely like to. You have no idea how much. It's all I've been thinking about tonight. Unfortunately, I'm stuck here with Dad. Ted's on a date. Mom had to babysit a couple of boys whose mother is in the hospital. The woman will be okay, but she's in a bind, and Mom thought it would be easiest on the kids if they slept in their own beds and all that."

Now who was babbling? "That's nice of your mom, but I won't pretend I'm not disappointed." Something about not having to look him in the eye made it easier to be bold. In person, she probably wouldn't have admitted her disappointment. Knowing her, she'd have just said that's fine and left it at that.

"Disappointed, huh? Why's that? Did you want some more?" His voice deepened to a seductive tone.

She closed her eyes as the parts of her body he'd kissed

so thoroughly that afternoon began to tingle again. "Yes." Her favorite word of the day.

"Mmm. You want some more right now, don't you?"

"Yes." She slid the hem of her dress up and lightly touched herself over her panties, remembering how he'd pleasured her. Just the thought of his tongue swirling and flicking made her moist.

"What are you wearing?"

That was the corniest line on the planet. Only creepy internet guys asked girls that. Did he think she was going to have phone sex with him? Well, maybe she was on the verge, until he ruined the moment with that cheesy line. She pulled her dress back over her knees and crossed her legs. "The blood of the last guy who asked that stupid question."

He died laughing. "Good girl."

"Yes. I am. Thanks for noticing."

"Kendal, I know you are…well…I don't want to call you a good girl for real, because you're not a girl anymore… you're a lady in every sense of the word, a true lady. You aren't sleazy or promiscuous."

"I'm being promiscuous with you, though, or trying to be."

"Does that bother you?"

"What, that we're f-buddies?"

"Whoa. We haven't actually f'd so let's not get carried away here. I mean…does it bother you that we're just fooling around, nothing serious?"

Yes. No? It was what she'd asked for, and she had a great time earlier today, an incredible time actually. Yeah, she'd rather be experiencing these things with someone she loved who loved her in return. However, she'd waited and wished for that for twenty-five years, and it'd never happened.

She wasn't going to feel guilty or embarrassed for taking steps to get over her strange anxiety about dating. Until she got a handle on that, she had no chance of falling in love with anyone.

She could relax with Dirk, maybe not a hundred percent, but more than she'd ever been able to before. This was a good thing. One day, she'd find love—once she built her confidence up, which was what she was working on. She'd stood up to her mother. She'd started dressing to flatter her figure and felt better about her appearance. But most importantly, she'd instigated a sexual relationship on her own terms. She was proud of herself and empowered.

Sure, right now, she wished her forever someone could be Dirk. She was totally crushing on him, big time. She'd even go so far as to so say she might be falling in love with him. But how stupid would it be to give up a chance to be with him now, because she couldn't be with him forever? Most people don't end up with the first person they make out with, and they survive it. So would she.

She chose her words carefully. "What I experienced with you today was incredible. It opened my eyes to how wonderful sex can be, and like you said, we haven't even had sex, fully. I'm glad you were my first. Well, first French kiss and kiss…down there." Her cheeks warmed. Good grief, she was blushing sitting alone in her own living room.

"I'm glad you feel that way. I've treasured our time together too. Are you sure you're okay with us seeing other people though?"

Why was he asking her that? Again. They'd been over this more than once. She'd convinced herself it was okay, but no, she wasn't thrilled with the idea. She'd rather date exclusively and not be so secretive about it. But if she told him that, he'd stop seeing her all together. She wasn't willing to give up being with him. Maybe by the end of the summer he'd start getting on her nerves like he had in the past or something, but right now, being with him was the highlight of her summer, her life. "I understand our arrangement, and I accept it." *I sound like I'm in court. Thank you, Judge Judy.*

"Do you want more?"

Did he mean more oral sex or more from the relationship? She was going to go with relationship since he didn't use his sexy-guy tone. "I don't know. Dirk, seriously, this is the closest I've ever been to a real relationship in my life. If navigating the whole dating thing was something I had a clue about, we wouldn't be doing this in the first place. You've made it clear what the limits are. Listen, being with you is good for me. I'm not looking to end it, if that's what you mean."

"I'm not looking to end it either. So, you think being with me is good for you?"

"Yes. Yes, I do. For many reasons."

"Tell me why."

"Oh Lord. Are you fishing for more compliments? Such a guy, needing your ego stroked." She loved teasing him, just like old times.

"I need something stroked all right, but it's not my ego." His low rumbly laugh made her smile. "I was just curious how you see things. But if it makes you uncomfortable, we can talk about something else."

Man, he was being so sweet tonight. Telling him why their fling was good for her didn't make her uncomfortable, per se, she just wasn't sure she could put it into words without sounding like a counselor.

"Sweetheart, I just want to know if you get more out of this than the physical connection."

"I do. I really do, Dirk. Here's the thing, though, being physical…it stirs up feelings…not gonna lie. I guess you could call it a longing, but that's not quite right either, because it feels like an emptiness is being filled. I can't explain it."

"You're doing fine, baby."

Hearing him call her baby and sweetheart was not helping her right now. She was trying to resist all those mushy emotions and be logical—analyze this thing and spell it out for him. "When you kiss me, all the patients in the asylum in my head take a nap." They both laughed. She continued. "There are no inner voices telling me I'm not pretty, that I'm strange, that no one will love me, that I don't know what I'm doing, that I'm so inexperienced I'll make a mess of things and do everything wrong, that—"

"Slow down. We don't want to wake those patients up." He chuckled softly.

She smiled and exhaled slowly. "When you kiss me, I float. You know how you feel when you float face up on the surface of the ocean with your ears beneath the water, and the world is kind of muffled? Your worries and stresses are somewhere on dry land, but you're not?"

"Yeah. It's awesome. Why do you think I surf every morning? It's very zen."

"Yeah. Well, when you kiss me, I feel kinda like that. When I float, I'm isolated and alone, in my own little world, and it's an awesome sensation. But…when you kiss me, I feel all zen like you said, but, in addition to that, all the loneliness I carry deep down inside disappears. And I think not feeling so lonely is good for me."

"I agree. And I get it. I'm lonely deep down too."

"You are? But you aren't an only child and your family is close. You have tons of friends."

"Well, you have friends and family too, but loneliness can be in many forms, like love."

She understood, even if he didn't elaborate. "Right. You can love your family, a friend, a song, a food, but when you love someone romantically, it's totally different. I haven't ever been in love, but I understand the concept."

"I've never been in love either."

"Really? I thought you were in love with Sarah, the girl you took to the senior prom."

"Sarah Fussell? Man, I haven't thought about her in ages. I did have it bad for her, you're right about that, but I wouldn't call it love. Sarah didn't have much patience with my dad. She couldn't stand when I had to cancel dates because of him. To keep from canceling, I invited him to hang out with us on the beach one day. Every time he forgot anything that had just happened, she cracked up and teased him about it. It pissed me off."

"Of course it did. That was mean."

"Right. Whatever romantic feelings I had for her dwindled after that experience. By the time we graduated, I didn't even want to lay eyes on the girl."

"I didn't know your dad was having trouble back then."

"Oh yeah. We weren't sure what was going on exactly, but we knew something was wrong. He got his diagnosis right after I graduated. I'd toyed with the idea of going to college, but I never could make up my mind what I wanted to be when I grew up."

"Dirk, a lot of people aren't sure what they want to major in when they start college. Even if they do declare a major, a good percentage end up changing their minds a year or two down the road."

"True. But, I opted to stay close to home and keep an eye on Dad. Turns out, Mom needed me, so I'm happy with my choices."

"You did the right thing." She admired his devotion to his family. The way he was pouring his heart out to her made her want to hug him close and tell him so.

"I know, but it's put a damper on my love life. I can't see anyone wanting to put up with the way I have to cancel out on things to look after him. Plus, who really wants a boyfriend who still lives with his parents and doesn't have a steady job?"

"Is that how you see yourself? As a bum who lives with his parents and can't hold down a job?"

"Well, it's kind of true."

"No, it isn't. You work more hours than lots of people with full time jobs. You aren't mooching off your parents. You pay your own way. If your dad was better, you wouldn't be living there. You aren't there because you can't make it on your own. You're there because that's where you're needed most. It's a sacrifice on your part, not a burden on them. There's a huge difference." Dang, that got her blood pumping. How could he look at himself that way? He wasn't a loser. Not by a long shot.

"Wow. I guess you set me straight on that one. Thank you. I…umm…that did my heart good to hear."

"I'm glad. Now, I never want to hear you even hint that you're the twenty-something loser who can't hold a steady job and lives with his folks. That is not you. That guy is someone who is lazy, doesn't work, plays video games all hours of the day and night, rarely lifts a finger around the house, and gets an allowance from Mommy and Daddy. And his folks are secretly scheming for ways to get rid of him. That is not who you are, Dirk Davis. Got it?"

"Yes, Ma'am. Got it." His soft sexy chuckle warmed her heart.

"The fact you put your family's needs first makes you a better man than most guys our age. I think you like to play the happy-go-lucky guy who goes with the flow, charming all the ladies, always joking around and making people laugh and smile, but really…you care deeply about others, and you bend over backwards to help everyone you know. You aren't so very laid back, not really. You're constantly looking around and making mental notes about ways you can make someone else's life a little brighter, a little easier."

"I never knew you paid such close attention to me."

"It's hard to miss. The fence at Bare Point needs repair. You show up with salvaged wood and fix it without anyone asking you. The door on Miss Judy's shack comes off. You bring your tools, and put it back up before anyone else even realizes there's a problem."

"How do you know about Miss Judy?"

"Oh give me a break. Myrtle posts all your good Samaritan deeds on her blog. Everyone on the island knows."

"No kidding? I'm going to have to pay more attention to Myrtle's blog then. To be honest, I don't follow it. I mean… it's just island gossip, anything I need to know, I find out eventually anyway."

"I remember when Megan needed a way to make money while she was in art school, you got the word out to all the people with fancy vacation homes in the area, told them she was the best mural artist around and available for hire on weekends. Now, she's making more money just working two days a week than she ever made working full time at her Dad's bar. Even recently, when Spike got loose. Carl called you to catch him. I could go on and on about how you take care of folks in the community."

"You need to stop. I'm going to get a big head, and you've already done that to me once today. Different head, but both massive."

"Dirk! I can't believe you just said that."

"What? That you made my head big today?"

She giggled. Oh God. Did she sound like Ashley? "I didn't know you were…turned on by doing that."

"You couldn't tell?"

"You seemed to be enjoying it, but as far as whether or not it turned you on…I wasn't sure. I didn't look to see how excited you were. I think my eyes were rolled back in my head so far seeing anything would have been impossible."

He chuckled. "Trust me, baby. I was hard as a rock from tasting you. I had to go for a swim to calm down and even that didn't work, until a shark swam toward me and scared my ass right out of the water. Then my hard-on inverted."

She jolted upright, to the edge of the couch. "You were attacked by a shark today, and you're just now telling me?"

"Hang on. I wasn't attacked. I just spotted a fin and got out of the water. It's not a big deal. There was no real danger."

"No real danger? Are you crazy? Shark is the definition of danger. Look it up in the dictionary."

"Relax, sweetie. I'm fine. But I have to admit, seeing how worried you are, I'm tempted to milk it for all it's worth to help me get to third base with you."

"You don't need to be put in danger to make a home run with me. You're safe."

"Very good. Baseball pun. I like it. I didn't think you were into sports."

"I'm not. But I like baseball uniforms. Something about those tight little white pants. Football too. I'm a fan of tight white pants, I guess."

"Ehm, as much as I like to give a girl what she wants, I have no intentions of wearing tight white pants. Ever. I'm not a ball player. The closest you'll ever see me in a uniform is when I wear my wetsuit. And that's pretty tight."

"I love the way you look in that suit. Mmmm, now I'm going to dream about you wearing that wetsuit to bed with me."

His breathing shifted. It became louder and faster. "You dream about me being in bed with you?"

"Yes. Lately, I dream about it every night. Do you ever dream about me being in bed with you?"

"I think I have that dream every four seconds of my life. If you saw what went on in my head, and the things I do to you in my fantasies, you'd probably hang up on me and call me a pervert."

Whew. Now she wanted to know what kind of fantasies he'd been having. Dang. They sounded hot. "Give me an example. I'm curious."

He sighed. "I'd rather demonstrate. But I tell you what. I'll give you a peek into my mind where you're concerned. I used to think you were a prim and proper perfectionist without much of a sense of humor. But lately, I've discovered you have a great sense of humor, when you relax and let it out. You were an A student, and you're naturally smart, but I don't think it's being perfect or getting an A that drives you. I think you love to learn new things. I noticed your book collection covered a wide range of topics. You even had a book on auto-repair. I would have never imagined you being interested in fixing a car."

"Oh, I got that so I could fix Mom's car. It made this funny whirring noise, and I was determined to figure out what it was. I asked Mazy about it, and she told me it was the timing belt. I wanted to see if I could replace that belt myself, so I studied and went for it. It wasn't that difficult. In fact, it was a lot easier than fixing the rotary valve on a French horn."

He cracked up. "I can picture you now, your Cookie Monster slippers and granny dress sticking out from under your mom's car."

"Don't you pick on my Cookie Monster shoes. They're awesome. Well, not really. They're hideous, but I can rock them."

"Ha. No, baby. You can't. No one can. But you're still adorable as all get out."

"Aww. You think I'm adorable."

"Hell yeah. I've always thought that. Even when we were kids. You have such an innocence about you."

"Innocence. My curse."

"No. God, no. It's part of what makes you so beautiful. You're innocent in many ways. I don't just mean about sex. You're not jaded about people. You're trusting. You don't view the world as some beast out to get you, or some villain that has done you wrong."

"You said I was beautiful, but I'm not. No need to exaggerate. I prefer honesty."

"Kendal. Holy crap. You're gorgeous. Jesus. Okay, I have to be honest, that's one of the things I *don't* like about you. You don't have a clue how lovely you are. I can tell you're starting to see it a little bit, but you haven't fully embraced it yet. And I'm not just talking about what you look like on the outside."

Not only were her cheeks warm, her chest, and ears, and arms were too. Full body blush. Was that even possible? Apparently, yes.

"Sweetie, when you helped my father the other day, you made him smile, sing, and play the piano. Through your gentleness and understanding you made his whole world light up. I saw the way that kid, Hunter, responded to you. Without saying a word, you were able to direct him away from a frustrating moment into a fun time at the piano. You handled two people with some truly special needs simultaneously and made it look like it was as easy as painting by numbers. You took my breath away that day. I couldn't take my eyes off of you."

"Aww." Oops. She didn't mean to let that out. It sounded like she was cooing over a puppy.

"Awe is right. I was in awe of you."

"Dirk, I don't know what to say. I'm flattered beyond belief."

"Oh, I'm not done with you yet. There's more about how attractive you are and you're going to hear it all. Remember the day I closed the bridge on that sailboat?"

"Of course." She stifled a laugh.

"It's okay to laugh. It's funny. But here's something I've never told another soul. I saw you on a paddle board, wearing a red bikini. You were paddling straight toward the bridge and I ogled you so hard, I didn't pay attention to what I was doing. I was so busy checking out your hellacious and curvaceous bod I'm now known as the island's weapon of mast destruction, again, thanks to you. I'm even known as Captain Crunch by a few others."

That was the first day she wore that bikini. She was paddle boarding near the bridge at the time of the accident. All the air left her lungs. Stunned. Speechless.

He laughed. "Yep. To say I think you look pretty damn good in a bikini is an understatement. I love your body."

Her heart was in her throat. He wasn't just flattering her, he was serious. She caused that fiasco on the bridge? Holy cow. She didn't know whether to feel guilty or pat herself on the back. All she knew was he was making her feel sexy as hell.

"Then the night of Megan's party you wore that tight little number and made me drool and nearly lose my mind. When you asked me to have a fling, it was all could do to keep from jumping you right there in the dunes."

"Maybe you should have." Oh my God. She covered her mouth. She was being a bit too bold.

"Oh don't worry. We still have time for all that. I'm looking forward to it more than words can express."

She clamped her legs together. He was making her want him so bad she was pulsating.

"But I have to say, in addition to finding you attractive on the outside, when I saw you in action, doing your thing with Hunter and Dad, I saw the most gorgeous woman in the world that day. And that woman was you."

A lump swelled in her throat. "Thank you." She couldn't say more without her voice cracking. His words touched her so deeply.

"I see your beauty inside and out, Kendal. I saw it when you played the piano for me. Your light was shining so bright I was drawn to it. I was compelled to kiss you. Hell, I want to kiss you right now. I wish I were holding you this very minute, smelling your hair, feeling your silky skin beneath my fingertips and the warmth of your soft body against mine."

"Mmm. That would be so nice." Her eyes fluttered closed as she imagined his touch.

"I'd let you put your head on my chest, and I'd run my fingers through your hair, press a kiss to your forehead, and listen to you breathe, waiting for you to fall asleep in my arms so I could stare at you and memorize ever curve and angle of your face. I'd study your fingers—those skillful, musical fingers, your delicate lips, the swell of your breasts and the valley between them that leads to your heart. And when you finally awoke, I'd kiss every inch of you. Every single inch."

He was turning her on again, but she was also getting sleepy. "Dirk, I'm—"

"Sleepy. I can tell. You're voice has gotten weaker. We've been talking a long time. It's been great, but you need to rest. Close your eyes, pretend your fingertips are my lips and press them against your mouth for a goodnight kiss."

She did as he instructed.

"Do it again. Let me hear it."

She held the phone close and kissed her fingertips, not a loud ridiculous sounding smooch, but a realistic, faint kiss.

"Mmm. Sweet dreams, pretty girl. I'll call you tomorrow."

CHAPTER SEVENTEEN
Broken Glass

Spencer reached for a vase, but she couldn't quite grasp it. "Benny, bring me the grabber." Her service dog trotted over to the wall where her extension gripper was hanging on a hook. The dog lifted the gripper with his mouth and walked it over to Spencer. "Good, Boy."

Removing the tool, she squeezed the handle and got the claw on the other end of the two-foot pole opening and closing then she lined up the opened pinchers with the vase she wanted. After a few more failed attempts at retrieving the vase, she pulled herself toward the edge of her wheelchair and tried again. Almost had it that time. She inched a little further to the edge of her chair and raised her arm, leaned forward and barely touched the vase. "Whoa." Out she fell, landing on the rug with a dull thud, pinning one arm beneath her. The vase shattered and lay in jagged pieces on the floor in front of her.

Benny circled her, stepped around the broken glass, and nudged her with his nose.

Spencer didn't think she was hurt too badly, she saw no blood and wasn't in severe pain, no need to alert 911 via the emergency call pendant around her neck. Instead, she petted her dog and said, "Benny, get help." He perked his ears then darted through the doggie door in the back of the shop and ran to her parents' house behind Big Kabloom.

Within seconds, her father burst through the back door, huffing and puffing. "Spencer, are you all right?"

She hated this. Yes, she was all right, but she despised having to summon help. "I'm fine. I was being stupid again. Sorry, Dad."

"Don't be sorry, sweetheart. I'm just glad you're okay." Her father lifted her off the floor and cradled her in his big strong arms like he'd done so many times throughout her life. He kissed her cheek and gently placed her back in her chair. Caressing her hair, he said, "Sweetie, you've had a bit of a leak. Why don't you go on over to the house and let your mom help you get cleaned up. I'll keep an eye on the shop."

She glanced down at the dark, wet spot on her pale green skirt. Her father had dealt with these types of incidents many times, but it still embarrassed her. "Thanks, Dad." Without looking him in the eye, she rolled over to the back wall, pushed the button to open the door and waited for the automated opener to do its thing.

Outside, her eyes misted. She hated having to rely on her folks. They let her be as independent as possible, but both of them had quit their jobs and found ways to make money from home after the car accident that left her paralyzed from the waist down. She'd be lost without her folks. She was grateful to have them in her life, but days like these were a constant reminder of her limitations, and it hurt to know this was how her life would always be.

When Spencer entered the house, her mother met her at the door. She eyed Spencer's lap, but didn't say anything about the obvious stain. "Are you okay, honey?"

"Yeah. I fell again, but I'm not hurt that I know of."

"Well, go on into your room, and I'll take a look at you and help you get all cleaned up."

"Thank you." She loved the fact her parents never fussed at her for doing things she knew better than to do. They accepted the fact that sometimes she pushed herself and made mistakes, but she didn't need to be chastised for it. She beat herself up about it enough as it was.

Her mother grabbed a beach towel that hung on Spencer's closet doorknob and spread it on the bed. She then assisted Spencer from her chair onto the towel and helped Spencer disrobe and clean up while also checking for any signs of scrapes or bruises and such.

Spencer stared up at the ceiling fan and imagined how horrible it would be if Earl had to do this for her. A deluge of questions flooded her mind. Was she being completely selfish for encouraging his affections? Did he really know what all was involved in being with her, really being with her? Did she have the courage to have that talk about some of the more unpleasant aspects of dealing with her situation, a talk she'd avoided having with anyone?

Tears pooled in the corners of her eyes again. No. She would not cry. She didn't do that. She was tough. Always. Grinding her back teeth as hard as she could, she stifled her emotions.

Her mother bent over her and gazed down into Spencer's face. Concern was etched into the lines across her mother's forehead and around the edges of her wide gray eyes, glassy with emotion. With her thumbs, her mom wiped away the tears that had rolled down Spencer's temples and said, "We'll have none of that, sweetheart. No sadness. This is the small stuff."

Yes, maybe it was the small stuff, but would it seem so small to Earl? What man would consider this level caregiving small? Thanks to the drunk driver who crashed head on into her, she'd never walk again, never feel anything below the waist. Never. If she had sex, she wouldn't be able to feel it.

She'd stopped being angry at the drunk driver years ago. Forgiving him had been a big step in her recovery. No one heals by harboring negative energy. But she'd be lying to herself if she didn't acknowledge that some of that old anger had taken root inside her heart once more. A normal life that included a healthy sex life and motherhood wasn't such a terribly big dream to have, but for her, it seemed to be the impossible dream.

The scent of powder brought Spencer's mind back to reality.

Her mom smiled. "There. Fresh as a daisy. I washed and dried some of your clothes today. Would you like to wear your favorite lavender skirt or would you prefer those new turquoise jeans?"

"The skirt, I guess." Spencer gazed at her slender mother, whose salt and pepper hair was pulled into a ponytail. Not a dab of makeup was on her face, no polish on her nails. She'd aged quickly this past decade since the accident, and she seemed older than her years.

Spencer could remember a time when her mother was glamorous, decked out in fine clothes, not a hair out of place, flawless makeup. Now, her beautiful mother had wilted like a flower. She no longer focused on herself, rarely purchased new clothes, hadn't worn makeup in ages. She was still pretty, in her own way, but she looked haggard.

Her dad had faired better, because he'd thrown himself into lifting weights and eating clean, being in the best shape of his life. He claimed it was because he wanted to keep his buff beach body as long as he could, but she knew the real reason. She'd heard him tell her mother. His biggest fear was not being able to care for Spencer as he got older, or worst of all—leaving her alone in this world.

After Spencer finished getting dressed with her mother's help, she held her mother's hands in hers. "Mom, I'll never be able to thank you enough for all you do for me. I'm so lucky to have you and Dad, and I'm so very sorry for the hardships I've caused you through the years."

"Hardships? Oh, baby, no. Please, never let me hear you say that sort of thing again. I thank God every day of my life that you survived that accident, that you're here. I cherish every moment with you, even if some of the things we face aren't particularly fun—I'm grateful for those moments. You are not a hardship. Never. You're a blessing in my life, and your father feels the same way." Her mother's chin trembled and Spencer knew better than to continue down this path of conversation. The last thing she wanted to do was to cause her mother to break down in tears. She'd caused too much sorrow in her mother's life as it was.

"Thank you, Mama. I love you very, very much."

"I love you, sweetness." Her mother placed a kiss on the top of Spencer's head. "Do you feel like going back to the shop, or would you like for me to call your father and see if he can fill in for you for the rest of the day? You haven't taken a day off in a long time."

"I'm fine. Working makes me feel strong. It keeps me busy, and I enjoy it. I'll go back to the shop. We're only open for three more hours anyway."

"Okay, dear. I'm making lasagna for supper. You're favorite."

Spencer smiled. She loved lasagna, but she wanted her mom to relax, stop working around the clock.

"Mom?"

"Yeah, honey?"

"Have you already started the sauce?"

"No. I just need to thaw it out, though."

"Well, how about you just relax for a while, nap, read, take a long bubble bath. Pamper yourself a little bit. You seem tired, Mama."

Her mother gazed into the mirror over the dresser. "I do look a fright, don't I? This is the first time I've even glanced at my own reflection all day."

"How about you get dressed up, and I get dressed up, and we talk dad into putting on a nice shirt and slacks, and we go out for dinner tonight, my treat."

Her mother smoothed her wrinkled house dress. "It's been so long since I put on a nice dress, I'm not even sure I have anything in my closet that will fit."

"You've lost a lot of weight, Mama. If you don't have anything to wear, come raid my closet. You always call me a clothes horse. You know I have plenty to spare."

"You are the sweetest daughter in the world. You know that?"

"Product of my upbringing. You produce good fruit."

Her mother laughed that silvery, tinkling laugh of hers, reminiscent of a delicate wind-chime dancing in a gentle breeze. A peaceful feeling fell over Spencer. As long as she could make her mother laugh, at least once a day, she knew everything would be just fine.

Tony Harris, Spencer's father, was crouched by the back counter, sweeping up broken glass with a whisk broom when Kendal stopped by Big Kabloom. Spencer was nowhere in sight. "Hey, Mr. Harris. Is everything okay?"

"Oh yeah, a vase just broke and Spencer took a slight tumble. She went to the house to get freshened up. She'll be back in a few minutes."

"Did she hurt herself?" Kendal pulled the plastic trashcan over to Mr. Harris so he could dump the glass shards he held in a dustpan.

"No. She's fine. Benny saved the day again."

"Benny is awesome." Kendal smiled at the thought of

Benny. He was the smartest dog ever. It never ceased to amaze her the things that dog could do, from opening doors for Spencer to retrieving items around the shop for her. He knew the names of all the tools she used. She'd ask for needle-nosed pliers, and he'd bring them. She'd ask for floral tape, and he'd get that too. Benny was the bomb dot com, as Leah would say.

The bell on the shop door jingled and in walked Leah. Talk about timing. Kendal grinned. "Oh my God, Leah, I was just thinking about you. That is too funny."

Leah pushed her sunglasses to the top of her head like a headband. Her dark hair fell in loose spiral curls past her shoulders. She had on a zebra print jumpsuit and red sandals, looking like she just stepped out of Vogue. "Hey, Kendal. Hi, Tony. Why was I on your mind, Kendal?"

"I was just thinking how you'd call Benny the bomb dot com."

Leah laughed. "I picked that saying up from Maggie. She says that all the time, crazy kid."

Maggie was Leah's nine year old niece.

Spencer entered the back door. "Wow, I leave for five minutes and look who shows up." Mr. Harris gave Spencer a peck on the cheek and whispered something in her ear then stood and addressed Kendal and Leah. "Nice to see you two again. I need to get back to the house and finish up my work for the day."

Leah and Kendal told him bye.

Once her father was gone, Spencer said, "What's new with you two?"

Kendal said, "I just stopped in to say hello."

Leah placed her hands on the counter and flashed them a mischievous grin. "I just swung by to place a flower order for Reel to Real Good. I needed to get out of there for a few minutes and recuperate from walking in on Myrtle stripping in front of the sinks in the ladies room at the restaurant, trying to remove a leather teddy with studs she'd worn under her dress. She said that damn leather getup was making her perspire so bad she couldn't stand it another second. I helped her with some of the hooks and buckles. Once she was naked, she backed up to the air dryer and turned it on with a look of pure bliss on her face. It was the funniest thing."

They all laughed at the mental image of Myrtle. Kendal caught her breath and said, "Where did she get a dominatrix outfit like that?" She didn't bother telling them she'd love to have an outfit like that and surprise Dirk. There were so many things she wanted to try.

"Kinky Joys in Wilmington most likely." Leah was just as deadpan as she could be. Was she serious? There was really a store called Kinky Joys? And it was just down the road? If Leah and Spencer hadn't been in the same room, Kendal would have jumped up and down, squealing like a giddy child.

Spencer put a hand to her cheek. "Oh my God. Tell me you are joking."

Kendal and Spencer established eye contact and giggled like teenagers.

"Y'all have never been there?" Leah looked stunned.

Kendal and Spencer shared a bug-eyed stare and said, "No," in unison.

Leah said, "We need to take a field trip, girls."

"Yay!" Kendal clapped her hands. Then caught a glimpse of the what's-wrong-with-you stare Spencer was shooting her direction. Kendal stuffed her hands in her pockets, but couldn't wipe the grin off her face. She was going to be ready for Dirk the next time he came over. Time to play! Heck yeah!

Mr. Harris stepped through the back door, his arms

loaded with a box of floral tape and foam. "I saw you were running low, and I thought I'd stock you back up before I forgot about it."

Spencer gave Leah and Kendal the no-kinky-joy-talk-in-front-of-my-dad face. "Thanks, Dad."

Leah winked at Spencer. "Tony, would you mind if I steal your daughter away for a couple of hours? I'd like to take her shopping in Wilmington. We haven't had an outing in a long time."

He beamed. "I think I could survive without her for a little while. My last client just postponed our Skype session, so my work's done for the day. Y'all go have some fun."

Spencer's brows rose and her mouth fell open. "Umm, well, okay…thanks." She gave Kendal a helpless look.

Kendal tried not to giggle again, but there was no holding it in, the expression on Spencer's face was priceless. The girl looked like she'd just stepped in poop or something.

Their fate was sealed. Destination Kinky Joys!

CHAPTER EIGHTEEN
Toys

Kendal wandered down the video aisle at Kinky Joys, perusing the tutorials. *How to Give a Mind Blowing Blow Job.* That video went into her shopping basket without a moment's hesitation. She wanted to give Dirk as much pleasure as he'd given her. Just because she was inexperienced didn't mean she had to be uneducated and inept.

She heard Leah's voice a few aisles over. "I had one of these sex swings years ago. They were so much fun. I bet you'd enjoy one, Spencer."

Spencer said something, but her voice was too low for Kendal to make out her reply.

Okay, how many different kinds of lubes are there? Holy Cow. The shelves were loaded with hundreds. Strawberry… yum. What's this warming-sensation stuff? She picked up the bottle to read the fine print more closely.

Leah's voice came from behind Kendal. "That stuff will make you burn down there, girl."

Kendal slammed that bottle back on the shelf and jerked her hand away from it. She didn't want to have anything to do with "burning down there" ever again. Thank you very much.

Leah looked in Kendal's shopping basket. "Good

choice." She turned around and pulled a box off the shelf and put it in Kendal's basket. "Get these too. Every girl needs a pair of these undies in her life."

"Grape flavored edible panties?" Kendal didn't want Dirk to eat her underwear, just her.

"Oh yeah. Trust me. You'll be thanking me later." Leah's expression said it all. She obviously had some great memories involving those undies.

Must be something to it. Kendal didn't argue. Might as well give them a try. Dirk said he could make a meal of her. Grapes had plenty of antioxidants. Maybe he'd get his daily serving of fruit. Passion fruit. Oh yeah.

Spencer zoomed toward them, her eyes wild. "Myrtle and Louise just came in the store. What are we going to do?"

Leah laughed. "Go say hello to them."

Spencer looked mortified. "I don't want to visit with Myrtle and Louise right now. They know my mother. And my father!" She put her hands over her face. "Have y'all lost your minds?" She mumbled through her fingers.

Kendal whispered. "They know my mom too, and y'all know what a prude Rita Duvall is." She directed her attention to Leah. "Is there a back door to this place?"

Leah went all wide-eyed. "I don't know, and I'm not going up to the drag queen behind the register and asking 'Have you got a back door?' Y'all can forget that."

It took Kendal a second to get what Leah was implying, and when she did, she said, "Oh. I see your point."

Kendal glanced at Spencer, who was scanning the area and damn near panting. Squatting beside Spencer's chair, Kendal made direct eye contact with her visibly frightened friend and said, "Don't worry. Breathe in. Breathe out. If anyone asks, I'll say I roped you into this."

Spencer frowned. "*You* were the one all excited about coming here, not me. No one even asked me if I wanted to come along."

Kendal stiffened. "We didn't force you here. If you didn't want to come, all you had to do was say so." This wasn't like Spencer. It was just the opposite of who she was. Spencer was usually the one who coerced Kendal into doing things outside of her comfort zone, not the other way around.

Without saying another word, Spencer rolled down the aisle at top speed and disappeared around the corner.

Leah nudged Kendal to turn around.

Oh God. Myrtle and Louise were walking straight toward them, waving and smiling. There was no way out of this.

Leah waved back and strolled their direction. Kendal knew she should follow, but her feet wouldn't move. Smart feet on a stupid girl. Yep. Stupid for coming here in the first place.

What if Myrtle and Louise asked questions or made fun of what she was buying? Wouldn't that be another humiliation highlight to add to her "The Summer I Lost My Virginity" diary. Maybe she should ditch the basket.

Myrtle swatted Louise's arm. "Louise, take them ding-dong anal beads off your neck. They aren't costume jewelry."

Louise removed the graduated anal beads from her neck in one long pull and scrutinized the string of bright blue spheres. "I was wondering why there wasn't a clasp. Who in their right mind would put these things up their—"

Myrtle stopped Louise from finishing her sentence by giving her "the hand."

"But—"

"Louise, we know where they go, you don't have to say it."

"But—"

"Yes. For crying out loud. People put them up their butts. Enough already."

"Well, I never." Louise plunked the beads onto the

nearest shelf.

Myrtle rolled her eyes. "Be grateful. They hurt like hell."

Leah did a 180, faced Kendal, and held her breath, blinking rapidly while clutching her stomach. Then all of the sudden a snorting laugh burst out of her and she stammered, "Oh my God. I think I'm going to die."

Myrtle chuckled. "That's exactly what I told him, honey."

That comment only made Leah laugh harder and her snort-laugh was contagious.

Myrtle put her hands on her hips. "When he told me he'd always wanted to try anal beads, I thought—sure, why not. Indulge the man's fantasies, if *he* wanted to try them. I didn't know he wanted to try them on *me*. Imagine my surprise."

Leah, Kendal, and Louise exchanged wide-eyed stares after they looked at Myrtle with her shoulders drawn toward her ears and her lips in a tight lemon-face pucker. Within seconds, all four of them were huddled together, laughing so hard they could scarcely breathe.

Louise waved her hand and said, "I gotta pee. I can't hold...too late." She dropped her hand. "Ahhh...thank goodness for Poise."

Myrtle cocked an eyebrow. "Thank goodness for boys? Girlfriend, you're too old for boys. You're way past cougar, more like three-toed-sloth."

Louise playfully shoved Myrtle. "At least I don't keep myself wrapped around Carl like he's a tree and I'm a koala bear."

Glancing toward the women, Leah shook her head as another fit of laughter overtook her full force. She leaned on a shelf, gasping for air. "I love you ladies. I haven't laughed this hard in a long time. Whew." She wiped her eyes.

It took a few minutes for the four of them to gain their composure. When they settled down a fraction, Myrtle said, "What brings y'all in here? Somebody got a new boyfriend, or did you wear out your battery operated ones?"

"We were just picking up some gag gifts for Mazy's bridal shower." Leah was a quick thinker.

Kendal exhaled a sigh of relief. She'd have to thank Leah later for that quick thinking. She scanned the area and didn't see Spencer. Where was she hiding? She could relax now, Leah covered for them beautifully. Myrtle and Louise seemed to buy the lie hook, line, and sinker.

Leah checked her watch. "Oh no. I gotta get going. I told Jack I'd only be gone about fifteen minutes, and it's been over an hour."

Leah turned her back to Louise and Myrtle and gave Kendal a wink.

Kendal was relieved to know Leah wasn't really panicking, and she played along. "Let's go ahead and check out then."

Leah faced the older women again, "Y'all coming to the restaurant for dinner tonight?"

Louise rubbed her belly. "You know it. Tonight's all you can eat crab legs, my favorite. I wouldn't miss it for the world."

Myrtle said, "Carl and I will be there around seven, when the band gets going."

"All right then. We'll see you two later tonight."

Kendal bid the ladies goodbye and followed Leah, who led the way to the register where Kendal bought her items. As they strode to the exit, Kendal checked every aisle, looking for Spencer, but she wasn't there.

Leah whispered, "She's probably outside."

When they stepped into the parking lot, Kendal spotted Spencer beside her van. Leah had driven it over there because it was easier to transport Spencer in it. As they neared Spencer, Kendal could tell she'd been crying. Her face was red, eyes were puffy, and mascara was smeared down her cheeks.

Kendal broke out in a sprint and ran over to her. "Spencer, are you okay?"

Spencer scowled in silence.

Kendal's stomach tightened. Had she done something to piss Spencer off? "What's wrong? Are you hurt, mad? What is it? Tell me."

"I'm fine. Let's go." Spencer's tone was harsh.

Kendal gently placed her hand on Spencer's shoulder. Spencer shoved her hand away and snipped, "Don't touch me. Just leave me alone."

Whoa. Spencer had never shut her down like that.

Leah came up beside them quietly. She unlocked the van, opened the side door, and lowered the lift.

No one said a word until after all three of them were seated in the van, and buckled in. As Leah pulled out of the parking lot, Kendal said, "Leah saved us. She told Louise and Myrtle we were buying gag gifts for Mazy's bridal shower."

Spencer said, "Quick thinking, Leah. Thanks." Her voice was still edged with anger.

Leah said, "You're welcome. I'm sorry I bulldozed you into this trip. I didn't realize it was something that would upset you."

Spencer blew out a breath. "I guess seeing all that stuff was too much for me. I mean...what the hell do I need a vibrator for...I can't feel it. That place was just a wall to wall reminder of how many things I'll never be able to do. Granted, I wouldn't want to do a lot of those lewd sex acts on display there, but it'd be nice to have the option." Spencer's voice trembled on those last few words.

Kendal's heart sank. Poor Spencer. Tears welled in Kendal's eyes at the thought of how her friend must be feeling. This must've been awful for her. Dammit. Why hadn't she even bothered to ask Spencer if she wanted to go?

Kendal had been so thrilled at a chance to take a peek into Kinky Joys, find some fun things to impress and inspire Dirk with, she hadn't even considered what this experience would be like for Spencer.

Leah flashed Kendal a concerned look. She pulled into a vacant lot, and parked under a shade tree. Kendal unbuckled, got on her knees in the passenger seat, and gazed over the headrest at Spencer. "I'm sorry, Spencer."

Leah faced Spencer. "Me too. I'm so sorry I put you through that."

"It's not your fault. Neither one of you did anything wrong. I should've said something. I was already in a bad mood when y'all stopped by." Spencer's chin quivered and within seconds she was sobbing, hard.

Seeing her in that much pain ripped Kendal's heart out. She got out of the van and entered the side door, crawling up beside Spencer to comfort her.

"I've got to break up with Earl." Spencer wailed then gasped for breath. "I can't expect him to…give up sex…for me." She quaked in Kendal's arms.

Whoa. Break up with Earl? That was a bit extreme. She and Earl were meant for each other. She couldn't go and do something like that. It'd kill him.

Leah reached back and held Spencer's hand. "Hey… hey…you can still have sex in your own special way. What makes you think Earl hasn't already got something in mind for ways to make your sex-life amazing?"

Spencer cried and cried, then finally caught her breath. "I know we can do a few things, but in that store…there were pictures of so many things…I'll never be able to do or feel. I don't want Earl to have to go without anything because of me. And I don't—"She balled her fist and hit it against the armrest of her chair. "I don't want to…God…I just can't stand the thought of…him having to deal with—"

"Shhh, shhh…" Kendal didn't know what to say, but she wished she could wave a magic wand and make everything better for Spencer, but she couldn't. All she could do was be there for her. One thing was clear though, she shouldn't break up with Earl.

She brushed the hair from Spencer's tear-filled eyes. "You've been in a wheelchair the whole time you and Earl have been dating. He's never once made any indication whatsoever that he has a problem with you being the way you are. You can't break up with him because you don't want to have a difficult conversation. You owe him the opportunity to talk this through with you. He gets a say in this. And if he wants to be with you, no matter what, let him be with you. Let him love you. You deserve love, Spencer. Don't push it away."

Leah nodded. "Kendal's right. And what's more, I've never seen Earl so gaga for a girl like he is for you. He's head over heels. I get jealous watching the two of you dance using that harness he made for you. Y'all gaze into each other's eyes like no one else is in the room. I envy you for having what I once had. But my soulmate passed away. I didn't have a choice, but to let him go. I miss him every single day. If you care for Earl half as much as you appear to, don't be so quick to turn him loose. Hang on to what you have for as long as possible. Talk to him about everything that's troubling you. Be brave."

Spencer's breathing returned to normal. Leah snatched up her purse. "I'm such a doofus. I forgot I have tissues in here somewhere." She rifled around in her handbag, pulled out a packet of tissues, and passed them back to Spencer and Kendal.

They both dried their eyes and blew their noses.

"So, what did y'all get Mazy?" Spencer sounded weak, but no longer angry.

Kendal shook her head with a grin. "Nothing. We high-tailed it out of there the first chance we had."

"Guess we'll have to come back another day then." Spencer sniffled.

"No. You don't ever need to go back into that store." Kendal hugged Spencer.

Spencer mumbled into Kendal's shoulder. "But what if I want one of those sex swings?"

Kendal pulled back and smiled at Spencer. "In that case, you just tell me when you're up to it, and we'll make a return trip."

Spencer gave her a half-hearted smile. "Do you really think Earl has thought about most of the awkward issues I'm worried about?"

"Honestly, yes. I imagine he's done some googling about all sorts of things in regards to your condition. He said he got the idea for the harness on the internet. That should tell you something. I'm pretty sure he's done quite a bit of research and has more of an idea of what all is involved in being with you than you realize. He's a lot smarter than people give him credit for."

Leah added. "Spencer, has he even tried to pursue sex with you?"

"No. He hasn't. We just kiss and cuddle, and it's wonderful."

Leah patted the back of Spencer's hand. "That speaks volumes. He's into you, whether he gets into your panties or not. Relax. When the time comes that you're both ready to take things a step farther, you'll know. And that's when you two can discuss all that heavy stuff you'd rather not dredge up. You don't have to have that talk today. Y'all haven't been seeing each other all that long. It's okay to take things slow."

"She's right." Kendal added.

Leah looked at Spencer. "Are you and Earl coming to Reel to Real Good for supper tonight?"

"I was going to treat my folks to dinner there, and I was hoping Earl could join us, but I haven't invited him yet. I'm not sure I want to now. Today seems to be my day for tears. What if I get to thinking about all this junk again and start crying? I don't want to freak him out."

Kendal said, "Go ahead and invite him. If you get emotional, you can blame it on me. I'll tell him you and I had a spat today. That'll shut him up real fast. Anytime Mazy and I argue, he tosses his hands in the air and says to keep him out of it."

Spencer laughed. "I do the same thing when you and Mazy bicker."

Kendal chuckled. "Oh yeah...you sure do. See, you and Earl are perfect for each other. You have so much in common." It was great to see Spencer smiling again.

Kendal was glad she chose not to tell Spencer about how Dirk had surprised her with the best sexual experience of her life. At the time, she'd chosen to keep it to herself, because it was such a private thing. But now, she realized there was more to it than that. Spencer didn't need to hear the details, or compare what she and Earl did or didn't do to what was going on between Kendal and Dirk. It was fine that they'd told each other about their first kisses, but that's as far as they needed to take it.

Kendal couldn't help but feel sad though, sad for the fact Spencer would never experience certain pleasures.

How Dirk had made her feel was indescribable. Her body called his name long after he'd left her apartment.

Kendal sat up straight as a naughty thought distracted her. She now owned a pair of edible panties. Would Dirk like that?

She stifled a snicker as the old Tootsie Pop commercial

played in her head. *How many licks does it take to get to the center?*

CHAPTER NINETEEN
Wink

Spencer sat across from her parents at Reel to Real Good. Her mother looked rested and beautiful in a coral strapless dress, her hair pulled into a high bun, and a pearl necklace and matching earrings. She'd put on makeup for the first time in ages, and Spencer's dad, who was in a button-down white shirt and khaki slacks, couldn't seem to keep his eyes off his gorgeous wife.

Her father asked her mother to dance, and her mom actually blushed. As he led her onto the dance floor, Spencer couldn't help but smile to see them so in love after all these years. She wanted a love like that in her life too. Maybe Earl was the one. It was too soon to tell, but she hoped he was.

"Sorry I'm late." She recognized Earl's voice without turning around. He sat in the seat beside her and took her hand in his. "Things ran later than I expected on my last call. I couldn't put it off 'til tomorrow, because, well, what kind of guy would I be if I left an eighty year old woman in a hot mobile home over night? So I stayed. I finally got her system running good as new. She was thrilled. She'll keep cool tonight."

Spencer squeezed his hand. "I didn't mind waiting. Mom and Dad and I have had a nice time together." She pointed to her folks on the dance floor. "They look cute together, don't they?"

He turned and gazed at her parents and smiled. "They're awesome together. Reminds me of my folks years ago, before Mom passed away. Dad used to crank up the music and dance with her in the kitchen. But when she got so sick, he changed. He was mad at the whole world. I guess that's a pretty helpless feeling, not being able to do a damn thing when the woman you love is withering away right before your eyes." Earl swallowed hard and took a deep breath. "Damn, I didn't mean to go all dark on ya. What the hell?"

Spencer lifted his hand to her lips and kissed it gently. "You can tell me anything and everything. I'll always be willing to listen."

Earl searched her eyes, then his gaze fell to her mouth. He leaned toward her and kissed her, ever so gently. "How about I tell you how beautiful you are, and how crazy I am about you?"

She grinned. "Oh, feel free, get it off your chest. How crazy about me are you?"

"So crazy I'd like to dance you around the room. Are you up for it?" He twisted around and put his hand on the harness he'd made her. It was hung on the back of her chair. "I see you came prepared for it. Good!"

Earl got her all strapped in and lifted her so they were heart to heart. He hooked the shoulder straps over his shoulders and she reached around and buckled them together at his lower back. He kissed her again and said, "We make a great team."

In his arms, eye to eye, his heartbeat in sync with hers, she knew she couldn't break up with him, didn't want to, ever. Things would work themselves out. She of all people should know you have to live in the moment, because everything could change in the blink of an eye. Don't worry about things yet to be, or things from the past. If happiness is staring you in the face, be happy, take it, live it, cherish it. Her happiness came in the form of a fiery redheaded man with blue eyes and the sweetest smile, and he was definitely staring her in the face. And she was staring right back, unafraid, drinking it all in, all of it—all of the love he was pouring out.

The song "Be Young, Be Foolish, Be Happy" came on the jukebox and Earl sang along with the Tams and looked deep into her eyes. "'Don't let love slip away…live your life for today."

She joined him. "Be young, be foolish, be happy."

Her parents danced up beside them and sang along. Next thing Spencer knew, it seemed like everyone in the restaurant was singing with them, smiling and enjoying the "now." All the stress from the day disappeared. There, in Earl's arms, surrounded by people she loved, she didn't view herself as handicapped at all. She was blessed, so very blessed.

During the band's first break, Kendal walked over to Mazy, who sat behind her drum set, and motioned toward Spencer and Earl, dancing with a lovestruck look in their eyes. "It's great to see Earl and Spencer having a good time."

Mazy beamed. "I've never seen Earl this happy. Ever. Spencer brings out the best in him. I'm so glad too. I've spent a lot of years worrying about him, but he's calmed down a lot since he and Spencer started dating. She's just what he needed."

Leah watched the happy couple dance and put a hand on her chest. "Earl is good for her."

"She's good for Earl. He's been an angry, lost soul for a

long time." Kendal could remember a time in Earl's life when he was miserable, fighting with his father, failing school, in trouble with the law. Now, he was almost done with tech school, starting his own business, getting along great with his dad, and head over heels in love. She was delighted to see the change in him. He deserved it.

Sam said, "I've always had a soft spot for Earl and Spencer both. They make an adorable couple."

"You ladies ready to eat?" Leah motioned to the table set for the band.

Mazy put her drumsticks away. "Heck yeah. I'm starving." Her hair was the same coppery shade as Earl's and seemed to glow due to the twinkling white lights draped on the dark navy curtain behind her. She wore a green sequined strapless top that reminded Kendal of the Little Mermaid.

Sam pulled her long blonde hair into a ponytail and secured it with an elastic band. She wore a navy and white striped tank dress that showed off her long legs and great body. In spite of her awesome tan, she looked a bit pale, especially around her lips. Beads of sweat dotted her brow. When she leaned over to place her bass in it's case, she staggered forward and had to put her hand down on the stage floor to steady herself.

Kendal rushed over to her. "Sam, are you okay? You look a little green around the gills."

Sam flashed her a fake looking smile. "Yeah. I'm fine, just clumsy."

Leah put a finger to her lips and shook her head no. What was she trying to tell her? No, what?

Kendal shrugged at Leah to indicate she didn't understand what she was trying to say. Leah gestured her over. "Sam's a bit under the weather, but she'll be okay."

Kendal didn't get why Leah was telling her that instead of

Sam. "Does she have the flu or something?"

Sam touched Kendal's arm. "No. I don't have the flu." She waved Mazy over and the four of them formed a tight circle on the stage, facing one another. Sam took a deep breath and in a low whisper, she said, "I've got something to tell you, but I want to keep it between us." She took a deep breath and released it slowly. "I'm pregnant."

Mazy gasped. Kendal studied Sam's face to see if she was happy about the pregnancy.

Sam offered a weak smile.

Leah didn't seem surprised by the news at all. She and Sam were close, so she'd probably already been told.

Sam wiped her brow with the back of her hand. "Listen, I don't want things to get all dramatic, but when I first moved here, it was right after a miscarriage I've never told you about. Well, Leah knew, but that's it. I hope you can understand why I don't want too much attention on my pregnancy just yet."

Kendal saw the sadness in Sam's eyes. "That must have been really hard for you, Sam. I won't say a word to anyone. Are there any complications with your pregnancy now?"

Sam placed a hand on Kendal's shoulder. "No complications whatsoever. Brock is doting on me."

Mazy grinned. "You and Brock are going to be the best parents."

"Thank you, Mazy." Sam touched her belly.

Mazy asked, "Boy or girl?" The way Mazy's eyes were twinkling, Kendal wondered if she was itching to have a child of her own.

"We don't know yet." Sam glanced toward the entrance. "Here's the thing, I may not be able to keep up with our current gig schedule, so I've invited a bass player from the studios in Wilmington to come check out the band. He's a solid bassist, and he knows all of our standard tunes. I think he could be a decent sub, should I need one."

Sub? They didn't need a sub. No one could take Sam's place. Kendal spoke up. "I can play all the bass lines with my left hand on my keyboard. It won't be as good as when you do it, but we can get by. You don't need to get a sub. Anytime you're not feeling up to it, just let me know. I'll cover your part."

Sam laughed. "Thanks, Kendal. I feel so dispensable."

Kendal's face became hot. "I'm sorry. I didn't mean it like it sounded. I just meant—"

"I know what you meant. It's fine. I appreciate it." Sam's eyes grew wide when a tall blond guy with tats all over his muscular arms strolled through the door.

Leah gestured toward the blond guy. "Is he the sub?"

Sam grinned. "Yeah. He's a hunk, huh? His name's Jacob."

Leah shrugged, seemingly not interested, which was a typical Leah response in regards to men. She claimed she had no desire to date, but Kendal thought she was just scared to open herself up again. Her husband had passed away nearly seven years ago, before Bikini Quartet was formed. Kendal hoped Leah would find the courage to move on, but that was going to have to be a decision Leah made on her own. It wasn't Kendal's place to say anything about it.

Kendal checked Jacob out. He was kinda hot, if you're into sexy bad boy. Dirk had a nicer face, leaner build, better hair. She loved the way Dirk's hair was sun-kissed and fell across his brow, curled up slightly around his collar. It was so silky between her fingers, long enough for her to get a good hold on his head when he....

Mazy snapped her fingers in front of Kendal's nose. "Earth to Kendal."

"Wha...did you say something, Mazy?" Kendal shook off the naughty visions she was reliving—Dirk's head between her thighs on the kitchen counter.

Mazy laughed. "Yeah. Sam and Leah already went to the table to eat. Are you going to join us, or stand there all night with your mouth wide open?"

Kendal closed her mouth. God, she must look like an idiot. She glanced over at Jacob, and he gave her a wink. She quickly turned her back to him. Had she been staring at him? Did he think she was ogling him? She hoped not. "Let's go eat." She clamored down the stage steps with Mazy right behind her.

She wasn't flirting with that guy. But, oh God, he was walking over to them, and he winked at her again! Does he have something in his freaking eye? Is he losing a contact? Enough with the winking already.

She checked her little black dress to make sure everything was covered. No cleavage showing. The dress was to the knee. It was form fitting, but fairly conservative. So why was that guy looking her up and down like that? He was giving her a complex.

Dirk slipped in the side door of Reel to Real Good to place a to-go order for him and his dad. Kendal bounced down the stage stairs, jiggling in all the right places in a sexy little black dress.

Who the hell was that blond guy winking at her? Dirk's jaw tensed.

When Kendal took a seat at a table near the bar, Dirk headed her direction. As he weaved through the crowd, he caught her eye. Her whole face lit up when she saw him.

He walked up behind the blond guy. Dirk pinched his nose and made a face behind the guy's back, pretending that the guy just broke wind. Kendal laughed. That's what he was going for. Score one for Dirk, Zero for Mr. Wink and Stink.

The blond guy turned around, and Dirk hopped up on a barstool and faced the bar as fast as he could. He kept an eye on blondie and Kendal in the mirror over the bar.

Just what Dirk suspected, the guy walked straight over to Kendal. Dirk scooted his stool back so he could eavesdrop. "Hey, you have a beautiful smile. I'm Jacob."

Kendal glanced over at Dirk then gave Jacob her attention. "Hi, I'm Kendal."

"Did I do something funny a second ago? I noticed you were laughing."

"Oh, I wasn't laughing at you. I just saw a lady drop a shrimp down her top, and it was funny."

Knowing Little House, a woman really had dropped a shrimp down her top. Nice cover.

"Shrimp have no business near cleavage. I agree. That's a man's territory." Blond guy laughed at his own dumb joke.

The look on Kendal's face was hilarious. It was a mixture of "you're weird" and "go away." Dirk loved it.

Sam interjected and introduced Jacob to Leah and Mazy. The three of them engaged in conversation Dirk couldn't quite make out, but Kendal didn't seem to be paying them any attention anyway, she was too busy giving Dirk the eye in the mirror.

Dirk texted Kendal: *Careful, babe. That alpha dog might pee on your tits to mark his territory.*

She pulled her phone from beneath her bra strap and read the screen, then burst out laughing. She kept her phone in her bra? Nice. He didn't hear the ringer, so she must have it on vibrate.

Damn it. Now he was imagining using a vibrator on her. *Don't go there. You're in public and must not get too excited here.*

Sam pulled Kendal into the conversation about songs choices or something like that.

Dirk placed his to-go order and engaged in small talk

with a few of the other patrons, but he tried not to draw too much attention to himself. He didn't want to get dragged out onto the dance floor or anything. He didn't have much time. Ted was watching his dad, but couldn't stay much longer, because he'd made plans with Heidi. If his brother hadn't already purchased nonrefundable concert tickets, Dirk would've reminded him that it was his turn to pull dad-duty.

Dirk greeted a few more friends then made eye contact with Kendal again. He glanced around to make sure no one was watching him too closely. Nope. Everyone seemed busy with their own chatter and having a good time.

He sauntered toward the bathroom, hoping Kendal would follow.

She did. When she rounded the corner of the alcove for the restrooms, he pulled her into a small broom closet and shut the door.

The room was pitch black and smelled like oranges, probably from a citrus cleaner of some sort. Before Kendal could say a word, he pressed against her and kissed her.

"Oww!" She pushed him away. "Losing my virginity to the handle of a plunger wasn't what I had in mind!"

"Sorry, baby. Not what I had in mind either. You okay?" He tugged her away from the shelf.

She went silent, then a snicker erupted from her.

He couldn't help himself. He laughed too. When he bent to kiss her, their lips got ever so close, then she started giggling again.

She whispered, "I'm sorry. I have a warped sense of humor. This is supposed to be sexy, isn't it?"

"No." He kissed her long and deep, then pulled back. "That was supposed to be sexy."

"Oh…" She sighed and her knees buckled. He wrapped his arm around her to support her and went in for another sizzling kiss.

It was several minutes before she tore her lips from his and said, "Somebody might catch us."

"I don't care." He mumbled against her mouth.

She moaned when he squeezed her bottom. "What do you mean you don't care?" Her body stiffened in his grasp and her voice sounded alarmed.

She obviously *did* care if someone found them together, in a compromising position. "Sorry, sweetheart. I got a little carried away." He kissed the tip of her nose. "I've been thinking about you all damn day. I couldn't hold it in any longer." He nibbled her earlobe.

"Me too." Her voice quivered. "I mean...I've been thinking of you."

He whispered, "Tell me exactly what you've been thinking." As he trailed a hand from her bottom to her breast, her back arched. He rasped her nipple with his fingertips, feeling it harden beneath the fabric of her dress.

She staggered, and he teased her nipple again, showing no mercy. He wanted to drop to his knees and dive in for another taste of her so bad he couldn't stand it. "Damn, I want you, Kendal." He covered her mouth with his.

Coming up for air, she breathed, "I want you too." She kissed him again, this time with more fire than she'd ever demonstrated. There was an urgency, a need in her now that she'd never displayed before. Maybe those orgasms on the kitchen counter had shown her what she'd been missing, and she wanted more. He certainly wanted to give her more. He could feel her heart pounding just as fast as his. If they didn't chill out, they'd be caught doing a lot more than kissing, and that wouldn't be cool. It'd embarrass her to no end—him too, for that matter.

Cupping her beautiful face in his hands, he stroked his thumb across her bottom lip. "We better take it easy here. We'll finish this tomorrow. In private."

"Tomorrow?" She clenched his shirt. "Why not tonight after the gig?"

"I wish I could, but Mom's watching Penny's kids again, and I'm keeping an eye on Dad."

"Let Ted stay with your dad. It's his turn, isn't it?"

Dirk took a deep breath. He wasn't being fair, expecting a girl to accept his crazy schedule. He was a fool to toy with the idea of establishing a serious relationship with the way his life was pulled in all directions.

Kendal kissed him again. "I'm sorry. I understand about your dad. I do. I'm just horny."

He laughed. He never dreamed he'd be hearing those words come out of Little House on the Prairie. "Me too." He kissed her back. "I can get the afternoon off tomorrow, if you can. Say around two o'clock?"

"That'll work out fine. I'll go to the nursing home a little earlier than normal. Both of my afternoon piano students canceled. They're on summer vacation. I'm all yours."

His mind was reeling. A whole afternoon to themselves. Oh, the things they could do together. Finally.

Voices came from the other side of the door, and he and Kendal both went rigid. When the voices moved away. He whispered, "See you tomorrow then."

"Okay," she whispered back and gave him another quick kiss.

He peered out the door. The coast was clear. He let her go out first, while he hung back a few more minutes so nothing looked suspicious.

When he sat back down on the barstool closest the band's table, he heard Sam ask Kendal, "What took you so long? It's time to go back on stage and you didn't even have a chance to eat yet."

Ha. Neither did he. And he'd wanted to eat…her.

Kendal stammered, "I had to go to the bathroom and

then Mama called and jabbered my ear off."

Sam said, "You don't usually blush like that when you're talking to your mother."

Dirk picked up his to-go order and paid, lingering by the bar, watching the girls in the mirror.

Mazy pointed across the restaurant and told Kendal, "Your mom has been talking to Myrtle for the past ten minutes. So, out with it. Who's the guy?"

Ha. Busted.

Kendal turned bright red. He felt sorry for her, but didn't dare say a word.

Leah spoke up. "Leave her be. When she's ready to tell us, she will."

The blond guy said, "Lucky guy, whoever he is."

As Dirk headed out, he couldn't help but grin.

Damn right, Mr. Wink and Stink. He is a lucky guy, luckiest guy in the world.

CHAPTER TWENTY
Ants

Kendal examined the grape edible panties, not sure if she should have them on when Dirk got there or not. They were flimsy and thin and reminded her of a fruit roll-up, which was *not* one of her favorite snacks. The thought of stopping Dirk in the heat of the moment to shimmy into these undies didn't seem like a good idea, so if she was going to wear them, she might as well don them now. She stepped into the strangely textured panties very carefully and eased them up her legs and into place.

Looking in the mirror, she frowned. These funky purple drawers were not flattering.

Opting to go braless, she slipped on a silky red robe that hit her mid thigh.

Should she wear high heels or not? Most of the pictures in Kinky Joys showed women in extremely high heels, even if they were naked otherwise.

There was a knock on the door. *He's here*. She padded to the kitchen and glanced at the clock, 1:45.

When she opened the door, Dirk gave her a sheepish grin. "Hope I'm not too early. I've been staring at my watch, trying to will it to move faster, but decided it must be broken. The past fifteen minutes felt like an hour." He gave her a kiss, sliding his hands up and down the back of her silky robe. "Mmm."

"You're right on time." She flashed her vixen-smile, the one she'd rehearsed while putting on her makeup.

He leaned in for a more passionate kiss. When he crushed her against his chest, his eyes grew wide. He'd obviously figured out she didn't have a bra on.

She pulled away from him before he could get his hands on her breasts. He stuck out his bottom lip and whimpered. Ha.

"I have big plans for you, Mister. Follow me." He didn't protest as she led him back to her bedroom.

Her heart actually fluttered with anticipation. This was the first time he'd been in her bedroom. Heck, it was the first time any guy had been in her bedroom.

She wanted him so much, and it wasn't just a physical want. Although, she was trying very hard to convince herself this was just about the sex.

She felt no need to rush, but she did want to show off some of the tricks she'd learned from that tutorial video and reciprocate the pleasure he'd given her. If she waited, she might be so caught up in the moment, she wouldn't be able to focus.

He faced her, and she moved in close and began tugging his T-shirt up his body. He helped her out and peeled his shirt off in a blur of movement then drew her to him for a scorching kiss.

His erection pressed into her belly, and she wanted to see and touch him there. Nervously, she fiddled with his belt buckle, but her hands were shaking so badly she couldn't manage to undo it.

He pressed his lips to the top of her head and took over. "I'll get that, sweetie." Within a few seconds his shorts were on the floor, his hardened length bared before her.

She stared, couldn't help herself. She'd never seen a cock

in the flesh—so rigid, thick, erotic. It was mesmerizing, jutting up toward her.

She touched it tenderly, her fingertips gently traveling over the smooth tip and down the veiny shaft. His breathing became shallow and his eyes filled with passion as he watched her explore his body.

Stuffing her nerves down as far as she could, she knelt in front of him and kissed the mushroom cap, running her tongue around the edge like the woman in the video had demonstrated. Dirk sucked in a breath and brushed her hair from her face. The desire in his eyes caused blood to rush to her womanhood, to the point she could feel her pulse throbbing between her legs.

Replaying the technique she'd learned from the video, she inched his beautiful cock into her mouth, making sure her lips were folded over her teeth and her tongue was softly petting. All the way down she went, until she couldn't breathe and had to relax her throat.

"Jesus, baby." His fingers clenched, until he had handfuls of her hair in his fists.

When she began to move her head up and down, he wobbled on his feet, and lowered himself to the edge of the bed, his legs spread. She crawled between his knees, using her hands to stroke and twist up and down his shaft while she worked his thickness with her mouth.

A low growl escaped his lips, and he gently tugged her head back and said, "You're gonna make me come."

"That's what I want." She pushed her head back down and found the rhythm that made his body tense with pleasure. She could tell by his breathing that was staggered with held breaths and throaty, manly moans, he was enjoying what she was doing. She felt in control, and loved it. Doing this to him was more exciting than she dreamed.

He nudged her head away just as he came in her hands.

He blinked his eyes and shook his head. "Oh my God, baby. That was amazing. Where'd you learn to do that?"

Yay. He liked it. Knowing that made her feel pretty damn amazing too.

There was a loud knock on the door.

She and Dirk locked eyes.

He whispered, "Are you expecting company?"

She shook her head. "No! Whoever it is, I'll try to get rid of them fast. Sit tight."

She darted out of the room, washed her hands, then zipped down the hall.

Her mother opened the back door and stuck her head in. "Yoohoo, Kendal."

By the time Kendal got to the kitchen, her mother had let herself in and was standing by the sink.

Shit! Kendal crossed her arms over her chest and tried to appear sleepy. She yawned and said, "Hey, Mama. I wasn't expecting you. What brings you by today?"

Her mother scrunched up her face. "Were you in bed? In the middle of the afternoon with all that makeup on your face?"

"Yeah. I *was*." Kendal resisted the urge to roll her eyes. Her mom had gotten a lot better about keeping her opinions to herself since their last confrontation when she'd invited the boy on the bicycle to dinner. But old habits die hard apparently.

With a half-hearted smile, her mother said, "That shade of red is pretty on you with your dark hair and fair skin. You look like a modern day Snow White. I don't care how old you get, you'll always be my little princess."

Wonder what she'd think if she knew what Kendal had been up to? It was sweet that her mother viewed her as a princess, but wasn't Kendal a little old for that? Disney. Really? And if they were Disney characters, who would her mother be? Ursula the Sea Witch? Kendal had to grit her teeth to keep from laughing out loud at that thought.

"I just came by to see if you'd like to go shopping. You said you had the afternoon off, and I thought we could go to Wilmington. There's a new boutique on the river that sells the prettiest dresses, like the pink and black one you like so much. I want to buy you one, your choice, of course."

That was really nice. Her mother had already mended the ripped garment and apologized profusely. "Mama, that's very generous of you, but you don't owe me a dress or anything. Really, let's just forget about all that negative stuff." If Dirk weren't waiting for her in her bedroom, she might have taken her mother up on her offer, but sexy man vs. new dress—no contest. Sexy man was the winner.

Her mother looked disappointed.

"I'd love to go to Wilmington with you though. Can I take a raincheck? I've been so busy lately, I'm exhausted. It's all catching up with me. All I want to do is go back to bed. I hope you understand." That wasn't a lie. She really did want to go back to bed.

"Of course, honey. I know you're schedule is crazy. I don't know how you do all that you do."

"I like it, so I don't mind, but yeah, it's tiring. Maybe we can go shopping next Monday. I have a day off."

"I'd like that. I miss you. I know it's good that you have this cute apartment and are on your own, but the house seems so empty without your smiling face and your piano playing." Her mother gazed at her with a strange look in her eye. "You've grown into such a gorgeous young woman. I can hardly believe we're related."

Kendal was moved by her mother's sweetness. She gave her a big hug. "I love you, Mama. I think you're pretty too. I've always thought so."

"Thank you, sweetheart." Her mother kissed her cheek.

"I'm going to get going and let you get some more rest.

When Kendal stepped back, she felt one of side of her underwear break. She squeezed her thighs together so her panties wouldn't fall off.

Her mom turned toward the back door.

She looked back at Kendal. "Honey, you really should keep your door locked. Please, dead bolt it after I go out."

"Yes, Ma'am." Kendal followed her mother to the door. As soon as Kendal stepped in front of the kitchen table, her edible panties hit the floor. Her mother's back was to her. Thank God. She kicked the undies under the table.

Her mother whirled around and said, "You may want to wash your face before you go back to sleep. It really isn't good for your skin to sleep in makeup. You have such a lovely complexion, you should take care of it."

"Yes, Ma'am." Kendal was panicked. If her mother didn't go in the next few seconds, Kendal feared she'd shove her out the door.

Her mother looked toward the table, squinted and bent her head.

No. God, no. Don't see those. Please, don't see those panties. Please.

"Kendal, what's under your table?"

Before Kendal could answer, her mother brushed past her and bent over and picked the panties up. "Fruit roll-ups! You hated these things as a kid."

"They taste better than they used to," Kendal said, as if she knew what they tasted like now. Roll-ups still grossed her out. If she'd have known the panties were made of the same stuff, she wouldn't have bought them. But she thought Dirk might like them. She remembered he used to eat roll-ups in school.

"They're made of sugar. You need to sweep your floor, keep your kitchen clean. You don't want to attract ants or roaches, do you?"

"No, Ma'am."

"Think of poor Pam downstairs, trying to run a candy shop and you drawing ants and roaches in the house. I thought I raised you better than that."

"You did, Mama. I'll mop the floor this evening."

Her mother marched over to the trash and threw the panties away. "Remember that summer we got overrun by sugar ants after your father left the cake uncovered on the counter while I was away visiting my sister? Remember what a time we had getting rid of those things?"

"Yes, Ma'am."

"Okay then. The best way to deal with pests is to keep them out of the house to begin with."

"Okay." Kendal let out a sigh of exasperation. She couldn't take anymore. Her mother needed to leave, before Kendal screamed.

"Alright, baby. Stop by the house any time. I'm looking forward to our shopping trip on Monday."

"Me too."

Her mother finally walked out the door, and Kendal locked the door behind her, When her mother disappeared down the steps, Kendal thudded her head against the door. The best way to handle pests is to not let them in the house. Excellent advice. She mumbled, "That woman is going to drive me crazy."

She took a deep breath, and rushed back to her bedroom. When she opened her door, disappointment washed over her. Dirk wasn't in there. Her window was opened, the ocean breeze blowing her curtains. She looked out the window onto her back deck. No sign of him. Damn it.

Her mother was right. She should have kept the door locked. If she had, her mom wouldn't have been able to come waltzing in uninvited. Oh, she had a pest problem all right. A big pest named Rita Duvall.

CHAPTER TWENTY-ONE
4th

Dirk recognized Rita Duvall's voice. Oh shit. She'd make life hell for Kendal if she found him there. That woman was too critical of her daughter. She was nice to everyone else, but she was damn hard on Kendal.

He could imagine the terror coursing through Kendal's veins right now. The back deck ran under Kendal's bedroom window. He could just step right out and sneak down the back steps. Done.

As he neared the back door of Laffy Taffy, he heard Pam, the candy shop owner, talking on her cell phone. She opened the back screen door and paused.

He ducked behind a yucca plant. Ouch! He cursed under his breath. Dang pointy spear-like leaves gouged his arm. Those plants ought to be illegal. He'd been pricked by those blasted things so many times doing landscape work it wasn't even funny.

Pam's feet were visible, but none of the rest of her, maybe she couldn't see him either. He hoped not.

Whew. She went back inside and shut the door.

Dragging himself to his feet with his heartbeat racing and sweat pouring down his body from the hundred degree humid weather, he sprinted to his car, which he'd hidden between the dumpster and Sushi Mama's.

Once safely inside his vehicle, he turned the AC on full blast and caught his breath. Relieved with the cool air blowing…speaking of blowing…he closed his eyes. His mind drifted and replayed the way Kendal had devoured him earlier.

She was a virgin? Never been kissed 'til he came along? Wow. How'd she know how to use her mouth like a pro? He'd expected her to be awkward, that he'd have to guide her through the BJ, and tell her what to do, at least a little bit. But dang if she didn't take charge and own him. He'd tried to hold back, but the way she took him deep into her mouth felt so good, too damn good.

He dropped his head to the steering wheel. How could one girl be so sweet, innocent, sexy, smart, and an incredible person to boot? It was gonna hurt like hell when she met Mr. Right.

As he drove home, he envisioned tearing Kendal's clothes off, groping and kissing her, their arms and legs braided together. He'd hold her up against the wall and take her hard and deep.

Pull yourself together, dude.

That wasn't how Kendal should lose her virginity.

Ha! She almost lost it to the plunger! He shook his head. Yep, he'd botched the closet seduction up too.

But eventually, if things went according to plan, he would be faced with the decision of how to "deflower" this wonderful woman. And he needed to treat the moment with the sensitivity it deserved. She didn't need to lose her virginity in a wild, manic, fit of passion. The wild, manic, passion could come later. Her first time ought to be romantic and slow. He didn't want to go gorilla on her and hurt her.

The moment needed to be as special as she was. He'd make love to her gently. And he'd get her all to himself where they could spend hours together, uninterrupted by anything or anyone.

Tonight wouldn't work, he was bartending at the resort 'til three in the morning. Tomorrow was the fourth of July, and he had a day full of various tasks all the way down to helping with the evening fireworks. The morning after, he'd be cleaning up the mess the fireworks made on the beach, but he could free up the rest of the day.

Before going inside his house, he texted Kendal instead of calling, because he wasn't sure if her mom was still at her apartment or not.

Dirk: *That was a close call with your mom. She still there?*

A few seconds later she texted back.

Kendal: *OMG! I nearly died! She's gone.*

Dirk called her. "Hey, sexy."

"Hey. I'm so sorry about Mom."

"No worries, just bad timing. Really bad timing. Listen, I just wanted to say…I don't know quite how to word this… but…yeah…that was the best blow job of my life. Ha. Sorry. I guess I could have phrased that more eloquently. I don't know how you knew what to do, but wow, baby."

Her soft laugh made him smile. Good. She wasn't offended.

She said, "Last night, I watched a tutorial video on how to…umm…do *that*."

He laughed. "*Good* video."

She had studied up for this. How many girls would do that? The fact Kendal did it for him, that she was that interested in how to please him…it made him fall a little harder for her. He was already jealous of the man who'd end up with her.

Truth was, if she'd fumbled the whole works, he would've still been into her. But she had gone out of her way to make sure he got his just as good as she could give it.

That spoke to her generosity. She wasn't self-centered. She was a giver in many ways. Knowing that made him want to shower her with affection while he had a chance. Guess that made him a giver too, but he already knew that about himself. She just brought out that part of him a little more strongly than anyone else ever had.

She whispered, "It makes me happy that you enjoyed that. I really wanted you to. You made me feel so good the other day."

"Mmm. I'll be doing that again. Don't you worry. And I have more tricks up my sleeve you might like even better."

The sexy, purr-like chuckle that came out of her let him know she liked that idea.

"Dirk, can you come back over. Now?"

"I better not. If we got going again, there's no way in hell I'd be able to pull myself away from you, and I'm scheduled to work the bar at the resort in an hour."

"Aww."

"Kendal, I've been thinking…I don't want to rush your first time. I'd like to take things nice and slow, no interruptions, no phone calls. Tomorrow is going to be crazy with all that's going on for the 4th of July. Can you clear your schedule for day after tomorrow? I'd like to steal you away…keep you to myself on the 5th."

"July 5th I'm all yours. I'll see you tomorrow, though, right?"

"Of course, but tons of people will be around, and we'll have to keep up the pretense that there's nothing going on between us."

"Oh yeah." He voice sounded darker. "Can't let anyone know."

Right. She wanted her privacy, and she deserved it. "Anyway, I've got one thing after the other lined up tomorrow, but I'll find you on the beach. I promise."

"Good." The sparkle returned to her voice.

"Well, let me get going then, before I change my mind and crawl back through your window."

She laughed. "I'll keep it unlocked for you."

"Don't tempt me, young lady."

"I'm not wearing anything but that silky red robe right now."

"Jesus, Kendal. You're killing me. You have no idea what seeing you in that slinky robe did to me today."

"Oh, I have an idea, pretty big one too."

Was she teasing him about his length? Ha. Hearing Little House on the Prairie making dirty jokes, something about that turned him on. Face it. Everything about her turned him on.

"See you tomorrow, Angel Face."

"Bye."

He clicked out. A few seconds later he got an incoming text.

Kendal: *(Kiss)*

He touched the word "kiss" on the screen and smiled.

Dirk: *(Kiss)*

Kendal locked Spencer's van while Spencer sat in her wheelchair on the sidewalk and got Benny's service harness all situated. They were parked in a handicap parking space close to the pier. Good thing she was with Spencer, because had she come by herself, she would've had to park a few blocks away, due to the crowd. People came from all over to be a part of the fourth of July festivities on the island.

Earl jogged toward them. "Bout time you two got here." He leaned down and gave Spencer a kiss, then hugged Kendal's neck. "I got the canopy all set up for us. Mazy and Trent are already on the beach."

Varroom. A loud motorcycle rounded the corner. Rafe Washington, Earl's father, was driving. A plump woman in stretchy white shorts and a skin-tight patriotic tank top was on the back of the bike, her arms wrapped around his waist. Spencer whispered in Earl's ear. "Looks like your dad has a new girlfriend."

The pudgy woman crawled off the motorcycle and removed her helmet. It was Rita Duvall. Kendal nearly passed out. "Mama?!"

Earl looked at Kendal with his eyes the size of silver dollars. He opened his mouth to speak and all that came out was, "Ahhhh. Da....ahhh—"

"Ma...ahhh...ma..." Kendal echoed Earl's speech impediment.

Spencer waved and smiled. "Hey, Mr. Washington. Hey, Mrs. Duvall."

Kendal's mother waved back and said, "Hey there, Spencer. You can call me Rita or Miss Hinton. I'm going to start using my maiden name again."

Oh no. Should Kendal read into that? Did her mother's choosing to go by her maiden name mean her mom wanted to let the world—namely Rafe—know she was a single woman? Mr. Washington was such a gruff man. And he cussed. A lot! What was her mother doing with him?

Earl shook his head and rubbed his eyes like he couldn't quite process what he was seeing.

When Kendal's mother got within arm's reach, she pulled Kendal tight against her soft bosom and whispered, "Turns out I didn't need a nice boy on a bicycle either. I needed me a bad boy on a motorcycle. Lord help me. You're mama's taking a walk on the wild side and loving it."

When she turned Kendal loose. Kendal couldn't seem to close her mouth. The images of her mother and Rafe Washington...together...really together...flooded her mind and darn near traumatized her.

Earl seemed to be having a similar reaction.

Rafe pushed his motorcycle out of the way, up close to the entrance of the Sandy Treasures beach shop.

"Mama, what are you doing with Rafe Washington?" Kendal couldn't get over this.

Her mother ran her fingers through her shiny hair that was devoid of its usual can of hairspray. It actually moved in the breeze like a normal person's. "My car broke down on the way home from your place yesterday. Rafe stopped to give me a hand. He couldn't get my car running, so he gave me a ride back to my house. I've never had such a big, roaring machine between my legs."

Kendal's jaw dropped again.

"I mean the motorcycle, honey. Not Rafe. Well, he's a big roaring machine too…nevermind." Her mother blushed.

Oh. My. God.

Earl must have overheard her mother cause he busted out laughing.

Rafe walked up. "What's so damn funny, Squirrely boy?"

"Nothing, Dad. I just can't get over you giving Rita a ride on the back of your Harley." Earl straightened up his face, but his chin quivered with bemusement.

Sure, Earl could think it was funny. His dad was a tough guy. But her mother didn't know what the heck she was getting herself into. Surely she wasn't really considering hanging out with Rafe on a regular basis, or doing *things* with him.

Rafe put his arm around Rita. "What you talkin' bout, boy? This woman loves to ride." He gave Rita a wink.

Rita cooed. "Oh my. We don't want to give the children the wrong idea."

Rafe looked at her like she was crazy. "Wrong idea? Dumplin', in case you haven't noticed, our kids aren't children anymore. I think they can handle it." He tossed a smile Kendal's direction. "Ain't that right, Kendal?"

"Yes, Sir." Kendal mumbled.

Rafe laughed. "Yes, sir? Holy shit. Nobody's said that to me in ages. Earl, you need to learn a few things from Kendal. She's got manners."

Spencer piped up. "Earl has manners!" She scowled at Rafe.

Rafe gave Spencer's nose a tweak. "I'm glad to hear it, cutie. Well, me and Rita are meeting some of my friends down by the lifeguard stand. We'll talk at you kids later on. Have fun."

Kendal watched her mother waddle away, arm in arm with Rafe Washington, and she had to lean on the parking meter to keep from keeling over.

Spencer giggled. "Y'all have been acting like brother and sister for years. Looks like there's a chance it might be made official. Can you imagine if Rita and Rafe were to get married?"

Earl and Kendal gawked at each other, then stared at Spencer and said, "Don't say that," in unison. When Kendal's gaze met Earl's again, they both started laughing.

Spencer beamed. "Well, you know what they say about how opposites attract. I don't think you can get more opposite than Rafe and Rita."

Spencer had a point there. Opposite was putting it mildly. Her mother and Rafe were practically different species.

Earl gave Kendal a hug. "Holy shit, sis."

She playfully punched his arm. "Let's get going and pretend we didn't just see that."

Earl nodded. "I agree."

As they made their way onto the beach, Spencer pointed up at the sky. A huge kite of Uncle Sam—his long legs dancing in the wind—hovered above the waves.

The beach was packed with people all decked out in red, white, and blue attire.

Mazy approached them with her pot-bellied pig, Rooster, on a red leash. He had on a pointy, blue party hat with a silver star topper. Mazy wore a red and white striped beach coverup. "Hey, y'all. Come on over and join us." She pointed to a canopy where Trent sat in the shade laughing with Brock and Sam about something.

Benny wagged his tail fast as lightning when he saw Rooster. As Benny pranced in the sand all happy to see the little pig, Rooster lifted his head and let out his infamous crow. Yes, it sounded more like a wounded animal than a rooster's cock-a-doodle-doo, but it was still cute as hell. The little pig gave it his all.

Earl told Mazy about Rafe and Rita and she seemed just a shocked as Kendal had been.

A pair of hands covered Kendal's eyes, and she heard a foreign accent whisper in her ear. "Guess who dis iz." It was Dirk being goofy.

She felt his hands. "Big bear paws." She reached back and tugged his ears. "Fuzzy bear ears." She felt his mouth. "Goofy grin. I'm going with Yogi Bear."

He chuckled. "You're right, Booboo." When he removed his hands from her eyes, she turned and smiled up at him. His whole upper body was painted in stars and stripes, including his face.

He quickly stepped away from her and spoke to Mazy and Earl. Spencer stared at Kendal and stuck out her bottom lip. Guess Kendal's disappointment that Dirk didn't have much to say to her was easy to read. Kendal shrugged and walked over to Spencer and stood behind her wheelchair.

Spencer looked back at her. "You okay?"

Kendal leaned close to Spencer and whispered in her ear, "Of course. It's best Dirk and I don't make it too obvious we're fooling around. You know how Myrtle and the gang can be."

Spencer didn't look too convinced, but she didn't argue the point.

Earl got Spencer and Benny all settled in the shade under the canopy.

Dirk chatted with Mazy as she walked Rooster over to Trent who held up a bottle of sunscreen.

Their friends greeted them as they sat in the empty chairs available.

Trent squirted sunscreen on Rooster and started rubbing it in.

Dirk laughed. "You're putting sunscreen on a pig?"

Mazy whirled around with her hands on her hips. "I'll have you know Rooster is fair skinned, and if we don't slather on the SPF he'll be peeling pork rinds tomorrow."

Dirk mumbled, "Pork rinds," and glanced over at Kendal. The moment her eyes met his, they both started laughing.

Everyone else laughed too, but when Dirk and Kendal didn't seem to be able to stop, everyone looked at them like they had lost their minds.

Spencer said, "What's so funny?"

Kendal shrugged. "Can you imagine Rooster peeling pork rinds? That's hilarious."

Spencer gave her a skeptical look and nodded.

Dirk put on a serious face, well as serious as a face can be with stars and stripes all over it. "I got to scoot on down the beach to get the line-up for the parade of animals underway. When y'all get Rooster and Benny ready, bring 'em on down." He waved—his gaze lingering on Kendal a few extra seconds—then he jogged away.

Kendal stared at his glistening, muscular back and that tight butt of his in those white swim trunks. She preferred tight white spandex pants like football players wore, but those white board shorts Dirk was sporting were mighty nice too. He filled them out just right.

She remembered how great he had looked naked the day before and for a split second, she seemed to have x-ray vision.

Spencer swatted her arm. "Kendal, are you sure you're okay? You look like you're doped up on crack."

Doped up on crack. Ha. Yep. Pretty much.

"Whew, Dirk takes my breath away sometimes. I'm going to have to get me a piece of that again, and soon." A female voice rang out.

Kendal spun around to find Ashley, standing behind her, wearing a microscopic flag bikini and sipping on a Diet Coke. Kendal wanted to tell her she better keep her damn hands off Dirk, but, once again, Kendal bit her lip and stayed quiet.

Ashley didn't keep quiet though. She kept on going. "Dirk sure knows how to give a girl an O, over and over. Have you ever been with a guy like that, Kendal?"

Kendal glared at her.

Spencer spoke up. "Ashley, all that bleach you put on your hair has taken its toll on your brain, if you think we care to hear about your sexcapades. Show a little more class and a little less ass, why don't ya?"

Dirk helped Carl get all the ostriches lined up for the parade of animals. Myrtle wore a statue of liberty crown and a silver bikini, and was sitting atop Robirrrda. Myrtle's skin sparkled like she'd slathered glitter lotion all over her wrinkled little body. And somehow, she'd managed to dye some of Robirrrda's wings red and blue. The other twelve ostriches were nose to tail feathers behind Robirrrda. Spike was the last one, and Louise was on top of him. Louise had on a Betsy Ross costume with a colonial flag tied around Spike's neck like a bib. The other ostriches were adorned with shiny patriotic garland and tiny Uncle Sam hats.

Earl had Benny on a blue leash and the dog wore a Benjamin Franklin wig with holes cut into the bald cap portion for his ears. He also wore round wire glasses and a ruffly ascot and doggie blazer. An old-fashioned kite was attached to a stiff wire and hooked to Benny's collar to make it appear as if Benny was flying the kite.

In addition to the blue pointy hat with the silver star on top, Mazy had put a red tutu on Rooster and had drawn kissy lips on him with red lipstick. Poor piggie. That had to be embarrassing.

All the other animals in the parade line-up were equally festive, including Tally the sea turtle, who had a stuffed bald eagle riding on its enormous shell painted like the American flag.

Everyone was all set. Dirk grabbed his pooper-scooper tools and got in the back of the line. Dirty job, but someone had to do it.

The parade began. When the guy carrying the boombox turned the music on, Dirk started dancing, keeping his eye out for messes to take care of. As they made their way down the beach, he tried his best to entertain the crowd with his dance moves and judging from the whistles and cheers coming from the crowd, they were having a ball. So was he, to be honest.

He spotted Kendal in her red bikini under the canopy with her friends. He was glad they were sitting so close to the parade line. He made sure to dance a little sexier for her benefit. When an old lady came up to him and tucked a twenty dollar bill into his swim trunks, he figured he might have overdone it.

But he saw the look in Kendal's eyes as she watched him

show off his best moves. She liked it. He saw her chest rising and falling like she was having a hard time catching her breath, and the way she bit her lower lip, not to mention how her nipples stood up at attention. Mission accomplished, and an extra twenty bucks was always a plus.

At the end of the parade, he was exhausted, but had to run back down the beach to help judge the sandcastle contest, then he was entered in the watermelon seed spitting contest, then there was the shagging on the beach contest—and he was the grand champion male dancer for that. It cracked him up that folks who weren't from the area thought the shagging contest would be some kind of public sex show. Did people really think just because the island had a nudist colony that they'd host something that obscene? Would something like that even be legal? He hoped not. Besides, this was a family festival.

Later, he would be walking the beach making balloon animals for the kiddies and manning one of the big grills for the burger cook-off. After that he had to get set up for the firework display. And somewhere in the middle of all of that, he wanted to fit in a little time to hang out with Kendal and his friends.

Kendal was playing with Bikini Quartet on the pier at dusk, and she was also running the apple pie booth that afternoon. It wasn't like she didn't have plenty to do too. But he really hoped they'd find a way to be around each other a little more, even though he'd have to act cool and pretend they didn't have anything going on between them.

He was tired just thinking about all the stuff he had to do today. He loved the fourth of July, but it kicked his ass.

He placed his vote for the sand sculpture that Brock and Sam had made. It looked like hatchling sea turtles crawling out of a double bass case, leaving tracks of music notes in the sand. The attention to detail was remarkable.

With just enough time to catch Kendal before the pies went on sale, he grabbed a beach bicycle out of the storage room beneath the pier and rode it back down to Kendal.

When he got to the canopy. Kendal was sitting alone with Ashley—who wore that teeny-tiny flag bikini again. Kendal looked pissed. What had Ashley been saying to her?

He leaned the bike against the fold out table where all the chips and snacks were spread out, and he walked under the canopy. "Hey, ladies. Where'd everybody go?"

Ashley jumped up from her low sitting deck chair and almost jiggled right out of her bikini top. She scampered his direction and threw her arms around his neck, gave him a hug, and said, "Hey, hot stuff." When she pulled away, some of the paint from his body was now on her. She looked down and giggled. "Seems you've left your mark on me. I guess I'm yours for the day, and night if you like."

Kendal folded her arms over her chest and yawned, then tugged her sun hat down as if she was going to try to catch a nap.

Dirk brushed by Ashley and sat beside Kendal. "Hey, Kendal. Did you get a chance to see the sand sculptures yet?"

She lifted her head and pushed her big floppy white hat back out of her eyes. "Yes." She was curt and didn't seem to want to talk.

"The one Sam and Brock made was awesome, wasn't it?"

"Yes." She rubbed her temples. "I don't mean to be rude, but I have a headache. Could you leave me alone for a bit."

Ashley had definitely been talking crap to Kendal. He'd bet money on it. "Sure. I need to head on over to the watermelon seed-spitting area anyway."

Kendal didn't respond, but Ashley said, "Are you competing?"

He said, "Yeah." But he wished he wasn't, he'd like to

pull Kendal off to the side and find out what had pissed her off.

When he got back on his bike to leave, Ashley hopped on the handlebars. "Give me a ride, baby."

Baby? Since when did Ashley call him that? And how the hell was he going to get out of this without coming across like an asshole? He couldn't. And from the evil eye Kendal was now giving him from under the brim of her hat, it wouldn't matter if he ditched Ashley or not at this point. Kendal had obviously already labeled him asshole of the day.

Screw it. "Ashley, I'm not your baby. Get your butt off my bike."

Ashley jumped to her feet and whirled around. "What the hell's wrong with you?"

"You. You're what's wrong. The way you drape yourself all over me and won't leave me alone is getting old. I'm sorry. I got a lot to do, and you're not on the list."

Ashley put her hands on her hips and stomped her foot, her blonde hair flailing around her scowling face.

Kendal pulled her hat back over her face. From beneath that sunhat came a snicker.

Ashley kicked sand her way. "Shut up, Kendal. This isn't funny."

CHAPTER TWENTY-TWO
Fireworks

Earl sensed something was troubling Spencer. He'd caught her staring off into space with a worried look on her face several times. She must have something bothersome on her mind, judging from how preoccupied she seemed in the midst of all the festivities.

When they were alone in the dunes at sunset, he decided to ask her about it. "Is something wrong, Spencer?"

She tucked a strand of dark curls behind her ear and gave him that award-winning smile of hers he loved so much. "No, not at all, I'm having a great time."

"Why do you seem so distracted then?"

She fell silent but eventually took a deep breath and said, "Earl, why haven't you tried to do anything more than kiss me?"

Wow. He hadn't expected that. Did she want him to do more than kiss her? "I've been waiting for you to let me know it was okay, I guess."

He wasn't ready to tell her that he had some issues of his own, that he sometimes failed to get or maintain an erection. That was embarrassing. For years, he'd been taking supplements that were supposed to fix the problem, but he still struggled with erectile dysfunction, not something he expected to be dealing with at age twenty-five. The doctor said his problem was more psychological than anything, that Earl put extra pressure on himself to perform and that caused him to lose his erection. Overthinking. He'd tried some prescription meds, but a four-hour boner was painful, and no woman really wanted things to last for hours either. Not to mention the drugs gave him heart palpitations that were unnerving, to say the least.

Between Spencer's condition and his own, he thought that taking things slow was probably for the best. Had his failure to try to move things along given her the impression he was disinterested?

"It's okay." Her voice was frail and trembling. Was she upset?

"It's okay that I've hesitated or it's okay to move forward?" He reached for her hand.

"It's okay either way. I just thought maybe I didn't...you know...didn't turn you on that way." Her eyes were downcast as if she was embarrassed to face him.

"Spencer, you turn me on. I think you're beautiful. I adore being around you." Yes, he'd had fantasies about being with her. He'd even googled how the two of them could have sex. When he discovered that women who'd endured a similar spinal injury as Spencer's could have orgasms—something about the nerves that signaled sexual pleasure found new routes outside of the spinal column—it fascinated him. He was hopeful that Spencer could enjoy sex to its fullest. He just hadn't wanted to ask her if she could have an O, because what if the answer was no and the question upset her? He'd feel like a real shit.

But another thing holding him back was his own shortcomings. The last two girls he was with blamed themselves for his lack of an erection. One said it was because she was unattractive, that she wasn't pretty enough or sexy enough, that she didn't touch him the right way. The other one said it was because he thought she was trash, had slept around too much, that she was cheap. He'd tried to convince them both otherwise, but he'd failed.

What if Spencer misread his body and assumed he wasn't attracted to her because she was in a wheelchair? Would he be able to convince her that wasn't so? If his track record was any indication, the answer was no. He didn't want to run the risk of hurting her unintentionally like that.

Limiting their physical contact to holding hands and kissing gave him the opportunity to shower her with affection and demonstrate how much he adored her. But apparently, she wanted more. So did he, but he was petrified. Things were going perfectly between them. Would altering their sexual dynamics ruin it?

But she wanted more and deserved it. He needed to step up. Satisfying her every need and desire was what he wanted to do, desperately. Maybe if he just let things flow naturally, it would be fine. No overthinking, no long discussion.

He was lost. What was he to do or say? How could he reassure her right this very minute that she was the only woman in the world he wanted to be with. She turned him on in all the ways that really mattered.

He picked her up, cradled her in his lap, and kissed her with all the love he had in his heart for her. She wrapped her arms around his neck and returned his kisses with just as much affection as he gave. They may not have been talking, but they were definitely communicating how they felt toward one another, and it was powerful. She made him want to be a better man, a better person, a better lover. Disappointing her was the last thing on earth he ever wanted to do.

As their lips parted briefly, he whispered, "Spencer, you're the girl for me. Never doubt that." Before she could respond, he claimed her mouth with his as the crimson horizon faded to a hazy lavender.

The ocean breeze swirled around them and rustled their hair. Their bodies were hot and moist from perspiration, but he continued to hold her close, and she hugged him tight against her. They were on their own tiny island in a sea of people, and he'd never felt more complete.

On her back on a blanket in the dunes Spencer stared up at the fireworks display. "Oh, I love the waterfall ones." She pointed at the white sparkles cascading from a huge firework burst.

Earl's mouth was by her ear, his fingertips caressing her collarbone. "I love the feel of your skin."

Her gaze met his as he rose onto his elbow and stared down at her. The loud explosions above echoed off the houses behind them. Percussive vibrations travelled through the sand and thudded against her back, but she could still feel her heartbeat as it seemed to clang inside her ribcage. The energy in the air between her and Earl ignited with desire that seemed on the verge of bursting like the fire flowers of red and green that now glittered in the darkened sky.

His mouth hovered above hers. His warm breath mixed with her own as he dragged his fingertips from her collarbone to her nipple. When he discovered her nipple was hard, he lightly pinched it, and whispered, "The things I want to do to you."

She lifted her head and kissed him. He slid his other hand beneath the back of her head and cradled it as he deepened the kiss.

Her sense of touch was heightened like never before. She wanted her breasts touched skin on skin. When she moaned into his mouth, he peeled the fabric of her sundress away from her breasts and pulled back. His gaze fell to her bosom, and he gently traced her nipples one then the other. A heady feeling came over her as he kissed her neck, his hand still exploring her breasts. She took in the colorful display in the sky and released the moans and sighs his touch drew out of her.

He replaced his fingers with his mouth and kissed her breasts, licking and suckling her nipples. She'd never experienced such intense pleasure.

The more he kissed her breasts, the more turned on she became, until her body tensed with a strange need that left her dizzy. When she looked down at Earl, his eyes met hers and she saw he had pulled her dress up and his hand was in her panties. Was that what had her feeling so incredible? Could she feel that?

"Earl? What are you doing?" She lifted onto her elbows, and he rubbed her faster down there and sucked one of her nipples harder, flicking it with his tongue. She couldn't tear her eyes away from watching his hand rubbing her. "Oh God. I think I can feel that somehow." Her breath quickened and he tugged her panties down and spread her legs, then supported her body so she could watch his finger slide over her clitoris.

"Feel that, baby?" He kissed her cheek, her neck, her nipple.

"Oh my God. I feel something happening. Jesus, Earl. It feels so good!" Was she about to come? She didn't think that was possible for her.

The finale fireworks exploded in rapid concession and she shuddered, as a heated release of tension flooded her body and caused her to cry out and go limp. Panting, and clutching Earl, she pulled his head back to hers and kissed him passionately.

He gently pressed her down so she was flat of her back once more. She felt content and had the odd sensation she was floating. Tears trickled from the corners of her eyes as the last of the fireworks dissipated in the sky.

She swallowed hard and whispered, "I'd heard that some women who'd suffered a spinal cord injury like mine could have orgasms. A few years ago, I'd touched myself to see if I was like that and nothing ever happened. I don't know what you did, but you triggered something."

He kissed her again. "I wasn't sure what would happen, but I wanted to try. I read the same thing about some women having orgasms."

She caressed his face. "Have you been doing a lot of studying about how to deal with my condition?"

"Yes, I have. I love being with you, Spencer. I want to learn everything about you, how to make you happy, how to make your life more enjoyable."

The tears could no longer be contained. "I can't believe you just made me come. I thought I'd never know…" the emotion took over, and she could no longer speak. As he kissed her palm, she felt his tears on her fingertips. The tenderness in his eyes overwhelmed her, and she continued to cry because her heart was so full. So very full.

He rolled onto his back, and pulled her close, so her head rested on his chest as they let the emotions wash over them both, his fingers stroking her hair.

The faint fragrance of Earl's cologne helped to mask some of the gunpowder odor that lingered in the sky. His heartbeat thumping in a calm steady rhythm soothed her. Dare she dream about a full sex life or the possibility of having children one day? Had she been wrong to cross those off the list of things she could have, things she desperately wanted, but had convinced herself were beyond her reach?

Earl made so many things possible that she'd given up hope of ever experiencing. In tandem with Earl, she now knew once more what it felt like to dance, to run on the beach, and to jump around while playing volleyball. And for the first time, she knew what it felt like to explode in an intense orgasm that seemed to create internal fireworks that reverberated through her entire body.

She wondered if she should touch him sexually, try to make him come. When she ran her hand over his chest, down his tummy and toward his fly, he grabbed her wrist and said, "We'll save that for another night. I just want you to relax right now, drink in this moment."

She couldn't deny remaining calm, in the comfort of his embrace was exactly what she wanted, but she didn't want to be selfish. His reassurance set her at ease and she sighed, snuggled close and secretly wished they could stay like that 'til morning.

CHAPTER TWENTY-THREE
Treehouse

The treehouse on the south end had seen better days. Its wood had weathered to a dark gray and some of the nails in the flooring were raised, protruding an inch or more. Dirk hammered all the loose nails, then gave the ceiling, walls, and floor a thorough sweeping. In a tent formation, he draped sheer white fabric and several strings of battery operated white lights from the center support beam. Once he'd inflated a full-sized waterproof air mattress, he covered it in white linens and tossed down a few pillows. Gardenia petals sprinkled across every flat surface available was the finishing touch. With stereo and CD's tucked in the corner and a cooler filled with food and drink, he was almost ready for Kendal's arrival.

According to the charts, high tide would roll in around 8:00 P.M. and would begin receding around midnight. This area of the beach wasn't accessible by land during high tide. Kendal was scheduled to join him at 6:00 P.M. That gave him enough time to wine and dine her a bit before they settled in for the main event.

People rarely came to this area, but when they did, it wasn't at night. He and Kendal would have plenty of privacy. Another bonus, the tree house was in a dead zone for cell service. No calls or intruders for several hours was just what he wanted. Ted and his mom were looking after his dad. Kendal's mother was hanging out with Rafe Washington. Everyone was well taken care of, and he and Kendal could disappear from the world for a few hours—all night if they so desired.

He'd created a path of gardenia petals flanked by seashells. The only other thing he had left to do was set up the archway at the start of the path and drape gauze fabric over it and wire on some freshly cut gardenia branches loaded with blossoms.

He worked hard and fast. Once he'd completed his tasks, he put on a fresh white button-down shirt, beige trousers, and a pair of brown leather flip-flops. As he rolled his sleeves, he stepped back to admire the archway.

"This is beautiful." Kendal's voice drifted on the breeze.

He turned toward her, and the sight of her took his breath away. "Thank you. You're the beautiful one." He picked a flower from the archway as Kendal—a vision of loveliness in a strapless floral sundress with a hemline that floated around her knees—neared. She'd curled her hair and put on makeup as if she were going somewhere special. In her hand, she carried a straw tote, big enough to be used as an overnight bag.

He hoped she planned to stay with him through the night. The thought of waking up at sunrise with her in his arms after a night of making love would be a dream come true.

When she reached his side, he tucked the flower behind her ear then took her hand in his.

She blushed a similar shade of pink as the sky above—on the brink of sunset. He pressed a kiss upon her brow and inhaled the apple blossom scent of her shampoo.

"Dirk, this archway is spectacular. I can't believe you did all this."

"You haven't seen anything yet." He led her down the path. Her brown eyes sparkled. "I love gardenias. They're my favorite flower."

"I can see why. They smell amazing. Better than roses, in my opinion." He couldn't wait to see her reaction when she saw the decor that awaited them.

At the base of the treehouse ladder, he took her bag. She ascended, and he climbed behind her with a great view of her backside. He caught a glimpse of her lace panties when the breeze blew her skirt. Knowing that in a few hours those panties would most likely be on the floor made him eager to get upstairs.

Once inside, she gasped with her hands folded over her chest. "What have you done? This is like something out of a magazine." Her eyes glistened as she turned to see the area from all angles.

He sat her tote next to the cooler and went to the stereo, turning it on. Van Morrison sang "Moondance," and Dirk gathered Kendal into his arms and danced her around the bed that was in the center of the room. When Van sang, "I wanna make love to you tonight," Dirk sang along and looked deep into Kendal's eyes. He was rewarded with her kiss, one that assured him her desire matched his own.

Dirk had gone to a lot of trouble to make this night memorable. It took all the strength Kendal had to restrain the heartfelt tears that welled in her eyes from how much his loving gesture moved her. He'd seemed delighted when she'd pulled out her phone and took pictures of his handiwork. She had to do it. She wanted to remember every detail. Never would she have imagined Dirk to be so romantic. Especially considering all these years they'd teased each other like bratty kids.

After having spent more time with him one on one, she'd discovered he was as far from a brat or kid as you could get. He was a man, a man who'd bent over backward to make this moment special for her. How many women experienced something like this? Not enough, that's for sure. Every woman should be so lucky.

The delicious meal he'd prepared of shrimp and lobster, Asian slaw, and watermelon salad would've been considered gourmet, something a five star restaurant would've proudly served. And he'd said he wasn't much of a cook? His strawberry and chocolate cake for dessert blew her mind it was so good.

Tonight, their conversation had flowed effortlessly. She hadn't been nervous or addled in any way. They'd kept things light, sharing stories about some of their mutual friends on the island. Remembering some of Myrtle's antics had kept them laughing off and on throughout dinner.

Now they were winding down, the hush of night surrounding them.

Seated on the edge of the mattress, she sipped champagne from a flute and closed her eyes, breathing in the aroma of the petals scattered about the room. The warmth of Dirk's body grew closer. He lifted the glass from her hand, set it aside, and kissed her as he lowered her back on the bed.

The canopy of gauze and white lights swayed in the cool ocean breeze. Lapping waves were merely a few feet away. She rested her arms overhead in surrender, surrendering not only her body, but also her heart. Did he have any idea how deeply she cared for him, or how she longed to be his? The words, "take me," rang in her head, but she kept them to herself.

He must have read her thoughts, because he pushed her dress up and peeled her panties off slowly. The crisp evening air on her moist flesh gave her goosebumps.

Gentle strokes of his fingertips caressed her legs up and down, then glided over her abdomen.

"Let me help you out of this, sweetheart." The tenderness of his drawl called to mind southern gentleman depicted in classic movies.

She sat up and lifted her arms as he pulled her dress over her head. Once she was nude, he reclined her back down and gazed at her, his fingers roving, touching wherever his gaze travelled.

"Kendal, you're gorgeous, delicate, soft, made of silk. I don't mean to stare, but I can't help myself. You take my breath away." His lips replaced his fingers, and he planted light kisses on her forehead, eyelids, nose, cheeks, mouth, chin, neck, then back up to her ear. "Do you want me to make love to you tonight? If you're scared or want to back out, you can tell me."

She looked up into his eyes and sensed he was nervous and needed reassurance. "I want you completely, Dirk. I want to be with you tonight more than anything in my life."

His mouth claimed hers once more as he unbuttoned his shirt. She ran her hands over his muscular chest. He tossed his shirt aside and within seconds his pants floated in the air and landed by the stereo. Old school love songs had been playing one after the other all evening. Now, Dusty Springfield sang "The Look of Love," and Kendal could relate to the lyrics on a deep level. The way Dirk was looking at her must be the look of love described in the song, because it filled her with such emotion. No one had ever gazed into her eyes like that. It was as if he'd unveiled a portal into her heart and had entered her soul quietly, his presence a comforting embrace from within. She wasn't self-conscious or the slightest bit scared. Instead, she welcomed his gaze, his touch, all the sensations he was awakening in her body, and most of all—the emotions he stirred within her heart.

When he kissed his way down her ribcage and along her hipbone, she arched and parted her thighs in anticipation. Caressing his hair, she held her breath as his tongue laved affectionately lower and lower until he cleaved her open in one long stroke from her opening to that tiny bundle of nerves that seemed to be singing his name. He'd found the center of who she was as a woman, a woman she didn't realize had lived inside of her for years, neglected, and withered, never allowed to bloom.

Her sighs filled the air and an urgency followed—quick breaths, whimpers, and moans.

He hummed, "Mmm," into her folds and pleasured her with his mouth more aggressively than he had the other day in the kitchen. The frenzy of his movements had her clawing at the sheets within a few minutes. This time, she understood how to relax into the sexual energy, let it buoy her up and up. Gyrating and mouth agape, her hips undulated in rhythm with his tongue. The muscles in her canal clenched and released, clenched and released.

As she climaxed, he rose onto his knees with a condom already on. She didn't know when he'd put it on, but she'd had her eyes closed, lost in his touch for several minutes. Holding her gaze with his, he entered her then stilled. Supported on his hands that pressed into the mattress on either side of her shoulders, he studied her face.

Penetration happened so quickly, her pain was fleeting. In its place was a fullness.

"Did I hurt you?" He nuzzled her neck.

"No. Well, it hurt a little at first, but there's no pain now."

He bent his head by her ear and whispered, "I'm glad. Pain is just the opposite of what I want you to feel."

When he began to move inside her, there was no real discomfort, but it wasn't arousing her either. There was a strange pressure, a stretching of sorts. She enjoyed the closeness of Dirk, their connection, but was there supposed to be more to it than this? What was the huge deal about this act? He'd done more to excite her with his tongue and fingers earlier. He was large. She expected it to be more painful. Maybe if she wrapped her legs around him the angle of his thrusts would hit something inside her. He was moving so slowly. Did that feel good to him, or was he just trying to be gentle?

When she opened her eyes, he was staring down at her, scrutinizing her face. She said, "Why are you looking at me like that?"

He whispered, "You're thinking too hard right now. I can almost hear your wheels turning. Relax."

"I'm trying, but I'm not sure what I'm supposed to be feeling. Should I be doing something?"

He slid out of her, and whispered, "No. You're not supposed to be doing anything that doesn't come naturally."

"Did you come already?"

He chuckled into the crook of her neck, "Not yet."

"Why'd you stop?"

"Because you weren't into it. It was written all over your face."

"Oh no, I ruined it for you. I'm sorry. I was into it. I was."

"Kendal, it's your first time. It's natural for your mind to go into overdrive. This is new for you. I thought maybe you'd like to talk about it a bit before we continue."

He'd pulled out to talk? Didn't most guys just pump away until they got off? She must be lousy.

"I'm bad at this, aren't I?" She covered her face, scared to see the answer in his eyes.

"Sweetheart, it's impossible to be bad at this." He placed a hand between her legs and began to stroke her gently. "You feel amazing to me—warm, wet, tight." As he said the word "tight," he slid a finger inside her, curled it and rubbed her upper wall in a c'mere motion, his thumb petting her clitoris. Her mind quieted and her arousal grew. She bit her lower lip and moaned softly.

"There you go, baby. Let it feel good." He rolled onto his side and turned her so her back was to his chest, his mouth at her ear. He entered her again, this time he kept his fingers swirling right where she needed his touch.

With her shoulderblades to his chest, she twisted slightly so she could see his face. When he pushed himself deep inside her, it felt different than before. His thrusts matched the speed of his fingers. The orgasmic tension built within her abdomen again and she rocked against him.

"Yes, sweetheart. That's it." He studied her carefully. His voice low and coaxing.

Her eyes fluttered closed and all she could think about was the pleasure he was giving her. He increased speed, driving himself deep. She loved the way he filled her completely. Her breasts bounced. The slapping sound of their bodies colliding heightened her excitement. His other hand came up and squeezed her breast, one then the other.

She was close to climax when his pounding came to a halt and he focused entirely on rubbing her swollen clitoris. Her eyes flew open as he took her over the edge. "Dirk…"

He groaned and began thrusting again, while her walls contracted around his shaft. It seemed like her body was milking him.

She looked into his eyes and whispered, "Come for me."

Letting out a low grunt, he plunged deep one last time and kissed her, his lips ravaging hers. Cupping a breast in one hand and her delicate folds in the other, he remained buried to the hilt, his lips moving against hers, his tongue caressing hers. She now knew why people called this act making love.

She wanted to profess her love right then and there, but was afraid she'd scare him off. This was supposed to be casual sex, but there was nothing casual about the way she felt.

She pulled her head back and whispered, "I love the way you make me feel." She'd played it safe, but hoped he got the message.

He swallowed hard. There was so much passion in his blue eyes. "I love…" He kissed her again before finishing his thought. "I love being with you, Kendal."

Dirk watched Kendal sleep in his arms, and he fought the urge to wake her up and tell her he loved her. She'd asked for a fling, and more specifically, she'd expressed her desire to lose her virginity. Now she had. Having sex had been the goal, hadn't it? She'd said nothing to indicate she wanted more. But the way she'd said his name and looked at him held more intensity and passion than he even knew was possible. It felt like more, a lot more, and he could become addicted to it in no time.

Why was being with her so much different than being with other women? He'd enjoyed sex with others. Sex was always good. What's not to like? But good sex and feeling *this* connected were not the same. When she'd trembled and came while he was inside her, the feeling had been so powerful. It'd been beyond physical, way beyond.

She stirred. He whispered, "Hey, beautiful."

With a smile on her lips, she opened her big brown eyes and caressed his face. "Hey, handsome."

He savored her precious touch. "Want to go for a walk along the beach? We could even go skinny dipping if you'd like."

She grinned. "Dancing, a fantastic meal, making love, waking up in your arms, a walk on the beach, a moonlit swim, this night just keeps getting more romantic by the second."

He kissed her then whispered, "If you'd like to make love again, we can do that too."

She released a raspy laugh. "I do want to do that again, but not right now, okay?"

He snuggled her close. "Okay by me, we have the whole night."

"We sure do. Let's take that walk." As Kendal rose from the mattress, he admired her curvy body. She was natural, soft, and so damn beautiful he could hardly stand it.

They got dressed and drank some water, ate a little fruit, then walked to the small porch with a panoramic view of the Atlantic. The moonlight kissed the ocean and the stars glittered in the darkened sky. He paused to appreciate the view, then turned and began his descent down the ladder.

Something cracked. A limb breaking? A rung gave way beneath his foot. He clung to the sides of the ladder. Another rung broke, then another like dominoes. The entire ladder wobbled, and he lost his grip. He was going down and fast. Kendal reached for him as he began to fall, but it was too late.

She screamed.

A sharp pain stabbed his thigh, then he hit the ground hard, knocking the wind out of him. There was such excruciating pain in his leg. Blood soaked his trousers, and a splintered board protruded from his thigh. Holy shit, he'd been impaled. The pain was unbearable, and he broke out in a cold sweat, his heartbeat accelerating by the second.

CHAPTER TWENTY-FOUR
Emergency

Kendal called, "Dirk! Are you hurt? Dirk?"

"Jesus!" His pain-filled cry sent chills down her spine.

"Hang on! I'm coming down."

The moon's illumination cast just enough light for her to make out a splintered piece of wood—about three inches long and one inch in diameter—protruding from his upper thigh, blood soaking his pants. Did he have a head injury or more puncture wounds? It was impossible to discern from her vantage point—about twenty feet above ground.

She dug around in her tote and frantically retrieved her phone. No service. *Damn it*!

The town council had put wifi in the bath house beside Miss Judy's shack, but she'd have to cross over forty feet of water to get there.

The ladder was in pieces on the ground. She had to get down, but when she did, she wouldn't be able to come back up. Whatever she could use to help Dirk had to be tossed down before her descent.

The waterproof air mattress could be a raft, ripped sheets could be used for bandages, fresh water would be needed to rinse the wound or drink, a knife to cut fabric, and a plastic bag to wrap his leg and protect it from the saltwater. She could tie the sheets together and make a rope. She yanked the sheets off the bed and pitched the mattress over the edge of the porch, aiming away from Dirk. It landed in a patch of seagrass about three feet from him. All the other items were then loaded into her tote. Once she'd zipped the bag, she threw it in the grass as well. Knotting the ends of the sheet together, she called, "Dirk?"

"Hurry."

"I am. I am."

With one end of the sheet tied around a porch post, she made several fat knots along the length of the fabric for holding points and lowered the makeshift rope. It didn't reach the ground, but got close enough, provided she had a good grip.

She held onto the rail and climbed over the edge of the porch where the ladder had been attached and grabbed the sheet. Wrapping her legs around the fabric while holding it tight, she worked her way down its length using her hands and feet to stabilize her against the various knots she'd made. When she reached the end, she dropped the rest of the way safely to the ground, landing near Dirk.

His face was pale. He'd lost a lot of blood. Shredding strips of cloth, she said, "We got to stop the bleeding."

"Shit. It's bad." Dirk's eyes were set to panic-mode.

Her heart slammed against her ribs, but she tried her best to appear calm.

She tore open his pant leg to inspect his injury. The injury was extremely bad. The wood had pierced straight through from the back of his thigh to the front. Judging from the color of the blood and the fact that it wasn't spurting, she felt sure he hadn't opened a main artery. Thank goodness for that.

He groaned and stared down at his leg with his hands hovering like he wanted to apply pressure to stop the bleeding but didn't know where to press with that stick in the way.

Deep breaths. Deep breaths. She had to think fast. Thank God she'd taken many CPR and first aid classes due to working with kids and helping out at the nursing home.

Tourniquet was a last resort. If applied improperly or left on too long, he could lose his leg. But he was bleeding so much. This *was* life or death, there was no other choice. She was going to have to apply that tourniquet, and fast.

Leaving the wood that had skewered him in place, because she was afraid if she removed it the outward blood flow would increase, she tied strips of muslin around his leg above the injury. Tugging the bandage as tight as she could get it, the blood was still pouring out. She wedged a broken rung in the tourniquet and twisted it to help her crank the tourniquet tighter.

Dirk put his hands over hers and helped her twist the bandage as tight as they could to stop the bleeding. He groaned and trembled. Sweat beaded on his brow. Together they tied the tourniquet.

She pulled a bottle of water from her bag with the intention of rinsing the wound. His blood was clotting around the splintered wood, so she decided to leave it alone, not wanting to liquify or wash away the forming coagulation. He fell back on the sand, and pressed his forearm to his brow. His eyes fluttered closed, and he let out another low groan, but he said nothing. When he opened his eyes again, they rolled around, and he seemed unfocused.

"Stay with me, Dirk. Fight!"

She had to get him on the mattress and across the water soon. He needed medical care immediately.

The Atlantic was beginning to rush back out to sea, creating strong currents.

Dirk murmured, "Kendal…" he mumbled something else, but she couldn't understand him.

"Yes. I'm here." She squeezed his hand. "Hang in there."

She released his hand, lunged for the mattress, and dragged it closer to him.

"I need to get you on the bed, Dirk. Can you help me?"

He nodded, but appeared to be having difficulty moving his head, as if he was so depleted of energy he was about to pass out. She stood behind him and hooked her wrists under his armpits, then lifted and tugged him as he used his hands to help pull himself onto the mattress.

Her heart felt for him amidst his grunts and groans that indicated he was in a great deal of pain. She could only imagine how much it would hurt to have a jagged piece of wood through your leg like that. She hated to move him in his condition. But she needed to get to a place where she could access cell service, which meant crossing over the water. There was no way she was leaving his side. What if he bled to death in her absence? Abandoning him, even for a few minutes, was not an option. She'd never forgive herself if he made a turn for the worse while she was gone. Bringing him with her was the only way she could keep an eye on him.

Between the two of them, they got him centered the bed. She weaved strips of the sheet under the mattress and across his body and tied him down to keep him from falling off should the waves toss them about. Once she'd wrapped the plastic bag around his wound as best she could, she tucked the tote under the ripped muslin straps she'd made.

Luckily, because of the tide, she only had to drag the mattress—made heavy from Dirk's body weight—a few feet before there was enough water to buoy the bed so she could then glide the bed across the water's surface.

Sweat trickled down her back and slicked her arms. She huffed and puffed with the bitter, chemical tang of adrenaline in the back of her throat. Driving her legs into the sand, she leaned into the water and pulled Dirk behind her.

Moving against the resistance of the water was slower going than she'd hoped, but she pushed onward with a strength she didn't even know she possessed.

The breakers threatened to snatch him away from her. While still trudging forward, she tore another long scrap of sheet and then another, knotted them together and wrapped one end around her waist, and attached the other end to the strip across his chest. She couldn't risk being separated from him.

The shoreline where she was headed was still a good thirty feet away, and the water was getting deeper. It wouldn't be long before she'd be unable to stand, she'd have to swim. In this current, with the raft pulling her with it, that was going to be next to impossible. Climbing onto the bed and paddling with her hands wouldn't work, the bed was too wide for her to paddle evenly, she'd end up going in circles. Plus, she could tip the mattress over in her attempt to climb aboard.

She didn't trust her ability to swim against the current, but she had no choice. Hopefully, there wouldn't be very many patches of deep water to deal with.

Submerged to her chin, she fought back the panic that continued to rise within her. Dirk gripped the sides of the mattress, his knuckles were white. "That's it, Dirk. Hold on tight."

With her head barely above the surface she trudged on. She coughed and sputtered as saltwater flooded her mouth and stung her eyes.

The ocean floor disappeared beneath her. She could no longer touch ground and the current was dragging her and Dirk out. Kicking with all her might and using her arms to propel her forward, she swam, hard, but it didn't feel like she was covering any distance. It seemed like she was staying in the same place.

She couldn't think about that. She had to focus on not being pulled out deeper. A wave began to crest and she positioned her body to ride that wave, let the water push her and Dirk. She felt the deep suction as the wave gathered more water into itself, then she grabbed the mattress as she and Dirk surfed that wave in, just enough for her to be able to touch bottom again.

With legs planted like steel rods into the sand, she resisted the hard pull of the ocean and held her ground. Another wave approached. Could she catch this one too?

Dirk said, "We got this one. Wait for it. Wait. Now!" She jumped and grabbed the mattress and the wave rushed beneath them and drove them closer to where they needed to be.

The waves and water made it difficult to hear. If Dirk had been saying anything, she didn't know it.

Once shoulder deep, she checked to make sure he was hanging in there. He blinked and ground his teeth. "We're almost there. Hold on." She tried to assure him, but she wasn't convinced she'd told the truth. The undertow was fierce.

He closed his eyes and grimaced, but didn't cry out, even though she knew he was in agony.

She came to a patch of jagged shells, but ignored the bite of the sharp edges digging into her feet. She stomped through those shells anyway. The pain they caused was nothing compared to what Dirk was enduring.

A silhouette moved on the shore, she couldn't make out who it was, but she yelled and waved her hand, hoping they'd see her.

The person waved their arms in response. She breathed a sigh of relief and pushed forward, ignoring the trembling muscles in her legs.

Once closer, she realized the figure was Miss Judy. The frail woman ran out into the breakers, her silver dreadlocks whipping in the wind, her thin arms flailing. She made her way over to Kendal, and grabbed the other side of the mattress.

The look on Miss Judy's face mirrored the horror she was seeing—all that blood, Dirk's pale face, his leg impaled. The woman didn't comment on those things. She held herself together, even though Kendal could sense her terror.

Miss Judy patted Dirk's arm, "You're going to be just fine, son. Just fine."

Dirk tried to speak, but his words were incoherent.

She gave Kendal a nod, determination in her steely gray eyes, her bony jaw set. Together they pulled Dirk ashore.

Panting, Miss Judy held up the life alert pendant hung around her neck, "I pushed the button when I saw you two coming across. The ambulance should be here any minute. They'll head straight for my place, but I'll flag them over." She smiled down at Dirk. "When you gave me this necklace, I doubt you expected me to have to use this gadget on you, but it's sure come in handy tonight."

A weak smile curled the corners of Dirk's lips as the sound of sirens rang out.

Kendal collapsed onto the sand. Miss Judy fished a bottle of water out of the tote and passed it to Kendal. "Drink this, honey, and catch your breath."

Dirk tried to sit up, but he was strapped down. "Kendal, Kendal...are you okay? Where are you?"

She rose to her knees so he could see her. She tried to smile convincingly, but she was too exhausted to do a very good job of it.

Miss Judy untied him from the mattress. "I'll make sure they find ya." She jogged off toward her little shack.

Dirk rose onto one elbow, reached for Kendal, and

pulled her against his chest.

She was so out of breath she couldn't speak. The comfort of his caressing fingers in her hair and the sound of his heartbeat soothed her ragged nerves.

Three paramedics ran toward them and in less than a minute they had Dirk loaded on a stretcher with huge wheels able to roll in the sand. They questioned Dirk and got all his information. She thought she recognized the female medic, but wasn't sure. Dirk seemed to know her though.

Kendal was extremely shaky, but she forced herself to stand. She wasn't about to leave Dirk's side. She staggered over to the stretcher and stood by his feet. The female medic with Carrie on her name tag asked Kendal, "Are you hurt? Let me take a look at you."

Kendal waved her away. "I'm fine. I'm just exhausted. Got room in the back of the ambulance for me? I'd like to ride with Dirk to the hospital, if you don't mind."

"Of course. Is he a relative?"

"No."

"We're friends." Dirk answered Carrie on Kendal's behalf.

Friends. Yeah, they were that, but was that all? Just friends?

Dirk smiled at the pretty blonde and, in a weak voice, he said, "Can I hitch a ride to the hospital with ya?"

She grinned. "I'm going that way anyhow. I see no reason why not."

Kendal felt invisible as the paramedics rolled Dirk to the ambulance. They moved faster than she was able to walk and a gap of several feet soon separated her from Dirk.

Miss Judy grabbed her hand. "He's going to be just fine. Don't you worry. Dirk's a strong young man."

Miss Judy was notorious for avoiding people, but apparently she had a soft spot for Dirk. Didn't everyone, especially the females?

Kendal squeezed the woman's hand in response then let go. She had to jog a few feet to make it over to Dirk.

When Kendal caught up, she climbed into the back of the ambulance. Dirk motioned her closer. She leaned down so he could whisper in her ear.

"It may be less suspicious if you don't go to the hospital with me."

She couldn't believe what she was hearing. "I don't care who sees me. I'm not leaving you."

He gave her an apologetic look. "It's best if you stay here."

What the hell? She must have frowned or looked upset, because Dirk said, "I'll send Ted to clear out our stuff in the treehouse. Ted knows about us. He's known for a while. He won't say anything to anyone. Never has before."

Never has before? Never talked about the women Dirk had been with before? This was ridiculous. She didn't give a crap about keeping up pretenses now. She just wanted to know Dirk was okay. And here he was more worried about people finding out what they were up to in the treehouse than getting his leg patched up. And it had a freaking board sticking out of it! For crying out loud. He could've died. She could've died.

Her pulse thudded loudly in her ears and her jaw clamped down. Was he actually ashamed for people to know about them? What made him think most folks hadn't figured it out already anyway? And Ted…Ted was going to clear things out? Ted already knew about her and Dirk. Did he know she lost her virginity tonight? Was she another notch in Dirk's bedpost?

She wanted to ask Dirk all of those questions one after the other like her mom had a habit a doing, but Carrie was staring at her.

Kendal stifled her fury and whispered in Dirk's ear. "Thanks for your consideration."

There was a sadness in his eyes she didn't understand. He was the one who came up with the elaborate scheme to keep her "hidden." Why did *he* look like she'd hurt *his* feelings?

Carrie closed one of the back doors, and Kendal crawled out of the ambulance before the other door was pulled shut.

As the sirens blared again, tears streamed down Kendal's face. When the vehicle drove away, she fell to her knees and sobbed for so many reasons. She'd just been through a grueling and frightening experience, worried that Dirk might die, still unsure exactly how extensive his injuries were. She'd lost her virginity to a romantic man who didn't want to be seen with her in public.

Kendal flinched when Miss Judy touched her, she'd forgotten the woman was there.

"You're a brave girl, so strong. It hurts to love. It hurts so bad sometimes you want to hide away from the world, shut it all out. But you love. You love. There isn't anything else worth living for. I know. I've tried. Go on and cry brave, brave girl. The ocean drinks your tears and the sun, it will dry them in the morning. You'll see."

Dirk's leg hurt like a bitch, but he tried to block it out and focus on Kendal. He wanted her at his side, but he couldn't be selfish. Coming out to others about their relationship was her call.

She would be humiliated if word got out she'd had sex with him in the treehouse. That was private information, sacred to him. Even if folks didn't know it was her first time, just knowing she and he had been together up there—with the way it was decorated, it was obvious it was a romantic encounter, not just friends hanging out.

He could make something up. Maybe he'd tell people he and Kendal had been scoping out the old fort for one of her teacher friends who wanted to take some kids in summer camp on a field trip there. Then he could just say that they got stranded over there during high tide and he fell from the treehouse. He needed to work out the details better, but he'd figure it out.

The harebrained plan of his *might* fool folks, but if she were to cling to his side all the way to the hospital and pace the hall while the doctors did their thing, rumors would start flying all over the island. She'd made it clear she didn't want that.

She'd saved his life. The least he could do was protect her privacy.

Carrie said, "Your girlfriend didn't seem too happy about you kicking her out of the ambulance."

"She's not my girlfriend." Those words hung in the air, taunting him. She wasn't his.

Would she ever be? On Labor Day, would she push him aside? Would things go back to the way they used to be, with the two of them ribbing each other, but rarely talking, really talking? He had so many questions, but the one that tortured him the most was whether or not he could be the man she deserved for the long haul.

He'd botched everything at every turn. Even tonight. What should have been the most incredible night of their lives, ended with *her* having to rescue him.

CHAPTER TWENTY-FIVE
Snoop

After searching the internet for more articles about women who were also paralyzed from the waist down and able to orgasm, Spencer came to the conclusion it was more common than she'd previously imagined. Hoorah. Why had she been so quick to believe *she* wasn't capable of it?

There was truth in that saying, "When at first you don't succeed, try and try again." She was ready to try again with Earl. Hell yeah. He didn't know it yet, but he'd just unleashed her inner sex kitten.

At the jingle of the bell on the shop door, she turned her laptop off.

"Spencer?" Kendal called from the main showroom.

"Be right there." She rolled around the corner. One look at her friend standing in the middle of the room in a red and white polka dot dress, her fists by her side and nostrils flared sent off alarms in Spencer's head. Kendal had either been pissed off or pissed on. "What's got your brows warring with each other like Siamese fighting fish?"

Kendal felt her forehead and relaxed the muscles in her brow so she looked more normal, but then drove her fingers through her long dark hair, leaving sweaty matted clumps poked out on top of her head like mouse ears. So much for normal. Minnie Mouse was having a break down.

"Spencer, Have you heard any more news about Dirk?"

"Not in the last fifteen minutes." Good grief. Kendal had just quizzed her about this on the phone. "Why don't you go to the hospital and visit him?" She'd just got finished telling her that Dirk was scheduled to stay at least one more night for observation, but he was in stable condition according to Myrtle, who'd just stopped by to pick up a dish garden to take to him as a get well offering.

"I can't just show up. I need to make sure it's okay with him first. I've tried to text, but he doesn't answer. I doubt he even has his phone with him. It's probably still in the treehouse."

"You can call his hospital room." This was crazy. She understood why Kendal was worried about Dirk, but dang, afraid to call his room? Really?

"What if his mom answers?"

"So what. You're a friend. Quit being neurotic and give the guy a call. He's probably wondering why you haven't done it sooner."

"I don't know his room number."

"You know darn well you can find that out easy enough. What's with you?" Spencer didn't get it. This was beyond ridiculous.

Kendal leaned against a showroom table and blew out a long breath. "Last night he and I had sex, Spencer. I lost my virginity to him, okay? It was beautiful." Tears streamed down her cheeks, and she was trembling. "But in the ambulance, he looked me straight in the eye and said it'd be less suspicious if I didn't come with him to the hospital. I felt like he'd slapped me in the face. He basically kicked me out of the ambulance. The medic said it was okay for me to ride with them. I'd already cleared that. Dirk didn't want me there. He didn't want to be seen in public with me." Kendal broke down.

Spencer could feel her friend's heartbreak. Damn. She didn't know what she'd do if Earl did that to her. She'd probably have ridden to the hospital anyway, just to defy him. She wasn't the obedient type. Her mother would attest to that.

So, Kendal and Dirk *had* finally gone all the way. That was huge. She wanted to ask her what it was like, but now wasn't the time. No time was appropriate for such a personal question, but she couldn't help but be curious. She'd planned to tell Kendal about her own beautiful moment, but she'd tuck that away for now.

Dang it, seeing Kendal cry was making her tear up too. But the two of them boohooing in her shop wasn't going to solve a darn thing. She turned her chair around and rolled to the back room. "I'm calling his room. Dammit."

She looked up the hospital's phone number on her computer, called the main desk and gave the lady who answered Dirk's full name. The lady told her he was in room 248 and forwarded her call.

"Hello?" Dirk sounded groggy.

"Hey, Dirk. This is Spencer. How are you doing?"

"Hey, Spencer. It's sweet of you to check on me. I'm doing better than the doctors expected, apparently. They're sending me home tomorrow. How are you doing?"

She smiled. It was weird to have a guy in the hospital asking her how she was doing. "I'm doing better than the doctors expected too." That orgasm was proof, but he didn't need to know that.

He laughed. "All right! We should party."

"Ha. Yeah, we should. Listen, Kendal's been worried sick about you."

"Aww, well she can relax. Because of her quick thinking, I'm still kicking. Well, just one leg right now, but you know."

His voice changed when he mentioned Kendal. It wasn't

as chipper. It was almost somber. "She's here, if you'd like to talk to her."

She heard voices in the background, but couldn't make out what was being said. "I'd love to, but they're gonna be running some tests on me right now. I gotta go. But thanks for the call. Really appreciate it."

"Oh, okay. Yeah. No problem. Glad you're still with us. See ya when you get home."

"Spence, Did…umm…nevermind…it'll keep. See ya tomorrow, hopefully." He hung up.

What was he going to ask her? Had he lied about needing to go because they were going to run tests on him? She had to wonder. Why didn't he say he'd call Kendal or that she should come by or call him later?

She rotated and found Kendal leaning on the doorjamb. "See. He didn't want to talk to me."

"He did, but it was just a bad time. He's coming home tomorrow. You can see him then."

"Yeah? Just go over to his house and knock on the door? I don't think so. He knows my number. When he wants to see me or talk to me, he can dial it." Kendal crossed her arms over her chest. "I need some air. Sorry, Spencer. I didn't mean to dump all my troubles on you. I'm just… just…I don't know what I am." Her eyes misted again. "I gotta clear my head, figure it out. I'll call you later." Her mouth fell open on a gasp. "Crap, I have a gig tonight."

"It'll be all right. Call me when you get home. I don't care how late it is. You hear me?"

"Thanks." Kendal sniffled and came over and gave her a hug before walking out the door.

Spencer could feel how much Kendal cared for Dirk. She hadn't announced it, but no one gets that upset about a guy being secretive when secrecy was a mutual goal. Obviously, this fling had grown into something far more for Kendal.

But Dirk didn't seem to share her sentiment. It looked like Kendal was headed into the danger zone, and Spencer had practically pushed her into it from the start.

Her phone rang. It was Earl. "Hi. I didn't expect to hear from you so early."

"My last call got cancelled. I'm now a free man and thought I'd take you out to dinner."

Earl seized any and every opportunity to take her places. He'd never hesitated for people to see them together. Poor Kendal. God. This sucked for her.

"Spencer, you there?"

"Yeah. I'm here. Sorry, just got distracted. I'd love to have dinner with you. Come on over."

"Let me shower first and then I'll be over and help you close shop. Spencer?"

"Yeah?"

"For the first time in my life I look forward to each day. And it's because of you. No matter what kind of shit I have to deal with, knowing I'll get to see you at some point helps me power through the crud, you know?"

Wow. Sometimes that man said the most romantic things. "I do know. I feel the same way about you. Now, hurry up and get yourself over here so I can give you a great big kiss."

"Say no more." He clicked out.

She stared at the phone and smiled. What would it be like to take a shower with Earl? She needed to add that to her to-do-list.

With his mom's help, Dirk maneuvered through the side door into the kitchen on his crutches. Kendal's "Brick

House" ringtone went off. He scanned the counters and spotted his cellphone plugged into the charger by the refrigerator.

How'd it get there? Ted. Had to be. Dirk had left his phone in the pocket of his work shorts, in the treehouse.

His mother placed her car keys on a tray by the door. "That blasted phone's been ringing off the hook today. You're very popular. Kendal texted you twice this morning." Hand to her mouth, her eyes grew wide, as if she realized she'd said too much.

"Mom, did you look through my text messages?" He wouldn't put it past her. She'd done it before, but he'd been a minor, sneaking out of the house in the middle of the night. She had a reason to snoop then. But not now.

She lowered her hand and shrugged nonchalantly without establishing eye contact. "Oh honey, don't be ridiculous. When you get an incoming text the person's name flashes on the screen. Besides, she's the only one you've set a ringtone for. It's kind of hard to ignore 'She's mighty, mighty, letting it all hang out.' Fun song, by the way."

The muscles in his mouth twitched, but he wasn't about to smile and let his mother think she was off the hook. Dammit. This was serious.

He limped over to her and stared down into her big blue eyes. "Mother, did you read my text messages, yes or no?" Since she hadn't admitted nor denied, he'd bet money she had gone through all the information on his phone, which meant, she'd seen the picture he took of Kendal while she slept in the treehouse and the one he took of her in that sexy bikini on July 4th. Kendal didn't even know he had those photos.

His mother just blinked up at him and swallowed.

"Kizzie, where'd you put the remote control?" His father hollered from the living room.

Shaking her head and waving her arms, his mom brushed by him. "I don't have time for your interrogation, son." She disappeared into the living room. "It's probably stuck between the couch cushions again, dear."

She'd snooped. Not a doubt in his mind.

Dirk scrolled through Kendal's texts.

Are you okay?

How are you feeling?

Give me an update.

What's the prognosis?

His index finger hovered over the display while he tried to figure out exactly how he wanted to respond to her texts. *I'm home. Come over. Now.* Yep, that pretty much summed up how he felt, but he knew better than to type that. It sounded bossy and rude.

His mother stepped back into the kitchen. "If you're texting Kendal, ask her to bring the sheet music to "Fly Me to the Moon" when she comes over for supper this evening. She mentioned she had it."

"She's coming over for supper? When did you arrange this?"

"I called her today. I got her number from your phone. Hope that's all right."

But she hadn't looked through his messages? Yeah. Right. He took a deep breath and ground his teeth. He was two seconds from reaming his mother out for her invasion of privacy.

"Dirk, don't give me that look. There's nothing wrong with me inviting the young lady over. I've always been fond of her. She's a darling girl. Besides, she helped your father and got him playing the piano again and she damn near saved your life. The least I can do is feed her a good home-cooked meal to show my appreciation. Plus, she said she'd give your dad a piano lesson tonight if he felt up to it."

Crap. What could he say to that?

His mother stared at him and grinned. "Shut your mouth, son. Text the girl or call her, but don't just stand there."

When his mom left the room again, he dialed Kendal's number. He was routed to voicemail when she didn't pick up. "Hey, I'm home. Mom would like for you to bring the sheet music to that fly on the moon song when you come over this evening." He paused trying to think of what else to say. *Beep.* He took too long.

Fly on the moon? Did he really just say that? Way to go, genius. Should he call back and correct his mistake, tell her he missed her, couldn't wait to see her?

"Did you call her back?"

He jumped. His mother was right behind him. He didn't even hear her walk up. "Yeah. I asked her to bring the music. What time will she be here?"

His mother glanced at the clock over the sink. "In about an hour. I moved some of your things into your old room so you wouldn't have to climb the stairs to the garage apartment. There's a nice shirt and pair of pants in the closet, if you'd like to change out of those shorts. It's up to you."

"Thanks." It was thoughtful of her to look out for him. He wasn't much up to climbing stairs. She was right about that, but he didn't like the idea of her going through his stuff, even though he had nothing to hide in his apartment. No, all his dirty secrets were on his phone, and she'd already helped herself to those.

What if she blabbed about Kendal and him?

He was being paranoid. That wasn't her style.

She'd warned him and Ted all their lives against gossiping or sharing personal information about other people and how it tended to turn around and bite you in the butt. Best to keep your mouth shut, that was the Davis motto.

But what if she let it slip about him and Kendal? It could happen. Anyone could make a slip up. "Mom, Kendal's a very private person and—"

"Say no more, son. Whatever you've heard about her or whatever she's shared with you in confidence is none of my concern. I respect a person's privacy."

Said the woman who helped herself to his contact list, read his text messages, and who knew what else.

Kendal wiped her sweaty palms on her cotton dress and knocked on the door of Dirk's house. Would he be happy to see her? Would he be furious? She used the sheet music to fan herself, but the flimsy paper was no match for the humid air.

Dirk hobbled toward the glass storm door on his crutches. When their eyes met, he broke into a wide smile. Thank God. He appeared genuinely glad to see her. Her heart jumped, and she took a deep breath.

He opened the door and invited her in. As she stepped into the foyer, he kissed her cheek. "God, you're a sight for sore eyes." He put his face in her hair and breathed in. "Mmm." His breath tickled her neck, and she wanted to wrap herself around him and breathe him in too.

Instead, she said, "How are you feeling?"

He stepped back. "Doing a lot better than I was the last time you saw me. You do realize you're my hero, right?"

She laughed. "You helped, if I recall. I'm just glad you're okay. I was really worried."

He cupped her face and tilted her chin up. "I mean it, Kendal. You're my heroine. I'm addicted to you."

She laughed and poked him in the ribs. "You know how that sounds."

"I need a fix. I need a big hit of Kendal." He glanced

over his shoulder then leaned down and kissed her mouth.

She got so swept up in his kiss, she dropped the sheet music. When they parted and she bent to pick up the paper, Dirk gently stroked her bottom and her legs quivered. She got tingles in places only he had ever explored.

As they stepped into the kitchen, Dirk's mother said, "Hi Kendal, so glad you could make it. George has been asking about you all day."

Dirk's dad sat at the table, sipping tea. He looked up and said, "There's my girl. Come sit by me." He patted the chair beside him.

Dirk smiled and stepped aside so she could move to the seat Mr. Davis intended her to sit in.

Once the family was all settled around the table, Kizzie smiled. "Hope everyone's hungry."

Kendal couldn't remember the last time she'd sat down for supper with a family. Her dad had always insisted on eating his meals in his chair in front of the T.V. After he left, Kendal's mother tended to do the same thing. Half the time they just ate frozen dinners warmed in the microwave, because her mom was too depressed to cook and Kendal was too tired to bother after all the chores she had to do. The only time her mom set the table was when she'd invited some guy over she was trying to fix Kendal up with.

But the Davises were a family that ate together. She could tell. This was normal for them, and she liked being a part of it.

Halfway through the meal, Kizzie turned to Kendal and said, "I'll never forget that time you came to Dirk's seventh birthday party and pinned the tail on Louise Moore's butt instead of the donkey, and Myrtle Pinkerton stood up in a room full of kids and said, 'Wups. Wrong ass.' The look on your mother's face. I nearly died."

Kendal laughed. "Mama got so mad at Myrtle for

cussing."

"I know. She wouldn't let you come to anymore birthday parties at my house."

"It wasn't just your house. She put a stop to my party going period."

"Aww. I didn't know that. I guess I blew that one. I was trying to recall funny stories, and I just opened an old wound. I'm sorry."

"No, Mrs. Davis. You didn't open an old wound. I want you to know, I still have all those party prizes you sent me after that. I keep them in a little cigar box I decorated with macaroni and glitter in the third grade."

"You kept those silly things? That's so sweet. I wasn't even sure the teachers would pass them on."

"Yep. Every year on Dirk's birthday, I got a little package from you. All the way up to middle school. It meant a lot to me."

Dirk said, "Mom, I didn't know you did that."

"Well, I felt like Kendal should be included, even if her mother didn't agree. All the other kids were getting prize packets. Seemed mean to leave her out."

Dirk smiled and looked at Kendal. She wondered if he realized how lucky he was to have such a loving family, but she knew the answer. They were lucky to have him too.

After supper, Mr. Davis escorted Kendal to the piano, where they played old songs and sang for a good solid hour before he yawned and stretched and said he was tired.

Kizzie ushered Mr. Davis down the hall.

Dirk whispered in Kendal's ear. "Alone at last." He led her over to the cream leather sofa in front of a large window with a view of the ocean, barely visible in the dim evening light. Their home had a casual beach vibe, decorated in serene blues and greens. Dirk motioned for her to sit on the sofa. She thought he might sit in the large chair upholstered in a shell motif fabric facing the couch, but he opted to sit beside her.

When he got situated and propped his crutches against the end table, he faced her and took both of her hands in his. "I'm so glad Mom invited you over. Sorry I didn't return your messages right away. My phone was here while I was in the hospital."

The messages weren't a big deal, she'd figured he didn't have his phone on him, but she'd tried anyway, just in case. "It was nice of your mom to extend the offer. No worries about the texts. I'm just glad you're okay and home safe and sound. What did the doctors say?"

"They said you were wise to leave the wood in place, and to make a tourniquet to stop the bleeding. They also said had you not done those things, I wouldn't be here today."

She was at a loss for words.

"The thing that gets me the most is how you managed to get me across the water like you did. My memory's a little blurry about everything, but I do recall you turning into Supergirl at some point."

She laughed. "More like Crabgirl."

He wrinkled his nose. "Crabgirl doesn't suit you. How 'bout I call you my mermaid, that's more like you. A siren who can swim like a fish. Mermaid's better than Little House on the Prairie, right?"

She smiled, but when she considered him giving her a new nickname, she didn't like it. "I don't mind Little House. I've grown used to it."

"But that title no longer fits." He kissed her knuckles.

She pulled her hands from his. What was he doing this for? Was he kissing her hands because he missed her, or was he just charming her, playing his role to keep the game going between them? Game. That term certainly fit their relationship. A game to make it to the next level sexually. A game to keep others from knowing what they were doing. He wasn't a game to her, not anymore.

He furrowed his brows. "What's wrong?"

"Dirk, what we shared in the treehouse was so special to me. So very special. Then you fell and I thought you might not make it." The night of July 5th had been the most monumental of her life. She could hardly absorb it all. "I stayed away from the hospital, but I've been a wreck worrying about you. To be honest, I don't know how to act around you now. I'm not sure if I should keep my distance, hug you, kiss you, pretend we hardly know each other."

"Act the way you feel, Kendal. You don't have to be on guard here. My family knows how to keep their mouths shut. Well, Dad doesn't, but no one takes what he says too seriously anyway. Ted knows about us. I'm pretty sure Mom's figured it out. Dad already thinks we're getting married."

"Ha. You're Dad is a trip." She gazed into his eyes. He opened his arms, and she dove into them.

"You can relax here. My family loves you." Dirk held her close, his fingers twined through her hair, his lips pressed to her forehead.

He nudged her head up with his fingers. Looking into her eyes, he drew her face close to his. He rubbed his nose against hers then kissed her mouth tenderly.

All those raging nerves and doubts—that had been churning inside like a fierce current for the past two days—calmed. On a sigh, her stress seemed to float out of her.

His kisses reassured her he cared, and no matter how they defined their relationship, this truth was all she really needed to know.

CHAPTER TWENTY-SIX
Cottage

Earl hadn't told Spencer that he'd recently moved into a nice furnished cottage, previously occupied by a wealthy woman who'd been confined to a wheelchair. The place was modified with every convenience Spencer could ever wish for, and he'd wanted to surprise her.

When they pulled up into the driveway of his new place, her eyes grew large. "You live here?"

"Yep. As of three days ago. I would have brought you over sooner, but it took me a little time to unpack and get settled in."

"This place is beautiful. I've always admired the landscaping. The woman who used to live here was one of the founders of the botanical garden in Crystal Cove."

"Millie Norris, yes, I know. She used to visit here often, but this wasn't her main house. The one in Crystal Cove is huge."

"I was sad when she passed away. She was such an inspiration, the way she grouped flowers together in unexpected ways. I love her artistry."

"I thought you'd like all the flowers around the place. When I first saw it, I thought of you."

"Did you buy this place?"

"No, not yet. I'm renting for now. Her kids are in some

sort of property dispute and aren't looking to sell."

"That happens a lot. Loved ones pass away, and the surviving family members end up getting into arguments over who gets what." She smiled. "Guess I'm lucky to be an only child."

He nodded. "When my mom died she made sure everything was divided evenly between me and Mazy. My dad got the short end of the stick, actually. It wasn't until recently that I discovered that had been his choice. A few years ago I ended up signing my property over to Mazy when I served time. I wanted to make sure she had something to sell, in case she couldn't make ends meet. She tried to sign it back over to me a few months ago, but I told her no. It didn't seem right. She's built a new house on the land, and she and Trent are getting married. I didn't want to move in right next door. I wanted them to have their space."

"That was nice of you. Not many people would have seen it like that."

"It's not all selfless love, trust me. That property holds a lot of memories, and not all of them are good ones. I wanted a fresh start. A place to create new, happy memories. And look at this place, all these bright flowers everywhere. Who couldn't be happy here?"

Spencer drove her chair up the ramp and Earl opened the front door.

Once inside, Spencer covered her mouth and gazed around the living room. He wasn't sure if she liked what she saw or was upset.

"You okay?"

She lowered her hand. "That huge picture behind the sofa is made from pressed flowers. The coffee table is redwood. I love it."

"Wait 'til you see the kitchen and the bathroom."

She rolled into the kitchen. When he flipped the switch

to lower the counter height, she let out a squeal. "Do it again. Do it again!"

He raised and lowered the counters again and grinned.

She rolled over to the sink that was open underneath to make room for her knees. "I can actually use this. It's perfect. I've not been able to wash dishes in the sink in such a long time. I'm shocked that I've missed it. Let's cook at home tonight."

She'd called this place "home." He couldn't have been happier.

She did donuts in her wheelchair and threw her hands in the air. "I love this kitchen!"

"Let me show you the bathroom." He guided her into the large wheelchair accessible bathroom with a tub that had a side door and a lift to help her get in and out of her chair for bathing. Everything was automated so she could do it herself.

She pulled herself up by the handle hanging near the tub, sat down in the lift, then hit the switch. The long metal arm moved her into the tub and gently lowered her to the seat. She closed the door on the side and reached the water spout easily. Without turning on the water, she pretended to shower using the hand held sprayer. "I can take a shower or a bath all by myself. No more having to get someone to help me."

He didn't realize she'd been relying on assistance for bathing, but he was glad she was so thrilled about the idea of being able to do it herself now. He didn't mind helping her, but he could tell being independent was a big deal for her.

"You need a roommate?" She grinned up at him.

He knew she was joking. She wasn't about to move out of her folks house so soon in their relationship, but the idea of living with her certainly appealed to him.

"This is a one bedroom cottage. We'd have to share a

bed."

She blushed. "Show me the bedroom, Earl."

That quiet command got his blood going. He wanted to make love to her for hours, but he was afraid his body would fail him. It was time to have that dreaded talk. "It's right this way."

He led her to the large bedroom with a view of the garden. Once he'd picked Spencer up and placed her in the middle of the bed with her head propped up on a mass of pillows, he stretched out beside her. "Spencer, there are some things I need to tell you."

Her eyes never left his. "I'm all ears."

"And cute ears at that." He tweaked one of her lobes, then ran a finger down her nose. "Everything about you is perfect to me."

Her smile revealed sadness. Didn't she believe him? "Really, Spencer, you're beautiful just as you are, inside and out. I never want you to doubt that."

Concern crept across her face, drawing lines in her forehead. "There's a but in there. I can feel it. What's wrong?"

He blew out a breath. "For a long time, I haven't felt like I measured up, like I wasn't good enough for anyone."

"But you are good enough. More than good enough."

"Well, here's the thing—all those insecurities have taken their toll on me, Spencer." How was he going to be able to phrase the fact that he had trouble getting it up without sounding like a douche?

She caressed his arm. "I know they have, but it's okay to move on."

"I'm trying. I really am. What I'm hem-hawing around about is…I suck in bed." There he said it, and yeah, he sounded like a douche.

She looked at him quizzically. "Says the man who gave

me my first orgasm?"

He couldn't help but grin. "I was using my fingers, babe. I'm good with my fingers and my mouth. My other head" He pointed to his crotch. "Well, it has a mind of its own."

"Hard-headed little rascal, huh?"

"Ha! I wish. That's the problem. Sometimes, I want it to be hard, and it just plays dead."

"Have you spoken to a doctor about it?"

"Yeah. He said it was psychological. But if my mind wants to have sex, why does my body refuse to respond? It makes no sense. I've taken supplements for it for years, but I can't tell that they've made much difference."

She pushed herself up so she was sitting more upright on the bed. "Okay. I want you to hear me out about this. If I had not been able to orgasm, would you have still wanted me?"

"Yes. I'm glad you can enjoy sex, but even if that hadn't been the case, I would have still wanted to be with you, in whatever capacity we could."

She grabbed his hands and pulled them to her chest. "I feel the same way about you, Earl."

"What do you mean?"

"I mean, even if we can't have intercourse, I want to be with you in whatever capacity we can. You're so much more than a sexual partner for me. I never thought a sex life was even possible for me, but I wanted to be with you. I had a crush on you for quite a while before I got the nerve up to get you to come over to fix the refrigerators, which weren't really broken, by the way. I can't tell you how bad I felt when you hurt your back over my deception."

"You had a crush on me? I'd had a crush on you too. I was so excited when you asked me to come look at the coolers."

"Everything happens how it's supposed to, they say. I

never viewed my accident as the loving hand of fate, but it has left its mark on my life, and I like who I've become. Just like your past has left its mark on you, and I like who you've become too."

"You always know what to say. I'm always such a bumbling idiot."

"No you aren't. I love how open and honest you are. Not many people reveal their weaknesses so freely. We all have things about ourselves that we'd like to change. Sometimes, those things are shallow and we're better off not focusing on them, other times we discover a chink in our armor that really does need repairing or rebuilding. I think it's good to strive to be your best self."

"You don't have anything that needs changing, Spencer. Trust me."

"We all have imperfections, Earl. But to find someone who accepts us completely as we are is rare. You accept me, completely, right?"

"Of course I do. I worship you, Spencer. You mean the world to me."

"Then you need to listen to me very carefully, I accept you as you are, Earl, completely. How we love and make love may not be typical, but screw being typical. I don't care about everything always running smoothly, no messes, no awkwardness. I don't care if we have starts and stops, nights we just hold each other, or nights when go without sleep because we can't stop touching each other. I want everything you have to give, in whatever form you're able to give it."

He froze. No one had ever said anything so profoundly beautiful to him. He knew he could always find a way to show her how much he adored her. His ways may not always be wild nights in the sheets, but he'd make sure she knew she was loved. Words were beyond his reach. What could he say? He didn't know. He did what his heart urged him to do.

He pulled her tight against him and kissed her until they were both left trembling and breathless.

Spencer pushed away slightly and tilted her head up to look into his eyes. "Earl, you aren't perfect, and that's okay, because you're perfect for me. As is."

CHAPTER TWENTY-SEVEN
Crabs

Dirk climbed the stairs to his apartment and didn't even need to use his crutches to do it. He grabbed a cold drink and took a seat in front of the T.V., propped his feet up and channel surfed. It felt good to be home and kicking back, even if home was just a few feet away from his folks. He eyed his ping-pong table and envisioned Kendal's yellow piano in its place. It'd fit just fine. Whoa. Where did *that* thought come from? One step at the time.

First step, get Kendal up here.

He'd avoided bringing girls home because he didn't want to run the risk of one of them upsetting his father like a couple of girls in high school had done. Also, he thought living at home made him look lame. He'd convinced himself that until he got his life together, he wouldn't be a good provider or "boyfriend" material.

But then came Kendal—soft, sweet, no demands, no judgment. He'd stopped feeling like he needed to get his life together. Face it, when was this so-called together life gonna happen? When they had to put his father in a home, or worse, his dad passed away? Dirk wasn't in a hurry for either of those options. Did that mean *his* life was going to be on hold indefinitely? That was crazy. Maybe working odd jobs wasn't such a bad thing. And maybe, just maybe, including a girl—Kendal specifically—in his life was a good thing. It sure felt good.

She had a way of making him believe that he was as together as he needed to be. She knew who he was and accepted him. Maybe it was time he accepted himself and let his heart take the lead for a change.

He kept on the lookout for her car. When she arrived, he met her in the driveway.

She got out of her car with a bright pink bag in her hand. Smiling at him, she said, "Hey, look at you without your crutches. Awesome."

He did a little foot shuffle and ignored the pain that shot up his leg. That's what he got for showing off.

"Woohoo. You sure got your groove back." She held up the bag and said, "Pam made a fresh batch of saltwater taffy. I thought you might like some."

"Sounds great." He walked over to her and gave her a hug. He wanted to do way more than that, but they were outside where anyone who happened by could see. A friendly hug wouldn't seem out of place. A kiss? No way to deny that one. Plus, the last time he'd attempted to kiss her in the driveway she'd squirmed away.

"I would like *some*." He scanned her body. She blushed and lowered her gaze to his lips. Good. They were on the same page.

He nudged her chin up with his finger and lowered his voice to a whisper. "Let's go hang out in my apartment and nibble on some of that sweet stuff you got there."

She stammered, "Your apartment?"

"Mmmhmm. We could do all sorts of nibbling in my lair."

She swayed and touched his chest to steady herself, her breathing was shallow, and her nipples were visibly hardened beneath her T-shirt.

He loved knowing he could get her stirred up so easily. He took her hand and led her upstairs.

When he opened the door to his bachelor pad, she said, "So this is where all the magic happens?"

He laughed. "If you call 'all the magic' snoring and watching sports on T.V., yeah."

"No, I meant this is where you lure your women."

"You're the only girl I've ever brought up here, Kendal." He watched her expression change from playful to skeptical then shift to tender. He added, "You're the only girl I've ever *wanted* to bring up here." That brought a trembling smile to her lips.

"I'm honored, Dirk. I just assumed a guy who'd…well, you know."

"A guy who'd been around the block as many times I had would've brought many girls home?"

"Yeah."

"I admit I've had my share of fun with the ladies, but I take my home and family seriously." He hoped she'd get the message that he was taking *her* seriously, very seriously.

Kendal watched Dirk peel open a piece of taffy, gently pulling back the waxed paper wrapper, carefully removing the soft pink candy, then neatly folding the paper and setting it off to the side. It reminded her of the way he'd undressed her in the treehouse, taking his time, handling her with patience and tenderness.

He slowly put the entire piece of taffy on his tongue, and she stared at his mouth working that candy the way he'd worked her.

"Mmm, strawberry." He raised his brows and caught her gaze in his. "Tastes like our first real kiss."

She tried to keep her breathing in check, but couldn't. Her mind was too busy remembering all the delicious things

Dirk had done to her, all the things she wanted him to do again.

Was he really just going to sit there on the couch with her and eat candy? No way. Was she going to have to instigate something else?

He gave her a knowing smile and winked.

Ha. That mischievous glint in his eye told her he knew exactly what she was thinking. He was such a tease.

He opened a yellow piece of taffy and ate it. "Mmm, lemon. Reminds me of the lemonade you made for our first picnic."

"Thank goodness Pam didn't make any cayenne pepper candies."

He laughed. "These are soft and sweet. Just the way I like them. Just like you." He pulled her dress up to her thigh and caressed her bare leg.

He opened a purple piece of taffy. She was dying.

"Mmm, grape."

"That flavor would have been a reminder of the edible panties I wore, if my mom hadn't interrupted us."

He nearly choked. He coughed for a few seconds then caught his breath and said, "Details, please."

"I had on a pair of edible panties that fell off in the kitchen while I was talking to Mama after she just popped in on us, and she thought the undies were a grape fruit roll-up."

He coughed some more with a big smile on his face. "What possessed you to buy edible panties?"

"Leah took me and Spencer to Kinky Joys. That's when I bought that how-to video."

He squirmed when she mentioned that video. "I see. Umm, Kendal. I was going to try not to jump your bones the minute I got you alone today, but you're making that very *hard*."

"How hard?"

He looked down and so did she. It was her turn to say, "Mmm."

They'd done nothing but talk and kiss for weeks while he was under his parents' roof, recuperating. She'd enjoyed getting to know him and his family better. She felt close to the Davis clan now, a part of it even. That was nice, great, fantastic, but dang it, she *wanted* him. *Now*!

Daring to be bold, she reached down and stroked him over his shorts.

He sucked in a quick breath. "Kendal, baby, I'm trying to —"

"Stop trying." She straddled him, careful to be gentle around his injury. He held her hips as she settled onto his lap. With her hair falling around their faces like a dark tent, they breathed as one, staring into each other's eyes. "I want you, Dirk, not the man you think you need to be. I want *you*, all of you."

Dirk closed his eyes when Kendal lowered her face to his and kissed him. Her fingers were in his hair and her plush mouth on his. Everything about her was soft, sweet, and loving. She fit in with his family. His crazy schedule didn't phase her, and she accepted him fully. He never expected to click with her so well. In the past, he'd always put up a front with girls, wanting to show them a good time, give them a few thrills and just as many laughs.

It wasn't like that with Kendal, at least not anymore. The past few weeks hanging out with her at his parents' house while his wound healed had given him time to break through her shell and his own. They were comfortable with each other in a way he'd never experienced. He didn't need to be "on." He could let his guard down. She was right. It was time for him to stop trying and just go with it.

He loved how relaxed she was in his arms, not trembling with a scared look in her eyes and a million thoughts whizzing through her head so fast he could almost hear her wheels turning. There was a peaceful easiness about her, a quiet surrender.

She peeled off her shirt and placed his hands on her breasts, over the cups of her white lacy bra. He gently squeezed, and watched in amazement as she unhooked the back of her bra and let it fall away from her breasts. Fondling her gently, he marveled at the delicate flesh in his grasp

"Yours," She whispered as he suckled her nipple, giving herself to him, making him hungry for all she had to offer, her body, her heart.

The thought of her being his for more than the summer had been keeping him awake at night. Was it what he really wanted, to be monogamous? Would she even consider it? Once he crossed that line with her, there would be no turning back. One of two things would happen; they'd either fall in love and make it work, or they were both headed for heartbreak. Neither one of them had experience in the relationship-zone. It would be the blind leading the blind, as the old saying goes.

Right now, he was going to go with it, not strike up a long discussion or lay down any new rules. There was no need to define everything he was feeling. At the moment, she was his, and he was hers. Even if that fact was unspoken, it was currently true.

She wrapped her legs and arms around him as he stood and carried her to bed. It was time find out what she liked best, and the only way to do that was to explore. He tossed her on the duvet and started with her mouth.

As soon as their lips locked, Dirk succumbed to the fire raging within Kendal. Her frantic movements to disrobe him showed him she was as hungry as he was.

They ravished each other, no holding back.

Naked with their bodies braided as one, he took her to the edge and beyond again and again. The way she trembled, the exquisitely erotic faces she made, the delight in her cries as her passionate voice ignited a primal need in him to make her his—these intense and uninhibited moments unlocked a part of him he'd never set free before. He couldn't take his eyes off her. Every time she said his name, he became stronger, because he became more secure in his role as her man. Even when he was being dominate, he was worshipping her, and he knew he'd never be the same. He was okay with that, more than okay.

The next morning, Kendal awoke with Dirk's hand cradled between her thighs. The warm weight of his palm was comforting and reassured her she was his. She stared at his face as he slept heavily next to her. His breathing was deep and steady. He'd given himself tirelessly through the night, and she'd taken greedily, until she was rendered boneless.

She had a morning piano student and needed to go home to clean up before heading to Crystal Cove. She wanted to kiss Dirk, but chose not to because she hadn't brushed her teeth yet. Besides, he was sleeping so peacefully, he would probably appreciate being left undisturbed. She slipped out of bed and dressed. After placing a note on his bedside table to let him know she loved spending the night with him, she quietly exited his apartment and crept down the stairs. She saw his mother Kizzie through the kitchen window. Kizzie smiled and waved. Surprisingly, Kendal wasn't embarrassed.

She returned Kizzie's smile and waved back as she headed toward her car.

Low on gas, she stopped by Filly's on her way home. Ashley was working her usual early morning shift.

When Kendal paid for her gas, a cup of coffee, and a muffin, Ashley said, "Have you seen Dirk lately?"

Kendal didn't answer. She didn't want to share any information about Dirk, and she didn't want to lie either. It was none of Ashley's business, so she simply kept her mouth shut and put cream and sugar in her coffee and hoped Ashley would assume she was not quite awake yet.

"I was only asking because I saw your car at his house this morning on my way to work."

Dirk lived on a dead end road. Ashley must've gone out of her way to find that information out. Again, Kendal chose to not say anything.

"He's good. I wouldn't blame you for getting some of that. I know I've indulged quite a bit. Whenever I'm in between boyfriends, Dirk's the first guy I call."

"Ashley, it's too early in the morning to have this conversation. "

"Stop being such a prude. Kendal. Has he blindfolded you and broken out the tickler yet?" Ashley looked at her with a wide-eyed innocent expression. Innocent. Right.

Dirk hadn't blindfolded Kendal, he'd gazed into her eyes with such intensity she felt naked to the core, and it was an amazing feeling to be that naked and feel that safe.

Kendal sipped her coffee nonchalantly. "I got to run, Ashley. Have a good day." Kendal was still basking in the afterglow of being with Dirk. Even Ashley's catty remarks to goad her couldn't roust her off her serene little cloud.

Once she'd gone home and taken a shower, however, Ashley's words kept ringing in her head and somewhere inside Kendal a roller derby girl began to skate furiously with the desire to knock Ashley on her ass. Visions of handfuls of blonde hair in Kendal's fists were so real she could almost feel the straw-like strands being yanked from Ashley's scalp.

Dirk appreciated the sweet note Kendal left him that morning, but it didn't satisfy his need to see her face and hold her in his arms. He felt off, waking up alone. He didn't like it. He'd always been alone in that bed, but this morning it felt too damn empty. The soft, warm, presence of Kendal was missing, and his whole day had been off kilter ever since. He had to see her.

With an hour to spare before his bridge tending shift commenced, he stopped by Kendal's apartment. She greeted him at the door with that sincere and radiant smile of hers. When he pulled her into his arms, all was right with the world again.

They shared a slow, romantic kiss. It wasn't sizzling with sexual energy or gentle and ultra-sweet. It was more like —"there you are, my other half. I'm now whole again."

After a few minutes of small talk on the couch, she said, "Ashley is driving me crazy. I can't stand when she talks about having sex with you."

Why would Ashley be saying anything about having sex with him? They'd only slept together three times in the past five years and the last time was over six months ago. "What was she saying?"

"She knew I slept at your place. So, she's obviously spying on us. No real surprise there. But this morning she asked me if you'd blindfolded me yet and used your tickler on me. I haven't been able to get the image of you and her doing that out of my head since."

Dirk recalled Ashley asking him to do that to her. He'd humored her, but it all felt kind of silly to him, contrived.

She'd squirmed and squealed in a fake sort of way, like she thought that was what he wanted to see. He hadn't been into it. It seemed more like a low-budget porn than anything. Had she been really into it, he may have felt differently, but he was pretty good at knowing when a girl was fully engaged and when she was putting on a show. Ashley was all about putting on a show.

The fact she was talking about him to Kendal at all irritated him, but for her to be saying shit like that pissed him off big time. He was going to have to shut that girl up once and for all. No, he wasn't going to punch her in the face or anything, but she obviously needed a stern talking to.

Dirk kissed Kendal's brow. "I'm sorry she's talking like that. Truth is, the blindfold thing was a huge turn off for me. It wasn't my idea and had she not worn a blindfold she would have seen me rolling my eyes. I'll straighten Ashley out. She's been after me all summer. I don't know what her problem is, but you best believe that's all about to get sorted once and for all." He wasn't sure how he was going to make good on that promise. It wasn't like he could control Ashley, but he could tell her off, and she deserved it.

"Thanks. I've been trying to not pour fuel on the fire with her. I've felt like confronting her many times, but I've always held to the belief that sometimes the best way to put out the fire is to be the water. But I have to tell you, my well is running dry where she's concerned. I may be kind of quiet and nice in general, but when provoked, I can be feisty."

"Feisty, huh?" She'd shown him she was strong when she rescued him, but she'd never really barked at him about anything, with the exception of threatening to take a blow torch to his dick after the pork rind incident. Looking back on that now, it cracked him up. She had a way of surprising him. It was pretty cool. "I'd like to see this feisty side."

A wicked little smile spread across her face. "That can be

arranged."

Damn. That look in her eyes was giving him naughty thoughts and he didn't have time to make good on them. "I'd like for you to come back over tonight, but I don't want you to disappear on me the next morning. I was kind of sad this morning when I had no Kendal to kiss."

"Aww. Consider yourself lucky on that one. I didn't have my toothbrush."

"Ha. Is that why you snuck off without kissing me goodbye?"

She blushed. "Yeah. I—"

"Pack a goodie bag filled with whatever you want to leave at my place. I don't want to ever miss out on a good morning kiss again. I'll clear out a drawer for you and make some room in my medicine cabinet. Okay?" He'd move all his stuff into the garage if she wanted his whole damn closet. He didn't care. As long he could wake up with her in his arms, he'd be a happy man. And the really weird part about this was—he wasn't freaked about this sudden change. It felt right. He was excited more than anything.

She stared at him, her mouth opened as she processed what his request implied. Then she beamed. "I don't need much space. Thank you." The kiss his request had earned him said it all. She seemed excited too. And happy. That was the main thing. She seemed happy.

Yep, all was right with the world.

A couple of weeks later...

"Ashley is just jealous, Kendal. You can't let her get to you." Spencer wanted to strangle Ashley for spreading lies about Kendal, saying she'd flipped when Ted started seeing

Heidi. According to Ashley, Kendal was spending a lot of time at the Davis' house lately so she could worm her way into Ted's life, toying with Dirk in hopes of making Ted jealous. Good thing everyone knew better than to listen to the wanna-be-Barbie anyway.

Kendal grabbed the broom and began sweeping up the flower cuttings on the floor in the back room. "I've been trying to ignore her. But what infuriates me most is the fact that she and Dirk *have* slept together. She knows him intimately, and she keeps saying stuff just to push my buttons."

"She doesn't know for a fact you and Dirk have been together. She only suspects. She's probably hoping by over-sharing in front of you that you'll announce whether or not you and Dirk have or haven't done the deed. Plus, I guarantee she's betting on the notion of you toying with Dirk to be enough to make him want to stay away from you."

"It's none of her business what goes on between me and Dirk."

"Exactly. And if she had an ounce of class, she wouldn't talk about what's gone on between *her* and Dirk."

"True. I was glad he called her on it and told her she needed to stop running her mouth. I thought that'd shut her up, but it's only made her gossip more. He claims she's been after him all summer, the more he says no, the harder she chases."

"She's used to getting any guy she wants. This is probably the first time she's been turned down, and she's not handling it well." Spencer knew Kendal's fuse had been lit, and she was close to exploding all over Ashley and blowing the girl out of the water. But a fight was just what Ashley wanted, and if Kendal snapped, she'd end up looking like a crazed drama queen and people would start wondering if Ashley was telling the truth. As long as Kendal acted like Ashley was being so ridiculous she wasn't worth her time, Ashley was the one creating the drama and folks would see right through it. The girl was jealous and talking smack.

Spencer wanted Kendal to hang in there and let Ashley throw punches in the air and wear herself out. "Don't worry. The minute someone else comes along for her to sink her claws into, she'll move on."

"You're right. I need to push her out of my thoughts. Let's talk bout something else. How are things going with you and Earl?"

Spencer told Kendal all about the cottage and how wonderfully things were going with Earl. She didn't pull an Ashley and go into the nitty gritty about their sex life. However, as it turned out, Earl's "issues" were gradually fading as the two of them spent more time together.

Spencer handed Kendal a box of patriotic ribbon and decor to be put on the top shelf. "Do you have plans this evening?"

"I'm meeting Dirk at nine, but I'm free 'til then. Why?"

"Feel like a quick return trip to Kinky Joys? I'd like to buy one of those sex swings."

Kendal nearly dropped the box she was holding. "Whoa. You caught me off guard with that one. But sure, I can run you to Wilmington this evening. We can grab some dinner while we're in town. My treat."

As Kendal stepped down, Spencer said, "I can't believe how this summer has panned out for both of us. I have to tell ya, I never dreamed I'd turn into a little nymphomaniac, but I'm having a blast."

Kendal laughed and wrinkled her nose, "I never expected to like sex so much either. I can't seem to get enough. I've been spending every night with Dirk for the past two weeks, and he claims he has a lot left to show me. I thought for sure we'd done it all by now, but apparently not, and I find that thrilling. I'm not gonna lie."

"I know what you mean." Spencer and Kendal shared a sincere, long smile. Spencer imagined her own eyes looked just as dreamy as Kendal's.

A tall dark-haired guy entered Big Kabloom. Kendal whispered. "It's that violin playing jerk from New York who thinks he's God's gift."

Spencer peered into the lobby at the preppy snob. "Did he move down here?"

"I hope not. He annoys the crap out of me."

Spencer shrugged. "I'll see what I can find out." She rolled into the showroom and smiled. "Afternoon. What can I do for you?"

"I'd like a dozen red long-stemmed roses, no vase needed. I'll be hand delivering these."

"Lucky girl."

"Yes, and hopefully with these flowers, I'll get lucky."

Yuck. This guy really was a jerk. The declaration he'd made was about the sleaziest she'd ever heard.

He took off his sunglasses, revealing his beady eyes. "Do you know Ashley, the young lady who works at the gas station on the corner?"

"Yeah. I've known her for years."

"Do you happen to know her last name?"

Kendal came up behind her. "Green. Her name's Ashley Green."

Dirk pulled a small, black velvet jewelry box from his pocket and opened the lid. Inside, the diamond heart-shaped necklace Miss Judy had given him glinted in the moonlight. She'd told him if he gave the necklace to the right girl on a full moon, that girl would cherish his heart forever. If he gave it to the wrong girl or at the wrong time, the girl would toss the necklace aside and fall in love with another. Crazy superstitious nonsense, maybe, but if there was the slightest chance of forever with Kendal, he was going for it.

He was tired of sneaking around, pretending they weren't a couple. His mother had told everyone Kendal was giving his dad piano lessons on a regular basis so folks wouldn't start wondering why she was spending so much time at their house, but he wanted people to know they were together. He wanted to parade around the island with her on his arm, take her to dinner, and let the whole world know he was crazy about her. But before he could tell the world how he felt about Kendal, he needed to tell her.

The full moon lit up the beach. He could see Miss Judy's shack in the distance. The south end, the old fort, he and Kendal had claimed this patch of land as their special place, their sanctuary.

Earlier that week, he'd beached a small motorboat and extra gas nearby so no one would ever be stranded here during high tide again. He'd also built sturdy steps to the treehouse, did away with the ladder, and attached an antenna to the roof so this area was no longer a dead zone for cell service.

This place was where he and Kendal made love for the first time. It seemed fitting that it should be where he professed his love for the first time.

Kendal came into view, her hair and dress fluttered in the wind, a bucket in her hand. Maybe she'd brought some drinks on ice. Smart thinking. He'd been so wrapped up in trying to figure out exactly what he wanted to say, he'd forgotten the wine he'd planned on bringing.

As she neared, he waved to her, but she didn't so much as smile. Was she in deep thought and hadn't seen him? But she was looking right at him. Something was wrong.

With no more than five feet between them, he could plainly see her eyes were set to battle-mode. No mistake about it. She was pissed.

"What's wrong, babe?"

Her jaw twitched, but she said nothing. He'd never seen her like this.

She marched toward him with such fury in her eyes, he thought she was going to strike him.

"Kendal, what the hell's wrong?"

Toe to toe, eye to eye, she tugged the waistband of his shorts and emptied the contents of the bucket down the front of his pants.

Ouch! Something pinched his balls. A blue crab scurried out of his pant leg and down his shin.

She glared at him. "Since you're going around telling people I gave you crabs, I figured I'd make an honest man out of ya. After all, I wouldn't want to see you ruin your reputation of being a man of your word!" She threw the empty bucket at him and ran off.

Before he could chase after her, something got a good grip on his manhood and brought him to his knees. He peered down his pants. Jesus. How many crabs did she have in that bucket? Ouch! Damn it! He dropped his drawers and got the crabs off him. Far as he could tell, there had been at least six of those suckers.

Tell people she'd given him crabs? What was she...? Oh shit. Paisley, the New York violin guy. But that happened months ago.

The jewelry box was opened on the sand. He picked it up. The necklace was gone. He looked around for it, but had no luck. As he put his pants back on, a crab pinched his big toe. He kicked and sent the crab flying. It landed in the water with a splash.

Miss Judy's words rang in his head. "If you give it to the wrong girl, or at the wrong time, she'll toss it aside and fall in love with another."

CHAPTER TWENTY-EIGHT
Race

Tourists flooded the island for the annual ostrich race. Instead of being a jockey this year, Dirk had the honor of being the MC. He didn't usually get nervous, but he was today. He'd never done much public speaking.

With a little time before the race started, he decided to get off by himself and practice his opening monologue. No one appeared to be hanging around the barn, so he walked over to the big red building and sat on a bench just outside the double doors leading to the ostrich stalls.

He caught a whiff of apple blossom fragrance, like Kendal's shampoo. A snatch of bright yellow cloth with pink flowers protruded from the corner of the building. Farther down were a pair of cute feet in brown sandals, toes painted pink. He recognized those sandals and that dress.

Not giving him a chance to explain about the crabs, ignoring his calls, now hiding from him?

He'd had enough of Kendal's evasive behavior.

Quietly, he walked through the barn and sneaked around the back. She was peering around the corner with her back to him. He crept up behind her and grabbed her arm. "Boo."

She jumped sky high then tried to pull away from him. "Let me go!"

He tightened his grip. "I need to have a word with you "

"Dirk, I'm serious. Let me go right this minute or I'll scream."

He looked around. Not a soul in sight, and loud music was playing by the stage. "Go on then. Scream if you want, but I'm having a word with you like it or not."

She glared at him.

"Kendal, we need to talk."

"No, we don't." She stomped her foot.

Oh well, she was going to hear him out whether she wanted to or not. He backed her against the barn and placed his hands on either side of her waist so she couldn't get away.

She squirmed and pushed at his chest. "What do you think you're doing?"

"I'm not letting you go until you hear what I got to say. Understood?"

She tried to wrestle free, but he didn't budge.

In a huff she said, "Fine. But make it fast, cause Myrtle's waiting for me to bring her back a saddle."

"You want it fast, huh? Okay then, here's the fast version. I played by your rules all summer long, trying my damnedest to make sure no one knew what we were up to. That meant, when some other guy came breezing into town with eyes for you, I couldn't tell him you were my girl, and he needed to move along. I couldn't even hold your hand in front of him so he'd get the message."

Her expression softened, but she remained silent.

"So how do you think I felt when some hot shot musician started asking about you? He was rich, talented, and you'd made it clear you were interested in doing some exploring, that we were free to see other people. The problem was, I didn't want you going off with that asshole."

"But that was for me to decide," she ground out.

"I'm aware of that. That's why I bit my tongue around

him. But when I was leading him to the bath house on my way back to the boardwalk the day your Mama popped in on us, and I still had your taste on my lips, he asked me what I knew about you. I didn't want to tell him a damn thing, so I didn't answer him. When he and I were getting ready to cross that patch of marsh grass where all the crabs like to hide, I told him to watch out for crabs. He assumed I meant you had them. I started to correct him, but then he said he'd already dealt with a bad case of crabs in high school, didn't want another, and he was no longer interested in hooking up with you. So, I let him think whatever he wanted to think. That's all there was to it."

"You never actually said I had crabs?"

"Hell no! Why would I say something like that? Even if you *had* given me crabs, I wouldn't have told anybody. I'd never say something that I knew would make you look bad, whether it was true or not."

She caressed his face.

That one gentle touch from her loosened all the knots in the back of his neck and he dropped his forehead to hers. "I'm not proud of how things went down, but —"

"It's okay, Dirk. I'm not particularly proud of dumping a bucket of crabs down your pants either." She smiled.

He laughed.

Carl drove up on his tractor pulling a livestock trailer. When Dirk waved to the man, Kendal scurried away and went behind the barn.

He helped Carl load Robirrrda into the trailer. "She's the last one." Dirk told the old man. "You need any help getting her saddled up or anything?"

"Nah. Ted's got all that under control. You ready for your big debut as MC?"

"Ready as I'll ever be."

"I really appreciate you doing this. The mayor left me in a

lurch by canceling at the last minute. He ain't been himself lately. I don't know what's going on with him, but I've a feeling your gonna be a bigger hit with the crowd than he was anyway."

"Hope the mayor's all right. So far as a bigger hit with the crowd than he was, I wouldn't put money on it. Kind of hard to top his world-class ostrich impersonation."

"Oh Lord, please tell me you aren't going to do the mayor's version of the ostrich strut. I've tried to tell the man it looked like he was doing the mating dance. Last year, it was all I could do to keep Spike from attacking him in a jealous rage after the mayor accidentally got Robirrrda all stirred up with his fancy stepping."

Dirk laughed. "I won't be doing the ostrich strut. Ever. No worries there. And for the record, I got some fresh funny-bone material." He patted his shirt pocket that was filled with various jokes and stories to entertain the crowd. Since the blow out he had with Kendal, he didn't trust himself to be naturally funny or witty under pressure, seemed like his sense of humor had gone on sabbatical.

"I got a story you can add to your stash." Carl took off his straw hat and wiped his sweaty, balding head with a red bandana. "One day this judgmental old biddy turned up her nose and asked Myrtle how she could stand dating an ostrich farmer, like I was the scum of the earth or something. Myrtle just smiled and said, 'He's surrounded by fast, long-legged chicks with big asses they like to shake in his face all day, and I get to ride a massive cock whenever I want. It's a win win situation.' Lord knows, when she told me that, I died laughing and fell a little more in love with her."

Dirk laughed hard. It was the first good laugh he'd had since he and Kendal had their spat, if you could call it that. But no, he wouldn't be adding that story to the list. Too many kids would be in the audience.

Carl wiped his eyes that were weeping from being tickled by his own story. "Welp, let me get on outta here. Text me if you need me for anything. I'll keep my phone on me."

Carl sped away and left a dust cloud in his wake as he drove across the field. Dirk looked in the barn and around back to see if Kendal was still there. She was nowhere in sight. Well, at least he'd straightened out that crab mess. He pulled out his notecards and sat on a bench in the shade. He had just enough time to do a tad more studying.

A crash came from the back of the barn. He stuffed his cards back in his shirt pocket and rushed to see what had caused all the commotion.

Kendal was hanging ass-out from the loft, the hem of her dress caught on something, and an ostrich saddle in her hands. Truth was, he couldn't see her face, but he recognized that yellow dress and that cute tush of hers. Plus, he didn't know any other girl who actually wore panties with song lyrics on them. These read : *But I won't do that* on the back. He knew the front read: *I will do anything for love.* The first time he'd seen those panties, he fell out of bed laughing, and she'd proceeded to break into a some sort of crazy Kendal dance while singing, "Can't Touch This." He proved her wrong though. He'd touched, and he wanted to touch right now. Damn, he missed touching her.

"Kendal, are you okay?" He tried to sound concerned, but he was smiling too hard to pull it off.

"Stop staring at my butt and give me a hand." Her voice was muffled.

He climbed up the ladder until he was eye-level with her gorgeous rump. At least she wasn't wearing her undies with *The answer is* on the front and *Blowin' in the wind* on the back.

He'd like to pretend she had "Bite Me" stamped on her bottom, because he wanted to nibble that sweet honey bun.

"Dirk, I can feel your breath where it doesn't belong."

"I'm just trying to read the fine print back here. You know…it doesn't say exactly what 'that' represents. What is the subtext for *But I won't do that?*"

"You know what it's implying. Now, would you please stop making like inspector 12 in the Hanes underwear factory and help me down from here?"

He smiled and blew cold air across her booty.

Goosebumps popped out on her legs, and she shivered. "Stop it! You're being such a pervert!"

Guilty. He put his mouth as close to her bottom as he could without touching and growled.

She let out a little squeal and giggled. "God, I hate you."

"Pass me the saddle, sweet cheeks."

"I can't. My arm is stuck in one of the stirrups."

"How in the world did you manage to do that?"

"I don't know. I was coming down and my foot slipped, my dress got snagged, and my arm shot through the stirrup when I panicked, trying to keep myself from falling. It all happened so fast."

He climbed up a couple more rungs, so his face was now at her lower back, and he slipped his arm around her waist. "You rescued me. I'm happy to have a chance to return the favor."

"Please stop talking. Your whiskers are tickling me."

He'd almost forgotten how ticklish she was on her lower back."

"I can't help it." He rubbed his chin against her delicate skin, and she flinched in his grasp.

"I mean it, Dirk. It's not funny."

He nodded yes, making sure to drag his stubble across her flesh. "Yes, Ma'am."

She erupted in a squirming fit of high-pitched laughter. "I can't take it. You're going to make us both fall."

All her wiggling caused him to struggle to hold onto the

ladder, and for a brief second, the fear of both of them tumbling to the ground made him freeze.

He had to dislodge the hem of her dress before he could bring her down, but he couldn't reach the edge of it. He grasped a handful of the flouncy skirt and gave the fabric a good tug, but it didn't come loose from whatever it was hung on.

"Just rip it." Her voice was low and breathy and made him come to a full salute below the belt.

He climbed up one more rung, his foot barely able to fit next to both of hers. With his mouth by her ear, he said, "You sure?"

She twisted slightly and looked him in the eyes, their mouths inches apart. He knew he was pressing his hardness against that soft rump of hers, but under the circumstances, there wasn't any way around it. And he was okay with that.

She didn't comment on his obvious erection, she just breathed, "Yes," on a sigh.

He wanted to kiss her so badly his brain was swimming with desire. "Kendal…"

She turned her face away. "Do it quick."

"You want a quickie?" He was stunned.

"No, Dirk. Geez. I was talking about the dress."

"Oh, right." He snatched her dress free and a long tearing sound ensued. "Sorry about that. Step on back. I got ya." He guided her back to safety.

Kendal tugged her arm free from the stirrup and smiled at him. "Thank you."

Did that mean he'd been forgiven? He sure hoped so. He was definitely ready to get back in the saddle, so to speak.

Mrytle's voice sounded over the speakers that were stationed around the farm for the day's event. "Calling Dirk Davis to the stage."

"Oh crap. I gotta go." He spun around, patting his shirt

pocket, making sure his cards were still there. With his mind in a whirl, he took off in a sprint toward the stage.

Kendal couldn't possibly let anyone see her now. The whole back of her dress was ripped wide opened. She spotted Carl's dune buggy behind the barn. The keys were in it. She tossed the saddle in the back and hopped in the vehicle.

As she traversed the dunes and made her way down the beach toward Laffy Taffy, she couldn't help but smile with the wind in her hair. She knew Paisley hadn't lied to her about the crab stuff. She could see the honesty in his eyes. That's what had upset her so badly to begin with. She'd been able to dismiss a lot of what Ashley had gabbed about, because she could tell a lot of her jaw-jacking was a load of b.s. The fact Paisley seemed to be so sincere, and what he'd claimed Dirk had said was so vicious, she'd allowed it to get to her. And it was true—Paisley hadn't flat-out lied—but he had misinterpreted Dirk. She should have known Dirk wouldn't say something so awful about her. Poor guy, the way he jumped around with those crabs pinching away. Guess she got him back for the cayenne pepper.

In a rush, she ran into her apartment and changed into a bright blue sundress then back out the door she went. She hauled buggy down the beach as fast as she could go. She didn't want to miss Dirk's big moment in the spotlight.

She searched out Myrtle, who was waiting behind the stage, moments from doing her own performance. "Myrtle, I got that saddle for you. Where do you want it?"

Myrtle barely gave the saddle a glance. "Just toss it over there by my golf cart. I'll get it later. Did you happen to run into Dirk in the barn?"

Uh oh. "Yeah, but he ran out of there the moment you called for him."

"Oh, I know he came running when I made the announcement. I was just trying to figure out why he was late to start with."

"I think he was practicing his jokes."

"Oh? Is that all he was practicing?" Myrtle gave Kendal a little wink, and Kendal's stomach churned. "I hope you were smart enough to talk to him, instead of avoiding him like you've been doing lately."

"I haven't been avoiding him."

"Child, I've had my eye on you two all summer long, and I've been trying to give y'all your space. I know how skittish you can be, pretty girl. I was happy to see you finally spread your wings a little bit and didn't want to do anything to cause you to crawl back in that shell of yours. But if you two can't get yourselves together, *together*, I'm going to have to intervene. And next time, I won't be as subtle as sending you to the barn for an old saddle." She dropped her chin to her chest and leveled Kendal with those blue eyes of hers, glassy as crystal balls able to forecast Kendal's future. They showed a life filled with public humiliation and torment in the form of a blog post if Kendal didn't patch things back up with Dirk.

Gulp. She better get to patching.

Dirk introduced Myrtle and her dancing ostrich, Jitterbug. Myrtle gave Kendal a satisfied nod and disappeared around the corner of the stage.

Kendal parked the dune buggy back where she found it and walked over to the bleachers, but there were no spaces left. She spotted Spencer sitting near the front with Earl.

They looked so happy together, Kendal found herself smiling. Mazy and Trent were cuddled up in lawn chairs on the other side of Earl. They looked just as happy. Brock and Sam were in the bleachers smiling away. Everyone was paired off and lovey-dovey. She didn't want to be a third wheel. Plus, she couldn't get over there to any of her friends anyway, not with everyone packed in so tightly. She resigned herself to peep between the shoulders and heads of the people standing along the sidelines.

The crowd laughed at Dirk and cheered him on as he danced with Myrtle and Jitterbug in the field. He was touching so many people in his own special way and brightening their day. Everyone loved him, including her. Especially her. But he wasn't the settling down kind of guy, and she knew that going in. She'd accepted it. In fact, it was partly why she'd chosen him for her summer adventure. He'd been the perfect choice. She just didn't expect to fall for him so hard.

At the beginning of the summer, she thought she knew him. They'd grown up together, for goodness sakes, but truth was, she hadn't known him at all. He wasn't the guy with the Peter Pan attitude, who never wanted to grow up. He was a family man, putting the needs of others above himself, taking care of the whole island, and wearing a smile while doing it. So many people did things begrudgingly, whined, complained, and drew attention to their sacrifice. Not Dirk. He gave of himself freely and generously, without expecting anything in return. His focus was never on himself, always on others, looking for what they needed most and trying to help them get it. Today, Carl needed an MC to keep the crowd laughing and enjoying themselves. Who did he turn to? Dirk. When she needed someone to help her get over her own issues, who did she turn to? Dirk.

Even if their relationship dwindled, she didn't regret

being with him. It'd changed her for the better. She was more comfortable in her own skin on many levels. Going into this fling with Dirk, she thought it was all about sex. Boy, had she been wrong. It'd been about crawling out of her shell and being vulnerable, learning that she was stronger than she realized and that the only way to truly live life to the fullest was to get out in it and not stay curled up in the shadows being a spectator.

Myrtle walked onto the stage and motioned for the crowd to quiet down. "Before we get the big race started, I need to make an announcement. For those of you who don't live on Pleasure Island, you might not think what I got to say effects you, but it does. You see, our mayor coordinates the majority of the events on the island, including this annual race, and ensures everything runs smoothly for all of us. But he couldn't be with us today. He's been battling lupus for years and his health has made a turn for the worse. He put in his resignation this morning and suggested we consider electing Dirk Davis to take his place."

Dirk grabbed his chest and all the color left his face. This was obviously the first he'd heard this news. Carl put his arm around Dirk and grinned like a proud father.

"Now, before some of you start saying Dirk is too young, let me inform you that there are hundreds of mayors all over the country younger than our Dirk. Just google it, if you don't believe me. I'm not saying we are appointing Dirk as mayor right here and now. I don't even know if he'd accept the position. I'm saying our mayor resigned, and he offered up a name of a person he felt would be well suited to perform the duties required. I'm simply honoring his wishes by sharing this information with y'all, and figured now would be a good time to do it, since most everyone is here. We'll hold a city council meeting next Saturday and present the names of the men and women Pleasure Island would like for us to consider for the position of mayor. Remember, only city council members are eligible for this position. To my knowledge, all adult citizens of Pleasure Island are, in fact, on the city council, and that's something we should all be proud of. Anyone listed who doesn't want the job will be given the opportunity to decline their nomination. Once we narrow it down to who is willing to accept the position out of the people you'd like to see take it on, we'll vote on it as a community."

A gentle hand touched Kendal's shoulder. "Dirk would make such a great mayor." Kendal recognized the female voice whispering in her ear. It was Leah.

Kendal faced her friend and said, "He would, but he looks like he's about ready to pass out at the thought of it."

Leah took off her straw fedora and used it as a fan to alleviate the sweltering heat. "He just needs a little encouragement. You up for the task?"

"Me?"

"I've held my tongue as long as I can stand it. Like a lot of folks, I've had my eye on you two this summer. Don't you think it's time y'all admitted to each other and everyone else that you're crazy about one another?"

Kendal didn't know what to say.

"Don't look so surprised. It's true. Most everyone knows about you two, but no one's wanted to say anything, because y'all seemed to *really* want your privacy. But if Dirk ends up being mayor, he's going to need a strong woman at his side, someone to help him watch over his dad, someone to attend the occasional political event with him. He's going to need a woman in his life he can be proud to show off—a smart, kind, classy young woman. He's going to need you."

"But I don't even know if he wants me, for real."

"Kendal, do you love him?"

"I'm not sure."

"You're not?" Leah raised her eyebrows in disbelief.

"Well, I am sure, but I'm not sure he feels the same way." Kendal worried her bottom lip between her teeth.

"Let me tell you a little secret. When you love someone, you tell them how you feel, not so they'll love you back, or say it back to you. You tell them because those words are meant for them to carry in their heart."

Just tell Dirk she loved him, just like that? Was it really that simple?

Leah put her hat back on and her expression grew grim. "My husband and I were bickering the week of his accident. I had many opportunities to tell him I loved him, but I was being stubborn and giving him the silent treatment. Now, it's too late. I can't tell him how much I love him. He's gone. And I've learned from that experience."

How sad. She didn't know Leah and her husband had ever fought. They had always seemed so happy. But then again, Kendal had just been a kid, and hadn't paid close attention.

Leah took Kendal's hand, as if she wanted Kendal to listen carefully. "I know what true sorrow and unbearable sadness is. It's all those 'I love you's' intended for someone else, trapped inside your heart, clawing to get out. I don't cry because he didn't say he loved me before he left the house for the last time. My heart aches, because of what I left unsaid. Even when I was upset with him, I loved him, but I didn't say it. I know you've been upset with Dirk lately, and I hope you two have worked it out, but even if you haven't, if you love him anyway, in spite of it all, you need to tell him."

Leah was the most level-headed, down to earth person Kendal knew. She never talked much about her husband or the pain of his loss, but Kendal knew she'd been hurting for years, a hurt that had caused Leah to wall off a part of herself. She hadn't even entertained the idea of dating again, and for such a beautiful woman with so much life ahead of her, that seemed a shame. Kendal understood Leah's pain a little better now, and she really appreciated her advice. Like always, she could count on Leah to steer her in the right direction.

Sorrow was all those 'I love you's' meant for someone else, trapped inside your heart, clawing to get out.

CHAPTER TWENTY-NINE
Heart

The big race began. All the people on the bleachers stood and cheered. The man directly in front of Kendal put his son on top of his shoulders so the small boy could see. Her view, however, was completely blocked.

Leah had gone back to the tent where she was selling refreshments, leaving Kendal alone in the noisy mob.

Kendal wormed her way through the sea of smiling faces and wedged herself between a chicken-wire fence and a livestock trailer.

Six ostriches were sprinting around the dusty track with their jockeys jostling about. One guy almost fell off, but managed to right himself and hang on, as his ostrich inched past another one. Spike led the pack, just like everyone had predicted. His jockey, Rudy, had taken home the trophy with every ostrich he'd ridden for the past ten years. Watching those massive birds running at top speed, feeling the earth shake as they neared, getting caught up in the energy of the spectators, Kendal's whole body tensed, and she shouted. "Come on, Spike!"

Something grabbed her by the hair. She spun around. Robirrrda had her neck stuck out of the trailer and was trying to munch on Kendal's tresses. "Ouch, Robirrrda! What are you doing?"

"You got some seed in your hair." Dirk climbed out of the trailer. He walked toward her and smiled, then reached up and picked out the seed.

She held her breath and stared into his eyes.

"You okay there?" He ran his hand down her arm.

She released her breath and nodded. *Say it. Tell him you love him. Do it now.*

But she couldn't just blurt it out. It didn't feel right. She had to lead into it somehow. "Are you considering being mayor?"

He backed up and leaned against the trailer. Tunneling his fingers through his hair, he blew out a breath. "Myrtle threw me for a loop with that one. I wish she would've warned me. I'm having a hard time processing it."

"I think you'd be a great mayor. You do more to take care of things around the island and the people who live here than anyone else does."

"Me? I do odd jobs here and there, but I'm no politician."

"We don't need a politician. We need an honest man."

He laughed. "Good point."

"You wouldn't be doing it alone, you know."

"Oh no? Somebody going to hold my hand?" He glanced down at her hand.

"Lots of people will. Mr. Peabody always handles the legal stuff, his law degree comes in handy. Myrtle does a good job at coordinating some of the meet and greets. And you've never met a stranger. You get along with everyone, rich folks, not so rich folks, doctors, farmers, even the hermit lady who rarely speaks to anyone."

"What about you?"

"Me? I'm just starting to come out of my shell. I don't have the outgoing personality you have."

"That's not what I meant. I meant, do I get along with

you?"

"You know you do."

"You had me wondering the past two weeks, Kendal. I didn't like being shut out like that."

She stepped toward him and rose up on her tiptoes, and placed her hands on his chest. "I'm sorry. I was being stupid." She lifted her chin to kiss him.

He backed away. "Hang on a minute. You do realize it's Labor Day. You said our fling would end on Labor Day, remember?"

She staggered backward. "Yeah. That's right." She felt like he'd just slapped her in the face. Tears welled in her eyes. Damn it. She was *not* going to stand there and cry in front of him. She's the one that set that day as the "expiration date." Holy crap, was she going to pass out, or be sick? Whoa, she was feeling a bit light-headed.

She turned away from him. This wasn't how she expected things to go. She was supposed to tell him she loved him, but she couldn't even speak right now. The lump in her throat was the size of a softball, and if she uttered a single syllable her voice would surely crack with emotion.

Walk away. Catch your breath.

One foot in front of the other, she made her way toward Leah's tent. Dirk came up behind her. She couldn't face him, she just couldn't. To keep from breaking down in front of all those people gathered to have a great time, she ran.

He chased her down, grabbed her hand and spun her around to face him. "Our fling is over. You hear me?"

God, yes, she got it. Did he have to embarrass her? Why was he being so cruel?

He placed his hands on her waist and brought his face close to hers. "No more fling, no more secrecy. From here on out, you're mine, and I'm yours. There is nothing casual about my feelings for you, Kendal Duvall. I'm very serious about you, very, and I don't care who knows it." He kissed her hard, right in front of everyone, and he didn't stop kissing her until her feet were off the ground, her arms were around his neck, and the crowd had erupted in a cacophony of whistles and cheers that had nothing to do with ostriches.

She looked around. Everyone was staring at her and Dirk, and she shouted, "I love you, Dirk." Leah was right, those words needed to be said. Kendal's heart felt free and happy, as if a million butterflies fluttered out of her chest at once in a swarm of colorful wings that kissed the sky.

Dirk lowered her to her feet, and cupped her face in his hands. "And I love you, Kendal."

Dirk took off his mayor's robe and carefully hung it on a hook in the treehouse.

"So, how does it feel to be mayor?" Kendal asked, as she put her arms around his waist and snuggled in close.

"I've only held the position for an hour, I need a little more time before I can answer that." He kissed the tip of her nose. "Feel like dancing?"

"You lead. I follow."

Kendal's apple scented shampoo that he'd come to love, the warmth of her soft body in his arms, the sound of her gentle voice in the darkness—these were things he could never grow tired of. The big ceremony where he was appointed to office had been a grand event with tons of people present, and that had been a lot of fun, but it paled in comparison to simply holding Kendal in his arms, in their own little corner of the world.

He turned on the stereo. "I Fooled Around and Fell in Love," came through the speakers. He sang along and meant every word. That was exactly what had happened to him, and he'd never been happier.

Here they were, in a place they'd visited so many times, but tonight, they could catch a glimpse of their future, a future together.

He could now say he had a career, and it felt good. And he was proud of how Kendal had come into her own. She was still introverted, that was just part of her nature, but she was friendly enough. What surprised him the most was that she no longer hesitated to dance—in fact, she was getting to be pretty good. If she kept improving at the rate she was going, they'd enter the shagging contest in the fall. They might even enter the big dance-off in Myrtle Beach.

He'd been so caught up in the ceremony for him, he'd failed to ask her about her day. "So, did you and Spencer have a chance to check out that commercial property today?"

"Yep. And it's perfect for my piano studio. I contacted the landlord, and she's meeting me tomorrow to talk over the lease."

"Awesome."

"I'm so excited. Looks like I'll have a full load of special needs students this year, thanks to Mindy Lancaster's help on getting the word out to the parents."

"I'm happy for you, baby." He kissed the top of her head.

"Your dad looked so proud of you tonight." She smiled up at him.

"He was having a good night. I haven't seen him talk to that many people and actually remember their names since I was in high school. I don't know what triggered his improvement, but it was great."

"I think all that positive energy did him good. He was watching his son rise to a respected position in the community, and he was surrounded by people who knew him and cared about him. Positive thinking is a powerful thing." Her brown eyes shined in the dim light of the moon.

"Your mom seemed to be having a lot of fun with Rafe too."

"I know. I can't believe how well they get along. I would have never imagined the two of them tolerating each other, but they seem to balance each other out. She's not nearly as uptight and controlling as she used to be, and he's a lot more polite. It's like they're better people now that they're together, better than they ever were by themselves."

"A good woman makes you want to be a better man. I can relate."

She beamed. "You say the sweetest things."

He dipped her and gave her neck a kiss then pulled her back up, eliciting a quiet laugh from her. "You know what I find odd?"

"What's that?"

"I feel like I'm finally figuring out who I am. I can't explain it very well, but it's like I'm finally meeting myself."

She nestled her head against his chest. "I know what you mean. I feel the same. But I don't think I'd be feeling that way had I not fallen in love with you."

He caressed her back. "Same here. I didn't know how lost I was until I found your love." Look who was getting poetic? Ha. Damn, that should be a lyric in a love song. Preferably *not* a song quoted on panties.

Mmm, that bit of poetry won him a dynamite kiss.

When the music stopped, Kendal stepped back. "Let's take a walk, whatdaya say?" She tugged his hand. They climbed down the new stairs he'd built for the treehouse. When they reached the water's edge, a light came on in Miss Judy's shack in the distance.

He was glad she'd made it home safely. "When Miss Judy came to the ceremony all dolled up, I nearly fell out. She looked good, and she was chatting up a storm."

"She wouldn't have left her shack for anyone but you, you know that, right?"

He did know that, and it warmed his heart. "Yeah. I know. I think the world of her too."

Something glittered in the seagrass. He walked toward it to get a closer look. To his surprise it was the heart-shaped diamond necklace, sparkling in the light of the full moon.

He could hardly contain his excitement when he picked it up and held it in his palm.

"What are you doing?" Kendal called to him.

"I was just looking at something." He walked up behind her and draped the necklace around her neck. "Lift your hair for me."

She did. Once he fastened the necklace she pinched the heart between her fingers and looked down at it. "It's beautiful!"

"My heart belongs to you." He meant those words with everything in him.

She looked up into his eyes and smiled. "I'll cherish your heart forever."

THE END

Connect with Lyla Dune
LylaDune.com

Other books in the Pleasure Island series:
Book One - Low Tide Bikini
Book Two - Rip Tide Bikini
Book Four - Even Tide Bikini will be out in the Fall of 2014

Acknowledgements

I'd like to thank my critique partner Joy Avery. She is a talented author of contemporary romance as well. Her most recent book is His Until Sunrise.

My beta readers: Whitney Belisle and Katrina Smith have once again been life-savers, helping me put the finishing touches on the book. I'm grateful to have both of these remarkable ladies in my life.

My dear friend Shelley Slater Davis has been one of my biggest supporters from the beginning stages of my journey. I send out a huge thank you to her.

Most of all, I thank my husband for his endless support and for believing in me.

www.ingramcontent.com/pod-product-compliance
Lightning Source LLC
Chambersburg PA
CBHW030418180626
46812CB00005B/2058